THE BLIND GODDESS

THE BLIND GODDESS

ANNE HOLT

TRANSLATED BY TOM GEDDES

ISIS
LARGE PRINT
Oxford

First published in Great Britain 2012
by
Corvus
an imprint of Atlantic Books Ltd.

Published in Large Print 2013 by ISIS Publishing Ltd.,
7 Centremead, Osney Mead, Oxford OX2 0ES
by arrangement with
Atlantic Books Ltd.

British Library Cataloguing in Publication Data
Holt, Anne, 1958–
    The blind goddess.
    1. Wilhelmsen, Hanne (Fictitious character) - -
    Fiction.
    2. Oslo (Norway) - - Fiction.
    3. Detective and mystery stories.
    4. Large type books.
    I. Title
    839.8'238–dc23

ISBN 978–0–7531–9114–9 (hb)
ISBN 978–0–7531–9115–6 (pb)

Printed and bound in Great Britain by
T. J. International Ltd., Padstow, Cornwall

The man was dead. Conclusively, beyond all reasonable doubt. She could tell instantly. Afterwards she couldn't really explain her absolute certainty. Maybe it was the way he was lying, his face hidden by the rotting leaves, a dog turd right by his ear. No drunk with any self-respect lies down next to a dog turd.

She rolled him over carefully. His entire face was missing. It was impossible to recognise anything of what must once have been a person with an individual identity. The chest was a man's, with three holes in it.

She had to turn away and retch violently, bringing up nothing but a bitter taste in her mouth and painful cramps in her stomach, letting the corpse fall forward again. She realised too late that she had moved it just enough for the head to land in the excrement, which was now spread all over the drenched dark-blond hair. That was the sight that finally made her throw up, spattering him with the tomato-coloured contents of her stomach. It seemed almost like a derisive gesture of the living towards the dead. The peas from her dinner weren't yet digested, and they lay there like toxic-green full stops over the dead man's back.

Karen Borg started running. She called her dog, and put it on the lead she always carried mostly for the sake of appearances. The dog scampered excitedly alongside her until it realised that its mistress was sobbing and gasping, and then it decided to contribute its own anxious whining and whimpering to a chorus of lamentation.

They ran and ran and ran.

MONDAY 28 SEPTEMBER, AND EARLIER

Police headquarters in Oslo, Grønlandsleiret, number 44. An address with no historical resonance; not like 19 Møllergata, the old police headquarters, and very different from Victoria Terrasse, with its grand government buildings. Number 44 Grønlandsleiret had a dreary ring to it, grey and modern, with a hint of public service incompetence and internal wranglings. A huge and slightly curved building, as if the winds had been too strong to withstand, it stood framed by a house of God on one side and a prison on the other, with an area of demolished housing on Enerhaugen at the rear, and only a broad expanse of grass fronting it as protection against the city's most polluted and trafficky streets. The entrance was cheerless and forbidding, rather small in proportion to the two-hundred-metre length of the façade, squashed in obliquely, almost concealed, as if to make approach difficult, and escape impossible.

At half past nine on Monday morning Karen Borg, a lawyer, came walking up the incline of the paved path to this doorway. The distance was just far enough to make your clothes feel clammy. She was sure the hill must have been constructed deliberately so that everyone would enter Oslo police headquarters in a slight sweat.

3

She pushed against the heavy metal doors and went into the foyer. If she'd had more time, she'd have noticed the invisible barrier across the floor. Norwegians bound for foreign shores were queueing for their red passports on the sunny side of the enormous room. On the north side, packed in beneath the gallery, were the dark-skinned people, apprehensive, hands damp with perspiration after hours of waiting to be told their fate in the Police Immigration Department.

But Karen Borg was late. She cast a glance up to the gallery round the walls: blue doors and linoleum floor on one side, and yellow on the other, southern, side. On the west side two tunnel-like corridors in red and green disappeared into nothingness. The atrium extended seven floors in height. She would observe later how wasteful the design was: the offices themselves were tiny. When she was more familiar with the building she would discover that the important facilities were on the sixth floor: the commissioner's office and the canteen. And above that, as invisible from the foyer as the Lord in His heaven, was the Special Branch.

"Like a kindergarten," Karen Borg thought as she became aware of the colour coding. "It's to make sure everyone finds their way to the right place."

She was heading for the second floor, blue zone. The three lifts had conspired simultaneously to make her walk up the stairs. Having watched the floor indicators flash up and down for nearly five minutes without illuminating "Ground," she had allowed herself to be persuaded.

She had the four-figure room number jotted on a slip of paper. The office was easy to find. The blue door was covered in paste marks where attempts had been made to remove things, but Mickey Mouse and Donald Duck had stubbornly resisted and were grinning at her with only half their faces and no legs. It would have looked better if they'd been left alone. Karen Borg knocked. A voice responded and she went in.

Håkon Sand didn't appear to be in a good mood. There was an aroma of aftershave, and a damp towel lay over the only chair in the room apart from the one occupied by Sand himself. She could see his hair was wet.

He picked up the towel, threw it into a corner, and invited her to sit down. The chair was damp. She sat anyway.

Håkon Sand and Karen Borg were old friends who never saw each other. They always exchanged the customary pleasantries, like *How are you, it's been a long time, we must have dinner one day*. A regular routine whenever they happened to meet, in the street or at the homes of mutual friends who were better at keeping in touch.

"I'm glad you came. Very pleased, in fact," he said suddenly. It didn't look like it. His smile of welcome was strained and tired after twenty-four hours on duty.

"The guy's refusing to say anything at all. He just keeps repeating that he wants you as his lawyer."

Karen Borg lit a cigarette. She defied all the warnings and smoked Prince Originals. The "Now I'm smoking Prince too" type, with maximum tar and nicotine and a frightening scarlet warning label from the Department of Health. No one cadged a smoke from Karen Borg.

"It ought to be easy enough to make him see that's impossible. For one thing, I'm a witness in the case, since I was the one who found the body, and second, I'm not proficient in criminal law. I haven't handled criminal cases since my exams. And that was seven years ago."

"Eight," he corrected her. "It's eight years since we took our exams. You came third in our year, out of a hundred and fourteen candidates. I was fifth from the bottom. Of course you're proficient in criminal law if you want to be."

He was annoyed, and it was contagious. She was suddenly aware of the atmosphere that used to come between them when they were students. Her consistently glowing results were in stark contrast to his own stumbling progress towards the final degree exam that he would never even have scraped a pass in without her. She had pushed and coaxed and threatened him through it all, as if her own success would be easier to bear with this burden on her shoulders. For some reason which they could never fathom, perhaps because they'd never talked about it, they both felt she was the one who had the debt of gratitude to him, and not the other way round. It had irritated her ever since, this feeling of owing him something. Why they had been so inseparable throughout their student years was something nobody understood. They had never been lovers, never so much as a little necking when drunk, but a mismatched pair of friends, quarrel-some yet bound by a mutual concern that gave them an invulnerability to many of the vicissitudes of student life.

"And as for you being a witness, I don't give a shit about that right now. What's more important is to get the man to start talking. It's obvious he won't cooperate until he gets you as his defence counsel. We can think again about the witness stuff when we have to. That'll be a good while yet."

"The witness stuff." His legal terminology had never been particularly precise, but even so Karen Borg found this grated on her. Håkon Sand was a police attorney, and his job was to uphold the law. Karen Borg wanted to go on believing the police took the law seriously.

"Can't you talk to him anyway?"

"On one condition. You give me a credible explanation of how he knows who I am."

"That was actually my fault."

Håkon smiled with the same feeling of relief he'd had whenever she'd explained something he'd read ten times before without comprehending. He fetched two cups of coffee from the anteroom.

Then he told her the story of the young Dutch national whose only contact with working life — according to reports so far — had been drug trafficking in Europe. How this Dutchman, now sitting as tight-lipped as a clam waiting for Karen Borg in one of the toughest billets in Norway, the custody cells in Oslo police headquarters, knew exactly who Karen Borg was

— a thirty-five-year-old very successful commercial lawyer totally unknown to the general public.

"Bravo Two-Zero calling Zero-One!"

"Zero-One to Bravo Two-Zero, go ahead."

The police officer spoke in hushed tones, as if he were expecting a confidential secret. Far from it. He was on duty in the operations room. It was a large open space with a shelved floor in which raised voices were taboo, decisiveness a virtue, and economy of expression vital. The duty shift of uniformed officers sat perched above the theatre floor, with an enormous map on the opposite wall to chart the scene of the main action, the city of Oslo itself. The room was as centrally positioned in the police headquarters building as it could be, with not a single window looking out onto the restless Saturday evening. The city night made its presence felt in other ways: by radio contact with the patrol cars and a supportive 002 number for the assistance of the public of Oslo in their moments of greater or lesser need.

"There's a man sitting in the road on Bogstadsveien. We can't get anything out of him, his clothes are covered in blood, but he doesn't look injured. No ID. He's not putting up any resistance, but he's obstructing the traffic. We're bringing him in."

"Okay, Bravo Two-Zero. Report when you're back on patrol. Received Zero-One. Over and out."

Half an hour later the suspect was standing at the reception desk. His clothes were certainly bloody:

Bravo Two-Zero had been right about that. A young rookie was searching him. With his unmarked blue epaulettes lacking even a single stripe as insurance against all the vilest jobs, he was terrified of so much possibly HIV-infected blood. Protected by rubber gloves, he pulled the open leather jacket off the arrested man. Only then did he see that his T-shirt had originally been white. His denim jeans were covered in blood too, and he had a general air of self-neglect.

"Name and address," said the duty officer, glancing up wearily over the counter.

The suspect didn't reply. He just stared longingly at the packet of cigarettes the young officer was shoving into a brown paper bag together with a gold ring and a bunch of keys tied with a nylon cord. The desire for a smoke was the only sign that could be read in his face, and even that disappeared when his eyes shifted away from the paper bag to the duty officer. He was standing nearly a metre away from the policeman, behind a strong metal barrier that came up to his hips. The barrier was shaped like a horseshoe, with both ends fixed into the concrete floor, half a metre from the high wooden counter, quite wide in itself, over which projected the nose and thinning grey hair of the police officer.

"Personal details, please! Name! Date of birth?"

The anonymous man smiled, but not in the least derisively. It was more an expression of gentle sympathy with the exhausted policeman, as if he wanted to indicate that it was nothing personal. He had no intention of saying anything at all, so why not just put him in a cell and have done with it? The smile was almost friendly, and he held it unwaveringly, in silence. The duty officer misunderstood. Needless to say.

"Put the bugger in a cell. Number four's empty. I've had enough of his insolent attitude."

The man made no protest, but went along willingly to cell number four. There were pairs of shoes in the corridor outside every cell. Well-worn shoes of all sizes, like door nameplates announcing the occupants. He must have automatically assumed the regulation would also apply to him, because he kicked off his trainers and stood them neatly outside the door without being asked.

The cell was about three metres by two, bleak and dreary. Floor and walls were a dull yellow, with a noticeable absence of graffiti. The only slight advantage he was immediately aware of in these surroundings, so far removed from the comforts of a hotel, was that his hosts were obviously not sparing with the electricity. The light was dazzling, and the temperature in the little room must have been at least twenty-five degrees Celsius.

Just inside the door there was a sort of latrine; it could hardly be called a lavatory. It was a construction of low walls with a hole in the middle. The moment he saw it, he felt his bowels knotting up in constipation.

The lack of any inscriptions on the walls by previous guests didn't mean there were no traces of frequent habitation. Even though he was far from freshly showered himself, he felt quite queasy when the unpleasant odour hit him. A mixture of piss and excrement, sweat and anxiety, fear and anger: it permeated the walls, evidently impossible to eradicate. Because apart from the structure designed to receive urine and faeces, which was beyond all hope of cleansing, the room was actually clean. It was probably swilled out every day.

He heard the bolt slam in the door behind him. Through the bars he could hear the man in the next cell continuing where the duty officer had given up.

"Hey, you, I'm Robert. What's your name? Why've the pigs got you?"

Robert had no luck either. Eventually he had to admit defeat too, just as frustrated as the duty officer.

"Bastard," he muttered after several minutes of trying, loud enough for the message to get through to its intended recipient. There was a platform built into the end of the room. With a certain amount of goodwill it might perhaps be described as a bed. There was no mattress, and no blanket lying around anywhere. Well, that was okay, he was already sweating profusely in the heat. The nameless man folded up his leather jacket to make a pillow, lay with his bloody side downwards, and went to sleep.

When Police Attorney Håkon Sand came on duty at five past ten on Sunday morning, the unknown prisoner was still asleep. Håkon didn't know that. He had a hangover, which he shouldn't have had. Feelings of remorse were making his uniform shirt stick to his body. He was already running his finger under his collar as he came through the CID area towards the police lawyers' office. Uniforms were crap. At the beginning, all the legal specialists in the prosecution service were fascinated by them — they would stand in front of the mirror at home admiring themselves, stroking the insignia of rank on the epaulettes: one stripe, one crown, and one star for inspector, a star that might become two or even three depending on whether you stuck it out long enough to become a chief inspector or superintendent. They would smile at the mirror, straighten their shoulders involuntarily, note that their hair needed cutting, and feel clean and tidy. But after an hour or two at work they would realise that the acrylic made them smell and their shirt collars were much too stiff and made sore red weals round their necks.

The chief inspector's duty was the worst of the lot. But everyone wanted it. The job was usually boring, and intolerably tiring. Sleep was forbidden; a rule most of them broke with a foul, unwashed woollen blanket pulled up over their uniforms. But night duty was well paid. Every legally qualified officer with one year's service got roughly one duty a month, which put an extra fifty thousand kroner a year in their pay-packets. It was worth it. The big drawback was that the shift began at three o'clock in the afternoon after a full working day, and as soon as it was over at eight the next morning you had to start on a normal working day again. At weekends the duties were divided up into twenty-four-hour shifts, which made them even more lucrative.

Sand's predecessor was impatient. Even though the shift, according to the rules, should change at nine, there was an unspoken agreement that the Sunday duty officer could come in an hour later. The person being relieved would always be drumming their heels. As indeed was the blonde female inspector today.

"Everything you need to know is in the log," she said. "There's a copy of the murder case from Friday night on the desk. There's always a lot to do on this duty. I've completed fourteen reports already, and two Clause Eleven decisions."

The devil she had. With the best will in the world Håkon Sand couldn't see that he was any more competent to make decisions about care proceedings than the child care authorities' own staff. Yet the police always had to sort things out when a juvenile caused bureaucratic inconvenience by needing help outside normal office hours. Two on Saturday, which meant statistically none on Sunday. He could but hope.

"And it's full out the back; you'd better make your round as soon as you can," she added.

He took the keys, fumbling as he attached them to his belt. The cashbox contained what it should. The number of passport forms was also correct. The log was up to date.

Formalities completed, he decided to go and collect some fines straight away, now that Sunday morning had laid its cold but calming hand on last night's revellers. Before going, he flipped through the papers on the desk. He'd heard about the murder on the radio news bulletin. A badly mutilated body had been discovered down by the River Aker. The police had no leads. Empty words, he'd thought. The police always have some leads, it's just that they're all too often very scanty.

The photo file from the scene-of-crime people hadn't been added yet, of course. But there were a few Polaroids lying loose in the green folder. They were grotesque enough. Håkon never got used to photographs of the dead. He'd seen plenty of them in his five years in the force, the last three attached to Homicide, A.2.11. All suspicious deaths were reported to the police, and entered on the computer under the code "susp." Suspicious death was a broad concept. He'd seen bodies that were burnt, deaths from exhaust fumes, stab wounds, bullets, drowning, or torture. Even the tragic elderly folk who were only victims of the crime of neglect, found when a neighbour in the flat below noticed an unpleasant odour in the dining room, looked up and saw a damp patch on the ceiling, and rang the police in indignation at the damage — even those poor devils were input as "susp" and had the dubious honour of having their final photographs taken postmortem. Håkon had seen green corpses, blue corpses, red, yellow, and multicoloured corpses, and the pretty pink carbon monoxide bodies whose souls had been able to endure no more of this world's vale of tears.

The Polaroids were stronger stuff than most of what he'd seen before, though. He threw them down abruptly. As if to forget them as soon as he could, he grabbed the report of the findings. He carried it over to

14

the uncomfortable "Stressless" posture chair, a cheap imitation-leather version of the flagship model from Ekornes, much too curved in the back, lacking support where the lumbar region needed it most.

The bare facts had been typed up in a style that could hardly have been more unhelpful. Håkon furrowed his brow in annoyance. They said the admission criteria for the Police Training College were getting steadily higher. Ability in written presentation was obviously not one of them.

He came to a halt near the end of the page.

"Present at the scene of the crime was witness Karen Borg. She found the deceased while walking her dog. There was vomit on the body. Witness Borg said it was hers."

Borg's address and occupation confirmed that it was Karen. He ran his fingers through his hair, regretting not having washed it that morning. He decided to phone Karen during the week. With pictures as gruesome as that, the body must have been an awful sight. He absolutely must ring her.

He replaced the file on the desk and closed it. His eyes dwelt for a moment on the name label at the top left: Sand/Kaldbakken/Wilhelmsen. The case was his, as prosecuting attorney. Kaldbakken was the chief inspector responsible, and Hanne Wilhelmsen the investigating detective.

It was time to sort out the fines.

There was a thick bundle of arrest sheets in the little wooden box. A full house. He skimmed quickly through the forms. Mainly drunks. One wife abuser, one obvious mental case who would have to be transferred to Ullevål Hospital later in the day, and a known and wanted criminal. The last three could stay where they were. He would take the drunks in turn. The point of fining them was admittedly rather unclear to him. The majority of the tickets ended up in the nearest litter bin. The few that were paid were charged to the Social Services. A merry-go-round of public money that made a contribution to employment of some sort, but could hardly be regarded as particularly rational.

One set of arrest forms remained. It had no name on it.

"What's this?"

He turned to the custody officer, an overweight man in his fifties who would never achieve more than the three stripes he had on his shoulders, stripes no one could deny him: they were awarded for age rather than merit. Håkon had realised long ago that the man was a dimwit.

"A nutter. He was in here when I came on duty. Bastard. Refused to give his name and address."

"What's he done?"

"Nothing. Found sitting in the road somewhere or other. Covered in blood. You can fine the sod for not giving his name. And for breach of the peace. And for being a scumbag."

After five years in the force Sand had learnt to count to ten. He counted to twenty this time. He didn't want to have a row just because of an imbecile in uniform who couldn't see that taking a person's liberty involved a certain responsibility.

Cell number four. He took a warder with him. The man with no name was awake. He stared at them with a despondent face, and was obviously in some doubt about their intentions. He sat up on the bed stiffly and spoke his first words in police custody.

"Could I have a drink?"

The language he spoke was Norwegian and yet at the same time not Norwegian. Håkon couldn't put his finger on it; it sounded accurate, but there was something not quite right. Could he be a Swede trying to speak Norwegian?

He was given a drink, of course. Cola, bought by Håkon Sand with his own money. He even got a shower. And a clean T-shirt and trousers. From Sand's own cupboard in the office. The custody officer's grumbling at the special treatment grew louder with every item. But Håkon Sand ordered the bloodstained clothes to be put in a bag, explaining as he locked the heavy metal doors behind him:

"These articles could be important evidence!"

The young man was certainly taciturn. A searing thirst after many hours in an overheated cell may have loosened his tongue, but it soon became clear that his need to communicate was extremely temporary. Having quenched his thirst, he reverted to silence.

He was sitting on a hard spindleback chair. Strictly speaking there was only space for two chairs in the eight-square-metre room, which also housed a solid and rather stately double filing cabinet, three rows of ugly painted-steel bookshelves full of ring-binders arranged by colour, and a desk. This was fixed to the wall with metal brackets, so that the desktop was on a slant. That's how it had been ever since the medical officer had had the idea of subjecting the staff to an ergonomics therapist. Sloping work desks were supposed to be good for the back. No one understood why, and most of them had found that their spinal problems were exacerbated by all the groping around on the floor for the things that slid off the desk. With an extra chair in the room it was hardly possible to move about without shifting the furniture.

The office belonged to Hanne Wilhelmsen. She was strikingly attractive, and newly promoted to Inspector. After coming out top of her year from police college, she had spent ten years at Oslo police headquarters marking herself out as a policewoman perfectly designed for an advertising campaign. Everyone spoke well of Hanne Wilhelmsen, a unique achievement in a workplace where ten percent of the day was spent running down your colleagues. She deferred to superiors without being branded an arse-licker, yet was not afraid to voice her opinions. She was loyal to the system, but would put forward suggestions for improvement that were usually sound enough to be implemented. Hanne Wilhelmsen had the intuition that only one in a hundred police officers has, the fingertip sensitivity that tells you when to coax and trick a suspect, and when to threaten and thump the table.

She was respected and admired, and well deserved it. But even so there was no one in that big grey building who really knew her. She always went to the annual departmental Christmas parties, to the summer party, and to birthday celebrations, was a fantastic dancer, would talk about the job and smile sweetly at everyone, and would go home ten minutes after the first person had left, neither too early nor too late. She never got drunk, and so never made a fool of herself. And no one ever got any closer to knowing her.

Hanne Wilhelmsen was at ease with herself and the world, but had dug a deep moat between her professional life and her private life. She didn't have a single friend in the police force. She loved another woman, a defect in this otherwise perfect human being, the public admission of which she was convinced would destroy everything she had spent so many years building up. A swing of her long dark-brown hair was enough to deflect any questions about the slim wedding ring that was the only jewellery she wore. She had been given the ring by her partner when they first moved in together at the age of nineteen. There were rumours, as there always are. But she was so pretty. So womanly. And the female doctor that a friend of someone's friend vaguely knew, and that others had seen Hanne with several times, was also very beautiful. They were really feminine women. So there couldn't be any truth in it. Anyway Hanne always wore a skirt the few times she had to dress in uniform, and hardly anyone did that, since trousers were so much more practical. The rumours were just malicious nonsense.

Thus she lived her life, in the knowledge that what is not confirmed is never regarded as actually true; but this made it even more important for Hanne to perform well in her job than for anyone else in the building. Perfection was her shield. Which was how she wanted it, and since she had absolutely no ambition to elbow her way to the top, but was only interested in doing a good job, there was no jealousy or envy to threaten her defences.

She smiled now at Håkon, who had seated himself in the extra chair.

"Don't you trust me to ask the right questions?"

"Relax. No worries on that score. But I have a feeling we're on to something bigger here. As I said, if you don't mind too much, I'd rather like just to sit in on the interview.

"It's not against the rules," he added quickly.

He knew she insisted on following the statutory procedures whenever possible, and he respected her for it. It was unusual for a police attorney to attend the questioning of a suspect, but it wasn't precluded. He'd done the same before on occasion. Usually to study the technique, but sometimes because he was particularly involved in a case. Normally the police officers didn't object to the presence of the prosecution staff. On the contrary, provided he kept a low profile and didn't interfere in the interrogation, most of them seemed quite pleased.

As if at a given signal, they both turned towards the prisoner. Hanne Wilhelmsen put her right arm on the desk and let her long lacquered nails play on the keys of an old electric typewriter. It was an IBM golf ball machine, very advanced in its time. Now it lacked the e, which was so worn that it produced only a smudged

20

black mark from the ribbon when you hit the key. It didn't really matter, since it was quite obvious what the smudge should be.

"It'll be a long day if you're just going to sit there and say nothing."

Her voice was gentle, almost indulgent.

"I get paid for this. Chief Inspector Sand gets paid. You on the other hand will just carry on being held here. Sooner or later we might let you go. Wouldn't you like to make it sooner?"

For the first time the young man seemed less confident.

"My name is Han van der Kerch," he said, after a few minutes' further silence. "I'm Dutch, but I'm residing in the country legally. I'm a student."

Now Håkon Sand had his explanation for the perfect yet not fully idiomatic Norwegian. He remembered his boyhood hero Ard Schenk, remembered himself as a thirteen-year-old thinking that the man spoke an unbelievably good Norwegian for a foreigner. And he remembered reading Gabriel Scott's *Dutchman Jonas*, a book he had loved as a child and which had contributed to his later unwavering support for the orange shirts in international football championships.

"That's all I'm prepared to say."

Once again there was silence. Håkon waited for Hanne Wilhelmsen's next move. Whatever it might be.

"Well, that's okay by me. It's your choice, and your right. But we'll be sitting here for some time in that case."

21

She had inserted a sheet of paper in the typewriter, as if she already knew that she would get something to take down.

"You might as well hear a theory we have."

The chair leg scraped on the linoleum as she pushed it back. She offered the Dutchman a cigarette, and lit one herself. The young man seemed grateful. Håkon was less pleased, and leaning back in his chair pushed the door ajar to create a through-draught. The window was already slightly open.

"We found a body on Friday evening," said Hanne Wilhelmsen in a soft voice. "It was a bit of a mess. He obviously hadn't wanted to die. At least not in such a horrible way. There must have been a lot of blood around. You were pretty well covered in it when we found you. We can be a bit slow here in the police sometimes. But we're still capable of putting two and two together. As a rule we get four, and we think we've got four now."

She stretched behind her for an ashtray on the bookshelf. It was a tasteless souvenir from southern climes made of brown bottle glass, featuring a faun in the centre wearing an evil grin and sporting an enormous erect phallus. Not exactly Hanne Wilhelmsen's style, thought Sand.

"I'll happily be more explicit."

Her voice was sharper now.

"We'll have a preliminary analysis of the blood on your clothes tomorrow. Which — if it matches the blood of our faceless friend — will be more than enough to justify keeping you in custody. We can have you in for interrogation whenever we like. Over and over again. A week might pass before you hear from us, then we'll suddenly turn up again, perhaps after you've gone to sleep. We'll question you for an hour or two, you'll refuse to say anything, we'll take you back, and then fetch you out again. It can be rather wearing. For us too, of course, but we can take it in turns. It's worse for you."

Håkon began to doubt whether Hanne deserved her reputation as a stickler for the rules. The method of interrogation she'd outlined was definitely not in the book. He was even more in doubt about the legality of threatening it.

"You have the right to a solicitor; the State will pay," he reminded him, as if to compensate for any possible illegality.

"I don't want a solicitor!" he exploded.

He took one last puff on his cigarette before stubbing it out emphatically and saying it again, "I don't want a solicitor. I'll be better off without one."

He threw a questioning, half-imploring look across at the pack of cigarettes on the table. Hanne Wilhelmsen nodded, and handed him both the cigarettes and the matches.

"So, you think it was me. Well, you may be right."

That was that. The man's basic needs had been satisfied at last: a shower, some breakfast, a drink, and a couple of cigarettes. Showing all the signs of having talked as much as he was going to, he slid forward in the chair and slumped back with a distant look in his eyes.

"Okay, then." Detective Inspector Wilhelmsen seemed fully in command of the situation. "Perhaps I should continue," she said, starting to turn over the pages of the rather slim file of papers beside the typewriter.

"So we found this repulsive-looking corpse. He had no documents on him, and his face had gone before him, so to speak, wherever it was he was going. But our man in the patrol car was fairly well acquainted with the drugs scene here in the city. The clothes, body, and hair were sufficient. Revenge killing, he thought. A not unreasonable assumption, it seems to me."

She linked her fingers and put her hands behind her head. She massaged her neck with her thumbs as she looked the Dutchman straight in the eyes.

"I think you killed the guy. We'll know better tomorrow, when the results come back from Forensics. But lab technicians can't tell me why. That's where I need your assistance."

The appeal seemed to be in vain. The man didn't move a muscle, he just retained his remote, slightly mocking smile, as if he had the upper hand. There he was mistaken.

"To be frank, I think it would be more sensible of you to give me that assistance," the Inspector went on. "Maybe you did it on your own. Maybe it was to order. Perhaps you were even forced into it. And that might have a decisive impact on what happens to you."

She paused in her steady stream of words, lit a new cigarette, and stared him in the face. He went on sitting there displaying absolutely no intention of talking. Hanne heaved a sigh and switched off the typewriter.

"It's not up to me to determine your sentence. If you're guilty, that is. But it could definitely be to your advantage if I was able to say something positive about your willingness to cooperate and so on when I have to testify in court."

Håkon recognised the feeling from when he was a child and had been allowed to watch a detective story on television. He would be dying to go to the loo, but didn't dare say so for fear of missing something exciting.

"Where did you find him?"

The Dutchman's question took Håkon completely by surprise, and he noticed for the first time a hint of uncertainty in the Inspector's face.

"Where you killed him," she replied, with exaggerated slowness.

"Answer me. Where did you find the guy?"

Both police officers hesitated.

"By the River Aker at Hundremanns Bridge. As you well know," Hanne said, holding him steadily in her gaze so as not to miss even a flicker of reaction in his expression.

"Who found the body? Who reported it to the police?"

This time Hanne Wilhelmsen's hesitation created a vacuum that Sand was sucked into.

"It was someone out for a walk. A lawyer, a friend of mine in fact. Must have been a dreadful experience."

Hanne was livid, but Håkon realised it too late. He hadn't picked up on her warning gesture as he started to speak. He flushed deeply at her fierce look of reproof.

Van der Kerch stood up.

"I would like a lawyer after all," he declared. "I want that woman. If you get her here, I'll think about talking, at any rate. If I can't have her, I'd rather have ten lonely years in prison at Ullersmo."

He went across to the door unbidden, stepping over Håkon Sand's legs, and waited politely to be taken back to his cell. Hanne Wilhelmsen escorted him, without a backward glance at her red-faced colleague.

The coffee had been drunk. It hadn't been particularly good, even though it was freshly made. Decaffeinated, Håkon Sand explained. There were six cigarette stubs in a tawdry brown and orange ashtray.

"She was bloody mad at me afterwards. Understandably so. It'll be some time before I'll be allowed to be present at an interrogation again. But the man won't be budged. It's you or no one."

He seemed no less exhausted now than when Karen Borg had arrived. He was massaging his temples and running his fingers through his hair, which was now quite dry.

"I asked Hanne to give him all the counterarguments. She says he remains adamant. I've kept well out of it. It'll smooth things over a bit if I can get you to help us."

26

Karen Borg sighed. For six years of her life she'd done little else but favours for Håkon Sand. She knew she wouldn't be able to refuse this time either. But she would play hard to get.

"I'm only agreeing to have a talk with him. I'm not promising anything," she said curtly, and stood up.

They went out the door, she first, he following. Just like the old days.

The young Dutchman had insisted on speaking to Karen Borg, with a vague intimation that he would open up to her. But that seemed to have been forgotten now. He looked full of bile. Karen Borg had moved over to Håkon Sand's chair, and Håkon had discreetly withdrawn. The lawyers' room in the custody suite was a miserable place, so in justified apprehension that she might renege on her promise to talk to the young Dutchman, he'd put his own office at her disposal.

Their suspect should have been handsome, yet was somehow unprepossessing. An athletic body, fair hair that looked as if it might have been expensively styled a month or so back. His hands were delicate, almost feminine. Did he play the piano? A lover's hands, Karen thought, with no idea of how she was going to deal with the situation. She was used to boardrooms, meeting rooms with heavy oak furniture, airy offices with curtains costing five hundred kroner per metre. She could tackle men in suits with fashionable or garish ties, and women with briefcases and Shalimar perfume. She knew all about the laws relating to shares and the formation of companies, and only three weeks ago had

27

earned herself a nice 150,000 kroner fee for checking over a comprehensive contract for one of her biggest clients. It hadn't involved much more than reading five hundred pages of contractual agreements, ensuring they contained what they purported to, and writing "OK" on the cover. That worked out to 75,000 kroner per letter.

The prisoner's words were obviously just as valuable.

"You asked to speak to me," Karen Borg began. "I don't know why. Perhaps we could take that as our starting point?"

He measured her up with his eyes, but maintained his silence. He kept tilting his chair backwards and forwards; up and down, up and down. That sort of thing put Karen Borg on edge.

"I have to say I'm not the right kind of lawyer for you. I know a few suitable people, and I can make some phone calls and get you a top lawyer in a matter of moments."

"No!"

The front legs of the chair hit the floor with a crash. He leant forward, looked directly at her for the first time, and said it again.

"No. I want you. Don't make any phone calls."

Suddenly it occurred to her that she was alone with a man who was presumably a murderer. The faceless corpse had been haunting her ever since she'd found it on Friday evening. Then she pulled herself together. No lawyer had ever been killed by a client here in Norway. Certainly not in a police station. She repeated this reassurance to herself three times and felt more relaxed. The cigarette helped too.

"Answer me then! What do you want from me?"

Still no response.

"You'll be up in front of the judge this afternoon for remand in custody. I'll have to refuse to meet you there unless I have some idea of what you're going to say."

Threats didn't have any effect either. Nevertheless she thought she could detect a glimmer of concern in his eyes. She made one last attempt.

"Besides, I'm running out of time now."

She glanced quickly at her Rolex. Her fear was giving way to irritation. Which was increasing. He evidently noticed it. He was rocking back and forth in the chair again.

"Stop that!"

The legs of the chair banged down on the floor a second time. She'd won a modest victory.

"I'm not necessarily asking for the complete truth." Her voice was calmer now. "I just want to know what you're going to say in court. And I have to know that right now."

Karen Borg's experience of criminals without white collars and silk ties was entirely limited to having yelled after a bicycle thief who was making off down Markveien with her new fifteen-gear bike. But — she had seen this on TV. Defence Counsel Matlock had said: "I don't want to know the truth, I want to know what you're going to say in court." Somehow it didn't sound quite as convincing coming from her own lips.

More hesitant, perhaps. But it might be a way of eliciting something.

Several minutes passed. The suspect had stopped rocking the chair, but was scraping it on the linoleum instead. The noise was getting on her nerves.

"It was me that killed the man you found."

Karen was more relieved than surprised. She'd known it was him. He's telling the truth, she thought, and offered him a throat pastille. He'd acquired the habit of smoking with a pastille in his mouth, just as she had. She'd started many years ago in the vague belief that it prevented the smell of smoke on the breath. By the time she'd realised it didn't, she'd already become hooked.

"I was the one who killed the guy."

It was as if he wanted to convince someone. It wasn't necessary.

"I don't know who he is. Was, I mean. That is, I know his name, and what he looks like. Looked like. But I didn't know him. Do you know any defence lawyers?"

"Yes, of course," she said, with a smile of relief. He didn't smile back. "Well, it depends what you mean by know. I'm not a personal friend of any, if that's what you mean, but it'll be easy to find a good defence counsel for you. I'm glad you realise what you need."

"I'm not asking you to get me another lawyer. I'm just asking you whether you know any. Personally."

"No. Well, a few of my fellow students went on to specialise in that field, but none of them is in the top league. Yet."

"Do you often see them?"

"No, only when I meet them by chance."

That was true. And a sore point. Karen Borg didn't have many friends now. They had slipped out of her life one after another, or she out of theirs, on paths that had become overgrown, only crossing now and again as polite exchanges over a beer in a pavement café in the spring, or emerging from a cinema late on an autumn evening.

"Good. Then I want to have you. They can charge me with the murder, and I'll be remanded in custody. But you must get the police to guarantee me one thing: to let me stay here in police headquarters. Anything to keep away from that bloody prison."

The man was certainly full of surprises.

The disgraceful conditions in the cells at police headquarters had hit the headlines from time to time in the newspapers, and with reason. The cells were intended for twenty-four-hour remand. They were scarcely even adequate for that. Yet they were where this prisoner wanted to stay. For weeks.

"Why?"

The young man bent forward confidentially. She could smell his breath, now rancid after several days without a toothbrush, and leant back in her own chair.

"I can't trust anyone. I have to think. We can talk again when I've worked some things out. You will come back?"

He was intense, verging on desperation, and for the first time she almost felt sorry for him.

She rang the number Håkon had written on a piece of paper.

"We've finished. You can come and fetch us."

Karen Borg didn't have to go to court, to her great relief. She had only once attended a court hearing. It was while she was still a student, and convinced she would use her law degree to help the needy. She had sat herself on the public benches in Room 17, behind a barrier which seemed to be there to protect innocent observers from the brutal reality in the room. People were being imprisoned at half-hourly intervals, and only one out of eleven had been able to persuade the judge that he couldn't possibly be guilty. On that occasion she had found it difficult to see who was defending and who was prosecuting counsel, so matey were they, laughing and handing one another cigarettes and telling crass courtroom jokes, until the wretched accused had been put in the dock and they went off to their respective corners to begin the contest. The police won ten rounds. It was swift, effective, and merciless. Despite her youthful urge to defend all the accused, she had to confess that she didn't particularly react against the judge's verdicts. Those charged had seemed to her to be dangerous, unkempt, unsympathetic, and too aggressive in their assertions of innocence and their resentment of the law, some in tears and many cursing and swearing. Nevertheless she had felt indignant at the convivial atmosphere that returned to the room immediately after a prisoner was led away shaking his head, a policeman gripping each arm, down to the holding cells in the basement. Not only did the two opponents, who only moments before had been impugning each other's honour, continue with their half-finished anecdotes, but even the judge craned forward to listen, smiled, nodded his head, and threw in an amusing comment, until the next poor devil was ready in the dock. Karen thought judges should remain aloof, and friendships be kept out of the courtroom. Even now she still had the same idealistic opinion. So she was glad that during her eight years in a law office she had never set foot in a courtroom, always managing to resolve matters before they got that far.

The custodial decision in respect of Han van der Kerch was a pure formality. He signed his written agreement to eight weeks, with a ban on visits and letters. The police had in some bewilderment granted his request to remain in the police headquarters cells. He was certainly an oddball.

So Karen Borg hadn't been required in court, and was back in her office. The fifteen commercial lawyers had their offices in the modern development at Aker Brygge on the waterfront, with an equal number of secretaries and ten clerks. The exclusive men's fashion boutique on the lower ground floor had gone bankrupt three times, and was eventually replaced by the larger fashion chain, Hennes & Mauritz, which was prospering. The cosy, expensive lunch bar had given way to a McDonald's. On the whole the premises hadn't lived up to their expectations at the time of purchase, but to sell now would involve a catastrophic loss. And it was a central location, after all.

Greverud & Co. was inscribed on the glass door, after old Greverud, who still, at the age of eighty-two, appeared in the office every Friday. He had established the firm just after the War, having built up an impressive reputation in the trials of collaborators. By 1963 there were five lawyers, but Greverud, Risbakk, Helgesen, Farmøy & Nilsen eventually became too much of a mouthful for the switchboard operator. In the mid-eighties they bought themselves into what everyone thought would become the mecca of capitalism in Oslo, and were among the few who had survived there.

In her third year as a student, Karen Borg had obtained her final summer job with this rock-solid firm. Hard work and an incisive mind were greatly esteemed at Greverud & Co. She was only the fourth woman ever to have had the opportunity, and the first to succeed. When she passed her exams a year later, she was offered a permanent position, interesting clients, and an immorally high salary. She fell for the temptation.

She'd never actually regretted it. She'd been sucked into the exciting world of capitalism, and was involved in the real-life game of Monopoly during its most thrilling decade. She was so talented that she was offered a partnership after a record three years. It was impossible to say no. She was flattered, pleased, and felt she deserved it. Now she earned one and a half million kroner a year, and had almost forgotten her reasons, all those years ago, for actually embarking on the study of law. Sigrun Berg ponchos had given way to elegant suits purchased for a fortune on Bogstadsveien.

The telephone rang. It was her secretary. Karen Borg pressed the loudspeaker button. This was uncomfortable for the person phoning, because her voice was surrounded by an echo that made it indistinct. She felt it gave her an advantage.

"There's a lawyer called Peter Strup on the line. Are you in, at a meeting, or have you left for the day?"

"Peter Strup? What can he want with me?"

It was impossible to hide her astonishment. Peter Strup was — besides much else — the chairman of the Defence Group, the special union of defence lawyers who regarded themselves as either too good or too bad simply to be members of the Norwegian Lawyers' Association like everyone else. A year or so previously he had been voted Norway's most eligible man, and was well known as one of the most frequent media pundits on just about any subject. He was in his sixties, but looked forty, and his time for the Birkebeiner Ski Race was up among the best. He was also said to be a friend of the Royal Family, though he would never confirm this in the presence of journalists.

Karen Borg had neither met him nor spoken to him. She had often read about him, of course.

"Put him through," she said, after some slight hesitation, and picked up the receiver in an unconsciously respectful gesture.

"Karen Borg," she said, in a flat and expressionless voice.

"Good afternoon, this is Peter Strup. I won't take up much of your time. I hear you've been appointed defence counsel for a Dutchman charged with last Friday's murder by the River Aker. Is that right?"

"Yes, that's correct as far as it goes."

"As far as it goes?"

"Well, I mean, it's true that I've been appointed, but I haven't talked to him very much yet."

She riffled involuntarily through the papers in front of her, the defence counsel's copies of the murder case. She heard Strup laugh, a charming laugh.

"Since when have you been working for four hundred and ninety-five kroner an hour? I didn't think legal aid rates would even cover the rent on Aker Brygge! Have things got so bad that you're having to poach on our territory?"

She didn't take offence at this. Her hourly rate was often well in excess of two thousand kroner, partly depending on who the client was. Even she had to laugh a little.

"We get by. It's purely a matter of chance that I'm helping this chap."

"Yes, that's what I thought. I've got enough to do, but I've been approached by a friend of his enquiring whether I can help the boy. An old client of mine, this friend, and we defence lawyers have to look after our clients, as you know!"

He laughed again.

"In other words, I don't mind taking the case on, and I can imagine you're not particularly keen on it."

Karen wasn't quite sure what to say. The chance to put the whole matter in the hands of the best defence

36

counsel in the country was very tempting. Peter Strup would undoubtedly do it better than she could.

"Thanks, that's kind of you. But he's insisted on having me, and in a way I've promised him I'll continue. Of course I'll pass on the offer to him, and I'll ring you back if he wants to take it up."

"Okay, we'll leave it at that, then. But you obviously appreciate I'll need to know soon. I'd have to familiarise myself with the case, and see if there's anything that can be done."

Their conversation drew to a close.

She felt a little perplexed. Even though she knew it was far more common among criminal lawyers to steal clients, or make strategic changes of lawyer, as it was more likely to be described, she was very surprised that Peter Strup had to have recourse to such measures. She'd seen his name recently in a newspaper report as one of three examples of the way cases were being delayed for months or even years because the most well-known lawyers had such long waiting lists. On the other hand, it was nice that he wanted to help, especially when the approach came at the instigation of one of Van der Kerch's friends. She could see the attraction of this caring attitude, though she herself kept all her clients at arm's length.

She closed the file in front of her, noticed that it was four o'clock, and decided to stop work, changing the board above the reception desk to indicate that she was the first of the lawyers to leave. She still couldn't avoid a slight prick of conscience every time there weren't at least ten names before hers under the "In tomorrow" sign. But today she managed to dismiss it easily, and walked out into the rain and caught an overcrowded tram home.

"I've taken on a criminal case," she mumbled between two mouthfuls of Frionor fish.

Karen Borg was from Bergen. She didn't eat fresh fish in Oslo. Fresh fish shouldn't have been dead for more than ten hours. Forty-eight-hour-old fish in the capital tasted like rubber, and the properly frozen output of a mass production line was actually better.

"Though it would be more accurate to say it was foisted upon me," she added as she finished chewing.

Nils grinned.

"Will you be able to cope with it? You often complain you've forgotten everything you learnt except what you've been doing for the last eight years," he said, wiping his mouth with the back of his hand, an annoying habit that Karen had been trying to eradicate for all of the six years they'd been living together, partly by drawing his attention to it, partly by pointedly laying large napkins by his plate. The napkin lay untouched, and he repeated the offence.

"Well, depends what you mean," she muttered, surprised at herself for feeling hurt, especially since she had had exactly the same thoughts earlier in the day. "Obviously I can, I'll just have to brush up a little." She resisted the temptation to add that she'd got a pretty good mark for her finals paper on criminal law.

She told him the whole story. For some reason she omitted the telephone call from Strup. She didn't know why. Perhaps it was because she felt uncomfortable about it. Ever since she was a child she had been reticent in matters that seemed complex. Anything dubious she kept to herself. Not even Nils really understood her. The only one who had ever come close to breaking through her defences was Håkon Sand. After he disappeared from her life, she became expert at sorting things out for herself in silence, and sorting things out for others for a living.

They'd eaten their meal by the time she'd finished talking. Nils began clearing the table, without seeming uninterested in her story. Karen sat down in an armchair, reclined the seat, and heard him loading the dishwasher. Eventually the rattling was accompanied by the gurgle of the coffee percolator.

"He's clearly scared to death," he shouted from the kitchen, then looked into the living room and reiterated it, "I think he's bloody scared of someone."

Brilliant. As if it wasn't obvious. Typical of Nils, he had an ability to come out with self-evident comments that for many years she'd found appealing, almost as if he were being deliberately sardonic. But lately she'd come to realise that he actually thought he could perceive what others couldn't.

"Of course he's scared," she murmured to herself, "but what is it he's scared of?" Nils came in with two cups of coffee.

"Well, he's clearly not afraid of the police," she said as she took the cup. "He wanted to be arrested. Just sat right down in a busy street and waited for them to arrive. But why wouldn't he say anything, why wouldn't he admit he'd killed the man by the River Aker? Why is he afraid of prison if he's not afraid of the police? And why of all things should he insist on having me as his lawyer?"

Nils shrugged his shoulders and picked up a newspaper.

"You'll find out eventually," he said, becoming engrossed in the comic strips.

Karen shut her eyes.

"I'll find out eventually," she repeated to herself, and yawned as she stroked the dog behind the ear.

TUESDAY 29 SEPTEMBER

Karen Borg had had a restless night. Not in itself an unusual occurrence. She was always tired in the evenings, and fell asleep within minutes of going to bed. The problem was that she always woke up again. Mostly at about five o'clock in the morning. She would still be tired and heavy with sleep, but incapable of drifting back into the world of dreams. Her problems seemed immense at night, even the ones that by day were little more than fleeting shadows. Things that were so easy to play down in the light of day as mundane, unthreatening, or mere irritations, became in this transition period before dawn pervasive menacing spectres looming over her. All too often she would lie there twisting and turning until half past six or so, and then drop into a deep unconscious sleep until the alarm clock jerked her out of it only half an hour later.

Last night she'd woken at two, drenched in sweat. She'd been sitting in an aeroplane with no floor, and the passengers were having to balance without safety belts on little projections attached to the aircraft walls. After clinging on tight until she was faint from exhaustion, she felt the plane go into a sudden steep descent towards the ground. She woke as it crashed into a hill. Dreams about plane crashes were supposed to be a sign of lack of control over one's life. But she didn't feel that could apply to her.

It was a bright autumn day for once. It had been pouring with rain all week, but last night the temperature had risen to fifteen degrees Celsius, and the sun was making a final effort to remind everyone that it was not so very long since summer after all. The trees on Olaf Ryes Plass were already turning reddish yellow, and the light was so strong that even the Pakistani shopkeepers looked pale as they set up their wares on the street outside their kiosks and grocery shops. There was a roar of traffic from Toftes Gata, but the air smelt surprisingly fresh and clean.

When Karen had become the youngest — and only female — partner in Greverud & Co. five years previously, she and Nils had seriously discussed leaving the Grünerløkka area. They could easily afford to, and Grünerløkka hadn't developed the way everyone was anticipating at the time she acquired a flat in a block then under threat of demolition but reprieved by the Oslo City Renovation Project. The rescue had been a half-hearted attempt at restoration, at an insane cost, and resulted in a fifteen-fold rent increase in three years. The least well-off had to move out, and had it not been for the fact that the creditors had nothing to gain by forcing the whole property company into liquidation, it might have been disastrous. But Karen had sold the flat at the right time, just before the big property crash in 1987, and had emerged with a reasonable sum for her new abode, a loft apartment in the adjoining block, which had miraculously escaped the Renovation

Project because the residents had themselves undertaken to carry out the City Council's area conservation plans.

Karen and Nils had really set their hearts on moving. But late one extraordinary Saturday night a year or so ago they had sat down and analysed their motives. They compiled a list of pros and cons, as if preparing an answer to an examination question. They ultimately concluded that they should use the money to extend their little flat instead. They strengthened the housing association's finances by purchasing the remainder of the loft, almost 200 square metres. It was very luxurious by the time it was completed and had risen enormously in value. They had never regretted it. When they'd both come to accept with remarkable equanimity that they would not have children, a tacit admission that had developed between them by the time they had been abstaining from contraception for four or five years without it leading to anything, they had started to forget all their friends' arguments about the pollution in Oslo city centre. They had a terrace with a Jacuzzi and barbecue, no gardening to do, and could walk to the nearest cinema without too much exertion. Even though they had a car, a Ford Sierra bought secondhand in view of the inadvisability of investing too heavily in a vehicle that would be parked in the street, they mostly used the tram or went on foot.

Karen had grown up in the pleasant residential district of Kalfaret in Bergen. It had been a childhood spent under the surveillance of the sophisticated local intelligence services, with agents peering out from behind curtains, always fully informed of everyone's slightest misdemeanours, from unwashed floors to extra-marital affairs. After a weekend visit home a couple of times a year Karen would be seized by a feeling of unbearable claustrophobia that she couldn't entirely account for, especially as she herself had never had anything to hide.

So Grünerløkka for her was a place of refuge. She and Nils had stayed put, and now had no intention of ever moving.

She paused in front of the little kiosk opposite the tram stop. The tabloid newspapers were piled high in their respective stands.

"Brutal drugs murder shakes police." The headline leapt out at her. She picked up a copy, went in reading it, and put the money on the counter with hardly a glance at the man behind the counter. The tram arrived as she came out. She stamped her ticket and sat down on a folding seat. The front page referred her to page five. Beneath a photograph of the corpse that she herself had found only four days ago, the text stated that "The police believe the brutal murder of an as-yet-unidentified man in his thirties to be a revenge killing in the drugs world."

No sources were given. The story was uncannily close to what Håkon Sand had told her.

She was infuriated. Håkon had emphasised that what had been said between them was not to go any further. The caution had been completely superfluous; there was no one Karen had less time for than journalists. She was all the more annoyed by the police's own bungling.

She wondered about her client. Would he get newspapers in his cell? No, he'd accepted a ban on letters and visits, and she seemed to recall that it also included a ban on newspapers, TV, and radio. But she wasn't sure.

"This will make him even more afraid," she thought, and turned her attention to the rest of the newspaper as the modern tram rolled and hummed along through the city streets with a smoothness so unlike the clatter of its predecessors.

In another part of the city a man was in abject fear of imminent death.

Hans E. Olsen was as ordinary as his name. Too much alcohol over too many years had left its mark on his face. His flesh was flabby and grey, with prominent pores, and always sweaty. But his permanently sour expression stemmed more from an innate bitterness than from his excessive consumption of alcohol. Right now he was sweating more than ever, and looked older than his forty-two years.

Hans E. Olsen was a lawyer. He had shown some promise in his early years as a student, and had attracted a number of friends. But his upbringing in a pious environment in southwest Norway had put a leaden weight on any vigour and *joie de vivre* he might have had. His childhood faith had been jettisoned after a few months in the capital, leaving the young man with nothing to put in its place. The concept of a vengeful and implacable God had never really lost its hold on him, and torn between his former self and the dream of

45

the student life of wine, women, and academic achievement, he had all too soon sought his consolation in the temptations of the big city. Even in those days his fellow students used to joke that Hans Olsen never used his cock for anything but peeing. But this was an assertion in need of qualification: he had discovered at an early stage that sex could be bought. His lack of charm and self-confidence had soon led him to the resentful realisation that women were not interested in him. He had become a frequent visitor to the red-light district around the city hall, and had thus accumulated a lot more experience than his fellow students gave him credit for.

His alcohol consumption, which increased so rapidly that by the age of twenty-five he was being referred to as an alcoholic — though from a medical point of view this was not strictly accurate — prevented him from passing his law examinations with a result commensurate with his original talents. He gained a mediocre degree, and took a job at the Ministry of Agriculture. He stayed there for four years before setting up on his own, after two years' practical work as an assistant judge in northern Norway, a period he now regarded with horror, but which had been a necessary evil to achieve his lawyer's licence and the freedom he felt he had always been seeking.

He had found a practice of three lawyers with a vacancy for a partner. They soon realised that he was an awkward character with an unpredictable temper. But they accepted him as he was, not least because, unlike others, he was always, without exception, up-to-date with the rent and his share of the joint expenses. They assumed this had more to do with his own modest expenditure than with any great earning capacity. Hans Olsen was, in a word, miserly. He had a predilection for grey suits. He had three — two of them more than six years old, and it showed. None of his colleagues had ever seen him in anything else. He spent his money on just one thing: alcohol.

For a brief period he had blossomed out, to everyone's amazement. The surprising turn in his life manifested itself in his more frequent hair washing, his use of an exclusive aftershave that for a short while overpowered the musty, slovenly body odour that permeated his office, and in the fact that he turned up one morning wearing a pair of new Italian, and, in his secretary's opinion, extremely suave, shoes. The cause of the transformation was a woman who was actually willing to marry him — after only three weeks' acquaintance, which in reality meant about fifty pints in the Old Christiania pub.

The woman was as ugly as sin, but those who knew her said she was warm, kind, and intelligent. She was a deaconess. That hadn't been a hindrance on the short path to their separation and divorce.

But Hans Olsen had one definite strength: criminals loved him. He stood up for his clients as few others did. Because he felt so strongly in their favour, he hated the police. He hated them without reservation, and never tried to conceal it. His ranting and raging had provoked countless prosecutors over the years, and usually resulted in his clients receiving sentences far in excess of the norm. Olsen hated the police, and the police hated him. Naturally enough this had an effect on the suspects he represented.

But now Hans Olsen was in fear for his life. The man standing in front of him was pointing a pistol at him of a type which he, with his limited knowledge of firearms, couldn't place. But it looked dangerous, and he'd seen enough films to be able to recognise a silencer when he met one.

"That was bloody stupid of you, Hansy," said the man with the gun.

Hans E. Olsen loathed the nickname Hansy, even if it was a natural consequence of his always including his middle initial when he introduced himself.

"I just wanted to talk to you about it," he croaked from the armchair he'd been ordered into.

"We had an agreement, Hansy," said the other man in an exaggeratedly restrained voice. "No one pulls out. No one squeals. We have to know that the operation is totally watertight. Remember it's not just us who're involved. You know what's at stake. You've never come up with objections before. What you said on the phone yesterday was a threat, Hansy. We can't tolerate threats. If one goes down, we all do. We can't afford that, Hansy. You know that."

"I've got documents!"

It was a last, desperate attempt to cling on to life. The room was suddenly filled with the unmistakable odour of excrement and urine.

"No, you haven't, Hansy. We both know that. Anyway, it's a chance I'll have to take."

48

The shot sounded like a small half-suppressed cough. The bullet struck Hans E. Olsen in the middle of the nose, which was completely shattered as the projectile bored right on through his skull and blasted out a crater the size of a turnip at the back of his head. Red and grey spurted over the little crocheted antimacassar on the chair, and splattered onto the wall behind it.

The man with the gun adjusted the tight rubber glove on his right hand, walked over to the door, and left.

THURSDAY 1 OCTOBER

The murder of Hans E. Olsen was given wide coverage in the newspapers. He had never reached the front pages while he lived, despite repeated ill-humoured attempts. In death he was the subject of reports on no fewer than the first six pages. He would have been proud of himself. His colleagues had shown their respect, even though most of them considered him to be a little shit, and the papers painted a portrait of a highly esteemed gentleman of the bar. Several found reason to criticise the police, once again utterly devoid of leads in a serious murder case. Though most seemed to agree that the lawyer had been removed by a dissatisfied client. With his fairly limited caseload, the hunt for the killer ought to be short and simple.

Detective Inspector Hanne Wilhelmsen didn't subscribe to that theory. She felt the need to air a few half-formulated thoughts with Håkon Sand.

They'd found themselves a place right at the back of the canteen, in seats by the window, with magnificent views over the poorer districts of Oslo. They both had cups of coffee, which both had spilt in their saucers. Their cups dripped as they drank. Between them was an open pack of chocolate caramels.

Hanne spoke first.

"To be honest, Håkon, I think these two murders are linked in some way."

She looked at him expectantly, unsure how her hunch would be received. Håkon dipped a chocolate in his coffee, put it in his mouth, and licked his fingers thoroughly. They didn't look particularly clean. He returned her gaze.

"There's not a single common element," he said somewhat morosely. "Different weapon, different method, different location, completely different characters, and a different time. You'll have problems convincing anyone!"

"But just listen — don't get too fixated on the differences. Let's see what similarities there might be."

She was very excited, and counted off the points eagerly on her fingers.

"First of all, there was a gap of only five days between the murders."

She ignored Håkon's sardonic smirk and raised eyebrows.

"Secondly, we have no explanation at the moment for either of them. Admittedly we've identified the man by the River Aker: Ludvig Sandersen, drug addict for years and a conviction record as long as your arm. He was released six weeks ago after his last sentence. But do you know who his lawyer was?"

"Since you ask in that triumphant tone, I'll guess at our deceased friend Olsen."

"Bingo! *That* at any rate is some sort of connection." Speaking more softly, she went on: "And not only was he Olsen's client, but he had an appointment with him the day he was killed! Heidi has Olsen's desk diary, and she spotted it straight away. Ludvig Sandersen had an appointment at two o'clock last Friday, and the next slot was crossed through. A long session, in other words. If it took place at all. We don't know that it did, of course. But I presume his secretary can tell us that."

Håkon had eaten most of the chocolate at breakneck speed, and Hanne had only managed to get a couple of pieces. Now she was shaping the gold foil into the form of a little bird while she awaited his response.

Suddenly they both started talking simultaneously, breaking off with a chuckle.

"After you," said Håkon.

"There's another thing." Her voice now was lower still, even though the canteen was almost deserted and their nearest neighbour several tables away. "I'm not going to commit any of this to paper. I'm not going to mention it to anyone at all. Only to you."

She made a gesture of putting her fingers in her ears, then leant towards him over the table.

"I had a guy in for questioning a short while ago about a rape. We brought him in purely on spec, because he's got a record that costs him a visit here whenever we have an unsolved sex case. We quickly eliminated him from the enquiry, but he was extremely nervous about something. I didn't pay much attention to it then — they're always up to one thing or another. But this bloke was really frightened. Before he'd actually sussed out what we wanted him for, he let out a few thinly veiled hints about a deal. He said he'd heard on the grapevine that there was a lawyer behind some of the large-scale drug dealing, though I can't remember his exact words anymore. You know what these people are like, they're ready to tell lies even faster than they commit felonies, and they'll try anything to get themselves out of a tight spot. So I didn't attach much importance to it at the time."

Hanne was really whispering now. Håkon had to lean across the table and put his head on one side to catch what she was saying. To anyone passing by they could have been lovers exchanging intimacies.

"I woke up in the night because I couldn't get him out of my mind," she said. "The first thing I did this morning was to dig out the old rape case file and check his name. Guess who his lawyer was."

"Olsen."

"Precisely."

They both sat staring out over the hazy vista of the city. Håkon Sand took some deep breaths and sucked in air reflectively between his front teeth. Though realising it sounded unpleasant, he soon stopped.

"What have we actually got?" he said, and took out a blank sheet of A4 paper. He numbered down the page.

"We have a dead drug addict. The self-confessed murderer under arrest refuses to give motive."

His pen scratched away on the paper, piercing the surface in his eagerness.

"It was such a thorough job that he wouldn't have survived even if he'd had nine lives. Then we have a dead lawyer, killed in a rather more sophisticated manner. We know that the two murdered men were acquainted. They had an appointment for a meeting on the very day that one of them bought it. What else do we have?"

He went on without waiting for an answer. "Some vague and highly unreliable rumours about an unknown lawyer's drug dealing. The rumour-monger's lawyer was our dear departed Olsen."

Hanne Wilhelmsen noticed that Håkon's chin was twitching at the side of his mouth, like a muscle spasm.

"I think you're onto something, Hanne. I think maybe we're onto something big. But what's the next step?"

For the first time in the conversation Hanne leant back in her chair. She drummed her fingers on the table.

"We keep everything under wraps," she declared. "This is the faintest scent I've ever had to base a serious investigation on. I'll keep you posted. Okay?"

The hit squad were the black sheep and also the great pride of the force. Usually in jeans, and in many cases long-haired or unkempt, these officers never felt bound by any dress code once they joined the squad. Nor did they need to. But at times they flouted other more sacrosanct rules and regulations, and were not infrequently carpeted by the head of personnel or even by the commissioner. They would agree to everything and promise to improve, but held up two fingers as soon as they were out of the door. Over the years some had gone too far and had been transferred to the most excruciatingly boring office duties, if only temporarily. Because actually the police loved their denim-clad

54

brethren. The hit squad were effective, industrious, and were subjected to constant visits by colleagues in Denmark and Sweden, who came to police headquarters with only vague concepts and left prostrate with admiration.

Just the previous week, during a visit by a group from the Stockholm police, a Swedish TV crew came out with them one night. The boys took the TV people to an address they knew they could bank on, a prostitute who always had a few grams of some substance or other lying around. It was easy to break down the door, because there wasn't much of the frame left after an earlier visit. They stormed into the darkened room with a cameraman in tow. On the floor was a middle-aged man in a bright red low-cut dress with a dog's collar round his neck. As soon as he saw the uninvited guests he burst into paroxysms of tears. The police tried to console him and assure him that it wasn't him they were after. But when they discovered four grams of hash and two fixes of heroin on bookshelves full of ornaments but devoid of books, they asked for the identity papers of the man on the floor anyway. Sobbing profusely, he fished out a khaki wallet. The policemen could scarcely suppress their mirth when they saw from the ID card that the man was an army officer. His despair was entirely understandable. Such circumstances, though not offences in themselves, had to be reported to higher authority on the seventh floor, the Special Branch. What happened to him then, no one in the hit squad knew; but the Swedish TV crew derived a lot of amusement from the incident, even though for the sake of decency nothing was ever broadcast.

The hit squad's role was implicit in its name. Their job was to turn up unexpectedly and create confusion in the drugs world, to prevent and to prosecute drug trafficking, and to discourage new recruits to the business. They weren't undercover agents in the American sense, so it wasn't essential for them not to be recognisable as police officers. The slovenly image that the majority of them had adopted was more to do with relating to the drugs environment than with pretending to be something they weren't. They knew about most of what went on in the Oslo underworld. But even if in that respect they were head and shoulders above other sections of the force, the problem was that all too often they couldn't prove anything.

Hanne Wilhelmsen could hear loud conversation and boisterous laughter from the squad's staff room well before she reached the door. She had to knock hard several times before someone finally opened up. The door was held ajar and a freckled man with greasy hair and a huge quid of chewing tobacco behind his upper lip gave her a crooked smile, revealing the tobacco trickling between his teeth on the left-hand side.

"Hi, Hanne, what can we do for you?"

He exuded affability, despite his surly body language and the fact that he was holding the door only just ajar.

Hanne smiled back, and nudged the door open wider. He let it go unwillingly.

Half-eaten remains of food, general detritus, and masses of paper, magazines, and soft porn lay scattered around the room. Reclining in a corner was a man with a shaven head, an inverted crucifix adorning one ear, heavy boots on his feet, and a thick Icelandic woollen sweater which looked as if it could stand up by itself. He went by the name of Billy T. He'd been at police training college with Hanne, and was regarded as one of the most effective and intelligent in the whole squad. Billy T. was a kindly soul, as gentle as a lamb, and had to live with an appetite for women which, combined with an enviable fertility, had given him no fewer than four children by an equal number of mothers. He'd never lived with any of them, but he loved his children, all boys, two of them near enough the same age. He coughed up his enforced maintenance contributions with no more than a muted curse every payday.

It was Billy T. who Hanne was in search of. She stepped over the mountains of clothes and papers in her path. He lowered the motorcycle magazine he was reading and looked up at her in mild astonishment.

"Could you spare me a minute in my office?"

An expressive gesture of her arm and head indicated what she thought of the possibility of any confidential conversation in these surroundings.

Billy T. nodded, abandoned his magazine, which was eagerly snapped up by the next reader, and followed her to the second floor.

Hanne Wilhelmsen pulled down a typewritten list from above her desk, letting a drawing pin fall to the floor. She didn't bother to retrieve it, just placed the list in front of Billy T.

"These are all the full-time defence lawyers here in the city, plus some others who don't specialise but take on quite a few criminal cases. There are thirty. More or less."

Billy T. shook his bullet-shaped head and scrutinised the list with interest. He had to squint slightly, because the type was small in order to fit on one sheet.

"What do you think of them?" Hanne asked.

"Think of them? What do you mean?"

He ran his finger down the page.

"He's all right, he's okay, he's a shit, she's very okay," he began. "Is that what you want to know?"

"Well, not exactly," she murmured, hesitating a little.

"Which of them has the most drugs cases?" she asked after a moment or two.

Billy T. took up a pen and put a cross by six of the names. He handed the sheet back to her and she studied it. Then she put it down and gazed out of the window before she spoke again.

"Have you ever heard rumours about any of these lawyers themselves being involved in the drugs trade?"

Billy T. didn't seem surprised at this. He nibbled his thumb.

"That's a serious question, I take it. We hear so damned much, and only believe half of it. But what you're asking is whether I personally have ever had my suspicions, right?"

"Yes, that's what I mean."

"Put it like this: we've had reason to keep people under observation now and again. The last couple of years there've been some odd fluctuations in the market. Maybe three years, in fact. Nothing concrete, nothing we can pinpoint. For example, the perennial problem of drugs creeping into the prisons. We don't know what to do. The checks get more rigorous all the time, but it doesn't seem to make any difference. And things change on the street too. Prices fall. Which means oversupply. Pure free-market economy, that is. Yes, we hear rumours. But vague and conflicting. So if you're asking whether I have suspicions about any of these lawyers, on the basis of what I know, my answer has to be negative."

"But if I ask about your innermost thoughts and instincts, and you don't have to give me any reasons, what would you say then?"

Billy T. from the hit squad rubbed his smooth head, picked up the paper, and placed a dirty index finger under one of the names. Then ran it down the page and stopped at another.

"If I knew something was going on, those two would be the first I would look into," he said. "Maybe because there's been talk, or maybe because I don't like them. Take that for what it is. And don't quote me on it, okay?"

Hanne Wilhelmsen reassured her colleague.

"You've never said it, and we've just been chatting about old times."

Billy T. nodded and grinned, rose to his full height of over six and a half feet, and ambled off back to the staff room on the fourth floor.

FRIDAY 2 OCTOBER

Karen Borg received several telephone calls as a result of her latest and highly unwelcome commission. That morning a journalist rang. He worked for the Oslo *Dagbladet*, and sounded far too aggressively charming and intrusive.

She was totally unused to journalists, and reacted with uncharacteristic caution, replying by and large in monosyllables. First there was a preliminary skirmish in which he appeared to be trying to impress her with everything he already knew about the case, which did indeed seem quite a lot. Then he started asking questions.

"Has he said anything about why he killed Sandersen?"

"No."

"Has he said anything about how they knew one another?"

"No."

"Do the police have any theory about the case?"

"Don't know."

"Is it true that the Dutchman refuses to have any lawyer but you?"

"So far."

"Did you know Hans Olsen, the murdered lawyer?"

She declined to assist him further, thanked him politely for calling, and replaced the receiver.

Hans Olsen? Why that question? She'd read the blood-curdling details in the daily papers, but had put it to the back of her mind, since it didn't concern her and she had no idea who the man was. It hadn't occurred to her that the case might have anything to do with her client. Of course it didn't mean there was any connection anyway; it might just have been a journalistic shot in the dark. She let it rest at that, though with a slight feeling of annoyance. She saw from the screen in front of her that nine people had tried to get in touch today, and from the names she could tell that she would have to spend the rest of the day on her most important client, Norwegian Oil. She pulled out two of the relevant files, bearing the bright red N.O. logo. Fetching herself a cup of coffee, she started making her calls. If she was finished in time she might manage a trip to the police station in the evening. It was Friday, and she had a bad conscience for not having visited her incarcerated client since that initial meeting. She definitely had to follow it up before the weekend.

Despite nearly a week in custody Han van der Kerch wasn't any more talkative. He'd been provided with a urine-stained mattress and a blanket. In one corner of the bunk-like platform he'd piled up a number of cheap paperbacks. They were allowing him one shower a day, and he was beginning to get acclimatised to the warmth, stripping off as soon as he came into the cell, and usually just sitting around in his underpants. Only when he was given the occasional opportunity for exercise, or a further attempt was made at questioning him, did he bother to dress. A patrol car had been out to his room in the student residences in Kringsjå to fetch him a change of underpants, some toilet things, and, rather excessively, his small portable CD player.

He was dressed now. Karen Borg was sitting with him in an office on the second floor. They weren't exactly having a conversation, more a monologue with intermittent mumbles from the other party.

"Peter Strup phoned me at the beginning of the week. He said he knew a friend of yours, and wanted to help you."

No reaction, just a darker and sulkier look around his eyes.

"Do you know Strup, the lawyer? Do you know what friend he's talking about?"

"Yes. I want you."

"Fine."

Her patience was nearly at an end. After a quarter of an hour of endeavouring to get something more out of him, she was on the point of giving up. Then the Dutchman unexpectedly slumped forward in his chair and in a gesture of despair sank his head in his hands, resting his elbows on his knees. He rubbed his scalp, raised his eyes, and began to talk.

"I can see you're confused. I'm bloody confused myself. I made the biggest mistake of my life last Friday. It was a cold, premeditated, and cruel murder. I got money for it. Or rather, I was promised money for it. I haven't seen a penny yet, and will probably have my own creditors on my back for years to come. I've been in this overheated cell for a week now thinking about what could have come over me."

Suddenly he burst into tears. It was so abrupt and unforeseen that Karen Borg was taken completely by surprise. The boy — for now he looked more like a teenager — was leaning over with his head in his lap as if he were bracing himself for a crash landing in an aeroplane, and his back was heaving. After a few moments he straightened up to get more air, and she could see that his face was already blotchy. His nose was running, and, being quite unable to think of anything to say, Karen pulled out a pack of tissues from her briefcase and passed it to him. He dried his nose and eyes, but didn't stop sobbing. Karen had no idea how to console a remorseful murderer, but nevertheless pulled her chair closer and took his hand.

They stayed sitting in that position for over ten minutes. It felt more like an hour — probably for both of them, Karen thought. At last the young man's breathing became somewhat less ragged. She let go of his hand and soundlessly pushed back her chair, as if to erase the short period of intimacy and trust.

"Perhaps you could tell me a bit more now," she said in a quiet voice, offering him a fresh cigarette. He took it with a trembling hand, like a bad actor. She knew it was genuine, and gave him a light.

"I don't know what to say," he stammered. "The fact is that I've killed a man. But I've done a lot of other things too, and I don't want to talk myself into a life sentence. And I don't know how to speak about one thing without revealing others."

Karen was in some perplexity. She was accustomed to treating information with the greatest discretion and confidentiality. She wouldn't have had many clients had she not possessed that quality. But confidentiality up till now had been about finance, industrial secrets, and business tactics. She had never received a confidence about anything unequivocally criminal, and was in a quandary about what she could keep to herself without falling foul of the law. But before she'd even thought through the problem, she decided to put the Dutchman's mind at rest.

"Whatever you say to me will be between the two of us. I'm your lawyer, and bound by the rules of professional confidentiality."

After a few final sighs he blew his nose vigorously into a wet tissue and began to tell her all about it.

"I was in a sort of syndicate. I say 'sort of', because quite honestly I don't know very much about it. I know of two others in it, but they're people at my own level: we collect and deliver, and sell a little now and then. My contact runs a secondhand car business north of the city centre, up in Sagene. But it's pretty big, the whole operation. I think. There've never been any problems getting paid for the jobs I've done. A bloke like myself can travel to the Netherlands as often as he wants without arousing any suspicion. I visited my mother every time."

At the thought of his mother he broke down again.

"I've never been in trouble with the police before, neither here nor back home," he sniffed. "Oh hell, how long do you think I'll get?"

Karen knew very well what a murderer could expect. And maybe even a drug courier. But she said nothing, just shrugged her shoulders.

"I've probably made about ten to fifteen runs in all," he went on. "Unbelievably easy job, in fact. I would be given a rendezvous in Amsterdam in advance, always a different place. The goods would be completely sealed. In rubber. I would swallow the packets, without actually knowing what was in them."

He paused for a moment before correcting himself.

"Well, I guessed it was heroin. Must have known it was, really. About a hundred grams each time. That's more than two thousand fixes. Everything went okay, and I got my twenty thousand on delivery. Plus all expenses paid."

His voice was thick, but he was explaining himself clearly enough. He sat tearing at the tissues, which were just about shredded to pieces already. He stared at his hands throughout, as if he couldn't believe they had so brutally killed another person exactly a week before.

"There must be quite a lot of people involved. Even if I don't know more than a couple myself. The whole thing's too big. One scruffy spiv in Sagene couldn't run it on his own. He doesn't look bright enough. But I haven't asked any questions. I did the job, got my money, and kept my mouth shut. Until ten days ago."

Karen Borg felt exhausted. She was caught up in a situation over which she had no control whatsoever.

Her brain registered the information she was receiving, while she simultaneously made febrile attempts to work out what she might do with it. She could feel her cheeks reddening and perspiration beginning to dampen her armpits. She knew she was going to hear about Ludvig Sandersen now, the man she'd found last Friday, a discovery that had haunted her at night and tormented her by day ever since. She clutched her chair tightly.

"I was up with the garage guy last Thursday," Han van der Kerch went on. He was calmer now, and had finally relinquished the remnants of the tissues and dropped them in the bin on the floor by his side. He looked at her for the first time that day. "I hadn't done a job for several months. I was expecting to hear something any moment. I've had a phone put in my room, so that I'm not dependent on the communal one in the corridor. I never pick up the receiver before it's rung four times. If it rings twice and then stops, and then rings twice more, I know that I have to meet him at two o'clock in the morning. Smart system. Not a single call is ever registered between us on my phone, yet he can contact me. Well, I turned up last Thursday. But this time it wasn't about drugs. There was someone in the syndicate who'd got a bit too big for his boots. Had begun to demand money from one of the guys at the top. Something like that. I didn't get to know much, just that he was a threat to all of us. I was terrified."

He smiled, a wry, self-deprecating smile.

"In the two years I've been doing this, I'd never really thought about the possibility of getting caught. In a way I felt invulnerable. Hell, I was shit scared when I thought someone might step out of line. It had never occurred to me that anyone from within might be a threat. It was actually the fear of being caught that made me say yes to the job. I'd get two hundred thousand kroner for it. Bloody tempting. The idea was not simply that he should die. It was also to act as a warning to all the others in the organisation. That was why I smashed in his face."

The boy began to sob again, but not so convulsively now. He could manage to go on talking while the tears were flowing. He kept pausing, taking deep breaths, smoking, thinking.

"But as soon as I'd done it, I got into a sweat. I regretted it straight away, and wandered round in a daze for twenty-four hours. I don't remember much about it."

She hadn't interrupted him once. Nor had she taken any notes. But there were two questions she had to ask.

"Why did you want to have me?" she enquired gently. "And why didn't you want to go into prison?"

Han van der Kerch stared at her for what seemed an eternity.

"It was you that found the body, even though it was well hidden."

"Yes, I had a dog with me. But so what?"

"Well, despite the fact that I knew next to nothing about the rest of the organisation, you come across things now and again. A slip of the tongue, a hint. I think, yes, I think there might be a lawyer involved. I don't know who. I can't trust anyone. But we wanted it

68

to take a long time before the body was found. The longer it took, the colder the trail. You must have found him only an hour after I killed him. So you couldn't be involved."

"And prison?"

"I know the organisation has contacts on the inside. Inmates, I assume, but it might be warders as well for all I know. The safest thing was to stay with the cops. Even if it is bloody hot!"

He seemed relieved. Karen, on the other hand, was depressed, as if all that had weighed on the young man for a week had now landed on her shoulders.

He asked what she was going to do. She gave him an honest answer: she wasn't entirely sure. She would have to consider.

"But you promised to keep all this to yourself," he reminded her.

Karen didn't reply, but drew her index finger across her throat. She called an officer, and the Dutchman was taken back to the miserable dingy-yellow cell.

Though it was gone six o'clock on a Friday evening, Håkon Sand was still in his office. Karen Borg realised that the weary lines he had in his face, that she'd thought on Monday were the result of living it up at the weekend, were actually permanent. She was rather amazed that he was working so late; she knew that no one got paid overtime in the police force.

"It's stupid to work so much," he admitted. "But it's worse to wake up in the night worrying about everything you haven't done. I try to get more or less

69

up-to-date every Friday. The weekends are more enjoyable then."

The big grey building was silent. They sat there with a feeling of unusual rapport. Then a siren broke the stillness, a police car being tested in the yard at the back. It ceased as abruptly as it had begun.

"Did he say anything?"

She had expected the question, knew it had to come, but having relaxed for a few minutes she was quite unprepared.

"Nothing in particular."

She noticed how difficult it was to lie to him. He always seemed to know what was going on in her mind. She could feel a flush creeping up her back, and hoped it wouldn't spread to her face.

"The Client Confidentiality Act," he said with a smile, and stretched his arms, linking his hands and putting them behind his neck. She could see sweat under his arms, but it didn't seem repulsive, just natural, after a ten-hour working day.

"I respect that," he went on. "Can't say much myself, either!"

"I thought the defence had a right to information and documents," she said reprovingly.

"Not if we think it might be detrimental to the investigation," he countered with an even broader smile, as if amused that they found themselves in a professional adversarial relationship. He got up and poured them some coffee. It tasted worse than on Monday, as if it was the same pot that had been on the hotplate ever since. She contented herself with one sip and pushed the cup away with a grimace.

"That stuff will kill you," she admonished him. He shrugged and reassured her that he had a cast-iron stomach.

For some reason she couldn't explain, she felt good. There was a tangible but oddly pleasant conflict going on between them that had never been there before. Never before had Håkon been in possession of knowledge she didn't have. Scrutinising him, she could see a glint in his eyes. His greying at the temples and his receding hairline made him appear not just older but also more interesting, and stronger. He had actually grown rather handsome.

"You've become quite good-looking, Håkon," she blurted out.

He didn't even blush, just looked her straight in the eyes. She regretted it immediately; it was like opening a chink in her armour that she had long recognised she couldn't afford, not for anyone. As quick as lightning she changed the subject.

"Well, if you can't tell me anything and I can't say anything, we might as well call it a day," she concluded, standing up and putting on her raincoat.

He asked her to sit down again. She complied, but kept her coat on.

"To be perfectly frank, this is a far more serious matter than we originally assumed. We're working on several theories, but they're fairly vague and without a shred of firm evidence to support them at the moment. I can at least tell you that it looks as if it might be drug dealing on a grand scale. It's too early to say how involved your client might be. But he's already in deep enough with murder. We think it was premeditated. If I can't say any more than that, it's not that I'm unwilling. We simply don't know, and I have to be careful, even with an old friend like you, not to come out with unfounded assertions and speculations."

"Has it anything to do with Hans E. Olsen?"

Karen had caught Håkon Sand off guard. His mouth dropped open and he stared at her. Neither spoke for half a minute.

"What the hell do you know about that?"

"Nothing at all," she replied. "But I had a call from a journalist today. A man called Fredrick Myhre or Myhreng or something like that. From the *Dagbladet*. He threw in a question about whether I knew the murdered lawyer. Right in the middle of asking me about my client. It seems that the journalists are fairly well informed about police activities, so I thought I should ask you. I don't know anything. Should I?"

"The bugger," said Håkon and stood up. "We'll talk about it next week."

As they went out the door, Håkon reached out to turn off the light after them. The movement brought his arm over her shoulder, and suddenly without warning he kissed her. It was a tentative, boyish kiss.

For a few seconds their eyes met, then he switched off the light, locked the door, and without saying another word led her out of the deserted building.

It was the weekend.

MONDAY 5 OCTOBER

Fredrick Myhreng, the journalist, didn't feel at all well. He tugged nervously at his rolled-up sleeves and began fiddling with a ball-point pen till he managed to break it and the ink oozed out, staining his hands blue. He looked round for something to wipe them on, but had to make do with sheets from his notebook, hardly ideal. He also got ink on his smart suit. He wore the sleeves turned back, as if he hadn't realised that this style went out of fashion when *Miami Vice* disappeared from Norwegian television. A long time ago now. The label on the outside of the right sleeve hadn't been removed; in fact, the turn-up was so contrived that it stood out like a hallmark. But it was no good; he still felt insignificant and uncomfortable sitting in Håkon Sand's office.

He had agreed to come willingly enough. Sand had phoned him early that morning, before the journalist's Monday-morning feeling after a lively weekend had worn off. Sand had been polite but firm when he asked him to present himself as soon as possible. It was ten o'clock, and he was feeling sick. Håkon offered him a sweet from a wooden dish, and he accepted it. He regretted it immediately after it was in his mouth; it was enormous, and impossible to suck without slurping.

Sand hadn't taken one himself, and Myhreng could understand why. It was difficult to talk with such an object in his mouth, and he felt it would look too childish if he started chewing it.

"You're working on our murder cases, I understand," Håkon said, not without a hint of arrogance.

"Sure, I'm a crime reporter," Myhreng answered curtly and with scantly concealed pride in his professional title. He almost shot the sweet out of his mouth in his eagerness to sound self-assured. Sucking it quickly back in again, he inadvertently swallowed it. He could feel its slow and painful progress down his gullet.

"What do you actually know?"

The young journalist wasn't really sure what to say. All his instincts prompted him to be circumspect, while his desire to exult in his knowledge was irresistible.

"I believe I know what you know," he declared, and thought he'd killed two birds with one stone. "And maybe a little more."

Håkon Sand sighed.

"Now look. I know you won't say anything about who and how. I know your warped sense of honour will never allow you to name sources. That's not what I'm asking for. I'm offering a deal."

A spark of interest showed in Myhreng's eyes, but Håkon didn't know how long it would last.

"I can confirm that you're onto something," he continued. "I've heard that you've apparently made a connection between the two murders. I also note that you haven't yet written anything about it. Which is

74

good. It would be detrimental to the investigation, to say the least, if it got into print. I could of course get the commissioner to ring your editor and put some pressure on you. But perhaps I don't need to."

The blond-haired journalist's interest was increasing.

"I promise you that you'll be the first to get what we have, as soon as we're able to say anything. But that's on condition that I can rely on you when I have to muzzle you. Can I?"

Fredrick Myhreng liked the way the conversation was developing.

"That depends," he said with a smile. "Let's hear some more."

"What made you link the two murders together?"

"What made *you*?"

Håkon took a deep breath. He rose, went over to the window, and stood there for a moment. Then he wheeled round again.

"I'm trying to come to an amicable arrangement," he said, adopting a harsh tone. "I could have you in for questioning. I could even bring a charge of withholding evidence pertaining to a criminal investigation. I can't torture you for information, I suppose, but I can make things hellish hot for you. Do I need to?"

His words had an effect. Myhreng squirmed in his seat. He asked for a further undertaking that he would be the first to know as soon as anything happened. He got it.

"I was having a drink in the Old Christiania the day Sandersen was murdered. In the afternoon, about three I think it was. Sandersen was sitting there with Olsen,

75

the lawyer. I noticed them because they were on their own. Olsen has a whole crowd he goes — sorry, I mean used to go — drinking with. They were there too, but at another table. I didn't think much about it at the time, but remembered it of course when the murders followed so closely on one another. I've no idea what they were talking about. But it was a bit of a coincidence! Beyond that, I know absolutely nothing. But I have my suspicions."

It went quiet in the room. They could hear the noise of the traffic in Åkebergveien at the back. A crow landed on the windowsill, expressing its complaints in raucous tones. Håkon Sand wasn't even aware of it.

"There may be a connection. But we don't know. For the moment there are only a couple of us here thinking along those lines. Have you talked to anyone else about it?"

Myhreng was able to reassure him on that score. He was only too keen to keep the story to himself. But he had begun some investigations of his own, he said. The odd question here and there, nothing that would arouse suspicion. And everything he'd learnt up to this point was only what he knew already. Hansy Olsen's alcohol problem, his predilection for his clients, his lack of friends, and his large number of boozing companions. What were the police doing?

"Very little so far," said Håkon. "But we've got going now. We'll talk at the end of the week. I'll be down on you like a ton of bricks, make no mistake about it, if you don't stick to our agreement. Not one word about

76

this in the paper, and I'll ring you as soon as we know any more. Right, you can go."

Fredrick Myhreng was elated. He'd done a good day's work, and had a broad grin on his face as he left police headquarters. His Monday-morning feeling had evaporated.

The big room was much too dim. Heavy brown velour curtains with tasselled edges absorbed what little light managed to find its way into the apartment on the ground floor of the old city block. All the furniture was made of dark wood. Mahogany, Hanne Wilhelmsen thought. It smelt as if it was always sealed up, and everything was covered in a deep layer of dust. It couldn't possibly have appeared in a single week, so the two police officers had to conclude that cleanliness had not been high on Hansy Olsen's list of priorities. But it was tidy. There were bookshelves right along one wall, dark brown with cupboards at the base and an illuminated bar cabinet at one end with cut-glass doors. Håkon Sand walked across the thick carpet to the bookshelves. He felt as if he was sinking into it, and his feet made no sound except for a slight creak of shoe leather. There was no fiction on the shelves, but the lawyer had an impressive collection of legal tomes. Håkon shook his head as he read the titles on the spines. Some of the books here would sell for several thousand kroner if they went to auction. He took one of them down, felt the good quality genuine calf of the binding, and registered the characteristic smell as he carefully turned over the pages.

Hanne had sat herself at the enormous marble desk with lions' claw legs, and stared at the leather armchair. There was a crocheted antimacassar over the back, covered in dark, congealed blood. She thought she could even discern a faint aroma of iron, but dismissed the notion as fanciful. The seat was stained too.

"What are we actually looking for?"

Håkon's question was pertinent, but received no response.

"You're the detective on the case: why did you want to drag me along?"

He still got no answer, but Hanne moved to the window and ran her hands along under the sill.

"Forensics have been over the whole place," she said at last. "But they were after murder clues, and they may have missed what we're looking for. I think there have to be papers hidden somewhere. There must be something in this apartment to give an indication of what the man was up to, apart from his legal practice, that is. His bank accounts, or at any rate the ones we're aware of, have been thoroughly scrutinised. Nothing suspicious at all."

She carried on feeling the walls as she spoke.

"If our rather flimsy theory is correct, he must have been pretty well off. He wouldn't have risked keeping documents at his office, because other people would be running in and out all damned day. Unless he had a hiding place elsewhere, there must be something here."

Håkon followed her example, and ran his fingers over the opposite wall, self-consciously recognising that he hadn't the slightest idea what a possible secret compartment might feel like. But they went on in silence until they'd duly felt round the entire room. With no result other than sixteen dirty fingertips.

"What about the obvious places?" Håkon wondered, and went over and opened the cupboards in the tasteless bookcase.

There was nothing at all in the first one. The dust on the shelves bore witness to its having been empty for a long time. The next was stuffed full of porn films, neatly arranged by category. Hanne took one out and opened it. It contained what it said it did, according to the enticing promises on the label. She put the film back, and took out the next one.

"Bingo!"

A slip of paper had fallen to the floor. She snatched it up, a neatly folded A4 sheet. At the top, written by hand, was the word "South." Below it followed a list of numbers, in groups of three with hyphens between them: 2-17-4, 2-19-3, 7-29-32, 9-14-3. And so it went on right down the page.

They stared at it long and hard.

"It must be a code," Håkon declared, regretting the words as soon as they left his mouth.

"You don't say," Hanne replied with a smile, folding the sheet carefully again and placing it in a sealable plastic bag. "We'll have to try to crack it then," she said emphatically, and put the bag in the case they'd brought with them.

Peter Strup was an extremely active man. He lived life at a pace which at his age would have made all the doctors' warning lights flash, if it weren't for the fact that he kept himself in such impressively good physical shape. He was in court thirty weeks a year. In addition to that he took part in protest meetings, TV programmes, and public debates. He had published three books in the last five years, two about his many exploits, and one pure biography. All of them, published just the right length of time before Christmas, had sold well.

He was in the lift on his way up to Karen Borg's office. His suit showed good taste, a deep reddish-brown flannel. His socks matched the stripes on his tie. He looked at himself in the huge mirror that covered the whole of one wall of the lift. He drew his fingers through his hair, adjusted his tie, and was annoyed to see a hint of grime around his collar. As the wood-trimmed metal doors slid open and he took a step out into the corridor, a young woman came through the big glass doors embellished with white numerals to reassure him he was on the right floor. She was fair-haired, quite attractive, dressed in a suit that was almost exactly the same colour and material as his own. Seeing him, she stopped in astonishment.

"Peter Strup?"

"Mrs. Borg, I presume," he said, offering his hand, which she took with only momentary hesitation.

"Are you on your way out?" he asked, rather superfluously.

"Yes, but only to get myself a few things. Come on in," she replied, turning back.

"Was it me you wanted to see?"

He confirmed that it was, and they went into her office together.

"I've come about your client," he said when he'd sat down in one of the deep armchairs with a little glass table between them.

"I really would be very happy to take him over from you. Have you discussed it with him?"

"Yes. He won't agree to it. He wants me. Would you like a cup of coffee?"

"No thanks, I don't want to take up too much of your time," Peter Strup replied. "Do you have any idea why he's insisting on having you?"

"No, I don't, actually," she said, amazed at how easily she found herself lying to this man. "Perhaps he simply prefers a woman."

She smiled. He gave a short but charming laugh.

"This isn't meant to sound insulting," he asserted, "but with all due respect, are you conversant with criminal law? Are you aware of all the courtroom procedures in criminal trials?"

She bristled angrily as she considered her response. Over the course of the last week she had been teased by her colleagues, bullied by Nils, and reproached by her snobbish mother for having taken on a criminal case. She was fed up with it. And Peter Strup would have to bear the brunt. She slammed her hands down on the desk.

"Quite honestly I've had just about enough of everybody pointing out my incompetence. I've had eight years' experience as a lawyer, following on from damn good results when I graduated. With all due respect, if I may use your own words, how challenging will it actually be to defend a man who has admitted to a murder? Won't it be fairly plain sailing, with a few well-chosen words about his difficult life before the summing up and sentencing?"

It was unusual for her to boast, and she wasn't normally short-tempered. But it gave her quite a buzz. She could see that Strup was uneasy.

"Of course, I'm sure you can handle it," he said soothingly, like a benevolent examiner. "I didn't mean to offend you."

As he went out he turned with a smile and added, "But the offer is still there!"

Having closed the door, Karen rang police headquarters. She eventually got a surly switchboard operator, and asked for Håkon Sand.

"It's Karen here."

He was silent, and for a fraction of a second she felt again the weird tingle of excitement that had arisen between them before the weekend, but that she'd almost forgotten about in the meantime. Perhaps because she preferred to.

"What do you know about Peter Strup?"

Her question broke the atmosphere of wariness, and she could hear the surprise in his voice as he answered.

"Peter Strup? One of the most competent defence lawyers in the country, maybe even the best; practising since time immemorial, and a damned nice guy, too! Clever, very well known, and not a skeleton in his cupboard. Married to the same woman for twenty-five years, three successful children, and a modest detached suburban house in Nordstrand. I read the last bit in the tabloids. What about him?"

Karen told her story. She was factual, adding nothing and omitting nothing. When she'd finished, she declared:

"There's something very fishy about it. He can't be short of work. And he went to all the trouble of coming to my office! He could have phoned again."

She sounded almost indignant. Håkon was immersed in his own train of thought, and said nothing.

"Hello?"

He came back to life.

"Yes, I'm still here. No, I can't explain it. He probably just called in because he was in your neighbourhood."

"Well, maybe, but then it was strange that he didn't have a briefcase or documents of any kind with him."

Håkon couldn't help but agree, though he said nothing. Absolutely nothing. But his brain was working so hard that Karen might almost have heard it.

WEDNESDAY 7 OCTOBER

"This is a book code. That much is self-evident."

The elderly man had the confidence of his expertise. He was sitting in the canteen on the sixth floor with Hanne Wilhelmsen and Håkon Sand.

He was good-looking, slim, and remarkably tall for someone of his generation. His hair might have been thinner than it once was, but there was still enough of it to present an imposing grey-white mane, combed back and recently trimmed. He had strongly defined features and a straight North European nose with reading glasses elegantly perched on the tip. He was neatly dressed, in a maroon sweater and stylish blue trousers. His hands were steady as they held the paper, and there was a narrow wedding ring tightly ingrown on the third finger of his right hand.

Gustaf Løvstrand was a retired policeman. His background was in military intelligence during the War and for a few years afterwards, until he turned to a more public-service orientated career in the police force. He was thoroughly dependable, well liked and highly respected by his colleagues before he was transferred to the Special Branch, where he had ended his career as a consultant. He'd had the unalloyed pleasure and satisfaction of seeing all three of his children in police-related jobs. He adored his wife and his roses, enjoyed his retirement, and was ready to assist anybody who regarded him as still having something to contribute.

"It's easy to see it's a book code. Take a look at the numbers," he said, laying the piece of paper flat on the table and pointing at the string of figures:

2-17-4, 2-19-3, 7-29-32, 9-14-3, 12-2-29, 13-11-29, 16-11-2.

"Absurdly simple," he went on with a smile.

The other two couldn't really see what he was talking about, and Hanne ventured to confess her ignorance.

"What exactly is a book code, and how is it so self-evident?"

Løvstrand glanced up at her for a moment, and then indicated the top line.

"Three numbers in each group. Page, line, and letter. As you can see, it's only the first one in each group that has any logical progression. It's either the same as the preceding first number or higher: 2, 2, 7, 9, 12, 13, 16, and so on. The highest number in the second group is 43, and it's rare for a book to have more than forty-something lines to a page. Once you identify the book it's based on, the puzzle should solve itself straight away."

He could only assume that it must have been devised by amateurs, since book codes were so easy to recognise.

"On the other hand, they're incredibly difficult to crack," he declared, "because you have to find the book! And if a prearranged code is used to denote it, you need an awful lot of luck to discover it. When you gave me this, I went down to the Central Library. I got a printout from the database that gave more than twelve hundred books with the word 'south' in the title. Good hunting! Anyway, that word could be a code too, and then you're no further on. Without the right book, there's not a hope of breaking the code."

He folded the paper and gave it back to Hanne, who looked dispirited. He wouldn't keep it, even though it was only a copy. His years in the secret service had had their effect.

"But since the code itself is so banal, I would suggest you try and track down what it's based on — search for the book near where you found this piece of paper. You might well stumble upon it. A lot of good police work comes from luck. I wish you plenty of it!"

The two officers sat in silence for a while.

"Look on the bright side, Håkon," said Hanne eventually. "At least we know we're onto something. Olsen would hardly have needed a code for writing his defence speeches. So it has to refer to nefarious activities."

"But what?" Håkon sighed. "Shall we go over everything we've got once again?"

An hour later they were both in a considerably better mood. It was not beyond the bounds of possibility that they might find the book. And since their last meeting they'd also had confirmation that Olsen had indeed seen his client on the day of the appointment. And that it had not taken place in his office, but in the unlikely and very public venue of the Old Christiania.

"That could of course mean that the meeting was entirely innocent," said Håkon rather glumly.

"Sure could," said Hanne, making ready to go.

"Why do you use so many American expressions?"

"I'm an America freak." She grinned, slightly embarrassed. "I know it's a bad habit."

They gulped down the rest of their coffee, and went their separate ways.

Later that afternoon two walkers were conversing on a fallen tree trunk in the wooded hills of Nordmarka just to the north of Oslo. The older of the two was sitting on a plastic bag as protection against the damp. The autumn was in its most typical phase, with the finest drizzle in the air, bordering on mist. Visibility was poor, but they hadn't come out to enjoy the view. One of them tossed a stone into the smooth surface of the forest lake, and they sat in silence watching the circular ripples spread out with the beauty of natural phenomena until the water was totally still again.

"Will the organisation collapse now?"

It was the younger one, a man in his thirties, who put the question. His voice was tightly controlled. He was tense, and it showed, despite the fact that he was trying to appear relaxed.

"No, it'll be fine," the older man reassured him. "There's a good solid structure in place. We've just hacked off one branch. Pity, in a way, because it was profitable. But it had to be done. There's too much at stake."

He threw another stone, with greater force this time, as if to emphasise his point.

"Well, the truth is," the younger man ventured, "it's been solid till now, we've always been careful, and the police have never got anywhere near us. But two murders are in a different league from our previous activities. However greedy Olsen may have been, I don't see why we couldn't simply have paid him off. Hell, it's given me the jitters!"

The older man got up and stood in front of him. He looked all around, to make sure they were alone. The mist had thickened, and visibility was down to about twenty or thirty metres. There was no one within that radius.

"Now see here," he hissed. "We've always been fully aware of the risks of this business. But we have to pull off a few more operations, so it doesn't look as if there's a connection between the supply of drugs and the murders. Then we'll get out while the going's good. But that means you'll have to keep a cool head and not let us down in the next few months. Because you're the one with the contacts.

"But we have a little spot of bother that might blow up in our faces," he continued. "Han van der Kerch. How much does he know?"

"Nothing, basically. He knows Roger in Sagene. Not much apart from that. But he's been part of the team for a year or two now, so he may have picked up a few bits and pieces. He can't have any knowledge of me. I haven't been as incredibly stupid as Hansy was, letting one of the runners into our secrets. I've stuck to the codes and written messages."

"All the same, he might be a problem," the older man persisted. "Your problem."

He lapsed into a meaningful silence without shifting his gaze from his companion. It was a threatening posture, with one leg on the tree trunk and the other firmly on the ground right in front of the younger man.

"There's something else you ought to remember. You're the only one who knows about me, now that Hansy has kicked the bucket. None of the boys lower down in the organisation is aware of my existence. Only you. That makes you rather vulnerable, my friend."

It was an absolutely blatant threat. The younger man stood up and put his face right up close to the other.

"That goes for you too," he said coldly.

SUNDAY 11 OCTOBER

Hanne Wilhelmsen had the same relationship with the police force that in her more romantic moments she imagined a fisherman had with the sea. She was indissolubly bound to the police, and couldn't envisage doing anything else. When she chose to go to police college at the age of twenty, she made a decisive break with the deep-rooted academic traditions of her family. It had been a protest against her professorial parents and thoroughly middle-class background. Her choice of lifestyle was met with deafening silence from the family, apart from a nervous clearing of the throat by her mother at one Sunday lunch. But they seemed to have accepted it with equanimity. Now she was a sort of mascot for them all, the one who had the most entertaining stories at Christmas. It was through her that the family could imagine they were keeping in touch with real life, and she loved her job.

At the same time she feared it. She had begun to notice what was happening to her soul as a result of this daily contact with murder, rape, violence, and abuse. It clung to her like a wet sheet. Even though she had got into the way of taking a shower when she came home from work, she sometimes thought the smell of death stuck fast, like the smell of fish guts on the hands of fishermen. And just as she imagined fishermen scanning the waters for direct or indirect signs of the presence of fish — gulls gathering, schools of whales hunting — almost as a reflex in their bones after generations at sea, that was how she let her subconscious roam over all her cases simultaneously. There was no information that didn't lead somewhere. The danger lay in the ever-present problem of overwork. Crime in Oslo was growing at a faster rate than the money allocated to police recruitment in the annual budget.

She constantly endeavoured to keep her caseload within a maximum of ten under investigation at any one time, a goal she all too frequently failed to achieve. Green files of differing thicknesses were heaped up in dangerously high and mutually threatening stacks on one side of her desk. Even in the extremely busy period that was now behind her, she had made time to go through them at intervals and try to attach the little A5 sheet bearing the words "Recommend no further action" to the greatest possible number of cases. With feelings of inadequacy and an absolute certainty of the suspect's guilt, she would go, weighed down with guilt herself, to get the necessary stamp from a police prosecution attorney, code 058, "Not proceeded with for lack of evidence." So another criminal went free, she had one less case to spend her time on, and she just hoped that she had mostly got her priorities right. The burden was made worse by the fact that she never encountered any resistance from the attorneys. They relied on her and only skimmed through the documents out of a sense of duty before invariably following her recommendations. Hanne knew that the stacks of green files were nightmares for them, too.

It was Sunday, and she had twenty-one files in front of her. She had sorted them according to the severity of the potential penalty. She felt paralysed for a while by an inability to act, but eventually managed to get herself going. None of the cases was a prime candidate for the archives. There were eleven Article 228/229s, assault and grievous bodily harm. Perhaps she should go for a fine on some of them, a legitimate and practical way of getting rid of them.

Three hours later she had proposed fines in seven cases, all involving greater or lesser degrees of violence perpetrated by drunken restaurant customers and churlish doormen. With a certain amount of goodwill two cases could be regarded as adequately investigated, even if more witness statements would undoubtedly have been valuable. Hoping the courts would be able to recognise a criminal when they saw one, she made recommendations to prosecute.

Sunday was a good day for working. No phones, no meetings, and only a few other colleagues to exchange smug words with in mutual admiration for being at work on their free day, without pay or recognition — only the knowledge that Monday would be that much easier.

She heard voices at the rear of the building, and glanced out of the window. A considerable number of press photographers were clustered outside, and she remembered that the minister of justice was coming that day. "Why on a Sunday?" their superintendent had asked grumpily when the notice of the proposed visit arrived from the commissioner's office. The only response he got was that it was not his concern. Hanne had a shrewd suspicion that the choice of day was not unrelated to the amount of space available in Monday newspapers, since all the major stories would have been hogged by the ubiquitous Sundays. The Monday papers had been getting thinner, and it was that much easier to get into print. The minister's visit was the result of repeated headlines about the high incidence of unsolved crimes, and he was also going to take the opportunity to discuss with the commissioner the alarming increase in street violence, what the media were fond of calling "unprovoked attacks" — not an accurate description if one had access to the relevant files, which journalists usually did not. So they didn't realise that the change was not the absence of provocation, but that it was now countered by knives and fists rather than by verbal abuse as in the old days.

Now she had got it down to twelve unsolved cases. She was closer to her target, and felt in a better humour. She selected the thickest of the files.

They weren't any nearer to finding an answer as to why Ludvig Sandersen had had to be despatched so brutally to what some maintained was a better place. Hanne hoped for his sake that she was the one who was wrong, and that he was now attired in white and seated on a cloud, indulging himself to the fullest on the greyish-white powder that had made his life on earth such a misery.

They had still not found any link between this case and Olsen's murder. She had chewed over the idea with Håkon Sand on Friday, and she felt they had enough now to make the connection official. But he had opposed the suggestion, and opted to wait a bit longer. However, she thought the time had come to start examining the two cases together. She pushed the pile of papers away, took her feet off the desk, and let her boots thud to the floor as she rummaged in her bag for her keys, which also fitted the doors of all the other investigators' offices. The file was with Heidi Rørvik, a few rooms further down the corridor.

There was no sign of anyone in the corridor as she came out. Everything was quiet, as it should be on a Sunday afternoon. But just as she was about to unlock the door of Rørvik's office, she felt rather than heard footsteps behind her. She swung round, a split second too late. The blow, with an object she couldn't identify, struck her savagely on the temple. Her head exploded in a violent flash of light and she knew she was already bleeding profusely even before she hit the ground. She had no strength in her muscles, so there was nothing she could do to break her fall. The left side of her forehead smashed to the floor, but she wasn't aware of it. She had already lost consciousness, momentarily experiencing only an intense feeling of life ebbing away, before she sank into a darkness that obliterated the pain. A gash like a broad, scornful sneer opened up on her brow.

★ ★ ★

She was roused by a desperate urge to vomit. She was lying on her stomach with her head twisted at an excruciating angle; the need was so overpowering that it fleetingly outweighed the sensation that her head was going to burst open. She hurt all over. Cautiously exploring with her fingers she realised with a dull sense of surprise that two big bleeding cuts, one on her forehead and the other above her right ear, were no more painful than the deep sharp stab emanating from somewhere inside, deep in the centre of her skull. She lay there fighting against the nausea for several minutes, but finally had to give in. As if by instinct, she found the strength and presence of mind to drag herself up onto her hands and knees, like a baby watching TV, so that she could vomit without swallowing anything. It helped.

She wiped her forehead, but couldn't prevent the blood running into one eye and obscuring her vision. She made an effort to stand up, but the blue corridor spun round and round, and she had to perform the task in stages. Finally on her feet again, she sagged against the wall, and only then did she start trying to understand what had happened. She couldn't remember a thing. She was seized by panic. She knew she must be at police headquarters, but had no idea why she was there. Where were the others? She staggered along to her own office and dialled her home number, smearing the telephone with blood in the process. She had to make numerous attempts; it was difficult to find the right buttons. The light from the window was unbearable, like being hit with a hammer behind the eyes.

"Cecilie, come and fetch me. I'm ill."

She dropped the receiver, and collapsed back into unconsciousness.

The darkness was comforting. Her head still ached, but where before there had been bleeding wounds, she could feel big soft bandages. The cuts weren't really painful, and she presumed she must have been given a local anaesthetic. The bed was a metal one, and after touching the bandages she discovered that a saline drip had been inserted into her hand. Hanne was in hospital, and Cecilie was sitting on the edge of the bed.

"It must hurt a lot," her partner said, smiling as she took hold of the hand that wasn't attached to the tube.

"I was very frightened when I found you," she continued. "But everything's all right. I've seen your X-rays myself, and there's no fracture. You've had a severe concussion. The wounds looked rather ugly, but they've been stitched and they'll soon heal up."

Hanne began to cry.

"I don't remember anything, Cecilie," she whispered.

"Slight amnesia, that's all. Loss of memory," Cecilie added with a smile. "It's quite normal. Don't worry, you just lie here for two or three days, then you can have a lovely couple of weeks off sick. I'll look after you."

Hanne was still crying. Cecilie bent over her, carefully, very carefully, and rested her face against the

96

bandaged head so that her mouth was level with Hanne's ear.

"That scar on your forehead will be terribly sexy," she murmured. "Terribly, terribly sexy."

MONDAY 12 OCTOBER

"It's not bloody good enough!"

Håkon Sand only swore when he was really furious.

"If we can't damned well be safe even in the office! And on a flaming Sunday as well!"

He spat out the words, accusations of incompetence, without knowing who to blame. He stood in the middle of the room and stamped his foot in time with his own outbursts.

"What the hell's the point of locked doors and security precautions when anyone can attack us whenever they like!"

The superintendent in charge of A 2.11, a stoical man in his fifties, listened to his ranting apparently unmoved. He said nothing until Håkon had calmed down.

"It's impossible to try and pin this on a particular individual. We're not a fortress, nor do we want to be. In a building with a staff of almost two thousand, anyone could have followed an employee through the staff entrance at the rear. It would simply be a matter of timing. You could just hide behind a tree near the church and walk in immediately after somebody who had a pass. You've probably held the door open yourself for someone following you, whether you've known them or not."

Håkon didn't reply, which the superintendent correctly took as an admission.

"And in principle anyone could easily hide in the building while it's open, in the toilets or whatever. It's easy to get back out again. Rather than trying to discover how, we should be asking ourselves why."

"It's bloody obvious why," Håkon raged. "This case, for God's sake. This case! The file's disappeared from Hanne's office. Not a disaster in itself, because we've got several copies, but someone's definitely trying to find out how much we know."

He cut himself short and looked at the clock. His outburst of rage was abating.

"I must dash. I've got to see the commissioner at nine. Do me a favour: ring the hospital and ask whether Hanne can receive visitors. Leave a note in my room as soon as you know."

Lady Justitia was magnificent. She stood some thirty centimetres high on the huge desk, the oxidised bronze redolent of considerable age. The blindfold round the eyes was almost entirely green, the sword in her right hand a reddish colour. But the flat bases of the two weighing pans were completely shiny. Håkon could see they were real scales, swaying slightly in the current of air created by his entry into the room. He couldn't restrain himself from touching the statue.

"Gorgeous, isn't she?"

The uniformed woman behind the huge desk was stating a fact rather than asking a question.

"Had it from my father as a birthday present last week. It stood in his office all his working life. I've admired it ever since I was a little girl. It was bought in the USA, in the late 1890s. By my great-grandfather. It may be valuable. Very attractive anyway."

She was Oslo's first female police commissioner. Her predecessor in the post, a fine upstanding man from Bergen, had been controversial and perpetually at odds with his staff. But he'd had an integrity and energy that had been lacking in the history of the force when he'd taken on the job seven years previously. He'd bequeathed a much better organisation than the one he'd inherited, but it had cost him dearly. Both he and his family were relieved when he retired, a little early, but with his honour intact.

The forty-five-year-old woman who now sat in the commissioner's chair was of a different calibre altogether. Håkon couldn't bear her. She was an arty-farty northerner from Trøndelag, more devious than anyone he'd ever met. She'd been manoeuvering herself towards the top position throughout her police career: keeping in with all the right people, going to all the right parties, and sipping drinks with the right colleagues at prosecution service meetings. Her husband worked in the Ministry of Justice. That had done her no harm either.

But she was undoubtedly very capable. If the old commissioner hadn't elected to retire as soon as he could, she would have taken up an intermediate post, that of public prosecutor. Håkon didn't know which would have been worse.

He made his report as factually as he could, but not in every detail. After a few seconds' thought he decided it would be wrong not to tell his most senior boss about the unofficial connection they'd made between the two murders. But he kept it brief. To his annoyance she grasped everything immediately, put a few pertinent questions, nodded at his conclusions, and finally gave her approval to the work he'd done so far. She asked to be kept fully informed, preferably in writing. Then she added:

"Don't speculate too much, Håkon. Get one murder out of the way at a time. The Sandersen case is in the bag. The technical evidence will support a conviction. Don't look for phantoms where there aren't any. You can regard that as an order."

"Strictly speaking it's really the public prosecutor who's my boss on investigatory matters," he parried.

In response, he was simply dismissed. As he was about to get up, he asked:

"Why does she have a blindfold over her eyes?"

He inclined his head towards the Goddess of Justice standing on her empty desk, attended only by two telephones.

"She mustn't let herself be influenced by either side. She has to exercise blind justice, impartially," the commissioner explained.

"But it's difficult to see when you're blindfolded," said Håkon, without eliciting a reply. The king, however, hanging with his wife in a gold frame behind the commissioner's shoulder, seemed to agree with him. Håkon chose to interpret His Majesty's inscrutable smile as support for his own observations, and got up and left the sixth-floor office. He felt even more bad-tempered than when he'd arrived.

Hanne was glad to see him. Even with the bandage above her eye and her hair shorn on one side, he couldn't help noticing how beautiful she was. Her pallor accentuated her large eyes, and for the first time since he'd learnt about the attack he recognised how worried he'd been. He didn't dare give her a hug. Perhaps it was the bandages that frightened him off, but on thinking about it he realised that it wouldn't have seemed natural anyway. Hanne had never invited intimacy beyond the professional loyalty she'd always shown him. But she was clearly pleased that he'd come. He wasn't sure what he should do with the bouquet of flowers, and after a moment's hesitation laid them on the floor. Her bedside table was over-full already. He drew up a tubular steel chair to the edge of the bed.

"I'm okay," said Hanne before he'd had time to ask. "I'll be back at work as soon as I can. If nothing else, this is proof positive that it's something big we've stumbled on!"

The gallows humour didn't suit her, and he could see that it hurt when she tried to smile.

"You're not to come back till you're completely well. That's an order."

He started to grin, but checked himself. It would tempt her to do the same, despite the pain. Her entire jaw was turning a blueish yellow.

"The original file has gone from your office. There wasn't anything in it we didn't have a copy of, was there?"

The question was meant as a hopeful statement, but she disappointed him.

"Yes," she said quietly. "I'd written a memo, just for myself really. I know what it said, so we haven't actually lost anything in itself. But it's a bit of a bugger that someone else will read it."

Håkon felt himself growing hot, and knew from experience that his cheeks would be turning a rather unbecoming pink.

"I'm horribly afraid that I'll have made Karen Borg an object of interest to the attacker. We've already discussed my view that she knows more than she's letting on. I made a few written comments to that effect. I also jotted down one or two words about the links we've made."

She looked at him with a grimace, and put her hand gently to her head.

"Not very good, is it?"

Håkon agreed. It certainly wasn't very good.

Fredrick Myhreng was rather demanding. On the other hand, he was right when he insisted that he had kept to his side of the bargain. He sat now like an eager swot noting down everything Håkon could tell him. The thought of being the first to run the story that the police were confronted not with two random murders in the increasing series of apparently motiveless killings, but with a double homicide linked to the drugs trade and possibly to organised crime — this thought made him sweat so much that his pantomime glasses kept sliding down his nose, despite the practical frames hooked behind his ears. As before, ink was going everywhere as he wrote. Håkon thought to himself that the journalist ought to be wearing oilskins, the way he handled his writing implements. He offered him a pencil as a replacement for the ball-point pen he'd just wrecked.

"How do you rate your chances of solving it?" Myhreng asked after listening to Håkon's carefully censored but nevertheless quite fascinating account. The bridge of his nose had turned blue from his continual adjustments to his spectacles. Håkon wondered if he ought to draw the man's attention to his odd appearance, but concluded that it would do him good to make a fool of himself, so restricted himself to the matter in hand.

"We certainly believe we'll solve it. But it may take some time. We've got a lot to follow up. You can quote me on that."

Which was all Fredrick Myhreng got out of Håkon Sand that day. But he was more than happy.

TUESDAY 13 OCTOBER

The headline was dramatic. The editorial desk had produced one of the pictures of Ludvig Sandersen's corpse they had used before, and mounted it beside an old archive photograph of Hans Olsen. It must have been taken more than ten years earlier, rather fuzzy and presumably an enlargement from what had originally been a group photograph. The lawyer had a surprised expression on his face, and was on the point of blinking, which gave his eyes a tired and vacant look. The caption was in bright red ink and covered part of the photo-montage.

"Mafia Behind Two Murders" it announced in trenchant terms. Håkon Sand found the story barely recognisable. He read the front page and the two full inside pages that the newspaper had devoted to the subject. Across the top of each page was a black strip with a white text: "The Mafia Affair." He ground his teeth in annoyance at the exaggerations, but on closer reading he could see that Myhreng hadn't promulgated any actual untruths. The facts were stretched, the speculations far-fetched and so well camouflaged that they could easily be taken for truth. But Håkon himself had been quoted accurately and so couldn't really complain.

"Well, it could have been worse," he said, passing the paper to Karen Borg, who was now sufficiently at home in his office to collect what passed for coffee from the anteroom herself.

"It's time you told me something about this client of yours," he demanded. "The man's still sitting around in his underpants refusing to talk. Now we know as much as we do, you ought in all decency to help us along a bit."

They stared at one another intently. Karen reverted to the type of silent contest they used to have when they were students. She held his gaze, held it so focused that everything except her grey-green eyes diffused in a mist. He could see the tiny brown specks in the iris, more in the right eye than the left; he couldn't blink, didn't dare to for fear that his own gaze would drop when his eyes reopened. Hell, he'd never managed to win this game. She always managed to outstare him until he lowered his eyes in embarrassment, the loser, the lesser of the two.

But this time she was the one who had to give in. He could see her eyes filling with water, she had to blink, and her gaze slid to the side as if nudged by the faint flush that had begun to spread over her left cheek. He was astonished at his own tenacity; she was exposed on the flank. But the victor did not exult; instead he took both her hands in his.

"I'm actually rather apprehensive," he admitted. "We don't know much about this gang, or mafia as they've now been called, but we do know they're not choirboys. The newspaper probably has some evidence for saying they'd go to any lengths to defend themselves and their own interests. We have reason to believe that they know that you know something. Or anyway that they suspect you do."

He told her about Hanne Wilhelmsen's memo, that must now be in the wrong hands. He could see that this made an impact on her. Her whole bearing was transformed as he'd never seen it before, as if she were looking to him for some kind of protection, to Håkon, whom she had protected and bullied through all their student years.

"We'll have no chance of protecting you unless you tell us what you know!"

He realised he was gripping her hands too hard. They'd gone white, with crimson indentations where he'd held her. He let go of them.

"Han van der Kerch has told me a little. Not much. He doesn't want it to go any further, but there is one thing I've got his permission to tell you. I don't know whether it's any use."

She had pulled herself together now. She was sitting up straight again, and her suit hung neatly in place.

"He was collecting the money for a delivery. As he counted the bundle of notes, he saw that one had been written on in ink. A telephone number. Which he's forgotten. But next to the number were three letters. He had the impression they might have been initials; they had full stops between them. He remembers the initials, because they were pronounceable: J. U. L."

"JUL?"

"Yes, with full stops. He had joked to the man who was giving him the money that he didn't want defaced notes. The man had snatched it back and been quite brusque with him."

"Have you thought about what it could mean?"

"Yes, I have."

There was silence for a moment, and they fell back into a familiar set pattern.

"What have you thought, then, Karen?" Håkon asked softly.

"It's occurred to me that there's a lawyer in Oslo with exactly those initials. And only one — I checked through the Lawyers' Association membership list."

"Jørgen Ulf Lavik."

Håkon's guess was not as impressive as it sounded. They'd both been students at the same time as Lavik, who was even then a popular character. Gifted, loads of friends, and politically committed. Håkon had thought for ages that Karen was in love with him, which she had dismissed at the merest hint. Lavik was fairly conservative, and Karen Borg had been the Socialist Front representative on the Faculty Committee. In those days such barriers were virtually insurmountable, and Karen had often described her fellow student as a reactionary shit in front of others and even Lavik himself. They'd only been on speaking terms a few times, once when they'd made common cause against restrictions on student numbers. He'd actually been to her parents' summer cottage out at Ula for what was intended as a student political seminar, but had turned

108

into purely a pleasure jaunt. She hadn't liked him any better after that.

"I don't understand what all this is about, but the newspaper insinuated that there might be lawyers behind some kind of gang. I can't really see Jørgen Lavik as a gang leader, but you're welcome to the information for what it's worth."

The information was worth quite a bit to Håkon. Its value rose when Karen added a few moments later, "You'll find this out for yourself, but to save you the trouble: Jørgen began his career as a lawyer's clerk with one of the big names. Can you guess who?"

"Peter Strup," said Håkon immediately, and his face relaxed into a huge grin.

Before Karen Borg left police headquarters that afternoon she was given a two-way radio on loan. She thought it resembled an old-fashioned walkie-talkie, larger and more awkward than a mobile phone. She had to twist a button, and it would rasp and scrape as in an American detective film. Then press another button and she would be in direct contact with the police operations room. She was BB 04, the ops room was 01.

"Keep it with you at all times," Håkon commanded. "Don't hesitate to use it. The ops room knows about you. The police will be with you in five minutes."

A lot can happen in five minutes, thought Karen Borg.

THURSDAY 15 OCTOBER

Once, a long, long time ago, she had flirted with him shamelessly. She was not commissioner then, but an inspector in the minor offences unit, and newly appointed to the prosecution service. They were travelling to Spain to gather evidence for an alcohol smuggling case, her very first foreign trip on official business. The man sitting in front of her now in the visitors' chair had been there as defence counsel. Gathering the evidence had taken three hours. The visit had lasted three days. There had been lots of good food, and even more good wine. He had been everything she admired: significantly older than herself, rolling in money, considerate, and successful. Now he was parliamentary under secretary in the Ministry of Justice. Not bad. During their trip ten years previously things had gone no further than a kiss and a cuddle. Which had not been her choice. So she felt slightly bashful now.

"A cup of coffee? Tea?"

He accepted the former, and declined a cigarette.

"Given up," he smiled, waving it away.

She could feel that her hands were damp, and regretted that she hadn't got out a few documents or something else to occupy them. Instead, she sat there twiddling her thumbs and rocking nervously back and forth in her enormous chair.

"Congratulations on your appointment!" he exclaimed. "Not bad, eh?"

"It was completely unexpected," she lied.

The fact was that she had been invited to apply. By the former commissioner. So it was no surprise to anyone when she got the job.

The under secretary looked at the clock, and came straight to the point.

"The minister is very concerned about this lawyer affair," he explained. "Very concerned indeed. What's it actually all about?"

She may have made blatant advances to the man many years ago, and still be very enamoured of him, a feeling in no way diminished by his rank, but she was a professional to her fingertips.

"It's a difficult case, and still rather unclear," she replied vaguely. "There's not much I can say. Beyond what's in the newspapers. Some of which is correct."

He adjusted his silk tie. He cleared his throat meaningfully, as if to let her know that he, as the minister's closest political subordinate, had a right to better information than appeared in the more or less (principally the former) unreliable tabloid press. But it was no use.

"Investigations are at a very early stage, and the police aren't yet ready to issue any information. If anything emerges during the course of the investigations that we think the Ministry's political office ought to know about, you'll hear from me immediately of course. I promise."

That was all he would get out of her. He was old enough to realise the fact. So he didn't persist. As he left the office, she observed that the extra kilos made his backside a lot less appealing. When the door had closed, she smiled, very pleased with herself. The ample bottom apart, he was still attractive. There would be other opportunities. A grey hair drifted silently down onto the desk, and she hastily pounced on it. Then she rang her secretary's number.

"Make an appointment for me at the hairdresser's," she said peremptorily. "As soon as possible, please."

Han van der Kerch was beginning to lose track of time. The lights were switched off to let the remand prisoners know when it was night, and the unappetising plastic-packed food was served punctually, dividing their lives into segments that fitted together to make a day. But without a glimpse of sun or rain, wind or cloud, and with far too much time that could only be used for sleeping, the young Dutchman had sunk into an apathetic state of semiexistence. One night, when five hours' sleep during the day resulted in unbearable nocturnal wakefulness, having to listen to painful sobbing from a young lad in the adjoining cell and piercing screams from a Moroccan with withdrawal symptoms further down the corridor, he thought he would soon go mad. He prayed to a God he hadn't believed in since he used to go to Sunday school as a child, prayed for daybreak and the bright ceiling light.

112

God had obviously forgotten him, just as Han van der Kerch had forgotten God, because morning never came. In his desperation he had flung his recently returned wristwatch against the wall and smashed it. Now he couldn't even follow the passage of time on its painful and relentless march towards a blank future without content.

The sturdy, myopic woman who brought the trolley of prison food round would occasionally give him a piece of chocolate. It made it feel like Christmas. He broke it up into tiny fragments and let them melt on his tongue one after another. The chocolate hadn't prevented him from losing weight; after three weeks' incarceration he was seven kilos lighter. His clothes no longer fitted him, but that was of little significance in his present circumstances, where he sat sometimes in his underpants, sometimes stark naked.

He was also afraid. The fear that had taken hold of him like an expanding cactus in his stomach as he stood over Ludvig Sandersen's disfigured body had spread to his limbs. His hands and arms were trembling and he was spilling all his drinks. At the beginning he'd managed to read the books he was allowed to borrow, but gradually his powers of concentration waned. The letters danced and leapt about on the page. He'd been given pills. That's to say, the warders had been given the pills, and they were handed to him one by one according to the doctor's instructions, with a plastic mug of tepid water. Tiny bright blue pills in the evening which helped him along the road to dreamland. Three times a day he had bigger white pills. They gave him a sort of breathing space as the cactus temporarily retracted its needles. But the certainty that they would return, stronger and sharper, was almost as bad. Han van der Kerch was starting to lose his grip on his own existence.

He thought it was day. He couldn't be certain of it, but the light was on, and there were noises going on all around him. A meal had just been served, though he wasn't sure whether it was meant to be lunch or dinner. Perhaps it was a late supper. No, it was too early, too much noise.

At first he couldn't see what it was. When the piece of paper dropped in through the bars it took him a while to work it out. He followed its progress; it was small and almost weightless and took ages to reach the floor. It fluttered like a butterfly, from side to side, as it bobbed down towards the concrete. He smiled, the motion was pleasing, and he felt it had nothing to do with him.

There it lay. Han van der Kerch left it where it was and raised his eyes again to follow the shadows of movement from the corridor. He'd just taken one of the white pills, and felt better than he had an hour ago. He made a laborious effort to stand up. He was dizzy, and had been lying for so long in the same place that his limbs had gone to sleep. They tingled uncomfortably as he hobbled the few steps to the door. He bent and picked up the piece of paper without looking at it. It took several minutes to get himself into a normal sitting position, without his legs complaining too much.

It was the size of a postcard, folded twice. He opened it up on his lap.

The message was clearly intended for him. A few words written in capitals with a broad-nibbed pen: "Silence is golden, talk and you're dead." It was rather melodramatic, and he began to laugh. His laughter was shrill and so loud that he startled himself and fell silent. Then a sense of fear came upon him that was utterly overwhelming. If a piece of paper could find its way through the bars of the door, so could a bullet.

He started laughing again, just as loud and shrill as before. The laughter echoed around the walls, bounced to and fro, and did a little jig around its performer before disappearing out through the bars and taking with it the last remnants of sanity from the Dutchman's mind.

FRIDAY 16 OCTOBER

Two murdered and two in hospital. And all we have to go on are some initials and the vaguest of suspicions."

It sounded as if they were wading through piles of crisp new banknotes: the yellowing maple leaves had experienced their first night of frost. Patches of fresh snow lay here and there, the nearest it had fallen to the city centre so far. They had arrived at the top of the hill in St. Hanshaugen Park, and the city lay spread before them in its frostbitten autumn pallor. It seemed as caught out by the sudden cold as the motorists on Geitemyrsveien, sliding into one another on their fully inflated summer tyres. The sky looked low. Only the church spires, the high one at Uranienborg and two shorter ones not so far away, were preventing it from total collapse.

Hanne Wilhelmsen had been discharged from hospital, but was hardly in a condition for lengthy walks in the woods. Nor should she really have been inflicting problems on her battered brain, but Håkon Sand couldn't resist the temptation when she rang and suggested going for a gentle stroll. She was still pale and bore clear signs of her ordeal. The blueness on her jaw had turned light green, and the enormous bandages had been exchanged for large plasters. Her hair was

116

completely lopsided, which surprised him. He'd thought she would have cut it all the same length to match the part that had been shaved smooth, a large area above one ear. When they met, with cautious smiles and a somewhat awkward pleasure at seeing one another again, she had immediately explained that she hadn't wanted to sacrifice the rest of her long hair. Even though it definitely looked very odd.

"Only one in hospital," she corrected him. "I'm on my feet again."

"Yes, from that point of view you're luckier than our Dutch friend. He's had a complete breakdown. Retroactive psychosis, the doctor says, whatever that may mean. Stark, staring mad, I should think. He's in the psychiatric wing at Ullevål Hospital now. Not that there's any reason to assume he'll be any more talkative after that. At the moment he's curled up in the foetal position and burbling like a baby. Scared stiff of everything and everyone."

"Very strange," said Hanne, sitting down on a bench. She patted the space next to her and he obeyed.

"Strange that it should happen after only three weeks," she went on. "I mean, we know what it's like in those cells. Not exactly a holiday camp. But people are always being held there too long. Have you ever heard of anyone going stir-crazy before?"

"No, but he probably has more reason than most to panic. A foreigner, feeling of isolation and all that."

"But even so . . ."

Håkon had learnt to listen when Hanne spoke. He hadn't pondered very much himself about Han van der

Kerch's mental state, just registered the fact resignedly; yet another door slammed in their face in an investigation that was more or less at a standstill.

"Could something have triggered it off? Could anything have happened to him in his cell?"

Håkon didn't answer, and Hanne said no more either. Håkon had that peculiar sensation of well-being he always experienced in Hanne's presence. It was something new in comparison with other women he'd met, a kind of comradeship and professional rapport together with the absolute certainty that they liked and respected each other. It occurred to him that they ought to become friends, but he rejected the thought. He realised intuitively that it was she who would have to take the initiative if they were to be more than colleagues. As he sat there now, on an ice-cold bench in St. Hanshaugen Park on a grey October day, he was more than happy with the feeling of being at one with this woman, who was so close and yet at the same time so remote, so intelligent, and so vital to the job he was trying to do. He hoped she wasn't having too bad a time.

"Was anything of interest found in the cell?"

"No, not as far as I know, and what the devil could there be anyway?"

"But did they look for anything?"

He ought to be able to answer. He missed her involvement, and he began to see why. He lacked the experience of direct leadership of an investigation; even though he was formally responsible for all the cases in

118

his name, it was rare for any of the police lawyers to take a direct part as he was now doing.

"I have to admit that was something I didn't think of," he said.

"It's not too late," she consoled him. "You can still check it out."

He accepted her reassurance, and to make up for his dwindling reputation as an investigator he told her about his enquiries on the subject of Jørgen Ulf Lavik.

Lavik had been fairly successful in quite a short time. After a couple of years with Peter Strup he had started up his own firm with two newly established lawyers about the same age as himself. They covered most aspects of the law, and Lavik himself had a caseload that was about fifty percent criminal with the other half spread over middle-ranging commercial law work. He had acquired a second wife, and had three children with her in quick succession. The family lived in a modest terraced house in quite a respectable part of the city. Their spending didn't seem on first appraisal to be any more than a man such as Lavik would be able to afford: two cars, a one-year-old Volvo, and a seven-year-old Toyota for his wife. No summer cottage, no boat. Wife at home, necessarily so, of course, with three boys of one, two, and five.

"Sounds like a pretty typical Oslo lawyer," said Hanne in a resigned tone. "Tell me something I don't know, pal."

Håkon thought she seemed exhausted. Her breath in the cold air was getting visibly faster, even though they'd been sitting still for a while. He stood up, brushed his hands over the back of his trousers as if to wipe off imaginary snow, and stretched out his hand to help her up. It was unnecessary, but she accepted it.

"Look into the commercial side of his activities," she instructed her superior. "And get a list drawn up of all his criminal clients over the last few years. I bet we'll find something or other.

"And also," she added, "put the cases together now. They're mine, both of them, I had the first one."

She looked almost joyful at the thought.

MONDAY 19 OCTOBER

It was only eight days since Hanne Wilhelmsen's brutal encounter with her attacker. She should have been on sick leave for at least another week. Considering the way she felt, she had to admit it would have been more sensible. She still had a slight headache, and was subject to episodes of giddiness and nausea if she overexerted herself. But she swore to everyone, including Cecilie, that she was in perfect condition. Just a bit tired. She consented to take half time off sick for a week.

She was greeted by applause when she went into the combined lunch and meeting room, and felt extremely self-conscious. But she smiled and shook all the extended hands. There were a few comments about her hairstyle; she parried the friendly teasing with self-irony, and everyone laughed. She was still wearing sticking plasters, and the lower part of her face was displaying various shades of yellow and green. That protected her from hugs, until the superintendent entered the room, threw his arms round her shoulders, and gave her an exuberant embrace.

"What a girl!" he bellowed into her ear. "My God, Hanne, you gave us all a fright!"

Hanne had to reiterate her insistence that she was fine, and promised to deliver the report he was expecting. They agreed on a time and place, and Chief Inspector Kaldbakken concurred.

Suddenly Billy T. was standing in the doorway. At six foot eight plus boots, his shaved head touched the lintel. Despite his broad grin, he was an intimidating sight.

"KO'd in the first round, Hanne? Thought you'd have been able to look after yourself better than that," he said, in a tone of mock disappointment. He had trained Hanne in self-defence himself.

"Are you going to sit there all day letting them sing your praises, or have you got a few minutes for some real work?"

She had indeed. Her desk was dominated by a huge bouquet of flowers. It was beautiful, but the vase rather spoilt the effect. It wasn't big enough either, and when she lifted it carefully to carry it to the windowsill the whole lot toppled over. The vase slipped out of her grasp and crashed to the floor. Flowers and water went everywhere. Billy T. roared with laughter.

"You see what happens when we show a bit of appreciation here in the office," he said.

He pushed Hanne aside, scooped up the flowers in one gigantic hand, and tried to sweep the water to the wall with his boots. Ineffectually. He sat down, tossing the flowers into a corner.

"I think I've got something for you," he declared, pulling out two pieces of paper from his back pocket. They were curved to the shape of his buttocks, like a man's wallet. They'd obviously been there some time.

"Seized last week," he said, as Detective Inspector Wilhelmsen unfolded them. "When we raided an apartment. Second time lucky. Twenty grams of heroin, four grams of cocaine. But it really was a stroke of luck, we'd only nabbed him for minor offences before. Now he's down below gnashing his teeth." He waved his arm with a flourish towards the window, indicating the rear of the building.

"And he'll be staying there till the main hearing, you can be sure of that — which may take a while," he added in a tone of great satisfaction.

The two sheets were very similar to the piece of paper from Olsen's porn video. Nothing but rows of figures, in groups of three numbers. Both were handwritten, and headed respectively "Borneo" and "Africa."

"He's singing like a lark, but he's sticking to his story that he doesn't know what these signify. We've been pushing him pretty hard, and he's given us a whole lot of useful information. More than necessary, in fact. Which makes me wonder whether maybe he's telling the truth when he says he's got no idea what the numbers mean."

They sat staring at the pieces of paper as if the secret would suddenly jump out and hit them right between the eyes if they concentrated hard enough.

"Did he say anything about how he'd got hold of them?"

"Yes, he maintains that he came across them accidentally, and that he kept them as a kind of insurance. We couldn't get any more out of him, not even what he meant when he said 'accidentally'."

Hanne noted the strange texture of the paper. It had a powdery coating, with a few scattered fingerprints faintly delineated in pale mauve.

"I've already had them tested for prints. Nothing of any use there," Billy T. volunteered.

He took the sheets from her and left the room, returning a couple of minutes later and handing her a copy of each, still warm.

"I'll keep the originals. You can have them if you need them."

"Thanks, Billy."

Her gratitude was genuine, despite her weary smile.

First she assured him that he was a witness, not a suspect. That scarcely made any difference to him, since he was already charged on another matter anyway. Then he was given a Coca-Cola, which he'd requested. He'd been allowed to have a shower before coming up. Hanne Wilhelmsen was friendly and open, and managed to indicate obliquely that a suspect in one case would benefit from being a good witness in another. He was not noticeably impressed. They made small talk. The break from the boredom of his cell was welcome; he looked as if he was actually enjoying himself. Hanne was not. Her headache was bad, and when she winced at the pain the stitches in her wounds pulled and made it worse.

"I realise I'll get several years for this."

He seemed more confident than Billy T. had implied.

"I might as well admit it to you: I'm not very interested in your own case. That can stay yours. I want to talk to you about the documents that were found on you."

"Documents? They weren't documents. They were bits of paper with numbers. Documents have rubber stamps and signatures and things."

He'd already drunk one bottle of Coke, and asked for another. Hanne pressed the buttons on the intercom and ordered it.

"Room service! Marvellous! Nothing like that where I am, you know."

"These documents, or sheets of paper," she tried again, but was interrupted.

"No idea. It's the truth. Found them somewhere. Kept them just as a sort of insurance policy. You can't be too careful in my line of business, you know."

"Insurance against what?"

"Just insurance, not for anything special. Have you been beaten up, or what?"

"No, I was born like this."

After three hours' work she was beginning to understand why the doctor had been so adamant that she should continue her sick leave. Cecilie had warned her about the headaches and the nausea, had outlined frightful scenarios of how everything could become permanent if she didn't take it easy. Hanne was beginning to think her partner might be right. She gently massaged the temple that wasn't plastered up.

"Can't say anything, you see."

He suddenly seemed a little more amenable. His bony frame was trembling, and he spilt some Coke as he tried to drink from the new bottle that had arrived within minutes.

"Withdrawal symptoms, you see. Ought to get me over to the prison. Plenty of dope there, you know. Couldn't you organise something for me?"

Hanne Wilhelmsen looked at him. Pitifully thin and pale as a ghost. His scanty beard wasn't sufficient to conceal all his spots; he had abnormally bad skin for a man over thirty. He must have been handsome once. She could imagine him as a five-year-old, dressed up for a photograph in a sailor suit and gleaming curls — a sweet child. She'd heard the lawyers at police headquarters complaining contemptuously about all the nonsense put forward by defence counsel. Wretched childhood, let down by society, drunkard fathers, mothers who drank a bit less to keep themselves just sober enough to prevent the child being taken into care, until by the age of thirteen it was totally uncontrollable and beyond all assistance from the child care authorities or any other well-meaning souls. They didn't stand a chance. Hanne knew the defence lawyers were right. She'd long realised that with ten years of frustration behind you, there was more than enough reason to turn bad. They'd all had a hell of a life. This guy too, presumably.

Like a thought-reader he started to whine in a quavering voice, "I've had a hell of a time, you know."

"Yes, I know," she replied dully. "I can't help with that now. Obviously. But I might be able to get you moved over there today, if you tell me where you got those documents from."

It was clearly tempting. She could see he was counting on imaginary fingers. If he could count at all.

"I found 'em. I can't say no more than that. I think I know whose they were. They're a dangerous lot, you see. They'll catch up with you wherever you are. No, I reckon those papers are still a good insurance policy, I really do. I'd rather wait my turn out the back; I must be well up the list now, I've been there five days already."

Detective Inspector Wilhelmsen didn't have the strength to continue. She told him to drink up the rest of the Coca-Cola. He obeyed, drinking it all the way back down to the remand cells. He handed her the empty bottle outside the door of his own cell.

"I've heard of you, you know. Honest and straight, that's what they say about you. Thanks for the Coke!"

The skinny man was transferred to prison the same day. Hanne was not too exhausted to pull a few strings before she went off duty. Even if she couldn't conjure up extra space in the overcrowded prison, she could influence priorities. He was even more delighted when later that day, having settled into a cell with a window and something that bore a remarkable resemblance to a bed, he received a visit from his lawyer.

They sat in a room by themselves, the smartly dressed lawyer and the man with withdrawal symptoms. It was off a larger hall where the lucky ones were visited by their families and friends, a bleak, inhospitable space that tried in vain to create a good impression by having a play area for the youngest visitors in one corner.

The lawyer riffled through various documents. His briefcase lay on the table. It was open, and the lid stood like a shield between them. He himself seemed more nervous than the prisoner, a fact the addict's state of health prevented him from noticing. The lawyer closed the lid and produced a handkerchief. He spread it out and proffered the contents.

There lay salvation, all the enfeebled man needed to get a few hours of well-deserved intoxication. He reached out for it, but the lawyer grabbed his hand as quick as a flash.

"What have you said?"

"Haven't said a word! You know me! Never say more than I have to, not this lad."

"Have you got anything in your flat that would give the police information? Anything at all?"

"No, no, nothing. Only some gear. Bloody bad luck, you know, they came just as I was gonna start my deliveries. Weren't my fault, that."

If the man's brain hadn't been so sluggish after twenty years' abuse of artificial stimulants, he might have said something different. If the glimpse of salvation in the lawyer's briefcase hadn't eroded the small amount of judgement he could still muster, he might have said that he was in possession of compromising material, papers he'd found on the floor in another visiting room, after another arrest. If he'd had his wits about him he would probably have realised that for the documents to fulfil their purpose as insurance papers, he should admit to possession of them. Maybe he could even have pretended that all would be revealed to the police if anything happened to him. He could have got some benefit from it at least. Perhaps it would have saved his life; perhaps not. But his mind was too befuddled.

"Go on keeping your mouth shut," the lawyer said, and let the prisoner help himself to the contents of the handkerchief. There was also a cylinder about the size of a cigar container, and with increasingly shaky hands the eager addict squeezed the supply into it. Unembarrassed, he pulled down his trousers and with a grimace pushed it up into his rectum.

"They search me before they put me back in the cell, but they'll never check my arse after a visit from a lawyer." He grinned happily.

Five hours later he was found dead in his cell. The overdose had sent him to his end with a beatific smile on his face. The remains of his fix were on the floor, a few tiny specks of heroin in a little piece of polythene. In the wet autumn grass two floors below the high barred window of the cell lay a little cigar-shaped case. No one was looking for it, and it would lie there through wind and rain until it was picked up by a security guard six months later.

The man's ageing mother wasn't told of his death until two days afterwards. She wept bitter tears and downed a whole bottle of aquavit for comfort. The boy's unwanted arrival in the world had caused her sorrow, and she had cried herself through most of his life. Now she grieved that he was gone. Otherwise there was no one, absolutely no one, who would miss Jacob Frøstrup.

The older man may have seemed threatening the last time they met, but this time his face was absolutely distorted with suppressed anger. Meeting as before in a car park way up in Maridalen to the north of the city, the two men had left their respectable-looking cars at opposite ends, making them very conspicuous because there were only three other vehicles on the whole plot, all side by side. Each had walked off separately into the woods, the older one suitably attired, as on the previous occasion, the younger one freezing in a suit and black leather shoes.

"What the hell are you doing turning up dressed like that?" the older man spat out when they were a hundred metres or so in among the trees. "Are you deliberately trying to draw attention to yourself?"

"Relax, nobody saw me."

His teeth were chattering. His dark hair was already wet, and the rain had soaked his shoulders. He looked like Dracula, a resemblance strengthened by his sharply pointed canine teeth, now quite distinct even when his mouth was closed, since his lips were tight with cold.

Not far off they heard the rumble of a tractor. They immediately hid themselves behind two tree trunks, a quite unnecessary precaution because they were at least a hundred metres from the track. The drone of the engine faded away into the distance.

130

"You know we never meet," the irate man snapped. "Now I've had to meet you twice in quick succession. Have you completely lost your senses?"

The question was superfluous. He looked drenched and dejected. His dishevelled appearance stood out even more in contrast to his expensive suit and fashionable hairstyle, both of which were gradually disintegrating. He made no reply.

"Pull yourself together, man!"

Now absolutely livid, he seized his companion by the lapels and shook him. The younger man offered no resistance, his head flopping about like a rag doll's.

"Now listen, listen to me."

The older man changed his tactic. He released him, and spoke slowly and precisely, as if to a child.

"We'll wind it up. We'll drop the idea of the several months I was talking about. We'll pack it in now. Do you hear? But you have to tell me where we stand. Does your jailbird know anything about us?"

"Yes. About me. Not about you, of course."

The avuncular tone was gone in an instant as the older man screeched, "What the hell did you mean when you told me you hadn't been as stupid as Hansy, then? You said you hadn't had any contact with the runners!"

"I lied," he said apathetically. "How the devil could I recruit them otherwise? I provided them with dope in prison. Not much, but enough to be able to control them. They run after dope like dogs after a bitch in heat."

131

The older man raised his fist to strike him, but a bit too slowly for any element of surprise. The younger man took a frightened step back, slithered on the wet leaves, and landed in a heap on the ground. He didn't get up. The older man kicked him contemptuously in the legs as he lay there.

"You'd better get things sorted out."

"I have," came a whimper from the rotting leaves. "I already have."

FRIDAY 23 OCTOBER

He didn't feel lonely, but perhaps a bit alone. The woman's voice on the *News at Six*, assertive and unpretentious, was okay company. He'd inherited the armchair from his grandmother. It was comfortable, so he'd taken it over even though his grandmother had gone to meet her Maker from the selfsame chair. On one arm there were still two bloodstains from where she had presumably hit her head on the bookshelf when her heart failed. It was impossible to eradicate them, as if she were still obstinately determined to lay claim to her right of ownership from her new existence on the other side. Håkon Sand thought it was homely. His grandmother had been as stubborn as a mule when she was alive, and the fading remains of blood on the pale blue velour upholstery reminded him of the splendid old lady who had won the War single-handedly, taken care of the sick and helpless, been his childhood heroine, and persuaded him to study law despite, to put it mildly, a poor head for academic work.

The apartment was tastelessly furnished, without any consistency or attempt at a homogeneous style. The colours clashed horribly, but paradoxically his little abode had a friendly, snug atmosphere. Each object had its own history, some were inherited, some bought

133

in the flea market, the lounge and dining-room furniture supplemented from Ikea. A man's flat, but cleaner and tidier than might be expected; Håkon, as the only son of a washerwoman, had learnt domestic skills early in life. He actually enjoyed housework.

The director of public prosecutions was making a vehement attack on the press treatment of criminal cases. The *News at Six* anchorwoman had a problem keeping the participants in check, and Håkon was sitting with his eyes closed and only lukewarm interest in the debate. The press won't allow itself to be subjected to controls anyway, he thought, and was just about to doze off when the telephone rang.

It was Karen Borg. He could hear the echo of his own ears buzzing in the receiver. He tried swallowing, several times. It was no use; his mouth was as dry as after a night on the tiles.

Having announced themselves, they could get no further. It was embarrassing to sit at a silent telephone without saying anything, and he cleared his throat a little awkwardly to fill the vacuum.

"I'm here all by myself," said Karen eventually. "How would you feel about coming over for a while?

"I'm a bit nervous," she added, as if to provide an excuse.

"What about Nils?"

"He's on a course. I can cook something interesting. I've got some wine. We can talk about the case. And about the old days."

He was willing to talk to her about anything. He was excited, happy, expectant, and scared. After a shower and a twenty-minute taxi ride he arrived in Grünerløkka, at an apartment the like of which he'd never encountered before.

The butterflies in his stomach settled down quickly, feeling cheated. Karen's welcome was not especially warm. She didn't even greet him with a hug, just favoured him with one of the formal smiles that he'd had so many of in the past. They soon fell into a natural conversational tone, and his pulse returned to normal. Håkon was used to having his hopes dashed.

The food wasn't particularly good. He could have done it better himself. The lamb chops had been fried too long before they were put in the casserole; the meat was tough. He recognised the recipe, and knew there was white wine in the sauce. Karen had poured too much in and it was over-dominant and acidic. But the red wine in their glasses was superb. They talked about this and that and about old student friends at inordinate length. Both were on their guard. The conversation flowed easily, but along fairly restricted lines, with Karen choosing the route.

"Have you actually got any further?"

The meal was eaten. The dessert had been more or less a failure as well, a lemon sorbet that had refused to stay set for more than thirty seconds. Håkon had smoothed things over and eaten the cold lemon soup with a smile of apparent appreciation.

"We feel we're getting somewhere, but we're light-years away from being able to prove anything. It's a bit monotonous now. Masses of routine stuff. We're gathering in everything that might be of any

135

significance at all and then sifting through it to see if there's anything useful. At the moment we've got nothing on Jørgen Lavik, but we reckon we'll have a better insight into his life in a few days."

Karen interrupted him by raising her glass. He took rather too big a gulp and coughed involuntarily before he'd finished swallowing. The red wine spattered the tablecloth, and he fumbled desperately for the saltcellar to retrieve the situation. She took his hand and looked into his eyes to reassure him.

"Relax, Håkon. I'll see to it in the morning. Carry on telling me about progress."

He put the saltcellar down and apologised several times before continuing.

"If you only knew how tedious it is! Ninety-five percent of the work in a murder case is utterly fruitless. Exploring every possible avenue. I get out of it, thank God — the purely practical side of it, that is. But I have to read it all. So far we've interviewed twenty-two witnesses. Twenty-two! Not one of them has had anything to contribute. What little physical evidence we have tells us nothing. The bullet that finished off Hans Olsen comes from a weapon that isn't even sold in this country. Which doesn't get us very far. We think we can see a pattern here and there, but it's as if we can't find the common denominator, the missing piece that would give us something to work on."

He tried to rub the salt into the tablecloth with his fingertip, in the hope that the old wives' remedy would be effective.

136

"Maybe we're going at it from completely the wrong angle," he went on, in a tone of resignation. "We thought we'd come up trumps when the records showed that Lavik was in the cells the very day your client lost his marbles. I was very excited, but the warder remembered the visit in detail, and was able to swear that the lawyer never spoke to anybody other than his own client. He was accompanied, like all other visitors."

Håkon didn't want to talk about the case. It was Friday, it had been a long, tiring week, and the wine was beginning to go to his head. He felt more at ease, and a warm glow was spreading through him and slowing his movements. He reached over for her plate, scraped the leftovers carefully onto his own, put both sets of cutlery on top, and was about to get up and take everything out to the kitchen.

That was when it happened. She suddenly stood up and came round the solid pine table, knocking her hip against the rounded corner. It must have been painful, but it didn't divert her from her purpose. She dropped down into his lap. He sat in helpless silence. His hands were moist and hung like lead weights on the ends of his arms, flaccid and weak; what should he do with them?

His eyes watered with trepidation and desire, and he was even more nervous when she dexterously removed his spectacles. He blinked in confusion, and an involuntary tear ran down his left cheek, small and solitary, but she noticed it, laid her hand on his cheek, and brushed it away with her thumb.

She put her lips to his and kissed him for what seemed an eternity. It was quite different from the light touch at the office; this was a kiss full of promises, desire, and longing. It was the kiss Håkon had fantasised about, yearned for, and always dismissed as nothing more than an idyllic dream. It was exactly as he'd imagined it. Totally different from all the other kisses he'd garnered in fifteen years of bachelor existence. This was the opposite, his reward for having loved one and only one, right from their first meeting at a lecture fourteen years ago. Fourteen years! He could remember it better than yesterday's lunch meeting. He had come scuttling into the auditorium in the west wing five minutes late, and had taken his place on a folding seat in front of an attractive blonde girl. As he pulled the seat down, he had trapped the girl's toes — she had been sitting with her feet up. She had cried out in agony, and Håkon had stammered an apology, flinching at the laughter and catcalls from the other students; but when he looked at his victim, he was overcome by a feeling of love from which he would never recover. Through all the years he had said nothing. His patient waiting had been painful and melancholy, seeing Karen's lovers come and go. This feeling of resignation had led him to believe that women were something he could interest for a month or two, for as long as novelty lent their games in bed some excitement. More than that it could never be. Not with other women.

He remained passive for a few moments, but gradually the endless kiss became mutual. His courage increased, and his hands were no longer so helpless, they felt less heavy, and he stroked her back as he moved his legs slightly to let her sit more comfortably.

They made love for several hours. A wonderfully close, intimate lovemaking, old friends with many years of shared experience who had never touched each other, never in this way. It was like walking through a cherished landscape scarcely recognisable in an unfamiliar season. Known yet unknown, everything where it should be, but in a different light, a landscape both unexplored and strange.

They whispered tender words and confidences, and felt remote from reality. Somewhere far off a tram rattled by. The noise forced its way into the cosy intimacy of the living-room floor, sniffed the dawn, and disappeared again into the distance, like a good friend who wished them well. Karen and Håkon were alone again; she confused, exhausted, and elated; he just very, very happy.

Hanne Wilhelmsen was devoting her Friday evening to entirely different pursuits. She was sitting with Billy T. in an unmarked police car with its lights off, at the roadside up at Grefsenkollen, in the hills northeast of the centre. The road was narrow, and in order not to obstruct what little traffic there was late on a Friday evening, they had parked so far off it that the car was leaning at a rakish angle. Her spine was protesting at having to sit with one buttock a lot lower than the other. She tried to straighten herself up, but couldn't.

"Here," said Billy T., reaching over for a jacket on the backseat and handing it to her. "Put that under one side!"

It helped, at least for the time being. They were eating the food she'd brought with them, neatly packed in clingfilm, six slices for Billy T. and two for herself.

"A picnic!"

Billy T. was loudly enthusiastic, and helped himself to coffee from the thermos flask.

"A relaxing Friday evening," said Hanne, grinning with her mouth full.

They'd been sitting there for three hours. It was their third evening on watch outside the terraced house where Jørgen Lavik lived with his family. The house was brown in colour, uninspiring, but with attractive curtains and a soft warm glow from the windows. The family went to bed late, and they had watched the lights go out around midnight every night so far. Up till now their vigils in the freezing car had been a thankless task. The Lavik family had a relentlessly normal routine. Through the living-room window the blue flicker of a television set could be seen from the children's programmes till the late evening news. In two rooms on the upper floor which they assumed were the children's the lights were turned out at about eight o'clock. Only once had someone emerged from the varnished door with its embellishment of geese croaking their welcome in Gothic script. Mrs. Lavik presumably, putting out the rubbish. It had been difficult to see her very clearly, but they'd both got the impression of a slim, stylish

140

woman, well dressed even when just spending the evening at home.

They were bored. Radios and cassette players were forbidden in police cars. The police radio, with its reports of the capital's Friday night crimes, both major and minor, was not especially entertaining. But the police officers were patient.

It had started snowing. The flakes were large and dry, and the car had been stationary for so long that the snow no longer melted on the bonnet. It was soon completely covered. Billy T. switched on the windscreen wipers for a few sweeps to improve their view.

"It's beddy-byes now," he said, gesturing towards the house as the lights went out in one room after another. A lamp continued to shine from one of the upstairs windows for a few minutes, but then there was only a kind of lantern by the entrance door to illumine the contours of the darkened house.

"Well, now we'll see whether our friend Jørgen has anything better to do than to snuggle down beneath the quilt on a Friday night," said Hanne, without sounding particularly hopeful.

An hour passed. The snow was still falling, silently and unhurriedly. Hanne had just aired the opinion that they might as well call it a day. Billy T. had snorted contemptuously. Hadn't she ever been on surveillance duty before? He was adamant that they should sit there for another two hours.

Suddenly someone was coming out of the house. The pair in the car almost missed it as they sat there sleepily with drooping eyelids. The figure — it was a man's —

shook itself against the cold, and fumbled with the lock for what seemed ages. He was wearing a long dark coat. When he turned, he held the collar up and kept his hands crossed over his chest. He half ran towards the garage, which was below the house by the road. The garage doors opened before he reached them. Remote control, evidently.

The Volvo was navy blue, but with its lights on it was easy to follow. Billy T. kept a good distance; the traffic was so sparse at this time of night that the danger of losing sight of the car was minimal.

"It's crazy to do a stakeout with only one patrol car," Billy T. muttered. "These guys are paranoid. We ought to have at least two."

"Money," Hanne replied. "Luckily this one's not used to the game; he's not looking over his shoulder at all."

They drove down to the main crossroads at Storo. The traffic signals were vacuously flashing amber like simpleminded Cyclopes, luring motorists to their doom. Two cars were slewed across the main ring road, one with its front severely damaged. The police officers couldn't get involved, and continued towards Sandaker.

"He's stopped," Hanne suddenly shouted.

The Volvo, its engine still running, was parked by a telephone booth in Torshov. Lavik was having problems getting into the booth; the hinges must be stiff after all the frost and snow. But he managed to make a gap just wide enough to squeeze through. Billy T. drove calmly on round the next corner and made a U-turn with a skilful slide on the snow. He came back to the junction and parked fifty yards or so from the man in the phone booth. The light was apparently causing him discomfort: he was bending forward to shield his eyes. He had his back towards the unmarked police car.

"Phone call from a box. Well, well. Friday night. Our suspicions were correct," said Billy T. with unconcealed delight.

"He might simply be having an affair," said Hanne, trying unsuccessfully to dampen his enthusiasm.

"And rings her from a phone box at two in the morning? Get real, Hanne!" he scoffed, with a conviction born of professional experience.

They were silent for a while. The street was almost deserted, just the occasional drunken night owl staggering home through the snow that now lay everywhere and gave the October night a Christmassy atmosphere.

All at once the man banged down the receiver and was off again. He was obviously in a hurry to get somewhere. He leapt into his car and the wheels spun as it pulled away and raced off down Vogts Gata.

The police car glided out of the junction and accelerated after it. The next stop came equally unexpectedly. In a side street in Grünerløkka the Volvo was almost thrown into an empty parking space. They parked the police car further along the street. Jørgen Lavik vanished round a corner. Hanne and Billy T. looked at one another, and got out of the car in tacit accord. Billy T. put his arm round his colleague, suggesting in a whisper that they pretend to be lovers, and they strolled off firmly entwined towards the little street where they'd seen the lawyer disappear. It was slippery, and several times Hanne had to hold on tight to Billy T. to prevent herself falling. Her boots had leather soles.

They turned the corner and spotted them straight away. Lavik was standing in muted conversation with another man, but their gesticulations revealed something of its content. It didn't look too amicable. There was a distance of a hundred metres between the police officers and the two men. One hundred long metres.

"We'll take them now," Billy T. murmured, as eager as a red setter with a scent of grouse.

"No, no," Hanne hissed. "Are you mad? On what grounds? There's no law against conversing at night!"

"Grounds? What the hell's that? We stop people every day just on a hunch!"

She felt her companion brace himself, and clutched at his coat. The other two had seen them. They were near enough now to hear the men's voices, without being able to distinguish the words. Lavik reacted to the spectators by raising his collar and making his way slowly but determinedly back to his car. Hanne and Billy T. camouflaged themselves in a passionate clinch, and heard the footsteps fading away behind them, towards the dark-blue Volvo. The unknown man still stood where he was. Suddenly Billy T. tore himself loose from Hanne's arms and charged after him. Lavik was already round the corner on the other side of the street and out of sight. The stranger ran off, and Hanne was left standing there, not knowing what to do.

Billy T. was in tip-top condition, and was catching up with his prey by a metre a second. After fifty metres the stranger dived into a doorway, and Billy T. was only ten metres behind. He got to the door a second before it closed. It couldn't possibly have been shut before, the man must have slammed it behind him. It was big and heavy, and slowed Billy T. down. By the time he was through the man was nowhere to be seen.

He rushed along the passageway, which issued on to an enclosed yard. It was fairly big, maybe ten metres square, and surrounded by three-metre-high walls. One wall looked like the rear of a garage or a shed; a sloping roof extended from the top of it. A flower bed had been built up in one corner, and the stringy remains of some flowers poked sadly up through the snow. There was a homemade trellis behind it, bare, the plants having only succeeded in reaching the bottom crosspiece. At the top was a man just about to scramble over the wall.

Billy T. took the diagonal across the yard in ten paces. He grabbed a boot. The fleeing man kicked out and his heel caught the officer on the forehead with a crack. But Billy T. didn't entirely let go — with his spare hand he tried to get a proper grip on the trousers higher up. But he was unlucky: the man gave a violent jerk and freed himself. He stood holding one boot, feeling rather foolish even before he heard the second boot hitting the ground on the far side of the wall. It took him only three seconds to follow, but his quarry had made good use of his advantage. He was already well on his way to another gate, this time giving onto the street. As he reached the archway in the house wall he turned to face Billy T. He had a gun in his right hand and was aiming it directly at him.

"Police!" yelled Billy T. "It's the police!"

He lurched to a halt. But his leather soles didn't. They kept going. His huge figure danced five or six steps to regain its balance, his arms flailing like a broken windmill. In vain. He fell backwards onto the ground with a crash, and only the fresh snow saved him from injury. His pride, on the other hand, had taken a considerable battering, and he cursed inwardly when he heard the outer gate slam shut behind the fugitive.

He rose to his feet, and had just brushed the snow off himself when Hanne landed on the ground from the wall behind him.

"Idiot," she said, at once reproachful and admiring. "What would you have charged the guy with if you'd caught him?"

"Unlawful possession of firearms," the bruised policeman muttered, knocking the snow off his trophy, a man's leather boot, size ten. He ordered a retreat. With rather ill grace.

MONDAY 26 OCTOBER

There was a whole pile of yellow message slips on the post shelf in her office. Hanne Wilhelmsen hated telephone messages. She was far too conscientious to throw them out, but knew that at least half of the eleven who had rung had nothing significant to say. The most enervating part of the job was having to respond to questions from the public, impatient victims who couldn't see why it should take more than six months to investigate a rape by a known assailant, irascible defence lawyers enquiring about prosecution decisions, witnesses who considered themselves of greater importance than the police gave them credit for.

Two of the messages were from the same person. "Ring Askhaug, Ullevål Hospital," they said, with a phone number. Hanne thought anxiously about all the scans they'd taken of her skull, and rang the number. Askhaug was there, even if Hanne did have to be transferred to three other numbers before she eventually got the woman on the line. Hanne introduced herself.

"I'm glad you phoned," chirped the woman at the other end. "I'm a nurse in the psychiatric department."

Hanne breathed a sigh of relief. At least her own head wasn't the problem.

147

"We had a patient here, a prisoner on remand," the nurse continued. "A Dutchman, I think he was. I was told you were in charge of the case. Is that right?"

"Yes."

"He was in a psychotic state when he was admitted, and went to Neurology for several days before we saw any improvement," the nurse explained. "We got his mental condition into some sort of order eventually, even if we don't know how long it will last. We put incontinence pads on him at first; it would have been too labour-intensive otherwise, you see."

The soft southern voice sounded apologetic, as if it was she alone who was responsible for the lamentable state of resources in the health service.

"It's normally the nursing auxiliaries who change the pads, you know. But he was thoroughly constipated until I happened to be on night duty. We take a turn too, with the patients, I mean. So I changed this man's pads. It's really the auxiliaries' job, you know."

Hanne knew.

"Well, I noticed a white, undigested lump in his stool. I wondered what it was, so I picked it out. We wear plastic gloves, you see."

A slight giggle came down the line.

"And?"

Hanne was getting impatient. She ran her finger rapidly to and fro over the stubble at her temple. Her hair was growing back, and it itched.

"It was a piece of paper. The size of a postcard, folded up, but the writing was still legible. Even after a

148

little wash. I thought it might be of interest, you see, so I rang you. To be on the safe side."

Hanne praised her profusely and hoped she would soon get to the point.

At long last she learnt what the message on the paper had been.

"I'll be with you in fifteen minutes," was Hanne's immediate response.

They had finally set up an incident room. That sounded pretentious, until you entered it. Twenty square metres had been left over at the furthest end of the northwest corridor after A.2.11 had been partitioned into rooms. It was impersonal and almost unusable. For bigger cases they called it the incident room, gathering both documents and personnel together in the one place. Quite functional, in a way. Two telephones, one on each of a pair of desks placed back to back beneath the window, with the same thin metal legs as in the rest of the building; the desktops sloping in opposite directions like a pitched roof. On the ridge was balanced a narrow board full of nibbled pencils, rubbers, and cheap pens. Behind each desk the walls were covered in shelves. They were empty, a reminder to everyone of how little they had on the case. A constant tiring hum emanated from an old photocopier in a small adjoining room.

Chief Inspector Kaldbakken was chairing the meeting. He was a slim man whose dialect contrived to make half his words stick in his throat in an indecipherable mumble. It could have been worse: at least they were all used to him, and could guess at what he was saying. Which wasn't much.

Detective Inspector Hanne Wilhelmsen was reporting. She was going over everything they had, separating fact from speculation, solid information from hearsay. Unfortunately most of it was speculation and hearsay. But it made an impact of sorts. There was little physical evidence, scarcely enough to convince anybody.

"Let's arrest Lavik," exhorted a young constable with a snub nose and freckles. "Stake everything on a single card. He'll crack!"

You could have heard a pin drop, and in the embarrassing silence the redheaded officer realised he'd made a fool of himself. He began to bite his nails in shame.

"What do you say, Håkon? What have we actually got to go on?"

It was Hanne who was asking. She looked better now, and had bowed to the inevitable and cut her hair short. It was a distinct improvement: the lopsided style of the past week had been rather comical. Håkon seemed somewhat distracted, but refocused his attention.

"If we could get Lavik to make a voluntary statement, it might possibly give us a lead. The problem is that from a tactical point of view we have to be certain the interrogation will be effective. We know . . ."

He broke off, and started the sentence again.

"We believe the man to be guilty: there are too many coincidences. The meeting in the middle of the night with the armed fugitive, the initials on the banknote,

150

the visit to the cells the day the warning note scared the shit out of Han van der Kerch. And another fact: he was visiting Jacob Frøstrup only a few hours before the poor chap did himself in."

"That doesn't actually prove anything," said Hanne. "We all know that prisons are full of drugs. The warders, for instance, can go in and out quite freely without any check whatsoever, directly from outside to an individual cell if they want to.

"Quite unbelievable," she added, after a moment's thought. "It's absurd that the staff of a department store like Steen and Strøm have to subject themselves to searches to prevent shoplifting, while prison staff have no inspection for drug-smuggling into prisons!"

"Unions, trade unions," muttered Kaldbakken.

"And Han van der Kerch's dread of the prison may have something to do with that. Perhaps he suspects people within the prison system," Hanne went on, not rising to the chief inspector's political views. "It seems unlikely to me that Lavik would take the risk of being stopped with a case full of drugs. Frøstrup's death is more an indication that Van der Kerch's fear of prison was justified.

"But this note here is Lavik's work. That much I'm certain of," she said, holding up a plastic envelope containing the undigested warning.

The writing was faint and half-obliterated, but no one had any difficulty reading the message.

"It looks like a poor joke," the redheaded man ventured again. "Bits of paper like that belong in crime

151

novels, not in real life." He laughed. He was the only one who did.

"Could a person really be driven into a psychotic state by such a note?" asked Kaldbakken sceptically. In thirty years he'd never come across anything like it.

"Yes, it literally frightened him out of his wits," said Hanne. "He wasn't in very good condition before, of course; a note like this could have been the last straw. He's better now, anyway, and back in a cell. Well, better doesn't mean much, he's sitting in a corner and refusing to say anything at all. Karen Borg can't get anything out of him either, as far as I know. He ought to be in hospital, if you ask me. But they'll throw him back at the prison service as soon as he can remember his name."

They were all very well aware of that. Prison psychiatry was a *perpetuum mobile*, to and fro, to and fro. The prisoners never really got any better. Only worse.

"How about asking Lavik in for a chat?" Håkon proposed. "We could take a chance on his not refusing, and see how it holds up. It might be the most stupid thing we could do; but on the other hand, does anyone have a more feasible suggestion?"

"What about Peter Strup?" It was the superintendent's first contribution to the discussion.

Hanne replied, "We've got nothing on him at the moment; in my notes he's just a big question mark."

"Don't leave him aside forever," the superintendent advised, closing the meeting. "Bring Lavik in, but don't push him too far. We don't want the whole legal profession on our backs. At least not yet. In the meantime, you" — he pointed at the young lad with the snub nose, and moved his finger along — "and you . . . and you . . . can do all the dirty work. Come with me and get your duties. There's a lot to be checked. I want to know everything about our two lawyers. Eating habits and deodorants. Political affiliations and women. Look out especially for common factors."

The superintendent departed, accompanied by the red-haired lad and the other two, roughly the same age, who'd had the sense to keep quiet during the meeting. It hadn't made any difference — the youngest always got the routine chores.

Hanne Wilhelmsen and Håkon Sand were the last to leave the room. She noticed that he seemed very satisfied, despite the situation.

"Yes, I do feel good," he responded to her friendly and surprised enquiry.

"In fact, I feel bloody good!"

Håkon Sand was begging to be allowed to attend. Detective Inspector Wilhelmsen was far from positively inclined. She hadn't forgotten the blunder with Han van der Kerch.

"I know the man," he argued. "My presence may put him more at ease. You've no idea what power competent lawyers think they have over inept ones. He may well get over-confident."

She finally conceded, in exchange for an explicit promise from Håkon to keep his mouth shut. He could speak if she gave him a sign, but even then should restrict himself to empty phrases or insignificant comments, nothing about the actual substance of the case.

"Let's do the good guy — bad guy routine," she said in the end with a grin.

She would be the surly one, he could contribute encouraging slaps on the back.

"But don't be too aggressive," Håkon warned her. "There's a risk he'll just get up and walk out, and we've got no adequate reason for holding him."

He came to the meeting with them voluntarily. No briefcase, but otherwise smartly and professionally dressed, in a suit and stylish shoes, too stylish for the slushy streets of Oslo. His trouser legs were wet, and the light brown leather of his shoes had a dark band along the sides, which would probably mean a troublesome autumn cold in store for him. The shoulders of his tweed coat were also wet, and Håkon glimpsed the exclusive label on the lining as Lavik took it off and gave it a shake before turning in search of a hook or coat hanger. He found neither, so draped it over the back of his chair. He was relaxed and cooperative, showing no sign of apprehension.

"I must say, I'm rather intrigued," he said with a smile, sweeping his hair back from his brow. It flopped forward again immediately. "Am I suspected of something?" he asked, smiling even more broadly.

Hanne reassured him: "Not at the moment."

Håkon thought she was taking a risk. But with the lesson of experience fresh in his mind, he said nothing. Neither he nor Hanne had anything to write with or on.

154

They both knew that the flow of speech could easily dry up at the sight of a tape recorder or writing implements.

"We're pursuing various lines of enquiry concerning one or two cases we're having trouble with," she admitted. "We have a feeling that you might have something to contribute. Just a few questions. You're free to leave whenever you like."

It was scarcely necessary to tell him.

"I'm fully aware of that," he said, good-naturedly, though they could discern a grittier undertone. "I'll stay till I feel like going. Okay?"

"Okay," said Håkon, hoping he was within his remit. He wanted to say something, if only to mitigate his sense of being superfluous. This it failed to do.

"Did you know Hans E. Olsen? The lawyer who was murdered recently?"

Hanne went straight to the point, but Lavik had obviously anticipated this.

"No, I can't say I did," he replied calmly. Not too fast, nor too falteringly. "I didn't know him, though of course I've spoken to him on occasion. We work in the same field — as criminal defence lawyers, I mean. I must have bumped into him in the law courts a few times too, and probably at meetings of the Defence Lawyers' Association. But as I say, I didn't really know him."

"What theories do you have about the murder?"

"The murder of Hansy Olsen?"

"Yes."

"Well, what theories . . ."

155

The hesitation was natural, he sounded reflective, as if he was trying to be helpful, like any innocent person making a statement to the police.

"To be honest, I haven't thought very much about it at all! It struck me it might be dissatisfied clients, which is the explanation that's going around in the profession, if I can put it like that."

"What about Jacob Frøstrup?"

Hanne and Håkon agreed later that they were almost sure they saw a flicker of uncertainty in the lawyer's manner when his unfortunate client was referred to. But since they had no tangible evidence for their impression they had to concede it was probably more a projection of hope than sound judgement.

"It was a dreadful shame about Jacob. He'd had a devil of a time from the moment he was born. He'd been a client of mine for many years, but he'd never been arrested for anything particularly big. I don't understand why he should get involved in something like this now. He didn't have long to go; he'd had AIDS for more than three years, I believe."

He'd been staring out of the window as he spoke. That was the only perceptible change since the beginning of the conversation. Apparently conscious of this, he turned to face his interviewers again.

"I heard that he died the same day I visited him. Very upsetting. He certainly seemed terribly depressed. He talked about taking his own life, didn't want to go on living, what with the pain, the shame, and now this charge on top of everything else. I tried to cheer him up a bit, and told him not to give in. But I have to say that the news of his death didn't take me entirely by surprise."

Lavik shook his head slowly in sorrow. He flicked at his shoulders as if to remove nonexistent dandruff; his hair was thick and lustrous and his scalp healthier than Håkon could boast of. Håkon, feeling defensive, looked down at his own black jacket and quickly brushed off the white flakes that stood out so embarrassingly against the dark background. The lawyer gave him a sympathetic and extremely condescending smile.

"Did he say anything about why he had such a large supply of drugs?"

"Frankly," said Lavik reproachfully, "even if he is dead, I find it highly irregular to be sitting here repeating to the police what he told me."

The two officers accepted his position in silence.

Hanne gathered her thoughts before playing her final card. She ran her fingers over the shaved area by her temple, a habit she'd developed over the last few days. It was so quiet in the room that she fancied that the others would be able to hear the rasping sound it made.

"Why did you meet a man in Grünerløkka at three o'clock last Friday night?"

Her tone was incisive, as if she were trying to make it sound more dramatic than it actually was. But he was ready for her.

"Oh that, that was a client. He's in deep trouble, and wanted immediate help. The police aren't involved yet, but he's afraid they will be. I just had to give him some advice."

Lavik smiled reassuringly, as if it wasn't unusual for him to drag himself out of bed in the middle of the night to rendezvous with clients in the city's less respectable districts. All in a day's work, his expression almost seemed to say. All in a night's work.

Hanne leant towards him and rapped the fingers of her left hand on the desk.

"And you expect me to believe that," she said in a low voice. "You expect me to believe that?"

"It doesn't matter to me what you believe," said Lavik, smiling again. "What matters is that I'm telling the truth. If you think otherwise, you'll have to try and prove it."

"That's exactly what I intend to do," Hanne replied. "You can go. For now."

Lavik put his coat on, thanked them, and said good-bye amicably, closing the door carefully and politely behind him.

"You had a lot to say," said Hanne in some annoyance to her colleague. "Not much point in having you here."

Her head injury had made her more irascible. Håkon ignored it. Her mood was simply the result of frustration at Lavik's excellent parrying of her questions. He just grinned.

"Better to say too little than too much," he retorted in his own defence. "Anyway, we know one thing now. The owner of the boot must have spoken to Lavik after the episode on Friday night. He was well prepared. Why didn't you say anything about the piece of paper, by the way?"

"I want to keep that in reserve," she said pensively. "I'm going home to lie down now. I've got a headache."

"They don't know anything!"

Lavik was intensely pleased with himself, and even through the distortion of the telephone line the older man could hear his exultation. He'd been worried about his younger colleague, who'd looked as if he might be on the verge of a breakdown at their last meeting in Maridalen. A confrontation with the police could have had catastrophic repercussions. But Lavik was utterly sure of himself. The police knew nothing. A shaven female and a dumbo of an old student contemporary of his — they'd just seemed puzzled, with no cards up their sleeves. Of course the events of Friday night were rather unfortunate, but they'd bought his explanation, he was certain of that. Lavik was absolutely delighted.

"I swear they know nothing at all," he repeated. "And with Frøstrup dead, Van der Kerch round the bend, and the police completely clueless, we're in the clear!"

"You're forgetting one factor," said the other man. "You're forgetting Karen Borg. We don't know what she knows, but it's almost definitely something. The police think so anyway. If you're right that they've got no leads, it means that she still hasn't talked. We don't know how long that situation will last."

Lavik didn't have much to say to this, and his jubilation abated somewhat.

"They may be wrong," he said, more meekly. "The police can get things wrong. She may not know

159

anything at all. She and Sand used to be as thick as thieves when we were all students together. I bet she would have told him if she'd had anything to tell. In fact, I'm damned sure she would."

He was sounding more confident again, but the older man could not be persuaded.

"Karen Borg is a problem," he stated emphatically. "She is and will remain a problem."

There were a few seconds' silence before the older man brought the conversation to a close.

"Don't ring me again. Not from a phone box, nor from a mobile. Don't ever ring. Use the normal method. I'll check every other day."

He slammed down the receiver. Lavik jumped at the other end as the noise shot through his ear. His ulcer gave a stab. He took out a packet of antacid powder from his inside pocket, bit off the end, and sucked in the contents. It left a white residue on his lips that would stay there for the rest of the day, but in just a few seconds he felt better. He looked carefully both ways as he came out of the phone booth. His euphoria had evaporated, and belching intermittently he made his way back to his office.

THURSDAY 29 OCTOBER

"Greed," he thought. "Greed is the criminal's worst enemy. Moderation is the key to success."

It was bitingly cold, and the snow had already been lying for weeks up here in the mountains. He'd changed over to winter tyres at Dokka, when he got to the northern end of Randsfjorden, having had a couple of alarming skids into the opposite lane. But he still had difficulty with the long, steep incline of the forest track only half a mile from the cottage. Eventually he'd had to reverse up the slope. Only once before had he had so much trouble, and the cottage had been in the family for more than twenty years. Was it the road conditions or was he losing his nerve? The little parking place was empty, and he could only just distinguish the dark outline of the four neighbouring cottages. There were no lights to indicate human habitation, but the moon came to his aid when crossing the two hundred metres to the cottage door in his snowshoes. His hands were frozen and he dropped the key in the snow twice before he finally got the door open.

It smelt mouldy and airless. He locked the door behind him, even though he realised it was hardly necessary. He had problems getting the wick to ignite in the paraffin lamp; it seemed wet from the dank air rather than with paraffin. He managed to light it after several attempts, but an ominous quantity of soot particles shot up to the ceiling. The solar energy unit had no electricity stored in it, though he couldn't see why. There must be something wrong with it. He hung his torch from the ceiling, removed his coat, and slipped on a thick sweater.

An hour later he had things organised. The paraffin heater was temperamental, and he finally abandoned it in favour of a good old-fashioned open fire. It was still far from warm, especially as he'd opened up the room to air it for half an hour. But the fire was burning fiercely and the chimney looked as if it was standing up to the blaze. The gas cooker was functioning, and he treated himself to a cup of coffee. He decided to let his business wait until the cottage had reached a reasonable temperature. The job was going to be wet and cold. There was a bundle of sixties comics stuffed in a basket, and he took one out and started turning the pages with his cold hands. He'd read it a hundred times before, but it would do to occupy him for a while. He was itching to get on with things.

It was midnight before he dressed to go out again. He took a pair of overalls from the cupboard, and his old national service boots that still fitted him, thirty years after he'd misappropriated them from the army. The full moon was still high in the southern sky, so the torch was superfluous at first. He had a coiled rope slung over one shoulder, and an aluminium snow shovel in his hand. He left his snowshoes against the side of the cottage; he could wade through the forty metres of snow to the well in his boots.

The well housing stood out like a huge landmark below the cottage in an area that could almost be described as marsh. They had been warned against taking water from there, but had never been affected by it. It always tasted fresh and sweet, with a distinct flavour of the seasons. Four stout poles were tied together at the top, like a rudimentary Lapp tent. Plywood panels had been nailed to each side, cut to an A-shape, with an aperture in one of them. A basic door arrangement, fastened with a padlock, had originally been quite small, just large enough to get the bucket through, but he had sawn it bigger four years ago. Now a man could just about crawl inside; the family thought it unnecessary, but it definitely made it easier to draw up the water.

It took almost a quarter of an hour to dig out the door enough to release it. He was sweating, and his breathing was laboured. He kicked the door firmly into an open position in the snow, crouched down, and squeezed his way in. The lowest part of the well housing was only just over a square metre, and the apex of the timber frame wasn't high enough for him to stand up. With a bit of a struggle he got the torch to shine down on the water. It was pitch-black and absolutely motionless. An old shoulder injury gave a twinge when he bent awkwardly, and he let out a fart and a groan under the strain. At last he focused the beam of light on the narrow ledge near the surface of the water. He lowered his foot tentatively, and as expected he could feel that the ledge was as slippery as soap. He kicked at the surface several times, and finally got a toehold. He repeated the exercise on the opposite side until he was standing with his legs astride, upright and reasonably stable. He took off his gloves and put them on a horizontal joist in front of him. Then he tried to roll up his overalls as far as they would go. It wasn't easy, they were too thick, and his fingers were already cold again. In the end he gave up, crouched down, and put his right arm into the freezing water while holding on to the bucket hook with his left hand. His arm went numb in seconds and he was aware of his heart beating faster and a tightness in his chest. He felt with his fingers around the sides of the well half an arm's length beneath the surface. He couldn't find what he was searching for. He cursed, and had to pull his arm out. Rolling the overall back down helped a bit, and he rubbed the sleeve against his skin and blew on his frozen hand. He waited a few minutes before he dared make another attempt.

He did better this time, feeling the loose brick almost immediately. He extracted it carefully and lifted it out of the water. His sweating back, freezing arm, and heavy thudding heart were all trying to persuade him to abandon the task, but gritting his teeth he thrust his hand down into the water again. Now he'd located the spot, he was able cautiously and delicately to draw out an object the size of a small but sturdy case. There was a handle on one end facing outwards, and he made sure he had a proper grip on it before pulling it out of the hidden cavity.

164

When the case, in fact a large box, came to the surface, his numbed fingers could cope no longer. He dropped his prize and lunged forward in a desperate attempt to catch it. But he lost his balance, his left foot slid off the ledge, and he disappeared under the water together with the box.

He couldn't see anything, and his ears, mouth, and nose filled with water. The cumbersome overalls were quickly sodden and he could feel his boots and clothing dragging him down towards the bottom. He was in a complete panic, a fear not so much for himself as for the box. But as its further descent was partially blocked by his own body, he was able to react fast enough to save it. With a supreme effort he stretched up and reached the edge of the door above and heaved the box out into the snow. He was really frightened now. He flailed around, but could already feel his movements becoming torpid, his arms and legs not obeying his commands. With another huge effort he grabbed the bucket hook again, mentally crossing his fingers for the bolts in the thin plywood to hold. Hauling himself upwards, he managed to get high enough to stretch one arm over the side of the door aperture. He took the risk of letting go of the bucket hook and thrust the upper part of his body through the opening. Moments later he was standing dripping wet and gasping for breath in the moonlight. His heart had intensified its protests and he had to clutch at his chest to ease the intolerable pain. Leaving the well door open, he picked up the box and staggered back to the cottage.

He ripped off his clothes to stand naked in front of the fire. He almost felt like climbing right into it, but in fact crouched down on the wide hearth as close to the flames as he could get. Eventually it occurred to him to fetch a quilt. It was cold and rough, but at least he wouldn't freeze to death. The clawing at his breast had stopped, though his skin was burning and prickly. His teeth were chattering as if possessed — he regarded that as a good sign. It was already at least fifteen degrees Celsius in the room, and in half an hour he'd recovered sufficiently to put on an old tracksuit, a sweater, woollen socks, and felt slippers. He got himself another cup of coffee, and settled down to open the box. It was made of metal but had a rubber seal and coating and a waterproof lock.

Everything was there. Twenty-three sheets of code, a bound nine-page document, a list of seventeen names. It was all in a plastic envelope, a safety measure that was redundant in view of the watertight nature of the box itself. He took the envelope out. Beneath it the box was completely filled by seven bundles of banknotes, two hundred thousand kroner in each. Five lay crosswise, the other two lengthwise. One million four hundred thousand kroner.

He extracted a quarter of one pack, at random, leaving the rest there. He locked the box carefully and set it back down on the floor.

The papers were totally dry. He looked first at the list of names, and then poked it into the fire. He held it until it burst into flames, and had to let go hastily in order not to scorch his still numb fingers. Then he turned to the nine-page document and started leafing through it.

The organisation couldn't have been simpler. He was the unknown godfather in the background. He had selected his two assistants with great care. Hansy Olsen because he had a useful relationship with the criminal classes, an innate understanding of money, and a flexible attitude to the law. Jørgen Lavik because he appeared to be Olsen's absolute antithesis: clever, successful, sober, and cold as ice. The young man's recent hysteria seemed to indicate that he had been mistaken. He had felt his way step by step, with extreme caution, as if he were seducing a virgin. An equivocal remark here, a few ambiguous words there, and in the end he got both of them. He had never participated in any of the actual work himself. He was the brains, and he had the investment capital. He knew all the names and planned all the moves. After long experience of defence cases he recognised where the traps lay. Greed. It was greed that caused their downfall. Smuggling drugs was easy. He had found out where the stuff came from, and what connections could be relied on. So many clients had told him mournfully about the little error that had brought them down: excessive greed. The answer was to keep every operation within limits. Not to aim too high. It was better to have a steady flow of modest earnings than to be tempted by a couple of successes to go for the "big haul."

No, the problem wasn't on the import side; the risks lay in the distribution. In an environment full of informers, stoned buyers, and avaricious pushers, you had to tread warily. That was why he'd never had any direct involvement with the lower echelons of the organisation.

Only once or twice had things gone wrong. The runners were caught, but the operation had been so small that the police didn't suspect a larger outfit behind it. The lads had kept their mouths shut, taken their sentences like men, and had a promise smuggled in of a significant bonus when they came out in the not-too-distant future. Four years was the longest sentence, but they knew they were earning a good salary for every year inside. Even if the runners had chosen to grass, they wouldn't have had that much to say. At least that's what he'd thought until a short while ago, before he'd realised that his two crown princes had exceeded their mandate.

He'd cleaned up a considerable amount of money. On top of a significant legitimate salary, it made him pretty well off. He'd used some of it gradually and circumspectly, but never in a way that couldn't be justified from his valid finances. The money in the well was his. There was also a corresponding amount hidden away in a Swiss bank account. But the major portion of the surplus was in an account he couldn't use himself. He could put money in, but not take it out. That account was for the Cause. He felt proud of it. The pleasure of being able to contribute to the Cause had effectively suppressed a lifetime's conviction of right and wrong, of criminality and legality. He saw himself as chosen, and doing what was right. Fate, which had held its protective hand over their operations for so many years, was on his side. The few mistakes they had made were inevitable, and recent events merely a warning from that same Fate to wind up the business. That could only mean that his task was accomplished. The greying man looked upon Fate as a good friend, and heeded its auguries. He'd earned countless millions; now others could take over.

The bonuses for the unlucky couriers had depleted the capital somewhat, but it was worth it. Only his two colleagues had known who he was. Olsen was dead. Lavik was keeping quiet. At least for the time being. He would take things slowly — he had plans for all eventualities.

Hansy Olsen was his first murder victim in peacetime. It had been remarkably easy. And it had been imperative, no different in essence from the occasion when two German soldiers had lain in the snow in front of him, each with a bloody hole in his uniform. He'd been seventeen then, making his way to Sweden. The shots had continued to ring in his ears as he searched them both for valuables and then trudged on full of national fervour to Sweden and freedom. It was just before Christmas 1944, and he knew he was on the winning side. He had killed two of the enemy, and felt no remorse over it.

Nor had the murder of Hans E. Olsen given him any sense of guilt. It had been a simple necessity. He'd experienced a kind of elation, a joy rather like the feeling of triumph after a raid on his neighbour's apple orchard over fifty years ago. The weapon was old, unregistered, but in perfect condition, bought from a long-deceased client.

He'd finished reading through the document. He rolled it up and screwed it round tight like a spill before throwing it on the fire. The twenty-three pages of code went the same way. Ten minutes later there were no documents anywhere in the world that could connect him to anything other than respectable activities. No signatures, no handwriting, no fingerprints. No proof.

He stood up and fetched some dry clothes from the cupboard. Replacing the box in the well was a more straightforward job than getting it out. He emptied the coffee grounds on the fire before changing back into the clothes he'd come in, hung his wet things in an outside shed, and locked the cottage. It was two o'clock, and he would be back in town in time to have a shower and turn up at the office. Cold and tired, admittedly, but that was acceptable. His secretary thought so, anyway.

TUESDAY 3 NOVEMBER

Fredrick Myhreng was in top form. While Hans Olsen was still alive, he had given him a few reasonable three-column articles, in exchange for a couple of beers. He'd sought out journalists with the enthusiasm of a small boy collecting returnable bottles. Even so, Myhreng preferred him dead. He had the full confidence of his editor, had been released from other work to concentrate on the mafia case, and met with encouragement from colleagues, who could see that he was making a niche for himself. "Contacts, you know, contacts," he grinned when people wondered what he was actually doing.

He lit a cigarette and the smoke blended with the exhaust fumes that formed a leaden haze to a height of three metres above the road. He leant against a lamppost, turned up the collar of his sheepskin jacket, and imagined himself James Dean. He breathed in a flake of tobacco as he inhaled and it caught in his windpipe, making him cough so violently that tears came to his eyes, his spectacles misted over, and he couldn't see a thing. Gone was James Dean, and he shook his head vigorously, opening his eyes wide to peer through the lenses.

171

On the opposite side of the busy street was Jørgen Ulf Lavik's office. A solid brass plate announced that Lavik, Saetre & Villesen occupied the second floor of the imposing turn-of-the-century brick building. Very central and very practical, only a stone's throw from the law courts.

Lavik was interesting. Myhreng had checked on quite a number of people now. Phoned around a bit, checked through old tax records, visited a few watering holes, and generally made himself amenable. He had started with twenty names on his pad; now there were five. It had not been easy sorting them out, and he had done it principally by instinct. Lavik became increasingly prominent, eventually heading the list. With a thick line underneath. He spent suspiciously little money. Perhaps he was just very frugal, but there were limits. His house and cars could have belonged to an average-income legal assistant rather than a partner in the firm. He didn't own a boat or a country cottage either, despite the fact that his tax returns for the last few years showed that the firm was flourishing. He'd done well out of a hotel project in Bangkok that he was still involved in. It looked as if it was going to be a sound investment for his Norwegian clients, and had led to further projects abroad, most of which had produced handsome dividends both for the investors and for Lavik himself.

As a defence lawyer it seemed he was quite successful. His reputation among colleagues was good, his statistics for acquittals were impressive, and it was difficult to find anyone who spoke ill of him.

172

Myhreng was not exceptionally intelligent, but he was clever enough to know it. He was also inventive and intuitive. He'd had a thorough training from a wily old fox of an editor on a local paper, and knew that investigative journalism consisted mainly of hard graft and failed leads.

"The truth is always well hidden, Fredrick, always well hidden," the old newspaperman had cautioned him. "There's a lot of muckraking before you get to it. Dress smartly, never give up, and have a thorough wash when you've finished."

It couldn't do any harm to have a chat with Lavik. It would be best not to have an appointment. Catch him on the hop. He stubbed out his cigarette, spat into the gutter, and zigzagged across the road between hooting cars and a stationary lorry.

The woman in reception was surprisingly plain. She was getting on in years, and reminded him of a librarian from an American children's movie. Reception-ists were supposed to be attractive and friendly — not this one. She looked as if she was going to tell him to be quiet as he tripped on the threshold and stumbled into the waiting room. But equally unexpectedly, she smiled. Her teeth were dull and unnaturally even. Obviously dentures.

"The door sill is too high," she apologised. "I'm always telling them. It's a wonder there hasn't been a real accident. Can I help you?"

Myhreng put on his flattering-old-ladies smile, which she immediately saw through, and her mouth contracted into a pattern of stern wrinkles like angry little darts.

"I'd like to speak to Mr. Lavik," he said without discarding his ineffectual smile. She consulted the book, but obviously couldn't find his name there.

"No appointment?"

"No, but it's rather important."

Fredrick Myhreng said who he was, and she pursed her lips even more. Without a word she pressed a button on her telephone and conveyed his message, presumably to the man in question.

She didn't come off the line immediately, but then with a quaint gesture she motioned him towards a row of chairs and asked him to wait. Mr. Lavik would see him, but he wouldn't be free for a few minutes.

It was actually half an hour.

Lavik's office was bright and spacious. The room had parquet flooring and just three pictures on the walls. The acoustics were poor, and more wall decoration might have helped. The desk was remarkably clear and tidy, with just three or four files on it. There was a solid wooden filing cabinet in one corner beside a small safe. The chair for clients was comfortable, but Myhreng could see that it was from a well-known furniture chain and cheaper than it appeared. He had the same kind himself. The bookcase contained very little, and Myhreng assumed the office must have its own library. He found it slightly bizarre that one shelf was full of old children's books, in enviably good condition, to judge from the spines.

174

He introduced himself again. Lavik gave him an enquiring look; the sweat on his upper lip was presumably caused by the malfunctioning room thermostat. Myhreng felt hot himself, and tugged at the neck of his sweater.

"Is this an interview?" the lawyer asked amiably.

"No, it's more a matter of a few preliminary queries."

"What about?"

"About your connection with Hans Olsen and the drugs case the police think he was involved in."

He could swear he saw a reaction. A slight, barely perceptible reddening of the throat and a movement of his lower lip to suck a few beads of sweat from the upper one.

"My connection?"

There was a smile on his face, but it looked rather forced.

"Yes, your connection."

"I had nothing to do with Olsen! Was he involved with drugs? Your newspaper gave the impression that he was the victim of criminals involved in drugs, not that he himself . . ."

"We can't say anything other than that yet, but we have our own theories. So have the police, I believe."

Lavik had had time to gather his thoughts. He smiled again, a little more relaxed now.

"Well, you're really off-target if you're trying to link me to that. I barely knew the man. Obviously I'd met him, around and about. But I couldn't say I knew him.

It was a tragic way to die, of course. He didn't have any children?"

"No, he didn't. What do you do with your money, Mr. Lavik?"

"My money?"

He sounded genuinely astonished.

"Yes, you earn enough, and you've been a good boy and given all the right information to the tax office. Almost one and a half million kroner last year. Where's it all gone?"

"That's got absolutely nothing to do with you! My conscience is completely clear, and how I invest my lawful earnings is hardly any affair of yours."

He stopped abruptly, his goodwill at an end. He glanced up at the clock and said he had to prepare for a meeting.

"But I've a lot more questions to ask you, Mr. Lavik, a lot more," the journalist protested.

"But I haven't got any more answers to give," said Lavik decisively, standing up and showing him the door.

"May I come back another day when it's more convenient for you?" Myhreng persisted as he walked across the room.

"I'd rather you rang. I'm a very busy man," the lawyer replied, putting an end to the conversation and shutting the door behind him.

Fredrick Myhreng was alone with the librarian. She had picked up on her employer's negative attitude and gave the impression she was going to refuse when

Myhreng asked if he could use the toilet. But common courtesy prevailed.

He'd noticed an opaque window in the corridor outside, near the entrance door. While he was sitting in the waiting room it had occurred to him that it must be a lavatory. That turned out to be not entirely correct. Behind the door bearing the familiar little porcelain heart was an anteroom with a washbasin, from which the cubicle was divided by a lockable swing door. He opened and closed the door, but instead of going in he took out a chunky Swiss Army knife. It had three screwdriver blades, and it wasn't difficult to loosen the six screws in the frame that held the window in position. He knew enough about carpentry to feel amused when he saw that the window was only screwed in; it should have been jointed together, otherwise it would warp. It hadn't been, however, presumably because it was an inside window and not exposed to the damp. He ensured that the screws were still caught by a couple of threads, and went quietly into the cubicle and flushed the cistern. Having washed his hands, he smiled pleasantly at the receptionist, who didn't even deign to say good-bye as he left the office. He didn't intend to lose any sleep over it.

The evening was well advanced and bitterly cold. But Fredrick Myhreng was not anxious to get into the warm. He was worried. His overconfidence of the morning had been replaced by growing uncertainty. He hadn't learnt anything about burglary or other illegal activities at the College of Journalism. Rather the reverse. He wasn't even sure how to begin.

The building had offices on three floors, and flats on the top two, as far as he could see from the names by the bells. In films the burglar would try all of them and say, "Hi, it's Joe," in the hope that someone would know a Joe and activate the door release. But that would hardly work here. The outer entrance door to the courtyard was very firmly closed. Going for the next best solution, he drew out a jemmy from his sheepskin jacket.

Getting in was a doddle. Two tugs and the door gave way. It didn't even creak on its hinges when he opened it just enough to slip through. To the left there was another door at the top of three little granite steps, already salted against the night frost. He was anticipating another obstacle, but to make certain he turned the door handle before he set to with his crowbar. Someone must have forgotten to lock it, because it opened outwards so easily and unexpectedly that he took an involuntary step back, found his foot in midair, and yelped as he touched the ground later than his reflexes had reckoned on. But it didn't detract from his delight at how well everything was going.

He bounded up the stairs in half the time it had taken him a few hours earlier. He stopped at the opaque window and stood for a moment to recover his breath, and to listen in case anyone had heard him. There was nothing except a faint ringing in his ears, so a moment later he took out a little tub of Plasticine and pressed the soft lump against the glass, using his thumbs to knead it into shape round the edges. It was difficult to know how much pressure he could exert without the window falling out, but when he was satisfied he repeated the operation with a new lump of Plasticine further down. Then he took hold of both lumps and pushed hard. The window wouldn't budge.

He was beginning to perspire and felt the need to dispense with his jacket. It was also hampering his movements, so after his second attempt on the glass he took it off. Despite his gloves, he had a firm grip on the Plasticine. When he put the whole weight of his body into his third attempt he could feel the screws giving way. Luckily the lower part of the window came loose first, and he was able to lift the frame at the same time as he clambered over the sill and into the little room. The window was completely free and all in one piece. He grabbed his jacket before removing the Plasticine, and eased the window back into position.

Cautiously he opened the door into the lobby. He was not so stupid as to assume there was no alarm. It didn't look very sophisticated: he could see a small box with a tiny red light above the window. He got down and squirmed his way across to the door of Lavik's office on his stomach. His torch was tucked into his belt and dug into him painfully with every ponderous movement. The door was open. He shone his torch round the room looking for a corresponding alarm box to the one in the anteroom. There wasn't one. Or at least the beam of his torch didn't pick anything out. He took a chance and stood up as soon as he was through the doorway.

179

Naturally he had no idea what he was looking for. He hadn't thought about it, and now he felt rather foolish standing there in an office he had no lawful right to be in, committing his first crime, but without any clear objective. The safe was locked. That was hardly suspicious. The filing cabinet was unlocked, however, and pulling out the drawers he found a sequence of cardboard folders, each with a little label projecting at one corner bearing a name written in a clear and elegant hand. The names meant nothing to him.

The desk drawer contents were what could have been predicted. Yellow message stickers, pink markers, a pile of ballpoint pens, and a few pencils. They lay in a tray subdivided into sections, supported by the sides of the drawer, to leave room for papers underneath, in the drawer itself. He lifted the tray, but the documents were of no interest. Star Tours' winter brochure, an A4 pad of preprinted fee notes. And a pad of lined paper. He put the pen tray back and closed the drawer. Beneath it was a low free-standing cupboard on castors, which was locked.

He ran his gloved hands along the underside of the desk. It was smooth and polished, and his fingers met no resistance. Disappointed, he turned again to the filing cabinet in the corner of the room. He walked across to it, bent down, and felt underneath it in the same way. Nothing. He lay flat and shone his torch systematically from one side to the other.

He almost missed it, because he wasn't expecting to find it. The beam had already gone past it before his brain registered what he'd seen, and in his slight confusion he dropped the torch, but it was still close enough for him to spot the little dark lump. He worked it free and stood up. The streetlights cast a pale glow into the room, enough to show him immediately what it was. A key, quite small, which had been attached to the bottom of the cupboard with tape.

He was inordinately pleased, and was about to put it in his pocket when he had a far better idea. He brought out a piece of Plasticine from the tub in his pocket, warmed it against his cheek, and fashioned it into two flat oval shapes. He pressed the key into one of them, long and hard. He had to take off his gloves to get it out again without damaging the impression. Then he did the same with the other side, and finally made an imprint of the diameter at the top of the first piece of Plasticine.

The tape was reusable, and he felt sure he'd got the key back in exactly the same place he'd found it. He put his jacket on, crawled out the way he'd come in, and fixed the window back on the inside without leaving any visible marks from the screwdriver. He brushed over the frame to get rid of possible splinters, and paused in the doorway of the waiting room to gather his breath for the big run. He counted down from ten, and on zero he shot like a rocket towards the entrance door, opened it, closed it behind him, and was halfway down the staircase before he heard the high-pitched shriek of the alarm. He was round the next block before anyone in the building had even got their slippers on.

"That'll give them something to think about," he thought triumphantly. "No sign of a break-in, nothing taken, nothing touched. Just an unlocked entrance door."

Fredrick Myhreng was used to feeling pleased with himself. This surpassed almost everything. He was humming as he skipped along, like a child who had played a successful trick, and with a yell to the driver and a huge grin on his face he just managed to catch the last tram home.

FRIDAY 6 NOVEMBER

She had developed a routine of calling in on her unfortunate client every Friday afternoon. He said nothing, but it seemed as if in some strange way he valued these meetings. Huddled up and thin as a rake, he still had the empty look in his eyes, but she thought she could detect a trace of a smile each time he saw her. Even though Han van der Kerch had so tenaciously resisted being transferred there while he had the mental capacity to say what he wanted, he was now in Oslo Prison. Karen Borg had permission to visit him in his cell, since it was impractical to bring him out to an interview room. It was lighter here, and the warders seemed both fair-minded and considerate, insofar as their workloads allowed. The door was secured behind her during every visit, and she felt an odd comfort from being locked in, the same feeling that had driven her into the cupboard under the stairs at home in Bergen as a child whenever the world seemed against her. The prison visits had become a time for contemplation. She sat there with the silent man in front of her, and listened to the orderly in the corridor clattering by with his trolley, the echo of obscene shouts and laughter, and the heavy jangling of keys whenever a warder passed the door.

He didn't look quite so pale today. He kept his eyes on her all the way to the bed as she sat down beside him. When she took his hand, she felt him squeeze hers in response; almost imperceptibly, but she was sure she had discerned a slight pressure. With hesitant optimism she bent forward and brushed his hair away from his forehead. It was growing too long, and immediately fell back again. She continued stroking his brow, running her fingers through his hair. It was evidently soothing, because he closed his eyes and leant towards her. They remained sitting like that for several minutes.

"Roger," he murmured, his voice a husky croak after not having been used for such a length of time.

Karen Borg didn't react. She went on caressing him and asked no questions.

"Roger," said the Dutchman again, a little louder now. "The guy at Sagene with the second-hand cars. Roger."

Then he fell asleep. His breathing became more regular, and his weight against her body increased. She rose carefully to her feet, moved him into a more comfortable position, and couldn't help kissing him gently on the forehead.

"Roger at Sagene," she repeated to herself, knocking softly on the door to be let out.

"Nothing. Absolutely nothing."

Håkon Sand took hold of the thick file and banged it down on the desk. It slipped out of his grasp and papers spilled out all over the floor.

184

"Damn!" he exclaimed, getting down to sort out the mess. Hanne joined in on all fours to help him. They stayed there on their knees looking at each other.

"I'll never get used to it. Never!"

He spoke with sudden vehemence.

"What?"

"That so often we know there's something crooked, that someone has committed a crime, we even know who's done it and what they've done, we know so bloody much. But can we prove it? No, we sit here like eunuchs, impotent, with all the odds stacked against us. We know, we're certain, but if we risked going to court with what we know, it would all be dissected by some defence lawyer devising a rational explanation for each single piece of evidence we produce. They pick and pick, and finally everything we knew becomes a mush of uncertain facts, quite enough to put it all in reasonable doubt. Hey presto, the bird has flown and the rule of law has been upheld. Whose? Not mine, anyway. The rule of law has just bloody turned into a useful tool for the guilty. It means putting as few as possible in prison. That's not rule of law! What about all the people who're murdered, raped, suffered child abuse, or are robbed or burgled? Hell, I should have been a sheriff in the Wild West. They took direct action when they knew who'd done it. Tied a rope to the nearest tree and hanged the criminal by the neck. A sheriff's star and a Stetson would have been a bloody sight better rule of law than seven years at law school and ten stupid jury members. The Inquisition. Now that's what I call a court. Judge, prosecutor, and defence counsel all rolled into one. There really was some action then, not a load of waffle about the rule of law for crooks and gangsters."

"You don't mean all that, Håkon," Hanne said soothingly, retrieving the last pieces of paper. She'd had to lie almost flat to reach an interview transcript that had lodged itself under the mobile shelving.

"You don't mean it," she repeated, half muffled under the desk.

"Well, not entirely. But almost."

They were both feeling frustrated. It was late on a Friday afternoon. There had been too many long days, working into the evenings, which she coped with better than he did. They sat and sorted the papers into their original sequence.

"Brief me," he demanded when they'd finished.

It didn't take long. He knew how little physical evidence they had, and their wider tactical investigations had ground to a halt. Forty-two witnesses had been questioned in all. Not one of them could throw any light on the case, not even a vague lead to follow up.

"Has anything come of the watch being kept on Lavik?" said Håkon, putting the papers to one side. He took a warm bottle of beer out of a plastic supermarket bag and knocked the cap off against the edge of the desk. The wood splintered slightly and he brushed a sliver of glass off the neck.

"It's the weekend," he said in excuse, raising the bottle to his lips. The foaming beer threatened to splash down his clothes, so he leant forward and shifted his legs. He wiped his mouth and waited for an answer.

"No, with the resources we've got it's impossible to mount twenty-four-hour surveillance on the guy. It's as chancy as a game of roulette. No point in following him at all if it's not effective. It just makes it more infuriating."

"What about the business side of his activities?"

"It would be an enormous task to get to the bottom of it. He's had some hotel projects in the Far East. Bangkok. Which isn't that far from the heroin markets. But the investors he's been working for are sound enough, and the hotels are already built. So there's nothing suspicious about the business itself. If you could wangle the expenses, I'd be delighted to go to Thailand and investigate further."

She pulled a face that clearly indicated what she thought of the likelihood of such budgetary extravagance. It had turned dark outside, and the weariness they both felt, together with the faint aroma of beer, made the little office seem almost cosy.

"Are we on duty now?"

He knew what she meant, shook his head with a smile, and handed her a beer, opening it in the same way as the first. Once again the desk suffered, but this time the neck of the bottle remained intact. She took it from him, then set it down and disappeared without a word. She was back in a couple of minutes and struggling to make two candles stay upright on his desk. They did so eventually, having dripped wax everywhere, each tilted at a slightly different angle. She switched off the main ceiling light and Håkon turned the desk lamp to the wall so that it cast a diffused glow into the room.

"If anyone comes now, the rumours will start flying."

He nodded in agreement.

"But it could only be to my advantage," he said facetiously.

They clinked their bottles together, a bit too forcefully.

"This was a good idea. Is it allowed?"

"I'll do what I like in my own office at half past six on a Friday evening. They're not paying me for being here, and I'm taking the train home. And there's nobody waiting for me there, either. What about you, is there anyone waiting for you?"

He intended it as an amicable enquiry, just an impulsive and well-meaning attempt to exploit the unusual atmosphere. But she clearly interpreted it as overstepping the mark, stiffened in her chair, and put her bottle of beer down. He could have kicked himself as he noticed her change of attitude.

"How about Peter Strup?" he said after an uneasy silence.

"We haven't seen much of him. Perhaps we should. But I just don't know what there is we can put our finger on. I'm more interested in what Karen Borg must know."

Even in the flickering candlelight she could see him flush. He took off his glasses to distract her attention, and wiped the lenses on his cotton sweater.

188

"She knows more than she's saying, that much is obvious. Presumably about criminal offences other than the one we've got Van der Kerch for now. We're holding him for murder. The forensic tests are complete, and enough to convict him. But if our theories are right, he may also be up to his neck in drug trafficking. It wouldn't exactly be favourable to his sentence to have that on top of a murder. She's got a duty of confidentiality, and she's a woman of principle, believe me. I know her. Or used to, anyway."

"Well, at least it doesn't look as if that memo of mine has caused any harm to come to her," said Hanne. "She hasn't been aware of anything unusual or worrying?"

"No."

He wasn't as confident as he sounded. He hadn't spoken to her for a fortnight. Not that he hadn't tried. Even though she'd kissed him to seal a promise that he wouldn't phone her, he'd broken it after just a couple of days, after he'd fallen down a loft ladder very early the Saturday before last. He'd tried her office number on the Monday morning, but had been turned away by a friendly-sounding woman on the switchboard. Karen Borg was busy, but yes, she would pass on the message that he'd phoned. She'd passed on four more messages since then, but none had elicited a response. He'd accepted it with his old feeling of resignation, but even so felt bitter disappointment whenever the telephone rang and he leapt to answer it, only to find that she must be sticking to her resolution not to speak to him for at least a month. There were still two weeks to go.

"No," he reiterated, "she hasn't noticed anything unusual."

The candles had made big circles of wax on the desk. Håkon put his hand protectively but unnecessarily behind the flames and blew them out, then stood up and turned on the ceiling light.

"So much for the *Vorspiel*," he said with artificial cheerfulness. "Now off to our respective weekends!"

SATURDAY 7 NOVEMBER

Even though winter had rattled its sabre, leaving the frost-bitten grass as the first casualty, it had had to surrender to a normal dreary autumn. The debris of these latest preliminary skirmishes had lain for a few days as dirty white patches everywhere; now all were gone. The rain was two or three degrees too warm for snow, but felt much colder. The asphalt, which a short while before had glittered at night as if studded with millions of black diamonds, now lay like a flat slobbering monster swallowing every morsel of light the moment it hit the ground.

Hanne and Cecilie were on their way home from an excellent party. Cecilie had drunk too much, and was flirtatiously endeavouring to hold Hanne's hand. They walked arm in arm for a few metres, between two streetlights, but as they came into the glow of the lamp Hanne pulled away.

"Coward," Cecilie teased her.

Hanne just smiled, and withdrew her hands into her sleeves, guarding them from further attempts at intimacy.

"We're nearly home," she said.

Their hair was already drenched, and Cecilie complained that she couldn't see anything through her glasses.

"Get yourself some contact lenses, then."

"Well, I can hardly get any at this very moment, can I? And it's now I need them! So I'll just have to take your arm. Either that or I'll break my neck and you'll be all alone in the world."

They walked on with their arms linked. Hanne didn't want to be all alone in the world.

The park ahead of them was very murky. They were both afraid of the dark, but it would save five minutes, so they decided to risk it.

"You're really witty sometimes, Hanne. You really are," Cecilie chattered on, as if the sound of their voices would ward off any evil powers that might be lying in wait on an autumn night. "Your jokes make me die. Tell me the one about the National Theatre in Gryllefjord. It gets funnier every time. And it's a nice long one. Go on!"

Hanne began it willingly enough. But when she came to the bit about their second performance at Gryllefjord town hall, she suddenly stopped. She made a quick imperative gesture and dragged Cecilie behind a giant maple tree. Cecilie misunderstood, and offered her lips for a kiss.

"Cut it out, Cecilie, keep quiet and control yourself!"

She extracted herself from the unwanted embrace, pressed up close to the tree, and peered out.

The two men had been incautious enough to position themselves under one of the few lamps in the entire poorly lit park. The women were thirty metres away and couldn't hear what was being said. Hanne could only see the back of one man, standing with his hands in his pockets and banging his legs against one another to keep warm. That might mean they'd been there for some while. All four of them remained where they were for what seemed an eternity, the men conversing in low tones, the women silent behind the tree. Cecilie had eventually realised it was a serious matter and accepted that now was not the moment for an explanation.

The man with his back to them was wearing ordinary everyday clothes. His jeans were tucked into a pair of down-at-heel snow boots. His jacket, also denim, had imitation fur on the lapels and collar. His hair was short, almost a crew cut.

The man whose face Hanne could see was wearing a light beige overcoat and was also bare-headed. He wasn't saying much, but appeared to be listening intently to the other's flow of words. After a few minutes he took a small folder from the other man, possibly a slim file. He flicked rapidly through it and seemed to be asking questions about some of the contents. He pointed several times at the documents and held them out under the lamp for them both to see. Finally he folded them lengthwise and thrust them with some difficulty into an inside pocket.

The light coming from directly above, like a weak sun at its zenith, turned his face into a caricature, looking almost diabolical. Even so, Hanne had recognised him immediately. As the men shook hands and went off in opposite directions Hanne let go of the tree and turned to her partner.

"I know who that one is," she said, in a tone of great satisfaction.

The man in the overcoat was hurrying off, his shoulders hunched, towards the far side of the park where he'd left his car.

"It's Peter Strup," she declared. "Peter Strup the lawyer."

MONDAY 9 NOVEMBER

The paintings hung on the walls in dense profusion. It made for a pleasing impression, even though they did rather overpower one another. She recognised some of the signatures. Well-known artists. One rainy evening she had offered the proprietor a tidy sum for an almost metre-square picture of Olaf Ryes Plass. It was painted in watercolours, but was not like any watercolour she had ever seen: it looked as if it had been done on brown paper which had not absorbed the paint. It was rough and violent, full of urban life and vigour. In the background you could see the block where she lived. But the painting hadn't been for sale.

The tables were too close together, which was the only annoying aspect of the place. It was difficult to conduct a private conversation when the neighbouring table was in such close proximity. There weren't many customers on a Monday; it was so quiet that they'd rejected the table to which they'd been ushered and insisted on one at the other side of the room. For the moment there were no fellow diners next to them.

The black oilcloth that covered the table was in elegant contrast to the white damask napkins, and the wineglasses were perfect, with no fussy adornment. The wine itself was superb; she had to give him credit for his selection.

"You don't give up," said Karen Borg with a smile after tasting it.

"No, I'm not renowned for surrendering, at least not to beautiful women!"

It would have been banal, even rather impertinent, coming from anyone else. But Peter Strup made it sound like a compliment, and she realised — not without a degree of self-reproach — that she felt gratified by it.

"I couldn't say no to a written invitation," Karen replied. "It's years since I last had such a thing."

The invitation had been on top of her pile of mail that very day. An ochre-coloured card of quality paper from Alvøen, deckle-edged and headed in fine print: *Peter Strup, High Court Barrister.*

The text itself was handwritten, in a manly but neat and legible hand. It was a humble request to meet him for dinner at a particular restaurant, considerately enough only two blocks away from where she lived. The time proposed was that same evening, and he had ended by writing:

This is an invitation in the best sense. With your polite rejection fresh in my mind, I leave it to you whether to accept. You don't need to let me know, but if you come, I'll be there at 7p.m. If you choose not to, I promise you'll hear no more from me — at least not on this matter!

He had signed off with his first name, like an American gesture of familiarity. It seemed a bit presumptuous, but only in this one respect. The note itself was tasteful, and gave her a free choice. She could turn up if she felt so inclined. She did. But before finally deciding she rang Håkon.

It was over a fortnight since she'd asked him to keep his distance. Since then she'd been wavering between a fierce desire to phone him and panic at what had happened. It had been the best night of her life. It threatened everything she had, and showed her that there was something inside her that couldn't be controlled, tempting her out of the secure existence she was so dependent on. She didn't want to have an affair on the side, nor did she want a separation, under any circumstances. The only rational conclusion was that Håkon had to be held at bay. But at the same time she was sick with desire and had lost several kilos in weight while striving towards a decision whose ramifications she still could not envisage.

"It's Karen," she said when she finally got through to him at the third attempt.

He gulped so hard that he started coughing. She could hear him moving the receiver away, but what she couldn't hear was that the cough and the excitement at her call had made him vomit, and he had to grab the wastepaper bin. The bitter taste was still burning his mouth when he was eventually in a condition to speak.

"I'm so sorry," he said, clearing his throat. "Something went down the wrong way. How are you?"

"I don't want to talk about that now, Håkon. We will talk about it, but later. I have to think. I need to work things out. Be a good chap. Give me a bit more time."

"Why are you phoning then?"

A mixture of despair and the faintest surge of hope made him sound unjustifiably impatient. He could hear it himself, and hoped the telephone line would take the sting out of his tone.

"Peter Strup has invited me out to dinner."

There was complete silence. Håkon was absolutely taken aback, and inordinately jealous.

"I see."

What more could he say?

"I see," he repeated. "Have you accepted? Has he given any reason for the invitation?"

"Not yet," she replied. "But I'm sure it has something to do with the case. I'm tempted to go. Do you think I should?"

"No, of course you shouldn't! He's a suspect in a serious criminal investigation! Have you gone completely crazy? God knows what he might be up to! No, you can't go. Do you hear what I'm saying?"

She sighed, and realised what a mistake it had been to phone him.

"You know he's not a suspect, Håkon. Go on, admit it. You've got nothing on the man at all! The fact that he's shown a peculiar interest in my client is hardly enough to put him in the spotlight. Actually, I'm rather keen to find out what's prompted this interest, and dinner with him might produce an answer. That would be advantageous for you too, wouldn't it? I promise I'll tell you whatever I can get out of him."

"We've got more on him," Håkon countered pathetically. "We have more than just this attempted poaching of clients. But I can't tell you anything. You'll simply have to take my word for it."

"I think you're jealous, Håkon."

He could hear that she was smiling, damn her.

"I'm not in the least jealous," he shouted, his gastric juices rising into his mouth again. "I've got a genuine professional concern for your safety!"

"Well, well," she said. "If I should disappear this evening, you can arrest Peter Strup. I'm going. I've made up my mind."

"Wait a minute. Where are you meeting him?"

"None of your business, Håkon, but if you really want to know: the Wine Bar on Markveien. Don't phone me. I'll phone you. In a while. A few days, or weeks."

She rang off and a derisive monotone buzz took her place.

"Damn," Håkon muttered. He spat again into the wastepaper bin and then removed the plastic liner, knotted it tight, and went off to dispose of its evil-smelling contents.

The food was out of this world. Karen enjoyed a good meal. Her own repeated culinary efforts were always a disaster. A metre of cookery books on the shelf hadn't made any appreciable difference. In the course of her years with Nils he had gradually taken over the cooking. He could make gourmet meals out of sachets of soup; she could ruin a prime steak.

Seeing him again, she thought Peter Strup more attractive than his photographs in the newspapers. According to the press he was sixty-five. He looked much younger in photographs, but it was probably because the numerous tiny wrinkles didn't show. Now, sitting across a table from him, she could see that life hadn't treated him as leniently as she'd previously thought. Nevertheless the lines on his face gave him more credibility, made him look more experienced. His impressive dark grey hair covered his head like a steel helmet. A Viking chieftain with a glint of granite in his eyes.

"How are you liking it as a defence counsel?" he asked with a smile over the port, after three courses and cheesecake.

"All right," she replied, not giving anything away.

"Is your client still in the same psychotic state?"

How did he know about the Dutchman's state of health? But the question slipped from her mind as fast as it had occurred to her.

"Yes. It's a shame for the poor chap. It really is. They haven't even arranged the medical for the court yet — he's too far gone for them to do it! He ought to be put away. But you know how it is . . . Frustrating. There's not much I can do for him."

"Do you visit him?"

"Yes, I do. Every Friday. It seems as if somewhere deep inside his disturbed brain he sets store by it. Strange."

200

"No, it's not that strange," said Peter Strup, gently wafting away the smoke of Karen's cigarette.

"Sorry, is that troubling you?" she asked apologetically, stubbing it out half-smoked.

"No, not in the slightest," he assured her, picking up her pack and shaking out another one to offer her. "It's not troubling me at all."

She declined the cigarette anyway, and put the pack in her handbag.

"It's not surprising that he welcomes your visits. They always do. You're probably the only one who calls. It's a glimmer of light in his existence, something to look forward to beforehand, and something to keep him going till the next time. However psychotic he is, he still registers what's going on. Does he talk?"

It was a totally innocent question, quite natural in the context. But it put her immediately on the alert, cutting right through the genial atmosphere and the comfortable mild intoxication induced by three glasses of wine.

"Only meaningless mumbling," she said in an offhand tone. "But he smiles when I go in. Or at least he makes a grimace that could be taken for a smile."

"So he doesn't say anything," Peter Strup continued casually, looking at her over the top of his glass of port. "What does he actually mumble about?"

Karen's jaw tightened. She could feel she was under interrogation, and didn't like it. Up to that point she'd been enjoying the meal, and felt at ease in the company of a courteous, knowledgeable, and charming man. He'd been recounting anecdotes from legal and sporting life, telling her jokes with triple layers of meaning, and spicing the whole with an attentiveness that would have made more attractive women than Karen feel flattered. She had opened up too, more than she usually did, and confided some of her misgivings about life as a lawyer for the rich and powerful.

Now he was cross-examining her. She wouldn't let herself be drawn.

"I don't want to talk about a specific case. Least of all about this particular one. I have my duty to my client to think of. Anyway it seems to me you owe me an explanation for your so patently obvious curiosity."

She had folded her arms, as she always did when she felt annoyed or vulnerable. Now she felt both.

Peter Strup put down his glass and sat like a male mirror image with arms folded and his gaze fixed on hers.

"I'm interested because I think I have an inkling of something that concerns me. As a lawyer, as a person. There's a possibility I could protect you, from something that *could* be dangerous. Let me take over the defence."

He unfolded his arms and leant towards her. His face was too close to hers, and involuntarily she tried to back away — in vain, as it happened, because her head was soon pressing against the wall.

"You can regard this as a warning. Either you let me take over the Dutchman, or you'll have to accept the consequences. I can assure you of one thing: you'd definitely do yourself a service by withdrawing. It's probably not too late."

It had become very hot in the room. Karen could feel her cheeks reddening and a rash starting on her neck from her slight allergy to red wine. The underwiring in her bra dug into the damp flesh beneath her breasts. She rose abruptly to get away from it all.

"And I can assure *you* of one thing," she said in a low voice as she reached for her handbag without taking her eyes off him. "I won't hand this man over for any amount of persuasion. He's asked for my services; I've been appointed by the Court; I'm going to help him. Regardless of any threats, whether from criminals or from high court barristers."

Even though she had spoken in subdued tones the scene had drawn a certain amount of attention. The few customers in the other half of the room had fallen silent and were openly watching the two lawyers. She lowered her voice even further, and said almost in a whisper, "Many thanks for the meal. It was very good. I don't expect to hear from you again. If I do hear a single word from you about this case, I'll report you to the Lawyers' Association."

"I'm not a member," he smiled, wiping his lips with the large white napkin.

Karen Borg stomped out to the cloakroom, threw on her coat, and got home in one minute and forty-five seconds. She was furious.

The night was still young when she woke up. The digital numerals on the clock radio shone the time at her in their fiery red glow: 02:11. Nils's breathing was slow and even, with funny little snores on every fourth breath. She tried to join in the rhythm, to link herself in rest to the big sleeping figure by her side, to breathe in unison, to force her smaller-capacity lungs to the same tempo as his. They protested by making her feel dizzy, but she knew from experience that after the dizziness sleep would usually return from its nocturnal elusiveness.

But not tonight. Her heart flatly refused to decrease its speed, and her lungs wheezed in protest against the change of rhythm. What had she been dreaming? She couldn't recall, but the feelings of grief and impotence and indefinable anxiety were so overwhelming that it must have been something quite sinister.

She gradually eased herself over to the edge of the bed, and reached down to the plug of the extension phone on the bedside table and extracted it. Then she slipped out of bed as gently as she could, without waking Nils — she had had countless nights of practice — and tiptoed from the bedroom, pausing at the door to take her dressing gown.

Only a little lamp above the telephone table made it possible to see anything at all in the corridor. Karen felt round the cordless phone and lifted it gingerly off its base. Then she went straight through the door on the other side of the living room into what they called the office. The light was on; books on psychology covered the large thick pine desktop that was attached to two square supports descending from the sloping ceiling. Bookshelves lined the room from floor to ceiling. But they weren't sufficient; in various places piles of books a metre high stood on the floor. This room was the snuggest in the house, and there was an armchair with a footstool and a good reading lamp in one corner. Karen sat down.

She knew his number by heart, despite having rung it only once in her life, just over two weeks ago. She still remembered the number he'd had as a student, having rung it at least once a day for six years. For some reason it seemed a greater act of betrayal to telephone him with Nils asleep three rooms away than to make love with him on the living-room floor with Nils out of town. She sat staring at the phone for several minutes before her fingers eventually, almost of their own accord, picked out the right digits.

After two and a half rings she heard a muffled hello.

"Hi, it's me."

She couldn't think of anything more original.

"Karen! What's the matter?"

He suddenly sounded wide awake.

"I can't sleep."

A rustling noise indicated that he was sitting up in bed.

"But even so, that's no excuse for waking you," she said apologetically.

"Yes, it's perfectly all right. Honestly, I'm glad you're phoning. You know that. You must always ring me if you feel the need. Anytime. Where are you?"

"At home."

There was silence.

"Nils is asleep," she explained, anticipating his question. "I pulled out the plug on the bedroom extension. Anyway he always sleeps like a log at this hour of the night. He's used to me waking up and wandering about. I don't think he'll be worried."

"How did the dinner go?"

"It was pleasant up till coffee. Then he started to go on and on. I don't understand why he's so interested in the boy. He was quite pushy, so I had to put him in his place. I don't think I'll be hearing from him again."

"Yes, you seemed pretty livid when you left."

"When I left? How do you know?"

"You left the restaurant at 22:04 precisely and virtually ran home, looking fairly irate."

He gave a little laugh, almost apologetic.

"You beast! Were you spying on me?"

Karen was both indignant and gratified.

"No, I wasn't spying on you, just taking care of you. It was a chilly way of passing the time. Three hours in a doorway in Grünerløkka isn't exactly enjoyable."

He had to stop and sneeze twice.

"Damn, I seem to have caught a cold. You ought to be grateful."

"Why didn't you show yourself when I came out?"

Håkon made no response.

"Did you think I'd be cross?"

"There was that possibility, yes. As you were yesterday, on the phone."

"You're sweet. You're really sweet. I definitely would have been hopping mad. But I'm very touched to think that you were standing there all that time keeping an eye on me. Were you being Håkon then, or a policeman?"

206

There was a subtle invitation in the question. Had it been daylight he would have given a clever and diplomatic answer, as he knew she would prefer. But it was the dead of night. Without really deciding, he said what he actually thought.

"A prosecuting attorney doesn't do bodyguard duties, Karen. A police lawyer sits in the office and doesn't bother with anything except documents and legal cases. It was me myself on watch. I was jealous, and I was concerned. I love you. That was why."

He felt satisfied and calm. Whatever her reaction might be. It came as something of a shock, and knocked him completely off balance.

"I'm probably a little in love with you, too, Håkon."

Suddenly she burst into tears. Håkon didn't know what to say.

"Don't cry!"

"I'll cry if I like," she sniffed. "I'm crying because I don't know what to do."

She began to sob convulsively. Håkon had difficulty catching what she said, so he waited till she'd stopped.

It took ten minutes.

"I shouldn't have wasted my phone bill on that," she sighed at last.

"You can talk forever for the price of one unit at night. You can afford it."

She was more tranquil now.

"I'm planning to go away," she said. "To the cottage by myself. I'll take the dog and a few books. It feels as if I can't think here in the city. At least not here in the flat, and at the office all I've got time for is the battle to get through my work. Can hardly even manage that."

She started snuffling again.

"When are you going?"

"I don't know. I promise I'll phone before I go. It might be a week or two yet. But you must promise not to ring me. You've been so patient."

"I promise. Word of honour. But — could you say it just once more?"

After a short pause, she did.

"I may be a little bit in love with you, Håkon. Maybe. Good night."

TUESDAY 10 NOVEMBER

"Talk about a waste of effort."

Hanne Wilhelmsen had sensibly put two thick elastic bands round the documents on the case. They looked like a rather attractive Christmas present. A package that would stand up to anything, even being thrown. She put it to the test. *Thud.*

"Now we've been through both Olsen and Lavik. Zilch."

"Nothing? Nothing at all?"

Håkon Sand was quite astonished. It was more extraordinary that there was nothing of interest than if they'd found the odd little nugget. Few people would withstand the critical scrutiny of the police without something crawling out of the woodwork.

"But there is one thing that puzzles me," said Hanne. "We haven't got access to Lavik's bank account, since we haven't charged him. But look at his tax returns for the last few years."

She put a sheet of meaningless figures in front of Håkon. They told him nothing — except that the guy had an annual income that would turn every employee of the prosecution service green with envy.

"It seems as if the money just disappears," said Hanne in explanation.

"Disappears?"

"Yes, there's simply no correlation between the amount he declares and his wealth. Either his normal living expenditure is prodigious, or he's salted the money away somewhere."

"But why should he salt away money honestly acquired?"

"There's only one good reason for it: avoidance of wealth tax. But with the level of wealth tax we have in this country it seems both silly and unlikely. It doesn't make sense to me that he would risk tax irregularities for the sake of a few miserable kroner. His accounts are in order and approved by an auditor every single year. But there's something here I don't understand."

They sat and looked at one another. Håkon put a wad of chewing tobacco in his mouth.

"Have you started that filthy habit?" said Hanne in disgust.

"Just to stop myself succumbing to cigarettes again. Purely a temporary measure," he said in excuse, spitting out the old tobacco into the room.

"It'll spoil your teeth. Anyway, it smells foul."

"There's no one to smell me," he retorted. "Let's bounce a few ideas around. What would make you hide money away?"

"I would do it with money earned from the black economy or illegally. Switzerland, probably. As in crime stories. We're powerless with Swiss banks. The accounts don't even have to be registered in a name, a number will do."

"Have we noted any trips to Switzerland?"

"No, but he doesn't need to go there. Swiss banks have branches in masses of the countries he's visited. And I can't get away from the idea that there may be something in his connections with the Far East. Drugs. That would fit in with our theory. It's a pity he's got a valid reason for his trips there — his hotels."

There was knock at the door, and a fair-haired constable opened it without waiting for a response. This annoyed Håkon, but he didn't comment.

"Here are the papers you asked for," he said to the inspector, and handed her five sheets of computer printout, leaving again without closing the door. Håkon got up and did it for him.

"No manners, the youth of today."

"Håkon, listen: if I had large sums of unlawfully gained money and were using a Swiss bank account, and if I were miserly, wouldn't I take my own legitimate surplus and send it the same way?"

"Miserly? Yes, you could call him that!"

"See what a spartan life he leads! People like that take delight in having a complete record of their money. I bet he's put it all in the same account!"

It wasn't a very convincing theory. But for the want of anything better it would do. A lust for money makes even the cleverest people commit blunders. Though blunder was hardly the word — it would be difficult to show anything illegal in having less money than appeared in the accounts.

"From now on we'll assume that Lavik has money stashed away in Switzerland. We'll see where that gets us. Not much further, I'm afraid. What about Peter

211

Strup? Have you made any progress on him since the mysterious meeting in Sofienberg Park?"

She handed him a slim envelope of her own. Håkon noticed that there was no case number written on it.

"My private file," she explained. "That's a copy for you. Take it home with you, and keep it in a safe place."

He glanced through the papers. Strup's CV was impressive. Active in the Resistance during the War, despite being only just eighteen when peace came. Member of the Labour Party even then, but didn't rise to any prominent role during the years that followed. However, he'd kept in contact with the lads from the wartime forests and now had a circle of acquaintances in influential positions. Close friend of several former party leaders, on good terms with the king, with whom he had sailed in his time (God knows how he'd fitted it all in), and met up with the parliamentary under secretary in the Ministry of Justice once a week, having worked with him at an earlier stage of his life. Freemason of the tenth degree, thus with access to most of the corridors of power. Had married a former client, a woman who had killed her husband after two years of hell, and who had then served an eighteen-month sentence before coming out to wedding bells and life on the sunny side of the street. The marriage was apparently a happy one, and no one had ever been able to pin an extramarital affair on him. His earnings were large, despite the fact that his fees were paid largely from the public purse. He paid his taxes willingly, according to his own repeated assurances in the newspapers, and they were no small sums.

"Not exactly the picture of a major criminal," said Håkon, closing the file.

"No, but it hardly looks law-abiding to rendezvous with people in murky parks late at night."

"Nighttime appointments with clients seem to be quite a feature of this case," he commented ironically, nudging the tobacco into place with his tongue.

"We must be careful. Peter Strup has friends in the Special Branch."

"Careful? We're being so careful it feels like total inertia."

With that he gave up the struggle with the recalcitrant tobacco and spat it into the bin. He was out of practice.

It was fantastically beautiful, and Hanne Wilhelmsen's only luxury item. Like most luxury items, there was no scope for it in a police inspector's salary. But with a contribution from a legacy she could experience the freedom of a 1972 Harley-Davidson for six months of the year. It was pink. Pink all over. Cadillac-pink, with shiny polished chrome. At the moment it was standing partly dismantled in the cellar, in a workshop with yellow walls and an ancient stove in one corner where she'd knocked through into the chimney breast without asking the housing association. Ikea shelf units along the walls, full of tools, and a portable television on the top shelf.

The whole engine was lying in pieces in front of her, and she was cleaning it with cotton buds. Nothing was too good for a Harley. March seemed such a long way off, she thought, already feeling a frisson of pleasure at the prospect of her first ride of the spring. It would be wonderful warm weather with dirty puddles on the road. Cecilie would be riding pillion, and the steady throb of the engine would fill their ears. If only it weren't for the damned helmet. She had ridden coast to coast in the USA many years ago, wearing a headband with the inscription "Fuck helmet laws." Here at home she was a policewoman, and had no choice. It wasn't the same. Part of the freedom was missing, part of the delight in danger, contact with the wind and all the scents it bore.

She dragged herself out of her reverie and switched on the TV to see the evening newsmagazine programme. It had already begun, and had reached something of a high point. Three journalists had jointly published a book about the Labour Party's relationship with the Security Services, and of course had made various allegations that were totally unpalatable to certain people. Only one of the authors was present, and he was given a hard time. Accusations of speculation and undocumented claims, of amateur journalism and worse, poured over the airwaves. The journalist, a handsome white-haired man in his forties, answered in such a measured voice that after only a few minutes Hanne was convinced by him. Having watched it for a quarter of an hour, she turned back to her work on the engine. The valves were always filthy after a long season.

Suddenly the programme caught her attention again. The presenter, who seemed to be biased in

214

favour of the author, was directing a question at one of his critics. He wanted an assurance that nothing was undertaken by or purchased for the Intelligence Services without the money coming out of the official budget. The man, a grey character in a charcoal-grey suit, spread his arms expressively as he affirmed it.

"Where on earth would we get any other money from?" he asked rhetorically.

That terminated the discussion, and Hanne carried on working until Cecilie appeared in the doorway.

"Come on, I'm dying to go to bed," she said with a smile.

WEDNESDAY 11 NOVEMBER

He was thoroughly peeved and fed up. His case, the Big Case, had run into the ground of late. He hadn't been able to wheedle anything out of the police. The probable reason was that the police were stuck. So was he. His editor was displeased, and had ordered him back to normal duties. It bored him to have to go to the magistrate's court and prise trivial details out of a taciturn police constable about stories that would hardly make a single column.

With his feet up on the desk he looked as sulky as an obstinate three-year-old. The coffee was bitter and only lukewarm. Even his cigarette tasted disgusting. And his notebook was empty.

He stood up so suddenly that he knocked the coffee cup over. Its dark contents quickly spread over newspapers, notes, and a paperback that was lying facedown to keep his place. Fredrick Myhreng stared at the mess for a few seconds before deciding to do absolutely nothing about it. He grabbed his coat and hurried off through the editorial offices before anyone had a chance to stop him.

The little shop was run by an old friend from his primary school. Myhreng called in now and then, to have an extra set of keys cut for his latest woman —

they never returned them — or to have new heels put on his boots. What shoe repairs had to do with key-cutting was incomprehensible to him, but his school friend wasn't the only one in the city running the same combination of business.

It was always "Hi" and "Great to see you" and "Take five." Fredrick Myhreng had an uneasy feeling that the shopkeeper felt proud of knowing a journalist on a national paper, but went along with the ritual. The tiny premises were empty, and the owner was busy with a black and very worn winter boot.

"Another new woman, Fredrick! There'll soon be a hundred sets of keys for that apartment of yours floating around town!"

He was grinning broadly.

"No, same woman as last time. I've come to ask for your help with something special."

He produced a little metal box from his capacious pocket. Opening it, he carefully drew out the two Plasticine moulds. As far as he could see, the casts were undamaged. He held them out to his friend.

"So, you've started indulging in illegal activities?"

There was a hint of seriousness in his voice, and he went on:

"Is it a registered key? I don't make copies of numbered keys. Not even for you, old chum."

"No, it's not numbered. You can see that from the cast."

"The cast is no guarantee. For all I know, you might have smoothed off the impression of the number. But I'll take your word for it."

"Does that mean you can make a copy?"

"Yes, but it'll take time. I haven't got the equipment here. I use manufactured blanks, the same as most of the others do. Cut and grind them with this fancy little piece of computer-controlled machinery here."

He gave an affectionate pat to a monster of a machine covered in buttons and switches.

"Come by in about a week's time. Should be ready then."

Fredrick Myhreng thanked him for being his saviour and was on his way out of the door when he turned and asked:

"Can you tell what sort of key it is?"

The key-cutter pondered for a moment.

"It's small. Hardly for a big door. A cupboard, perhaps? Or maybe a locker. I'll think about it!"

Myhreng sauntered back to the newspaper office, feeling rather more cheerful.

Perhaps the guy in the twilight zone would welcome some fresh air. Hanne Wilhelmsen was inclined to have another try, anyway. Reports from the prison seemed to indicate that the Dutchman had improved a bit. Though that wasn't saying very much.

"Take the handcuffs off him," she ordered, wondering silently whether young policemen were actually capable of thinking for themselves. The apathetic, skeletally thin figure before her wouldn't be able to do much against two strong constables. It was doubtful whether he could actually run at all. His shirt hung loose on him, his protruding neck reminiscent of

218

a Bosnian in Serb custody. His trousers must have fitted him once; now they were held up by a belt drawn tight into an extra hole that had been pierced in it, several centimetres beyond the other ones. The hole was off-centre, so the end of the belt projected upwards and then dangled down again under its own weight, like a failed erection. He wasn't wearing any socks. He was pale, unkempt, and looked about ten years older than when she'd last seen him. She offered him a cigarette and a throat pastille. She had heard of his habit from Karen, and he gave her a weak smile.

"How are you?" she enquired in a friendly manner, without expecting a reply. Nor did she receive one.

"Is there anything I can get you? A Coke, something to eat?"

"A bar of chocolate."

His voice was frail and cracked. Presumably he'd hardly spoken for several weeks. She ordered three bars of chocolate over the intercom. And two cups of coffee. She hadn't put any paper in the typewriter. It wasn't even plugged in.

"Is there anything at all you can tell me?"

"Chocolate," he whispered.

They waited six minutes. Neither of them said a word. The chocolate and the coffee were served by one of the women from the office, slightly peeved at having to act as waitress. She was disarmed by Hanne's expressions of gratitude.

To watch the Dutchman eating chocolate was a remarkable sight. First he opened the chocolate carefully along the glued join, trying not to damage the wrapper. Then he broke the bar meticulously into its manufactured segments, laid the wrapper on the desk, and moved them all an equal millimetre apart. He set about eating them in a pattern, like a children's game, starting in one corner, then taking the one diagonally above it and working his way in a zigzag to the top. Resuming from there, he ate his way down in a similar formation till all the chocolate was gone. It took him five minutes. Finally he licked the wrapper clean, smoothed it out with his fingers, and folded it up to a precise design.

"I've already confessed," he said eventually.

Hanne was startled; she had been totally absorbed by the eating ritual.

"No, strictly speaking you haven't, not yet," she said. Avoiding abrupt movements, she put into the typewriter the sheet of paper that she had already prepared with the requisite personal details in the top right-hand corner.

"You don't need to make a statement," she said calmly. "And you also have a right to have your lawyer here."

She was going by the book. She thought she saw the glimmer of a smile cross his face when she mentioned his lawyer. A positive smile.

"You like Karen Borg," she remarked amiably.

"She's nice."

He had broached the second bar of chocolate, and was following the same procedure as the first.

"Would you like her here now, or is it okay if we have a chat on our own?"

"Okay."

She wasn't entirely sure whether he meant the former or the latter alternative, but she interpreted it in her own favour.

"So it was you who killed Ludvig Sandersen."

"Yes," he said, more concerned with the pattern of the chocolate. He had knocked a piece out of alignment and spoilt the layout, which obviously upset him.

Hanne sighed and thought to herself that this interview would be of less value than the paper it was recorded on. But it was worth making the attempt.

"Why did you do it, Han?"

He didn't even look up at her.

"Won't you tell me why?"

Still no answer. The chocolate was half eaten.

"Is there anything else you'd like to tell me?"

"Roger," he said, loud and clear, with a steady gaze for a fraction of a second.

"Roger? Was it Roger who told you to kill him?"

"Roger."

He had a faraway look in his eyes again, his voice reverting to that of an old man — or a child.

"Is he called more than Roger?"

But his communicativeness had come to an end. He seemed totally distant. Hanne called the two burly officers, forbade handcuffs, and gave the Dutchman the last bar of chocolate to take away with him. He looked content, and left smiling serenely.

The slip of paper with a note of the telephone number was hanging on the cork noticeboard. She got a response straightaway, and introduced herself. Karen Borg sounded friendly, if surprised. They talked for several minutes before Hanne came to the point.

"You don't have to answer this, but I'll ask anyway. Has Han van der Kerch mentioned the name Roger to you at any point?"

It was a hole-in-one. Karen was silent. Hanne said nothing either.

"All I know is that he may live in Sagene. Try there. I think you can look for a car dealer. I shouldn't be saying this. I haven't said it."

Hanne promised her that she hadn't heard it, thanked her profusely, cut the conversation short, and dialled a three-figure number on the internal phone.

"Is Billy T. there?"

"He's off duty today, but I think he'll be dropping by later."

"Ask him to contact Hanne when he does."

"Will do."

The downpour was lashing the car windows obliquely, like furious scrawled invective from on high, the sleet adhering to the glass despite the valiant efforts of the wipers. The autumn had been unusual, alternating between unseasonally severe cold with snow and rain, and temperatures rising to eight degrees. For several days the thermometer had stuck defiantly somewhere in the middle, hovering on zero.

"You're putting heavy demands on an old friendship, Hanne."

He wasn't annoyed with her, just rubbing it in.

222

"I work for the hit squad. Not as odd-job-boy to Her Royal Highness Hanne Wilhelmsen. And today was my free day. In other words, you owe me a day off. Write that down."

He was having to lean his huge body right over the wheel to see anything at all. Had it not been for his size and his shaven head he could have been taken for one of those ladies in BMWs from the posher part of town who had just acquired a driving licence in their forties.

"I shall be forever in your debt," she assured him, jumping as he braked hard at a sudden shadow that turned out to be a reckless teenager.

"I can't see a damned thing," he said, trying to rub off the mist that kept coating the inside of the windscreen as fast as he wiped it dry.

Hanne adjusted the heater control, but with no discernible effect.

"Typical public service tat," she muttered, making a mental note of the number of the vehicle so that she could avoid it next time she had to take a trip in the rain.

"I found only one Roger in the motor trade in Sagene, so we won't have to hunt far, anyway," she said, in an attempt to console him.

The car veered up onto the pavement, and Hanne was flung against the door, bruising her elbow on the window handle.

"Hey — are you trying to kill me?" she cried, before she realised they'd arrived.

Billy T. pulled up beside a grey concrete wall displaying a prominent "no parking" sign. He switched off the engine and sat with his hands in his lap.

"What are we actually going to do?"

"Just take a look. Get him a bit worried."

"Am I a cop or a robber?"

"Customer, Billy, you're a customer. Unless and until I say something different."

"What are we looking for?"

"Whatever there is. Anything of interest considered."

She got out and locked the door rather unnecessarily; Billy T. just slammed his shut without further ado.

"No one will nick that old wreck," he said, turning up his collar to protect himself against the rain gusting straight at them round the corner of the building.

"Sagene Car Sales." In English. She guessed the name even though some of the neon letters had evidently been out of action for a long time. In the crepuscular half-light she could only see "Sa ene Ca S les."

"International business, that's for sure!"

A bell rang somewhere out the back as they went in the door. There was a smell of old Volvo Amazons, a suffocating perfume emanating from the largest selection of so-called air-purifiers that Hanne had ever seen. Four cardboard Christmas trees, fifty to sixty centimetres high, stood side by side on a five-metre-long counter. The trees were decorated with smaller trees on glittering threads and luscious comic-strip women inset with the same thread. An army of plastic tortoises exuding Magic Tree fragrance encircled the trunks of the trees like little

224

Christmas presents, doing their bit to ensure that the air in the vicinity of the cash register was the purest in the whole city. Their heads were mounted on springs, and they were all nodding a welcome in the draught from the door.

The rest of the place was filled with every conceivable object connected with four-wheeled vehicles. There were exhaust systems and petrol caps, nylon leopard-skin seat covers, furry dice, and spark plugs. Between the shelf units, where there was no room for any kind of rack, hung old calendar pin-ups of semi-nude women. Their breasts took up three-quarters of the picture and the actual calendar dates were relegated to a superfluous narrow band at the foot.

A man emerged from the back rooms a few moments after the bell had rung. Hanne had to dig her fingernails into her palm to stop herself from giggling.

The guy looked an absolute stereotype. He was short and stocky, scarcely more than five foot six. He was wearing brown Terylene trousers with a sewn-in crease. The seam had come undone at the knee to present a really comical sight, a long sausage of a seam that vanished into a thin loose thread over the knees and then recommenced higher up. The trousers must have dated back to the seventies; that was the last time she'd seen a sewn-in crease.

The shirt was what at school she would have called spotty, light blue with polka dots, and the tie, also light blue, was evidently chosen to complement it. On top of all this magnificence he was wearing a black-and-white check suit jacket, missing a button — which didn't matter, since it was much too tight to fasten anyway. His hair reminded her of a hedgehog.

"Can I help you, can I help you?" he asked in a loud and affable voice, looking with some misgiving at the figure with the earring. Hanne's presence must have allayed his qualms, because his face lit up as he turned to her and repeated his greeting.

"Yes, we'd like to look at some secondhand cars," Hanne said, rather hesitantly, glancing over the little man's shoulder through a door with a glass panel that hadn't been cleaned for at least a couple of years. She guessed it probably led to a showroom.

"Secondhand cars, well, you've certainly come to the right place," the man said with a smile, even more amicable now, as if he'd thought at first that all they wanted was a spark plug and now saw the chance of a more significant sale.

"Follow me, madam, sir! Just follow me!"

He led them out through the filthy door, and Billy T. noticed a similar door adjacent to it, opening into some kind of office.

The smell of oil was refreshing after all the Christmas trees; the proper smell of real cars. It was obviously a business with no aspiration to be a specialised dealership; there were Ladas, Peugeots, Opels, and several four- or five-year-old Mercedes in apparently good condition.

"Look around and take your pick! May I ask what sort of price you had in mind?"

226

He smiled hopefully and glanced towards the nearest Mercedes.

"Three or four thousand kroner," Billy T. muttered, and the man puckered his wet lips uncertainly.

"He's joking," Hanne reassured him. "We've got about seventy thousand. But we don't have a fixed limit.

"My parents might chip in too," she whispered confidentially into his ear.

The car salesman's face brightened and he took her by the arm.

"Then you ought to cast your eyes over this Opel Kadett," he said.

It looked in pretty good condition.

"Nineteen eighty-seven, only forty thousand kilometres on the clock, *guaranteed*, and only one owner. Well maintained. I can give you a keen price. A very keen price."

"Lovely car." Hanne nodded, giving her putative husband a meaningful glance. He took the hint and asked the chequered man if he could use the toilet.

"Just through there, just through there," he replied in a benevolent tone, and Hanne began to wonder whether he had some kind of speech defect that made him repeat everything. A sort of sophisticated stammer, perhaps. Billy T. went off.

"Nervous stomach," she explained. "He's got an interview for a new job later this afternoon. This is the fourth time, poor man."

The salesman expressed his sympathy, and persuaded her to sit inside the car. It certainly was a nice model.

227

"I'm not familiar with this make," she said. "Would you mind sitting in it with me and going over the controls?"

"No trouble at all. No trouble at all." He turned on the ignition and demonstrated all the finer points.

"Beautiful motor," he said emphatically. "Well maintained. Between you and me, the previous owner was a bit of a skinflint, but that means he looked after it all right."

He stroked the newly polished dashboard, flashed the lights, adjusted the seat-back, switched on the radio, put in a cassette of Rod Stewart, and spent an inordinately long time fastening the seat belt round Hanne.

She turned towards him. "And the price?"

None of the cars had price labels on, which she found peculiar.

"The price . . . Yes, the price . . ."

He smacked his lips and sucked the air in through his teeth for a moment before giving her a smile she presumed was meant to seem friendly and confidence-inspiring.

"You've got seventy thousand and nice parents. For you I could say seventy-five. That includes the radio and new winter tyres."

They'd been sitting there for more than five minutes now, and she was beginning to wish Billy T. would return. There was a limit to how long she could haggle over a car without suddenly finding that she'd bought it. Another three minutes passed before he tapped on the window.

"We'd better go. We've got to fetch the kids," he said.

"No, I'll fetch them, you've got your interview," she corrected him.

"I'll ring you about this car," she promised the man in Terylene, who could barely conceal his disappointment at losing what he'd thought was going to be an easy sale. He recovered himself and gave her his card. It was as tasteless as its owner, dark blue artificial silk with his name on in gold, "Roger Strømsjord, Man. Dir." Pretentious title.

"I own the place," he explained with a modest shrug of his shoulders. "Don't take too long making up your mind! I have a fast turnover with cars like these. Very popular. Very popular, I have to say."

Rounding the corner, this time with the wind behind them, they returned to their own car and collapsed in shrieks of laughter.

When Hanne had dried her tears, she asked, "Did you find anything?"

He leant forward at an angle to fish out a notebook from his back pocket, and slapped it into her palm.

"The only thing there of any interest at all. It was in his wind-cheater pocket."

Hanne was no longer laughing.

"You idiot, Billy! That's not what we learnt at police college. And it's bloody stupid if it does have something important in it and we can't use it in evidence. Unlawful seizure! How will you explain that?"

"Oh, leave off. This little book isn't going to put anyone behind bars. But it might help you along the way. Perhaps. I don't know what's in it, I only had a brief glance. Phone numbers. Be a bit grateful, please."

Curiosity had dispelled her anger. She began looking through it. Naturally enough it smelt of Magic Tree. And it did indeed contain masses of telephone numbers, the majority entered after a name, in alphabetical order for the first five or six pages and then absolutely random. The ones at the end had no names, a few had initials, most of them just small incomprehensible signs.

Hanne was taken aback. Some of the numbers started with figures that didn't exist as first digits in Oslo, and there were no area codes given. Turning the pages, she came to a halt at four initials.

"H. v. d. K.," she exclaimed. "Han van der Kerch! But I don't recognise the number . . ."

"Check in the phone book," said Billy T., but snatched it from the parcel shelf before Hanne could get to it. "What's Van der Kerch under, Van or Kerch?"

"No idea, try both."

He found it under Kerch. It was quite different from the one in the notebook. Hanne was disappointed, but thought there was something about the two numbers that she couldn't quite perceive. Some relationship, almost, even though they were completely different. It took her thirty seconds to work it out.

"Got it! The phone book number is the notebook number minus the next number in sequence, including negative numbers but ignoring the minus!"

Billy T. didn't get it.

"What the hell are you on about?"

"Haven't you ever played those party games with numerals? You're given a sequence of numbers, and you have to work out the pattern and supply the last one. A kind of IQ test, some would call it, but I think it's more of a party trick myself. Look: the number in the notebook is 93 24 35. So 9 minus 3 equals 6; 3 minus 2 is 1; 2 minus 4 is minus 2, but forget about the minus; 4 minus 3 is 1; and 3 minus 5 is minus 2. From 5 take away the first figure, 9, and that makes minus 4. The number in the phone book must be 61 21 24."

"That's right!"

He was really impressed.

"Where on earth did you learn how to do that?"

"Huh, I once contemplated studying maths. Numbers are fascinating. This can't just be chance. Look up Lavik's number."

She used the same method, with complete success. The number was in code on page eight of the notebook. Billy T. started the car with as triumphant a roar as it was possible to get out of a tired Opel Corsa and sped off into the grey afternoon.

"Either Jørgen Lavik buys lots of secondhand cars, or this is the most promising lead we've got so far," said Hanne with new confidence.

"You're a genius, Hanne," said Billy T., grinning from ear to ear. "A bloody genius!"

They drove for a while in silence.

"I actually quite fancied that Kadett," Hanne murmured wistfully as they juddered into the garage beneath police headquarters.

THURSDAY 12 NOVEMBER

Jørgen Ulf Lavik was just as confident as last time. Håkon Sand felt ill-at-ease in his baggy corduroy trousers and a five-year-old sweater adorned with a threadbare, crumpled crocodile that hadn't adapted well to life in the washing machine. The lawyer's suit starkly negated any suggestion that he was a miser.

"Why is he here?" Lavik asked, turning to Hanne Wilhelmsen with a nod towards Håkon. "I thought it was the real police officers who did the donkey work."

Both of them felt offended. Which was presumably the intention.

"So what's my status today then?" he went on, without waiting for an explanation of Håkon's presence. "Am I a suspect, or still just a 'witness'?"

"You're a witness," Hanne replied curtly.

"May I enquire what I'm supposed to be a witness to? This is the second time I've been asked here. I'm well-disposed towards the police, as you know, but I'm afraid I'll have to decline further meetings of this nature if you don't soon come up with something more specific to question me about."

Hanne stared at him for several seconds, and he had to avert his gaze — which he turned disdainfully on Håkon.

"What's the make of your car, Lavik?"

The man didn't even need to think about it.

"As if you didn't know! The police saw me meet my client the other night! A 1991 Volvo. My wife has an old Toyota."

"Were they bought new or secondhand?"

"The Volvo was bought new. Standard estate model. The Toyota was bought a year old, as far as I recall. Maybe eighteen months."

He still seemed very sure of himself.

"I presume you bought the Volvo from the main dealership," said Hanne.

That was correct. And the Toyota had been bought privately through a colleague.

The window was only about a centimetre ajar; at intervals the gale raging outside made a long plaintive whistle, almost like a faint howl, as it blew across the metal sill and into the room. In its way it was quite soothing.

"Do you know a guy who sells cars up in Sagene?"

She regretted it the moment she'd spoken. She should have been more circumspect, should have laid a more sophisticated trap. This wasn't a trap at all. What a novice! Was she losing her grip? Had her head injury affected the cunning she had been so proud of? The gaffe made her bite her nail. The lawyer had the time he needed to collect his thoughts — in fact, he considered at length, obviously more than was strictly necessary.

"I don't normally reveal my clients' names, but since you ask — I have a long-term client called Roger who runs a small car firm, and it may well be in Sagene. I've never been there myself. I'd rather not say any more. Discretion, you know. You have to be discreet in this business, otherwise you don't keep your customers."

He crossed his legs and clasped his hands round his knee. Victory was his. They all knew it.

"Funny that he keeps your telephone number in code," Hanne tried, but in vain.

Jørgen Lavik switched his smile back on.

"If you only knew how paranoid some people are, it wouldn't surprise you in the least. I once had a client who insisted on going over my office with a bug detector every time he came for a consultation. I was helping him with a tenancy agreement. A tenancy agreement!"

His laughter was loud and boisterous, but not infectious. Hanne had no further questions. She had taken no notes. She had to admit defeat. Lavik was free to go. As he was putting his coat on she stood up quickly and thrust her face right up to his.

"I know that you've got a lot of irons in the fire, Lavik. And you know that I know. You're enough of a lawyer to realise that we in the police know much more than we ever use. But I promise you one thing: I'll be watching you. We still have our sources, information already gathered, and facts we haven't revealed. Han van der Kerch is in our custody. You're aware that he's not saying much at the moment. But he has a lawyer he's talked to, a lawyer of a totally different ethical calibre from your wretched hole-in-the-corner activities. You haven't a clue how much she's heard, nor the faintest idea of what she's told us. That's what you've

234

got to live with. So keep looking over your shoulder, Lavik, I'm out to get you."

His face had turned crimson, but deathly pale around his nose. He had not retreated even slightly from Hanne, but his eyes seemed to have sunk into their sockets as he hissed:

"Those are threats, Constable. Those are threats. I shall submit a formal complaint. Today!"

"I'm not a constable, Lavik. I'm a detective inspector. And this detective inspector is going to haunt you like a shadow till you break. So complain away."

He looked almost as if he was going to spit at her, but he brought himself rigidly under control and left the office without a word. The door slammed behind him. The bang reverberated through the walls for several seconds afterwards. Håkon's jaw dropped and he was stunned into silence.

"You look mongoloid with that expression!"

He pulled himself together and closed his mouth with a snap.

"What was the point of that? Do you want to put Karen's life in danger? He will file a complaint, you know!"

"Let him."

Despite her serious error of judgment, she seemed pleased with herself.

"I've given him a severe fright, Håkon. And frightened people make mistakes. It wouldn't surprise me if your friend Karen were to get yet another criminal lawyer among her suitors. If so, that would be a major blunder on his part."

"But what if they do something to her?"

"Karen Borg won't be harmed. They're not that stupid."

For a brief instant she felt a cold tingle of doubt, but dismissed it equally fast. She rubbed her temple and drank the remains of her coffee. From the top drawer of the desk she took out a handkerchief and a resealable polythene bag, and picked up the coffee cup Lavik had drunk from very carefully by its handle.

"He wrapped his hands round the whole cup," she said gleefully. "It pays to keep the office rather on the chilly side. He must have wanted to warm his poor little fingers."

The cup went into the bag, and the handkerchief back into the drawer.

"Something bothering you?"

"You don't deserve your reputation. That's not the way we take fingerprints."

"Article 160 of the Penal Code," she retorted off pat. "No court order needed for taking fingerprints if he's suspected of criminal activities. I suspect him. You do too. So we've complied with the law."

Håkon shook his head.

"That's the most literal interpretation of the law I've ever heard. The guy has a right to know that we've taken his fingerprints. He's even got a right to have them destroyed if the suspicion proves unfounded!"

"That'll never happen," she asserted unequivocally. "Back to work!"

236

They'd forgotten his belt. He wasn't supposed to keep anything. Why had they forgotten the belt? When he was about to go to be interviewed by the policewoman with the chocolate, his trousers had fallen down as he stood up. He'd tried holding them together at the front, but when they put the handcuffs on him, the trousers kept on slipping. The two blond men had sent the corridor attendant to fetch his belt, and had pierced an extra hole in it with a pair of scissors. That was thoughtful of them. But why hadn't they taken it away from him afterwards? That must be an oversight. So he removed it and hid it under his mattress. He woke several times during the night to make sure it was still there and he hadn't dreamt it.

It became a little treasure hoard for him. The secret belt made the Dutchman quite elated for more than twenty-four hours. It was something the others didn't know about, something he'd got which he shouldn't have. He felt as if he had the upper hand. Twice in the course of the day, immediately after the check by the warder through the door, he'd tried it on very quickly, skipping some of the loops in the waistband because he was in a hurry, and leaping around the room with his trousers firmly held in place and a broad grin on his face. But only for a few minutes, then off with it again and under the mattress.

He tried browsing through the magazines he'd been given. *Men Today*. He felt more on top of things, though unable to concentrate, his mind fixed only on what he was going to do. But first he had to write a letter. It took a long time. Perhaps she would be pleased? She was nice, and had kind hands. The last two times she'd been there he'd smiled as he slept. It was lovely being stroked on the back, so good to be touched.

The letter was finished. He moved the stool by the little desk over to the window high in the wall. Stretching up as far as he could, he was just able to pass the belt round the bars. He tied a knot in it and hoped it would hold. He'd put one end through the buckle first, so that it made a noose. A fine stiff noose, easy to get over his head.

His last thought was of his mother in Holland. For a split second he regretted his decision, but by then it was too late. The stool was already toppling beneath him, and the belt tightened in a flash. There were five seconds in which he had time to realise he hadn't broken his neck. Then everything went black as the blood flowing into his head through the carotid arteries was prevented from returning to the heart by the crushing loop of the belt. Within minutes his tongue, purple and engorged, was protruding from his mouth, and his eyes bulged like a stranded fish's. Han van der Kerch was dead, at the tender age of twenty-three.

FRIDAY 13 NOVEMBER

Billy T. had called the place an apartment. The term was quite unmerited. The block could be categorically described as being in one of the worst locations in Oslo. Built in the 1890s, long before anyone could have imagined the monstrous volume of traffic that would later eat into its surroundings, it was wedged between Mosseveien and Ekebergveien, looking like something spat out as inedible, but still standing there, clinging on in a state totally unacceptable to all except the local inhabitants of park benches, for whom the alternative would have been a container on the quayside.

It smelt stuffy and oppressive. There was a bucket just inside the door containing what looked like the remains of ancient vomit and something else undefinable but presumably organic. Hanne Wilhelmsen ordered the snub-nosed redheaded constable to the kitchen window. He shoved and heaved at it, but it wouldn't budge.

"This window hasn't been opened for years," he panted, getting a little nod by way of response. He took that as permission to abandon the attempt.

"What a dump this place is," he exclaimed, fearful of moving lest he come into contact with lethal and unknown germs. Too young, thought Hanne, who had seen all too many of these dreadful holes that somebody called home. A pair of rubber gloves flew through the air.

"Here, put these on," she said, pulling some on herself.

The kitchen was immediately to the left after the narrow entrance hall. There were dirty dishes everywhere, weeks old. A couple of black rubbish bags stood on the floor and Hanne had to use the toe of her shoe to clear enough space to get by. The stench wafted out into the room, making the constable retch.

"Sorry," he choked, "excuse me."

He rushed past her and made for the door. She grinned and went into the living room.

It was hardly more than fifteen square metres, and part of it was taken up by a makeshift construction serving as a sleeping alcove. There was a post right in the centre from floor to ceiling, and a curtain of cheap brown cloth drawn back against one wall and attached with nails to a bar on the ceiling, itself erected so crookedly that it might have been the work of a drunk.

Behind the curtain was a homemade bed, as broad as it was long. The bedclothes couldn't have been washed for years. She lifted the quilt with her gloved fingers. The sheet was like a paint palette, shades of brown interspersed with red splodges. A half bottle of aquavit lay at the foot. Empty.

There was also a narrow shelf behind the curtain. Astonishingly enough it had books on it, but closer inspection revealed them to be Danish pornographic paperbacks. Part of the shelf was taken up by empty or

240

half-empty bottles, a few souvenirs from Sweden, and a small, rather indistinct photograph of a boy of about ten. She picked it up and studied it carefully. Did Jacob Frøstrup have a son? Was there a little boy somewhere who would have been fond of the wretched heroin addict who'd ended his days in Oslo Prison from an overdose? Absentmindedly wiping the dust off the glass with her sleeve, she made a bit more space for it and put it back.

The only window in the room was between the alcove and the living area. And it opened. In the courtyard, three floors below, she could see the young constable leaning on one arm against the wall with his face pointing towards the ground. He still had his rubber gloves on.

"How's it going?"

She didn't get an answer, but he straightened up and gave her a reassuring wave. A few moments later he was standing in the doorway again. Pale, but recovered.

"I've had to go through this five or six times," she said, with a consoling smile. "You get used to it. Breathe through your mouth and think of raspberries. It helps."

It didn't take more than fifteen minutes to search the flat. They turned up nothing of interest. Hanne wasn't surprised: Billy T. had told her he'd searched thoroughly and there was nothing there. Well, nothing visible, anyway. They would have to start looking for the invisible. She sent the young man out to the car for tools. He seemed grateful for another opportunity to get some fresh air. He was back in two or three minutes.

"Bere shall be start?"

"You don't need to breathe through your mouth when you talk; you don't breathe in as you speak, do you?"

"I'll be sick if I do't ho'd by dose all de time, ebed bed I talk."

They began with the panel that seemed newest, the wall behind the sofa. The young lad got a good grip on it with the jemmy and worked up a bit of a sweat, but it actually came off fairly easily. Nothing there. He hammered it in place again and pushed the sofa back.

"The carpet," Hanne ordered, bending down in one corner. It might once have been green, but now it was encrusted with dirt and grime. The two police officers had to avert their faces from all the flying dust. But they managed to roll it up right across to the sofa. The floorboards underneath looked positively antique, and could probably be nicely restored with a good sanding down.

"Dook, dat one's dot so b'ack," exclaimed the constable, pointing to a short floorboard projecting about twenty centimetres from the wall.

He was right. The board was noticeably lighter in colour than the rest of the filthy floor. And the solid muck between the boards that gave the floor a level surface was completely missing in the gaps here. Hanne took out a screwdriver and began to prise the board loose. She lifted it up carefully to reveal a small compartment, entirely filled with something packed in

242

a plastic bag. The redheaded constable got so excited that he forgot to breathe through his mouth.

"It's money, Inspector Wilhelmsen, look, it's money! And what a hell of a lot!"

Hanne stood up, took off her soiled gloves, threw them in a corner, and put on a new pair. Then she squatted down and fished out the package. He was right. It was money. A fat bundle of thousand-kroner notes. At a quick guess she estimated it to be at least fifty thousand kroner. The constable had taken out a polythene bag from his inside pocket and held it open for her. It was just about big enough.

"Well done, Henriksen. You'll make a good Sherlock Holmes."

Hanne's praise heartened the youngster, and in his delight at the prospect of getting out of the fetid place he cleared everything up himself and locked the door behind them, leaping down the stairs after his superior like a puppy with its tail wagging.

THURSDAY 19 NOVEMBER

None of them had expected the result they got. To tell the truth, no one but Hanne Wilhelmsen had expected any result at all. Håkon Sand had dismissed Lavik's coffee cup with a shrug of his shoulders the previous Thursday. Han van der Kerch's death had overshadowed everything. There had been a hell of a fuss about the belt — rather unnecessarily, since the chap could have used either his shirt or his trousers for the same purpose. Experience showed that it was impossible to stop a determined suicide once he'd made up his mind. And Han van der Kerch certainly had.

"Yes!"

She bent forward at the waist, clenched her fist, and brought down her arm as if she were pulling an imaginary steam whistle.

"Yes!"

She repeated the movement. The others in the incident room watched her in silence, somewhat embarrassed.

Detective Inspector Hanne Wilhelmsen flung a document on the desk in front of the lanky chief inspector. Kaldbakken picked it up calmly, in mute reproof of her unseemly outburst of emotion. He took his time. When he put it down there was the faintest trace of a smile on his rather equine face.

"This is quite gratifying," he said, clearing his throat, "quite gratifying."

"Aw, come on! What an understatement!"

Hanne would have welcomed a more enthusiastic response. Jørgen Lavik's fingerprints, clearly delineated on a coffee cup from the police canteen, were identical to a beautiful complete print on a thousand-kroner note found under a floorboard in the nauseating flat of a deceased drug addict on Mosseveien. The report from Forensics was unambiguous and unassailable.

"It can't be true!"

Håkon Sand snatched the report so fast that it ripped down the middle. It was true.

"Now we've got the bugger," the ginger-haired constable cried out, bursting with pride at his contribution to the discovery. "All we've got to do is bring him in!"

Far from it, of course. The fingerprints proved nothing. But they were a damned good indication of something. The problem was that Lavik would almost certainly be able to concoct a whole host of explanations. His link to Frøstrup had been legitimate enough. The prints weren't adequate on their own. Everyone in the room, with the single exception perhaps of the over-eager young constable, was agreed on that. Hanne set up a flip chart in front of the group and picked up a red and a blue marker. Neither worked.

"Here you are," said her young colleague, tossing a new black spirit marker across the room.

"Let's list what we've got," said Hanne, starting to write. "First of all: Han van der Kerch's explanation to his lawyer."

"Has she told us what he said?"

Kaldbakken was genuinely taken aback.

"Yes. You'll find it in Doc. 11.12. The Dutchman left a letter, a sort of suicide note. A farewell message for Karen Borg. She was able to report what he'd told her — we interviewed her all day yesterday. It was exactly as we thought, but it was wonderful to get it corroborated! And the main thing is that we now have it in writing."

Without further comment she turned to the board and wrote:

1. H.v.d.K.'s statement (Karen B.)
2. Link Lavik — Roger Car Salesm. (phone no. in bk)
3. Lavik's fingerpr. on banknote at Frøstrup's (!!!)
4. Code list found at J.F.'s same as one at Hans Olsen's
5. Lavik's visit to cells on day H.v.d.K. lost his mind
6. Lavik's visit to prison on day of Frøstrup's overdose

"Han van der Kerch's statement is important," she said, using a broken ruler as a pointer to tap the first item on the chart. "The only, and perhaps rather ticklish, drawback is that we don't have it from the man himself. Hearsay evidence. On the other hand: Karen

246

Borg is an extra-credible witness. She can verify that Kerch had been involved for several years. He also confessed to his association with Roger the car salesman, and he'd heard rumours about lawyers lurking in the background. Rumours are a rather insubstantial basis for arrest, but all the trouble he went to in his choice of lawyer seems to imply that he had fairly reliable information. Anyway, Karen Borg's statement means we've got Roger in the bag."

She exchanged the ruler for a marker pen and underlined Roger's name heavily.

"And we're getting closer to our friend Jørgen."

Heavy underlining beneath Lavik's name.

"The connection here is wafer thin, even if we've established that they knew one another. Lavik has admitted it once, and will doubtless do so again. He'll say it was more meetings with clients, but there's still the incontestable fact that it's rather odd to keep phone numbers in code. A lot of trouble, and not undertaken without good reason.

"Also," she added emphatically, putting a thick ring round item three on the list to reinforce her words, "also, we've discovered Lavik's fingerprints on Jacob Frøstrup's banknotes. The fact that *he* was a drug-runner has been proved sixteen times over. In court. Besides, I always thought it was lawyers who received money from their clients, not the other way about. Lavik would definitely find that hard to explain away. Our strongest card, if you ask me."

She waited as if to allow for objections. None came, so she resumed.

"Item four takes us further into the unknown. This is very significant for the wider context, and I'm convinced that these codes could tell us quite a lot if only we could crack the damned things. But since we don't intend to charge Lavik with murder, I'm not sure we should put too much weight on them now. We might need an ace up our sleeves at a later stage. As for Lavik's presence at critical moments in the lives of Van der Kerch and Frøstrup, that too is slightly more peripheral and can be put on hold. For the time being. So we're back to items one to three as the basis for a possible arrest."

She paused again.

"Would that be sufficient, Håkon?"

He looked at her, and knew that she knew. It was nowhere near enough.

"Arrest for what? For murder? No. For drug dealing? Not really. We've got no grounds at all when it comes down to it."

"Well, yes we have," Kaldbakken objected. "The find at Frøstrup's wasn't totally lacking in significance."

"Use your imagination, then, Håkon," Hanne appealed with a wry smile. "You could make something out of it, couldn't you? The charges you come up with are often inaccurate and riddled with holes, yet you seem to get custody orders in their hundreds."

"You're forgetting one thing," said Håkon. "You're forgetting that this man is a lawyer himself. No court will ignore that. This wouldn't be a twenty-minute conviction. If we try to bring the bastard in, we've got

248

to be sure it will stick. There'll be a huge outcry anyway. If he's released, there'll be hell to pay."

Despite Håkon's scepticism, Kaldbakken was convinced. And none of the others could argue with the irascible authoritarian chief inspector on matters of professional police work. The seven officers went through the case again as it stood, item by item, sifted out the untenable, made a list of what more was needed, and at the end had the outline of a charge.

"Drugs," said the chief inspector in conclusion. "It's drugs we'll have to take him on. We don't need to wade in too heavily in the first instance, perhaps we should make do with the twenty-four grams we seized at Frøstrup's place."

"No, we'd have to broaden it out beyond that. If we only go for that amount, we're denying ourselves the opportunity to use things not specifically connected with it. If we're to have any chance at all here, we have to throw in everything we've got. There's so much on the list which is pretty worthless that we have to be able to put it before the Court all together."

Håkon seemed more confident now. His heart was thumping like a helicopter rotor at the thought that they were finally on the verge of a breakthrough.

"We'll draw up a charge of a general nature, with unspecified times and unspecified quantities, and we'll go for the gang theory, relying on Han van der Kerch's statement that there actually is a syndicate behind it. Go for broke."

"And we can say we've had tip-offs!" The snub-nosed young constable couldn't restrain himself. "It usually does the trick in drugs cases, so I've heard!"

There was another painful silence. Hanne calmly intervened before Chief Inspector Kaldbakken could demolish him.

"That we *never* do, Henriksen," she said firmly. "I'll assume your zeal is getting the better of you. I'll put it down to the same reason as your nausea. But you won't ever get beyond the novice stage if you don't learn to think before you open your mouth. We can take short-cuts, but never cheat. Never!

"Anyway, it's a complete fallacy. The worst possible thing in a magistrate's court is anonymous tip-offs. So now you know," she added.

The lad had been sufficiently rebuked, and the meeting was brought to a close. Hanne and Håkon stayed on.

"This will have to be cleared with the commissioner. And with the public prosecutor. And to cover our backs I should really check with the palace."

It was plain that Håkon wasn't entirely happy at the thought of what lay ahead. Dejection had set in once the beating helicopter rotors had come to a standstill. What he wanted most was to ask Hanne if she would apply for the arrest warrant.

She sat down beside him on the little sofa. To his amazement she placed her hand on his knee and leant familiarly against his shoulder. A faint aroma of a perfume he didn't recognise made him take a deep breath.

250

"Now it's really beginning," she said in a low voice. "All we've done so far is collect tiny fragments, a bit here, a bit there, so minute that it hasn't been worthwhile trying to fit the jigsaw together. It's now we have to get started properly. There are still loads of pieces missing, but can't you see the picture, Håkon? Don't give up! We're the good guys. Don't forget that."

"It doesn't always seem like it," Håkon replied sullenly.

He put his hand on hers, which was still resting on his knee. To his even greater astonishment she didn't withdraw it.

"We'll have to try, anyway," he said wanly, letting go of her hand and standing up. "Make sure you get everything done that's necessary for the arrest. I assume you want to arrest him yourself."

"Yeah, you bet your bottom dollar I do," she said vehemently.

They were all there. The commissioner, in a newly pressed uniform, serious and stiff-backed, as if she had lain awkwardly during the night. The public prosecutor, a flabby little fellow in a pilot shirt with small shrewd eyes behind pebble lenses, had got the best chair. The head of the drugs squad — who was only deputising, because the real one was acting chief constable in Hønefoss, where the chief constable himself was deputising for the public prosecutor, now on temporary appointment as a high court judge — had also ironed his uniform for the occasion. It was rather skimpy, and his shirt was hanging out untidily over his pot belly. He looked benevolent, like a jovial P. C. Plod, with a round red face and thin grey curly hair. Lady Justitia was on the table in her customary position, with her scales held high and sword poised for execution.

One of the clerical staff knocked on the door. She served coffee without a word, in plastic cups. Hanne Wilhelmsen and Håkon Sand were served last. Nor did they get full cups. It hardly mattered; Hanne didn't even have a sip of hers before she stood up. It took about half an hour to present the case. The content was the same as earlier in the day, though more structured. But since then she had also got something else. She smiled for the first time as she added:

"A sniffer-dog has identified the money!"

The head of the drugs squad gave a nod of acknowledgement, but as both the commissioner and the public prosecutor looked uncomprehending, she elaborated further.

"The money has been in contact with drugs. Or most probably: someone has touched the money immediately after handling drugs. That's a little piece of the jigsaw we really needed. Unfortunately it wasn't the note that had the fingerprints on, but even so . . ."

"About the fingerprints," the public prosecutor interrupted. "From a legal viewpoint, you haven't got Lavik's fingerprints. So we have to ignore everything that depends on them when we consider the issue of the arrest warrant. Have you taken that into account?"

He looked at Håkon, who rose from his seat and joined Hanne at the flip chart.

"Yes, indeed we have. We bring him in on the second charge, take his fingerprints immediately, and arrange with Forensics for them to have an official report ready on Monday morning. That should fit in. We plan to arrest Lavik and Roger the car salesman tomorrow afternoon. No one could expect us to have the committal application ready by Saturday in a case of this magnitude. So we'd have till one o'clock on Monday to draw up an application that will hold water. From that point of view, Friday afternoon is the optimum time for the arrest."

There was silence. The commissioner, who looked nervous and unwell, was sitting bolt upright in her chair with her back unsupported. This case might prove a burden for the police that they could well do without. The commissioner's job had turned out to be a lot more arduous than she had imagined. Problems and criticism every single day. This was an affair that could really blow up in her face. An artery throbbed uncomfortably in her gaunt neck.

The head of the drugs squad still retained his inappropriate smile. With his sheep-like grin and squinting eyes he didn't give an impression of great intelligence. The public prosecutor got up and crossed to the window. He stood with his back to them and spoke as if his audience were on scaffolding outside.

"Strictly speaking we ought to have the approval of the Court for an arrest," he said loudly. "All hell will be let loose if we don't go to the Court first."

"But we never do that," Håkon protested.

"No," said the public prosecutor, swinging round. "But we ought to! But . . . it's you who'll take the rap. Have you worked out how you're going to defend yourselves?"

Strangely enough, Håkon was gradually becoming less nervous. The public prosecutor was actually on his side.

"Well, the situation is this: we won't get an arrest if we don't include the fingerprints; we won't get the fingerprints before we've arrested him. Hopefully his defence counsel will have more than enough to do over the weekend, far too much to concern himself with formalities. I'm willing to take any flak afterwards. And since it's up to us to gauge the need to involve the Court in seeking an arrest warrant, it's not something we can really be hauled over the coals for. We'll just be severely reprimanded. I can take that."

The little man in the safari shirt smiled and addressed himself to Hanne.

"What about you? Have you completely recovered from the attack now?"

She felt almost flattered, and was annoyed with herself.

"Yes, I'm fine, thanks. But we still don't know who was behind it. We presume it has something to do with this case, so perhaps we'll uncover some clues along the way."

It was beginning to get dark, and the humid November air was pressing against the sixth-floor windows. From the depths of the building they could hear faint martial music. The police band was having a practice session. They had all sat down again, and Hanne was in the process of packing up the thick bundle of files.

"Just one more thing, Sand: have you decided how you'll word the charge against Lavik? Quantity unknown, place unknown, time unknown, and so forth?"

"We'll charge him with the quantity we found at Frøstrup's apartment. Twenty grams of heroin, four grams of cocaine. Not a lot, but more than enough to establish the next link. Much more than enough for remand in custody."

"Put a second count in the charge," the public prosecutor directed. "For 'having in recent years imported an unknown quantity of drugs.' Or some such phrase."

"Certainly," Håkon indicated his assent.

"Another thing," said the public prosecutor, turning to the head of the drugs squad. "Why is Eleven dealing with this case? Shouldn't it have been handled by A 2.4? It's developed into a drugs case, even if the murders are connected."

"We're cooperating," Hanne interjected unhesitatingly, without waiting for a response from the head of the drugs squad. "Cooperating very effectively. And the murder cases are the fundamental aspect, as you know."

The meeting was over. The commissioner had said barely a word since she opened the session. She shook the public prosecutor's hand as she showed him out of the room; the others had to make do with a nod. Håkon was the last to leave, and in the doorway he glanced back again at the beautiful sculpture. The commissioner noticed, and smiled.

"Good luck, Håkon. I really wish you luck."

It actually sounded as if she meant it.

FRIDAY 20 NOVEMBER

He couldn't have looked more astounded if he'd seen little red-eyed green Martians. Even Hanne Wilhelmsen was momentarily assailed by doubt. Jørgen Ulf Lavik, his eyes almost popping out of his head, stood in the office of his legal practice alternately staring at Hanne and reading the blue sheet again and again, emitting small plaintive whimpers. His face had turned crimson and puffy, and he seemed in imminent danger of a heart attack. Two plainclothes police constables had taken up position in front of the closed door of his office, feet apart and hands behind their backs, as if they were expecting him to attempt to rush past at any moment and escape to a freedom he must now fear might only lie in the dim and distant future. Even the ceiling lamp flickered and trembled in its fury and agitation as a heavy articulated lorry sped over the crossroads outside to catch the amber light.

"What the hell is this?" he squeaked, having read it at least six times. "What the devil does it mean?!"

He smashed his fist down on the desk with a mighty thwack. It obviously hurt, and the pain made him shake it involuntarily.

"It's a warrant for your arrest. You're being arrested. Taken into custody, if you prefer."

Hanne gestured towards the sheet of paper lying on the desk, torn nearly to pieces after the lawyer's outburst.

"The reasons are given there. You have all the time you want to respond. All the time you want. But for now you're coming with us."

Seething with anger, Lavik fought to keep himself under control. His chin was working, and even the men posted at the door could hear his teeth grinding. He kept flexing his hands rapidly until he calmed down.

"I must phone my wife. And I'll have to get myself a lawyer. Will you leave the room for a moment?"

Hanne smiled.

"From now on and for some good while I'm afraid you won't be able to talk to anyone without a police presence — except for your lawyer, of course. But it'll have to wait till we get to the station. Put your coat on. Don't make trouble; it won't help any of us."

"But my wife!" He sounded almost pitiable. "She's expecting me home in an hour!"

It couldn't do any harm for him to speak to her. It would spare them from criticism in that respect, anyway. Hanne picked up the receiver and handed it to him.

"Say what you like about the reason for your not coming home. You can tell her you've been arrested if you wish, but not a word about why. I'll cut off the call if you say anything I don't approve of."

She indicated the receiver rest with a warning finger and let him dial the number. The conversation was brief, and he told the truth. Hanne could hear a wailing voice at the other end of the line asking "Why, why?" Admirably enough he managed to retain his composure and ended by promising that his lawyer would contact her in the course of the evening. He banged down the receiver and stood up.

"Let's get this farce over with," he said grimly, and threw his coat on inside out, cursed when he saw what he'd done, and spoke to the two men in the doorway as he went out. "Aren't you going to clap me in irons too?"

They ignored the sarcasm. A quarter of an hour later he was in a cell in the police station. He had been there before. Things had seemed very, very different then.

Jørgen Lavik's choice of lawyer had surprised them all. They had expected one of two or three superstars, and prepared themselves for a rough ride. But at about six o'clock that evening Christian Bloch-Hansen had turned up, very correct and softly spoken, called on Hanne and Chief Inspector Kaldbakken, and politely requested a chat with Håkon Sand before he met his client. Which of course was granted. He had taken the slim file of copies of the charge documents with slightly raised eyebrows, but accepted without complaint Håkon's explanation that they were unfortunately the only documents he could give him without prejudicing the investigation. Bloch-Hansen wasn't annoyed. He'd been in the business for thirty years and was well known and respected. His was not a household name, however, because he'd never sought publicity. Indeed, it always seemed as if he deliberately avoided drawing attention to himself, which further strengthened his reputation in the courts and in the prosecution service, and had led to numerous commissions and special briefs, all discharged with thoroughness and professional competence.

Håkon's immediate relief at his agreeable opponent would gradually give way to the recognition that he'd got the worst imaginable adversary. Christian Bloch-Hansen was not a barrister who would rant and rave; he wouldn't want to inflate matters into bellicose headlines in the tabloid press. Nor would he dwell on inessentials: he would simply tear them to shreds. Nothing would escape him. He was expert at criminal trials.

In half an hour the neat middle-aged lawyer had gathered all the information he required. Then he went off to sit with his client in a separate room for a couple of hours. After he'd finished, he asked if the interrogation of Lavik could be postponed until the following day.

"My client is exhausted. You probably are too. I've had a long day myself. When would it suit you to begin?"

Overwhelmed by Bloch-Hansen's gentlemanly manners, Hanne let him choose the time himself.

"Would ten o'clock be too late?" he asked with a smile. "I like to have a more leisurely breakfast at weekends."

It was neither too late nor too early for Hanne Wilhelmsen. The interrogation would commence at ten o'clock.

SATURDAY 21 NOVEMBER

A shrill diabolical sound penetrated his consciousness. At first he couldn't make out what it was, and rolled over in confusion to squint at the alarm clock. He had an old-fashioned clockwork one that ticked, with a face of ordinary numerals and a key on the back that reminded him of the screw-on ice skates of his childhood. It had to be wound up tight every evening until it groaned if it wasn't to stop by about four in the morning. It was ten to seven, and he lashed out at the big bell on the top. It made no difference. He sat up in bed to clear his mind and realised it was the telephone ringing. Groping clumsily for the receiver he knocked the whole instrument to the floor with a clatter. He finally succeeded in getting hold of it and blurrily announced himself.

"Håkon Sand. Who's calling?"

"Hello, Sand. It's Myhreng here. Sorry to . . ."

"*Sorry?!* What the hell do you mean by ringing me at seven in the morning — no, *before* seven on a Saturday morning? Who do you think you are?"

Crash! He couldn't make the receiver stay on its rest, so in a savage temper he got up and wrenched the contact out of the wall. Then he fell back into bed bristling with indignation until sleep overcame him as

261

heavily as before. For an hour and a half. Then there was a furious and determined ringing at the door.

Half past eight was an acceptable hour to wake up. Nevertheless he didn't hurry himself, in the hope that whoever was there would lose patience before he got to the door. As he was cleaning his teeth it rang again. Even more aggressively. But Håkon took his time washing his face, and felt a sense of relaxed and demonstrative freedom as he wrapped his dressing gown round him and put on the kettle before going to the entry phone.

"Yes?"

"Hello, it's Myhreng here. Can I talk to you?"

This bloke didn't give up. But nor did Håkon Sand.

"No," he said, replacing the receiver firmly.

But a second later the raucous noise was reverberating again through the flat like an enraged hornet. Håkon pondered for a moment before picking up the entry phone again.

"Go and buy some fresh rolls from the 7-Eleven round the corner. And fruit juice. The sort with real fruit in. And newspapers. All three."

He meant *Aftenposten*, *Dagbladet*, and *VG*. Myhreng brought *Arbeiderbladet* and the latter two. He also forgot the bit about the real fruit.

"Damn fine flat," he declared, taking a long look into the bedroom.

As inquisitive as a policeman, thought Håkon, closing the door.

He ushered Myhreng into the living room, and went to the bathroom and put out an extra toothbrush and a

262

very feminine bottle of perfume left behind after a relationship a year ago. It was as well not to appear too pathetic.

Fredrick Myhreng hadn't come just for a chat. The coffee hadn't even brewed before he was in full flood.

"Have you brought him in, or what? I can't find him anywhere. The woman in his office tells me he's out of the country, but at home there's just a young boy who says his father can't come to the telephone. Nor his mother. Wondered whether I should ring the child care people when I got nothing but a five-year-old or whatever on the line half a dozen times."

Håkon shook his head, fetched the coffee, and sat down.

"Are you some kind of child abuser? If it occurred to you that we'd arrested Lavik, shouldn't it have dawned on you that it wasn't particularly pleasant for the boy or the rest of the family to be harrassed by you on the telephone?"

"Journalists can't afford to be too considerate," Myhreng retorted, seizing an unopened can of mackerel in tomato sauce.

"Yes, fine, you can open it," said Håkon sarcastically, after half the contents of the can were already on Myhreng's roll.

"Mackerel burger! Brilliant!"

With his mouth full of food and tomato sauce dripping onto the white tablecloth he babbled on.

"Admit it, you've brought him in. I can see it in your face. Thought there was something funny about that guy all along. I've worked out quite a lot, you know."

The look in his eyes above his ridiculously small glasses was challenging but not entirely confident. Håkon allowed himself a smile, and didn't hurry with the margarine.

"Give me one good reason why I should tell you anything at all."

"I can give you several. For a start, good information is the best protection against misinformation. Secondly, the newspapers will be full of it tomorrow anyway. And you can be bloody sure that the other papers won't let the arrest of a lawyer go unnoticed for more than a day. And thirdly . . ."

He interrupted himself, wiped the tomato off his chin with his fingers, and leant across the table ingratiatingly.

"And thirdly, we've worked well together in the past. It would be to our mutual advantage to carry on."

Håkon Sand gave the impression that he'd been persuaded. Fredrick Myhreng took more credit for this than was his due. Fired by the promise of exciting information, he sat waiting as obediently as a schoolboy, while Håkon took a long and invigorating shower. The file that he'd sat up with until late into the night went with him to the bathroom.

The shower took almost a quarter of an hour, and in that time Håkon had sketched out in his mind a newspaper story that would instil terror in the person or persons out there in the November gloom nervously biting their fingernails. For he was convinced there was someone. It was simply a question of luring — or rather, frightening — them out.

264

MONDAY 23 NOVEMBER

It was like some outlandish circus. Three television cameras, countless press photographers, at least twenty journalists, and a huge crowd of curious onlookers had assembled in the entrance hall on the ground floor of the courthouse. The Sunday papers had tried to outdo one another, but on closer analysis they had little more to say than that a thirty-five-year-old Oslo lawyer had been arrested on suspicion of being the organiser of a drugs syndicate. That was all the journalists knew, but they'd certainly filled up enough space. They'd made a sumptuous repast of the scanty ingredients, and been greatly assisted by Lavik's colleagues who, in lengthy interviews, were highly critical of the monstrous action of the police in arresting a popular and respected fellow lawyer. The fact that these honourable colleagues knew absolutely nothing about the matter did not deter them from availing themselves of the widest possible range of expression to articulate their concern. The only one who remained silent was the one who actually knew something: Christian Bloch-Hansen.

It was difficult to carve a path through the crowd obstructing the entrance to Court 17. Even though no more than two or three of the journalists present could have recognised him, the crowd reacted like a flock of pigeons when a TV reporter held out a microphone to him. The reporter was attached by a cable from his microphone to the photographer, a man over six feet tall who lost control of his legs when the interviewer suddenly whipped the flex taut. He struggled for some seconds to keep his balance and was momentarily held upright by the throng around him. But only briefly before overbalancing and bringing down several others with him, giving Bloch-Hansen the opportunity to slip into Court 17 in the ensuing chaos.

Håkon Sand and Hanne Wilhelmsen hadn't even tried. They sat behind the dark-tinted windows of the Black Maria until Lavik had been taken into the entrance at one side of the main door, with the customary jacket over his head. Hardly anyone bothered about poor old Roger from Sagene, looking rather comical with his beige parka pulled up round his ears. The whole crowd had swarmed into the court after them, and Hanne and Håkon were able to sneak in through the back door reserved for the police. They came directly up into the courtroom from the basement.

A frail court attendant was having his work cut out endeavouring to keep order in the room. It could be no more than an attempt: the elderly uniformed man hadn't the slightest chance of holding out against the crush from the multitude outside. Håkon saw the consternation in his face and used the phone on the magistrate's bench to call for reinforcements from below. Four constables soon succeeded in ejecting everyone for whom there was no space on the single public bench.

The magistrate was delayed; the session was meant to start at one o'clock sharp. He arrived at four minutes past, without so much as a glance at anybody. He placed his file in front of him; it was marginally thicker than the one Bloch-Hansen had been provided with three days previously. Håkon stood up and gave the defence counsel some additional documents. It had taken him seven hours to sort out what he wanted to present to the Court, which was not allowed to have more documents than were given to the defence.

Turning to Håkon, the magistrate asked for the defendant. Håkon nodded towards the counsel for the defence, who rose.

"My client has nothing to hide," he said in a loud voice, to make certain that all the journalists heard him, "but his arrest has obviously had a devastating effect, both on himself and on his family. I would ask that the committal proceedings be conducted in camera."

A sigh of disappointment, of resignation even, passed through the little group of spectators. Not because of their dashed hopes for open proceedings, but because they had expected it to be the police closing the doors against them, as more often happened. This laconic, discreet defence lawyer did not augur well. The only one to react with a smirk was Fredrick Myhreng, who felt sure he would be furnished with a continuing flow of information anyway. The *Dagbladet* had been fuller yesterday than its competitors. He had enjoyed the hour before the court session, exulting in the fact that

267

older colleagues were sidling up to him with enquiring looks and oblique questions, reluctant to admit to their own inadequacies but with a transparent desire for information that boosted his feelings of self-importance.

The magistrate struck his gavel on the desk and cleared the court for discussion with counsel. The court attendant stepped out triumphantly behind the last reluctant journalist and hung up the black sign with white lettering: *In Camera*.

There was of course no discussion. With a whimsical glint in his eye the magistrate stood up, walked the few paces to the adjoining office, and returned with a ready-prepared ruling.

"I assumed as much," he said, signing the paper. Then he leafed through the case file for a couple of minutes before picking up the ruling again and going out to announce to the crowd outside what they already knew. When he came back in he removed his jacket and hung it over the bar. He sharpened three pencils with the utmost concentration before leaning over to the intercom.

"Bring Lavik up," he ordered, loosening his tie and smiling at the woman sitting rigidly erect at the computer.

"It's going to be a long day, Elsa!"

Even though Hanne had warned him in advance, Håkon was shocked at Lavik's appearance when he entered through the door at the back of the court. If it weren't a physical impossibility, he could have sworn that Jørgen Lavik had lost ten kilos over the weekend.

His suit hung baggily and he had a sunken look about him. His face was alarmingly ashen and his eyes were red-rimmed and swollen. He had the air of a man on the way to his own funeral, and for all Håkon knew that might be closer than anyone dared to suppose.

"Has he been given anything to eat and drink?" he whispered in a concerned tone to Hanne, who gave him a dispirited nod.

"But all he would take was some Coke. He hasn't eaten a scrap of food since Friday," she said in an undertone. "It's not our fault, he's been given special treatment."

Even the magistrate seemed worried about the defendant's condition. He scrutinised him several times before telling the two police guards to remove him from the witness box and bring a chair. The stern computer operator relaxed her image momentarily to emerge from her enclosure and offer Lavik a plastic cup of water and a paper napkin.

When the magistrate had satisfied himself that Lavik wasn't as close to death as his appearance suggested, the proceedings finally commenced. Håkon was to speak first, and received an encouraging slap on the thigh from Hanne as he stood up. It was harder than intended and the pain made him want to pee.

Four hours later both prosecuting and defence counsel had followed the magistrate's example and discarded their jackets. Hanne Wilhelmsen had taken off her sweater, but Lavik looked as if he were freezing. Only the lady at the computer appeared to be unaffected.

They'd had a short break an hour ago, but none of them had risked showing themselves to the wolves in the corridor. Whenever the courtroom went quiet they could hear there was still a considerable crowd outside.

Lavik was willing to speak in his own defence, at excruciating length because every word was weighed so carefully. There was nothing new in his story — he denied everything and stuck to the statement he had made to the police. He even had an explanation of sorts for the fingerprints: his client had simply asked him for a small loan, which Lavik maintained was not unusual. In response to a caustic question from Håkon as to whether he was in the business of handing out cash to all his more indigent clients he replied in the affirmative. He could even provide witnesses to the fact. He couldn't of course explain how a lawfully acquired thousand-kroner note came to be in a plastic envelope with drugs money under a floorboard on Mosseveien, but equally they couldn't hold it against him if his client did strange things. The connection with Roger had been explained perfectly clearly before: he happened to have assisted the chap with a few minor matters, income tax returns and three or four traffic offences. Håkon's problem was that Roger had said exactly the same.

The explanation for the thousand-kroner note rang rather more hollow, however. Even though it was impossible to read anything in the magistrate's impassive face, Håkon felt certain that this element in the indictment would hold up. Whether it would be sufficient in itself was another question, which would

270

be resolved in an hour or so; the case would stand or fall by it. Håkon began his summing up.

The money and the fingerprints were the vital elements; after that he went over the mysterious relationship between Roger Strømsjord and Lavik and the encoded telephone numbers. Towards the end he spent twenty-five minutes on Han van der Kerch's statement to Karen Borg, before concluding with a pessimistic tirade about the likelihood of destruction of evidence and the risk of disappearance.

That was all he had. His final thrust. Not a word about any links to Hans Olsen through the murdered and faceless Ludvig Sandersen. Nor about the lists of codes they had found. Nothing whatsoever about Lavik's presence at the time of Van der Kerch's derangement or Frøstrup's fatal overdose.

He'd been so sure yesterday. They'd discussed and debated, analysed and argued. Kaldbakken had wanted to go ahead with everything they'd got, invoking Håkon's own absolute certainty of the same course only a few days earlier. But the chief inspector had eventually given way; Håkon had been both confident and persuasive. He no longer was. He racked his brain for the incisive punch line he'd practised the previous night, but it had gone. Instead he stood and swallowed a couple of times before stuttering that the police reaffirmed their application. Then he forgot to sit down and there were an awkward few seconds until the magistrate cleared his throat and told him he didn't need to continue standing. Hanne gave him a faint smile of encouragement and poked him in the ribs, more gently this time.

"Sir," began the counsel for the defence even while he was rising from his seat, "we are indubitably embarking on a very delicate case, one which concerns a lawyer who has committed the gravest of crimes."

His two adversaries couldn't believe their ears. What on earth was this? Was Bloch-Hansen stabbing his client in the back? They looked at Lavik for a reaction, but his weary, pallid face betrayed no emotion.

"It's a good maxim not to use stronger words than one can substantiate," he continued, putting on his jacket again as if to assume a formality that until then had not been required in the big hot room. Håkon regretted not having done the same; it would just look foolish now.

"But it is quite deplorable . . ."

He paused for effect to emphasise his words.

"It is quite deplorable under any circumstances that Karen Borg, a lawyer whom I know to have sound judgement and a reputation as a very capable barrister, does not seem to have realised she is guilty of contravening Article 144 of the Penal Code."

Another pause. The magistrate was looking up the relevant section, but Håkon was transfixed until he'd heard how Bloch-Hansen would continue.

"Karen Borg is legally bound by the Client Confidentiality Act," he went on. "She has infringed it. I can see from the documentation that she has based her position in this serious breach of the law on her deceased client's quasi-consent. This cannot suffice. I

272

have to stress first and foremost her client's demonstrably psychotic state, which rendered him incapable of determining his own best interests. Secondly I would draw the Court's attention to the so-called suicide note itself, Document 17-1."

He paused, and turned up the copy of the hapless letter.

"From this wording it is somewhat — no, extremely — unclear whether the formulation as a whole could be seen to exempt her from her duty of confidentiality. As I read it, it is more in the nature of a farewell note, a rather emotional declaration of affection to a lawyer who has obviously been extremely kind and sympathetic."

"But he's dead!"

Håkon was unable to hold his tongue, half rising and gesticulating with his arms. He dropped back into his seat again before the magistrate had time to call him to order. The defence counsel smiled.

"I refer you to Law Reports 1983, page 430," he said, going round the bar and putting a copy of the judgement on the magistrate's desk.

"One for you, too," he said, proffering a copy to Håkon, who had to stand up and go over to take it himself.

"The majority view was that the duty of confidentiality does not cease when the client dies," he explained. "The minority view concurred, come to that. There can be no doubt on the subject. And so we come back to this letter."

He held it up at arm's length and read it out:

"You've been very kind to me. You can forget what I said about keeping your mouth shut. Write to my mother. Thanks for everything."

He put the letter back with the other papers. Hanne didn't know what to think. Håkon had gooseflesh and could feel his scrotum contracting into a delicate little bulge of masculinity as it did when bathing in ice-cold water.

"This," Bloch-Hansen continued, "this is far from granting exemption from the duty of confidentiality. Karen Borg as a lawyer should never have made a statement on the matter. But since she has erred, it is essential that the Court does not do likewise. I would draw your attention in this respect to Article 119 of the Penal Code and point out that it would conflict with that provision if the Court were to allow Borg's statement."

Håkon turned the pages of the offprint he had in front of him; his hands were trembling so much that he had difficulty coordinating his movements. He found the relevant paragraph at last. Hell's bells! A court could not accept a statement from lawyers of information received in the course of their professional duties.

Now he was seriously worried. He didn't give a damn about Lavik, drug-runner and possible murderer Jørgen Ulf Lavik. All he could think of was Karen Borg. Perhaps she was in deep trouble. And it was entirely his fault: it was he who had insisted on getting her statement. Admittedly she had offered no protest, but she would never have provided it if he hadn't asked her for it. Everything was his fault.

On the opposite side of the room the counsel for the defence had packed up his papers. He'd gone to the end of the bar nearest the magistrate and was leaning with one hand on the top of the bench.

"And that, sir, leaves the prosecution with nothing at all. No particular significance can be attached to the telephone numbers in Roger Strømsjord's notebook. The fact that the man has a penchant for playing with numbers is not proof of wrongdoing. It is not even an indication of anything unusual — other than that he might be an eccentric. And what of the fingerprints on the banknote? We know very little about that. But, sir, there is nothing to show that Mr. Lavik isn't speaking the truth! He could have lent a thousand to a client he felt sorry for. Not particularly sensible, of course, since Frøstrup's credit rating was not exactly flawless, but the loan was without doubt a generous act. No special significance can be attached to that either."

A wave of his arm denoted that he was about to make his concluding remarks.

"I shall not comment further upon the grave impropriety of incarcerating my client. It would be superfluous. None of this even approaches reasonable grounds for suspicion. My client must be released forthwith. Thank you."

It had taken exactly eight minutes. Håkon had taken one hour and ten minutes. The two police constables who were in charge of Lavik had been yawning throughout the hearing. During Bloch-Hansen's defence they perked up considerably.

The magistrate was far from perky. He made no effort to conceal the fact that he was worn out, tilting his head from side to side and massaging his face. Håkon wasn't even offered his right of reply. He didn't care. He felt a sinister void in his stomach and was in no condition to say any more. The magistrate looked at the clock. It was already half past six. The news would be on in half an hour.

"We'll continue with Roger Strømsjord right away. It probably won't take so long now that the Court is familiar with the facts of the case," he said optimistically.

It took less than an hour. Hanne couldn't help feeling that poor Roger was only being seen as an appendage of Lavik. If the decision went against Lavik, it would go against Roger. If Lavik went free, Roger would do likewise.

"You'll have a judgement today, I hope, but it may not be until midnight," the magistrate declared as the hearing at last came to an end. "Will you wait, or may I have a fax number for each of you?"

He certainly could.

Roger was escorted back to the basement, after a whispered conversation with his defence counsel. The magistrate had already gone into the adjacent office, and the typist had followed him. Bloch-Hansen put his shabby but venerable document case under his arm and went over to Håkon Sand. He seemed more friendly than he had reason to be.

276

"You can't have had much when you arrested them on Friday," he said in an undertone. "I wonder what you would have done if you hadn't found the notebook and been lucky with the fingerprints. Or to put it more bluntly, you must have been miles away from reasonable grounds for suspicion when you took them both in."

Håkon felt faint. Perhaps it was obvious to the other two, because the lawyer was quick to reassure him.

"I'm not going to make any fuss about it. But if I can offer you a word of friendly advice: don't get involved in things you can't handle. That holds good for all aspects of life."

He nodded curtly but politely and went out to meet those journalists who had not yet lost patience. There were quite a few. The two police officers were left alone.

"Let's go and get something to eat," Hanne suggested. "Then I'll wait with you. I'm sure it'll be all right."

That was a barefaced lie.

Again he noticed the subtle fragrance of her perfume. She'd given him a hug of consolation and encouragement as soon as they were by themselves. It hadn't helped. When they emerged from the grand old courthouse, she remarked on how sensible it had been to wait for half an hour. The inquisitive crowds had long gone off home to the warmth. The television people had had to bow to their fixed schedules and hurry back with what little they'd got. The newspaper reporters had also vanished, after having obtained a

277

short statement from the defence counsel. It was already quarter past eight.

"Actually, I haven't eaten all day," Håkon realised in some astonishment, feeling his appetite sneaking back after having cowered in a corner of his stomach for over twenty-four hours.

"Nor have I," Hanne replied, even though it wasn't entirely true. "We've got plenty of time. The magistrate will need at least three hours. Let's find somewhere quiet."

They walked arm-in-arm down a little hill, trying to evade the heavy splashes from the roof of an old building, and managed to get a secluded table in an Italian restaurant just round the corner. A handsome young man with jet-black hair escorted them to their places, plonked a menu down in front of them, and asked mechanically whether they wanted anything to drink. After a moment's hesitation, they both ordered a beer. It was delivered in record time. Håkon drank half the glass in one gulp. It revived him, and the alcohol made an immediate impact — or perhaps it was just the shock to his atrophied stomach.

"It's all disintegrating," he said, almost cheerfully, wiping the froth from his upper lip. "It'll never get through. They'll walk straight out and back to their old games again. Mark my words. And it's my fault."

"We'll worry about it if it happens," said Hanne, though she was unable to disguise the fact that she shared his pessimism. She glanced at the clock. "We still have an hour or two before we may have to admit defeat."

278

They sat there for quite a while without saying anything and with a faraway, unfocused expression in their eyes.

Their glasses were empty by the time the food came. Spaghetti. It looked appetising, and was piping hot.

"It's not your fault if it hasn't worked out," she said as she struggled with the long white strands covered in tomato sauce. She'd tucked her napkin into her collar with an apologetic gesture to protect her sweater from the inevitable accidents.

"You know it isn't," she added emphatically, scanning his face. "If it goes wrong, we've all failed. We were all agreed on trying for custody, no one can blame you."

"Blame me?"

He banged his spoon on the table so that the sauce spattered everywhere.

"Blame me? Of course they'll blame me! It's not you or Kaldbakken or the commissioner or anyone else who was wittering on for hours in there! It was me! I was the one who messed it up. They have every right to blame me."

He suddenly felt full and pushed the half-eaten food away, almost in distaste, as if the mussels might be concealing an unpalatable release order.

"I don't think I've ever performed so badly in court, believe me, Hanne."

He took a deep breath and beckoned to the sleek young man for a bottle of mineral water.

"I'd probably have done a better job if I'd had a different defence counsel. Bloch-Hansen makes me nervous. His ultra-correct, factual style throws me off balance. Maybe I'd prepared myself for a bloody and open battle. When my adversary challenges me to an elegant fencing duel instead, I just stand there like a sack of potatoes."

He rubbed his face vigorously, grinned, and shook his head.

"Promise me you won't say nasty things about my performance," he begged.

"I can assure you of that on my word of honour," Hanne promised, raising her right hand to confirm it. "But you really weren't *that* bad.

"By the way," she went on, changing the subject, "why did you tell that *Dagbladet* reporter about a possible third person still at liberty? It sounded as if we had someone specific in mind. At least, I assume he got it from you?"

"Do you remember what you said when I was so shocked at the way you treated Lavik in the last interview before we arrested him?"

She frowned in concentration.

"Not really."

"You said that frightened people make mistakes. That was why you wanted to frighten Lavik. Now it's my turn to play the bogeyman. It may be a shot in the dark, but on the other hand it may hit someone out there who's scared. Very, very scared."

The bill arrived within seconds of Håkon's discreet signal. They both reached for it, but Håkon was the quicker.

280

"Out of the question," Hanne protested. "I'll pay — or at any rate let me pay half."

Håkon clutched the bill to his chest with a pleading expression.

"Let me feel like a man just once today," he begged.

It wasn't much to ask. He paid, and rounded it up with a three-kroner tip. The oily-haired waiter showed them out into the darkness with a smile, and hoped to see them again soon. His sincerity wasn't very convincing.

Weariness enveloped his brain like a tight black cowl, and his eyelids drooped whenever he stopped speaking for a few moments. He took out a small bottle of eyedrops from his jacket pocket, bent his head back, pushed his glasses to the end of his nose, and poured the drops liberally into his eyes. He'd soon used up the whole bottle; it had been new that morning.

Håkon Sand rotated his head in an effort to loosen up his neck muscles, which felt as taut as harp strings. Twisting a bit too far, he felt a sudden spasm of cramp on the left-hand side which made him flinch.

"Aaaah!" he yelled, massaging the painful area vigorously.

Hanne looked at the clock for the umpteenth time. Five to midnight. It was impossible to know whether it was a good or bad sign that the decision was taking so long. The magistrate would have to be especially punctilious if he were going to send a lawyer to jail. On the other hand he would hardly be less careful with a decision to release. It was probably obvious that the judgement would go to appeal, whichever it was.

She gave a yawn so enormous that her slim hand couldn't cover her entire mouth, and as she leant back Håkon noticed that she had no amalgam in her molars.

"What do you think of those white fillings?" he asked, and she stared at him in astonishment at the incongruity of the question.

"White fillings? What do you mean?"

"I can see that you haven't got any amalgam in your teeth. I've been thinking of getting rid of mine, since I read an article about how much rubbish there is in the 'silver' ones, mercury and the like. I've read that people have even been made ill by them. But my dentist advises me against the new composites and says that amalgam is much stronger."

She bent towards him with her mouth wide open and he could see quite clearly that it was all perfectly white.

"No cavities," she said with a smile and a touch of pride. "Of course, I'm a bit too old to belong to the 'no cavities' generation, but we had well-water where I grew up. Lots of natural fluoride. Probably dangerous, but there were sixteen of us kids in the neighbourhood who grew up without ever having to visit the dentist."

Teeth. Something to talk about anyhow. Håkon went over to check the fax machine again. It was still on and working okay, just as it had been the last time he'd checked and the time before. The little green light stared up arrogantly at him, but to reassure himself he had to verify once more that there was paper in the feed tray. Of course there was. He could feel a yawn coming on, but he suppressed it by clenching his jaws. Tears came to his eyes. He picked up a well-thumbed pack of playing cards and cast an enquiring glance at Hanne. She shrugged her shoulders.

"I don't mind, but let's play something different. Casino, for instance."

They finished two games before the fax emitted a promising trill. The green light had changed to yellow and a few seconds later the machine sucked in the top blank sheet of paper. It remained in the machine for a moment before its head emerged on the other side, neatly printed with a fax cover sheet from Oslo Magistrates Court.

They both felt their pulses racing. An uncomfortable tingling crept up Håkon's back, and he had to shake himself.

"Shall we take it out page by page, or wait till the whole lot has arrived?" he asked with a wry grin.

"Let's go get ourselves a cup of coffee, then when we come back, it'll all be there. It's better than standing here waiting for it page by page."

They had the feeling they were absolutely alone as they left the room and walked along the corridor. Neither of them said anything. But the coffee in the anteroom had gone, so someone must have been in, because Hanne had put a fresh jug on less than an hour before. Håkon went into his office instead, opened the window, and brought in a plastic bag that had been hanging on a nail outside. He took out two half-litre bottles of orangeade.

"The only fizzy drink that quenches nothing but your thirst," he quoted sardonically.

They clinked bottles in a gloomy toast. Håkon did nothing to suppress a loud and substantial belch, while Hanne gave a tiny burp. They returned to the incident room. Very slowly. There was a smell of polish, and the floor gleamed more than usual.

When they came into the room the evil green eye had taken over again from its yellow counterpart. The machine had reverted to its somnolent hum, and the out-tray now contained several sheets of paper. Håkon picked them up with a hand trembling more from fatigue than tension and quickly perused the top final page. He sank down onto the small sofa and read aloud:

"The defendant Jørgen Ulf Lavik will be remanded in custody until the Court or the prosecution service deems otherwise, though no later than Monday 6 December. Visits and correspondence will be prohibited for the duration of custody."

"*Two weeks!*"

His tiredness was swept away on a rush of adrenaline.

"Two weeks for Lavik!"

He sprang up from the settee, staggered past the coffee table, and flung his arms round Hanne, scattering the papers.

"Let go of me," she laughed. "Two weeks is literally only half a victory; you asked for four."

"It'll be pushing it, certainly, but we can work round the clock. And I swear" — he thumped his fist on the table before going on — "I'll bet a month's salary that we have more on that bastard before the fortnight's out!"

His childlike optimism and enthusiasm didn't immediately rub off on Hanne. She gathered the papers together and put them in sequence again.

"Let's see what else the magistrate has to say."

On closer inspection the decision couldn't even be described as half a victory. At most an eighth, perhaps.

Christian Bloch-Hansen's views on Karen Borg's witness statement had found support, by and large. The Court shared his interpretation of Van der Kerch's farewell letter as not in itself exempting her from her duty of confidentiality. The Dutchman's intentions had to be subjected to fuller appraisal, an appraisal in which particular emphasis had to be given to the question of whether promulgation of the information would be to his advantage. There was some indication that this was not the case, since the statement actually incriminated him to a significant extent, and would thus harm his posthumous reputation. In the opinion of the Court the interview conducted by Karen Borg was too short in this respect. The Court therefore proposed to ignore the statement at present, since it might conflict with statutory trial procedures.

Nevertheless, with some reservations, the Court found that there were reasonable grounds to suspect that a felony had been committed. But only with regard to the first charge of the indictment, the specified quantity of drugs that had been discovered in Frøstrup's apartment. There was no reasonable cause, in the Court's opinion, to suspect the defendant of anything more, in view of the inadmissibility of Karen Borg's statement. In one simple phrase the magistrate had conceded that there were grounds for believing that the defendant might tamper with evidence. Two weeks' remand in custody could not be regarded as disproportionate to the severity of the charges. Twenty-four grams of hard drugs was a substantial amount, with a street value of about two hundred thousand kroner. A fortnight behind bars, then, was the outcome.

Roger Strømsjord would go free.

"Oh, shit," they exclaimed simultaneously.

Roger was implicated solely on the strength of the statement from Han van der Kerch. As long as that was inadmissible, the Court had only the coded telephone numbers, which were inadequate evidence in themselves. He was to be released.

The telephone rang. They both leapt up, as if the gentle burbling were a fire alarm.

It was the magistrate, to check that the fax transmission had functioned properly.

"I suppose I can expect an appeal from both sides," he said in a weary voice, though Håkon thought he could detect a trace of humour in it.

"Yes, I want to appeal against the release of Roger Strømsjord, anyway, and seek a stay of execution. It would be a catastrophe if he were let out tonight."

"You shall have a stay of execution," the magistrate promised him. "Now we'll all turn in, shall we?"

That was one thing they could all agree on. It had been a long, long day. They put on their coats, locked the door carefully behind them, and left the half-empty bottles of orangeade standing in splendid isolation. The slogan was right: it had quenched nothing but their thirst.

TUESDAY 24 NOVEMBER

It was like waking up with a bad hangover. Hanne Wilhelmsen hadn't been able to sleep when she got home. Despite hot milk and a shoulder massage. After only four hours of intermittent dozing she was jerked into to full consciousness by a wretched news programme on her clock radio. Lavik's remand in custody was the first item. The commentator considered the hearing equivocal, and was extremely doubtful about the tenability of the police case. Of course, they didn't know the reasons for the decision, and therefore spent several minutes speculating on why the car salesman had been released. The speculations were fairly wide of the mark.

She stretched herself dispiritedly and forced herself up out of the warm bedclothes. She had to skip breakfast, because she'd promised Håkon she'd be at work by eight o'clock. It looked as if it was going to be yet another long day.

In the shower she tried to concentrate on other things. She rested her forehead against the shiny tiles, and let the scalding water run down her back and turn it bright pink. She couldn't get the case out of her mind. Her brain had gone into overdrive and was carrying her along with it. Right now she almost wished she could be the subject of an immediate transfer. Three months in the traffic police would be ideal. She might not be the type to run away from a difficult task, but this case was completely monopolising her. There was no peace, all the loose threads kept going round and round, weaving themselves into new solutions, new theories. Even if Cecilie didn't complain, Hanne realised that she herself was at the moment neither good friend nor good lover. At dinner parties she would sit staring mutely at her glass and being politely formal. Sex had become routine, without much evidence of either passion or involvement.

The water was so hot that her back was going numb. She straightened up and winced in agony when it scalded her breasts. As she adjusted the mixer control to escape being boiled alive, a thought suddenly struck her.

The boot. Billy T.'s hunting trophy. It must obviously have a twin somewhere or other. Locating a specific size ten winter boot in Oslo at this time of year might seem like a hopeless exercise, even if the owner hadn't dumped it. But the number of current owners couldn't be so immensely great and it might just be worth a try. If they managed to get hold of the other boot it should bring them someone virtually guaranteed to be involved in all this. Then they would see how tough he was. Loyalty had never been a strong point among drug dealers.

The boot. It had to be found.

★   ★   ★

The day was just dawning. Even though the sun had not yet risen over the horizon, the luminosity behind Ekeberg Hill to the southeast of the city centre seemed to promise fine cold November weather. The temperature had fallen below freezing again. The local radio stations were broadcasting warnings to motorists and predicting delays and overcrowding on buses and trams. A few workers on their way to another day's toil paused outside the *Dagbladet* offices to scan the pages of the newspaper displayed in the window.

Once again his case was the main headline. Myhreng had made a covert record in his notebook that very morning of his twelfth front page in less than a year. A bit immature perhaps, but it was good to have an overview, he thought proudly. After all, his position was only temporary. Almost like a probationary period.

The key was burning a hole in his pocket. Taking no chances, he'd had three more copies made and hidden them safely away. His key-cutting friend hadn't been of much assistance in the end. Apparently it might be almost anything. Nothing bigger than a luggage deposit locker. Maybe a cupboard, but definitely not a full-size door. So it was a pretty vague thing to track down.

He'd had no luck at the left-luggage lockers in the most obvious places. The key didn't fit at the Central Station or either of the airports, nor in the big hotels. And since there hadn't been a number on the key it wasn't likely that it was for use in any public facility.

Should he give it to Håkon Sand? The police were presumably under pressure now, since two weeks wasn't much, and the way the courts were handling appeals suggested that they might not even get as long as that.

There was a lot to be said for helping the police. They had resources that would make it far more effective for them to look for somewhere the damned key would fit. He also needed to build up some more goodwill. Definitely. He could do a lucrative deal. In fact, when he thought about it, it wasn't exactly wise to carry something about with him that could be crucial evidence in a case of this significance. Murder and stuff. Was it a punishable offence? Withholding evidence? He wasn't entirely sure.

On the other hand, how to explain his possession of the key? The break-in at Lavik's office was an offence in itself. If his editor got to hear of it, he could kiss his job good-bye. For the moment he couldn't think of any alternative story that would hold water.

The conclusion was obvious: he would have to hunt around on his own. If he succeeded in finding the cupboard or locker or whatever it might be, he would go to the police. If it contained anything of interest, that is. Then his dubious methods would probably be overlooked. Yes, the sensible thing was to keep the key to himself.

He hitched up his trousers and went into the big grey building where his newspaper had its home.

The broad expanse of the desk was completely covered in newspapers. Peter Strup had been at the office since half past six. He too had been woken by the news of the court ruling. He had bought seven different papers on the way to work, all of which had devoted sizeable headlines to the case. On the whole the articles had little to say, but they all took different angles. *Klassekampen* described the custody order as a victory for the rule of law, and had a leader on how reassuring it was that the courts occasionally demonstrated that they were not merely perpetuating class justice. Strange, he reflected grimly, how the same people who bring out their heavy artillery against the primitive need of a corrupt society for imprisonment as vengeance change their tune when the same system targets someone from society's sunnier climes. The tabloids had more pictures than text, apart from the huge headlines. *Aftenposten* had a sober report, really rather tame. The case certainly deserved a more adequate coverage than that — perhaps they were afraid of libel action. It all seemed a long way from a conviction, and it was obvious that Lavik would take cruel revenge if he were found not guilty.

His old-fashioned fountain pen scratched across the paper as he took notes at lightning speed. It was always difficult to follow the legal arguments from newspaper articles. Journalists confused concepts and blundered around the legal landscape like free-range hens. Only *Aftenposten* and *Klassekampen* were competent enough to realise this was a court ruling that was being challenged, not a conviction subject to appeal.

Finally he folded all the newspapers together, with pages hanging loose where he'd cut out the most significant bits. The whole batch went into the wastepaper basket. He clipped the cuttings to his

292

handwritten notes and put them in a plastic folder in a locked drawer. He buzzed his secretary and instructed her to cancel his engagements for today and tomorrow. She was manifestly astonished, and began to counter with ifs and buts before restraining herself.

"Very well then. Shall I arrange new dates?"

"Yes, please do. Say that something unforeseen has cropped up. Now I have to make one or two important phone calls and I don't want to be disturbed. Not by anyone."

He stood up and locked the door to the corridor. Then he took out a neat little mobile phone and went over to the window. After a couple of rings he was through.

"Hello, Christian, it's Peter here."

"Good morning."

His voice was sombre, the tone at variance with the words.

"Well, it's not exactly good for either of us. But I'd better congratulate you, if I've got it right from the newspapers. One discharged and the other in custody for half the length of time demanded could be seen as a favourable result."

His voice was flat and expressionless.

"This is one hell of a mess, Peter, a real bugger of a mess."

"I agree."

Neither said anything more, and the crackling on the line became intrusive.

Peter Strup wondered if the connection had been broken. "Hello, are you still there?"

"Yes, I'm here. Quite frankly, I don't know what's best — for him to stay there or be released. We'll have to see. The result of the appeal won't come much before the end of the day. Or maybe tomorrow. Those chaps aren't renowned for working overtime."

Peter Strup bit his lip. He shifted the telephone to his other hand, turned round, and stood with his back to the window.

"Is there any chance at all of stopping this avalanche? In a reasonably respectable way, I mean."

"Who knows? For the moment I'm preparing myself for anything. If it explodes, it'll be the biggest bang since the War. I hope I can avoid being nearby when it happens. Right now I sincerely wish you'd kept me out of it."

"I couldn't, Christian. The fact that Lavik chose you was a fantastic stroke of luck in the midst of all this misfortune. Someone I could rely on. Absolutely rely on."

It was not meant as a threat in any way. Nevertheless Christian Bloch-Hansen's voice sounded sharper.

"Let's get one thing crystal-clear between us," he said firmly. "My good nature isn't inexhaustible. There has to be a limit. I thought I made that clear to you on Sunday. Don't forget it."

"I'm hardly likely to," Peter Strup replied stonily, ending the conversation.

He stayed where he was and leant back against the cold glass of the window. This wasn't just a sticky mess, it was a bloody swamp. He made the other call, which was over in two or three minutes. Then he went to get himself some breakfast. With no appetite whatsoever.

Karen Borg was sitting at a pine table by a lattice window with red-striped curtains, eating with a very hearty appetite. The third slice of bread was already on its way down, and her boxer dog lay with its head on its paws looking up at its owner with a melancholy pleading expression.

"Stop begging," she admonished it, turning her attention again to the novel on the table in front of her. The unobtrusive tones of the morning radio programme provided background entertainment from an old-fashioned portable radio on a shelf above the kitchen bench.

The cottage was on a rocky mound, with a view she had imagined as a child stretching all the way to Denmark. When she was eight years old she had conjured up a picture of the flat land down there in the south, and she could actually *see* it, with its beech trees and gentle people. The image refused to budge, despite her elder brother's teasing and her father's more scientific attempts to persuade her that it was all in her own mind. By the age of twelve it had begun to fade, and the summer before she started at secondary school the whole of Denmark sank into the sea. It had been one of the most painful experiences of growing up, the realisation that things weren't the way she'd always visualised them.

She'd had no particular trouble getting the place up to a comfortable temperature. It was well insulated against the winter cold and connected to the electricity supply; and there was still heat left from Sunday when the entire cottage had been nicely warmed through. She hadn't dared switch on the water pump, because she wasn't sure whether the pipes had frozen. But it didn't matter, since the well was only a few steps from the door.

After two days she was more relaxed than she had been for many weeks. Her mobile phone was on, of course, to make her feel more secure, but it was only the office and Nils who had her number. He had left her in peace. These last weeks had been a strain for both of them. She winced at the thought of his injured enquiring look, his helpless attempts to understand her. Rejection had become a habit. They talked politely enough about their jobs, about the news and all the necessary, everyday things. But with no intimacy, no real communication. Perhaps he even felt relief when she decided to go away, though he'd tried to protest, with tears in his eyes and forlorn appeals. In any event, there had been no word from him since she'd made the obligatory call to assure him of her safe arrival. However glad she was that he had acceded to her wish to be left in peace, it hurt her a little to think he was actually managing it.

She shrugged and slopped some tea into her saucer. The dog raised its head at the abrupt movement, and she threw it a piece of cheese that it caught in midair.

"You don't need a second invitation!" she said, shooing the dog away but failing to persuade it to give up hope of catching another piece in its slavering jaws.

Suddenly she sprang to her feet and turned up the volume control on the radio. It must be working loose, she thought, judging from the crackling noise as she turned the knob.

Lavik in custody! God, what a triumph for Håkon. Another fifty-two-year-old man had been released, but both rulings were being challenged. That must be Roger. Why had they released one and held the other? She had been so certain that they would either both be put inside or both be freed.

There was little further information given.

Only gradually did her conscience begin to prick. She had promised Håkon that before going away anywhere she would phone him. She hadn't. Couldn't face it. Maybe she would phone him this evening. Maybe.

The meal was eaten, and the dog given a couple more scraps. She would wash the dishes before walking the kilometre or so to the shop for the newspapers. She wanted to keep up with what was going on.

"Where the bloody hell *is* the woman?!"

He threw the receiver down on the desk. It cracked.

"Oh, damn," he said, staring at it foolishly and a little apprehensively. He put it to his ear to test it: yes, he could still hear the dialling tone. A rubber band would have to do as a temporary repair.

"I don't get it," he said, calming down. "At the office they say she won't be available for a while. At home there's no reply."

And I'm definitely not ringing Nils, he thought to himself. Where could Karen be?

"We have to find her," declared Hanne rather unnecessarily. "We need a new statement urgently. It would have been best to get it done today. If we're lucky, the result of the appeal won't be announced till tomorrow, and we could let them have a new statement then, couldn't we?"

"I suppose so," Håkon muttered.

He didn't know what to think. Karen had promised to let him know when she was going to her cottage. With commendable self-restraint he had kept to his side of the bargain. Not phoned, not called on her. It was unusual for her not to reciprocate. If she really had gone away, that is. There were numerous possibilities. For all he knew, she might be having a discreet meeting with a client. Nothing to worry about. However, he'd had an uneasy gnawing suspicion since Sunday. The comforting feeling of at least being in the same city as Karen had vanished completely.

"She's got a mobile with an ex-directory number. Use all the police pressure you can bring to bear and get hold of it. Telecom, her office, anywhere. Just get me the number. It shouldn't be all that difficult."

"And I'll continue the search for the bootless man, however hopeless it seems," said Hanne, and went back to her own office.

The silver-haired man was afraid. Fear was an unfamiliar enemy for him, and he resisted it stubbornly. Even though he had scoured all the newspapers, it was impossible to get any real idea of what the police actually knew. The article in the *Dagbladet* on Sunday had been very alarming. But it couldn't be right. Jørgen Lavik had protested his innocence — that much was clear at least. Ergo, he couldn't have squealed. No one else knew his identity. So there couldn't, there just *couldn't* be any danger ahead.

Yet his consuming fear was not so easily assuaged; its bloodied talons had a tight grip around his heart, and the pain was intense. His breathing was reduced momentarily to a series of short gasps, and he struggled to regain control. Groping feverishly for the bottle of pills in his inside pocket, he fumbled with the cap and shook out the contents to put one under his tongue. The relief was immediate. His breathing became more regular again, and he managed to suppress his panic.

"Good Lord, whatever's the matter?"

His neatly attired secretary stood horrified in the doorway before rushing over to him.

"Are you all right? You look ghastly."

Her concern seemed genuine, which it was. She idolised her boss, and she also had an innate horror of grey, clammy skin ever since her husband had died in bed beside her five years ago.

"I'm better now," he assured her, brushing her hand away from his brow. "Truly. Much better."

She bustled out for a glass of water, and by the time she came back some of the natural colour had returned to his face. He drank it eagerly and with a tremulous smile asked for more. She rushed off to refill the glass, which he downed with equal alacrity.

After further affirmation that all was now well, his secretary withdrew to her adjoining room. Obviously reluctant, and with a worried frown, she left the door ajar, as if assuming he would at least make some kind of noise before expiring. He stood up with difficulty and closed it behind her.

He had to pull himself together. Perhaps he should ask for a couple of days off. But the vital thing was to maintain a completely detached attitude to events. They couldn't arrest him. It was essential not to allow his mask to slip. For as long as was humanly possible. He must, he really *must* find out what the police knew.

"How much money is there actually in drugs?"

The question was surprising coming as it did from an investigator who had been working on a drugs case for weeks. But Hanne Wilhelmsen had never been shy of asking obvious questions, and just recently she'd begun to wonder. When eminently respectable men with what she regarded as generous incomes were willing to risk everything for the sake of some extra dough, the sums involved had to be pretty substantial.

Billy T. wasn't in the least taken aback. Drugs were a vague and imprecise concept for most people, even within the police force. For him, though, it was straightforward enough: money, misery, and death.

"This autumn the various drugs squads in the Scandinavian countries have seized eleven kilos of heroin in the course of six weeks," he replied. "We arrested thirty couriers in Scandinavia. All the result of Norwegian narcotics intelligence."

He sounded proud, and had good reason to be.

"One gram provides at least thirty-five individual fixes. One fix costs two hundred and fifty kroner on the street. So you can calculate what sort of money we're talking about."

She scribbled the figures down on a napkin, tearing it in the process.

"About eight thousand seven hundred kroner a gram! That's . . ."

With her eyes closed and her lips in silent motion she gave up on the napkin and worked it out in her head.

"Eight point seven million kroner a kilo," she said, opening her eyes. "Nearly a hundred million for eleven kilos. Eleven kilos! That's not much more than a washing machine load! But can there be a market for such vast quantities?"

"If there wasn't a market for it, it wouldn't have been brought in," said Billy T. dryly. "And it's so damned easy to smuggle it in. Our borders are so vulnerable, with any number of approaches by sea, so many flights, not to speak of the amount of road traffic thundering through the frontier posts. It's virtually impossible to keep up any effective control procedures. But fortunately it's the distribution that's more problematical for them. They have to operate in an environment that's rotten to the core — which is what plays into our hands. In drugs investigations we're heavily dependent on informers. And thank God there's plenty of them."

"But where does it all come from?"

"Heroin? Mainly from Asia. Pakistan, for instance. Sixty, maybe seventy percent, of Norwegian heroin emanates from there. As a rule it'll have been on a tour of Africa before it finally reaches Europe."

"Africa? That's a roundabout route!"

"Well, geographically, perhaps, but there are plenty of willing runners. Pure exploitation of poverty-stricken Africans who have nothing to lose. In The Gambia they even teach them how to do it! 'Gambian Swallow School.' Those boys can swallow huge quantities of the stuff. First they make little balls of about ten grams each, wrap them in clingfilm, and warm them up to seal them. Then they stuff a condom full of them, grease it with something or other, and swallow the whole lot. It's quite phenomenal what they can get down. And after anything from one to three days it plops out at the other end; they dig it out of the crap, and there you are: riches galore!"

Billy T. spoke with a mixture of passion and disgust. He'd almost finished eating, a great pile of thick slices of dark-brown bread. The only items he'd treated himself to from the canteen counter were two half-litres of milk and a cup of coffee. It was all going down in record time.

"As Galen said: 'Slow eating is sensible eating.'"

Billy T. stopped chewing for a moment and looked at her in amazement.

"The Koran," said Hanne.

"Huh, the Koran . . ."

He went on chewing obstinately at the same speed.

Hanne hadn't had time to have breakfast that morning, nor to make herself a packed lunch. A dry open sandwich of peeled prawns on white bread lay

302

unfinished on the plate in front of her. "Not exactly suffering from overload," Billy T. had remarked with a nod at the sparse topping. The mayonnaise was stale. But the worst of her hunger was appeased. The rest could wait.

"Cocaine, on the other hand, usually comes from South America. There are entire regimes over there thriving on the fact that our society creates a need for drugs in so many people. The worldwide drugs trade is a multi-billion-dollar one. Even in this country the turnover must run into several billion kroner a year. We think. With seven thousand addicts feeding a habit that costs up to two thousand kroner a day, it amounts to quite a hefty sum. Of course we don't know exactly how much. But big money? You bet it is. If it weren't illegal, I'd have started up myself. No hesitation!"

She didn't doubt it; she was well aware of Billy's burdensome maintenance contributions. But a man of his appearance would be a rather obvious target at border crossings. He would certainly be the first one *she* would have stopped.

The canteen was beginning to fill up. It was getting on towards the lunch hour. Since a number of people were showing signs of heading in their direction, Hanne decided it was time to get back to work. Before she went, Billy T. solemnly promised to search for the missing boot.

"We're all keeping our eyes peeled," he grinned. "I've distributed a picture of the item in question to all units. The big boot hunt is on!"

He gave her an even broader grin and a Scout salute with two fingers up to his bald pate.

Hanne smiled in return. There wasn't really much of a policeman about the guy.

The room was guaranteed bug-free. Needless to say. It was right at the end of a corridor deep inside no. 16 Platou Gata on the second floor. The building looked thoroughly uninteresting and anonymous on the outside, an impression reinforced in the minds of the few who were granted access. It had been the headquarters of the Intelligence Services since 1965. It was small and cramped, but served its purpose. Discreetly enough.

The office itself wasn't very big either. It was bare, apart from a square laminated table in the centre with four tubular steel chairs along each side. There was also a telephone on the floor in one corner. The walls were unadorned and dirty yellow, adding quite an echo to the voices of the three men around the table.

"Is there even the remotest possibility of you two taking over the case?"

The man asking the question, blond and in his forties, was an employee of the Service. So was the dark-haired man in sweater and jeans. The third, older than the other two and wearing a grey flannel suit, was attached to the Police Special Branch. He was sitting with his elbows on the table, tapping his fingertips rhythmically together.

"Too late," he stated tersely. "We could perhaps have done it a month ago, before it took on such wide ramifications. Now it's definitely too late. It would arouse far too much attention."

"Is there anything that can be done at all?"

"Hardly. As long as we ourselves aren't sure of the full extent of the case, I can only recommend that you maintain contact with Peter Strup, keep an eye on our friend, and in general try to stay one step ahead of everybody else. But don't ask me how."

There was no more to be said. The chair legs made a screech of protest on the floor as the three men rose simultaneously. Before they headed towards the door, the visitor shook the hands of his two hosts as if they'd all been attending a funeral.

"This isn't good. Not good at all. I pray to God that you're wrong. Best of luck."

Ten minutes later he was back on the inaccessible top floor of police headquarters. His boss listened to him for half an hour; then gazed at his experienced colleague for over a minute without saying a word.

"What a bloody mess," he said. Vehemently.

The commissioner felt slightly aggrieved that the parliamentary under secretary wouldn't succumb. On the other hand, perhaps he was actually just using the case as a pretext for contacting her. It was a flattering notion. She looked in the mirror, and turned up her mouth in an unbecoming grimace at what she saw. Disheartening. The slimmer she got, the older she looked. Over recent months she'd been getting steadily more nervous as she approached her next period, each a little less reliable than the last. They were slightly late, unpredictable, and had diminished from a four-day flood to a two-day trickle. The pains had decreased too, and she missed them. She was horrified to notice instead the onset of hot flashes. She saw in the mirror a woman whom nature was mercilessly consigning to the status of grandmother. With a daughter of twenty-three it was far from merely theoretical. She gave an involuntary shiver at the thought. Well, she would just have to keep trying.

From her desk drawer she took out a jar of moisturiser, "Visible Difference." "Invisible difference" had been her husband's sarcastic comment one morning a few weeks ago, his mouth flexed beneath his razor. She'd given him such a vicious punch that he'd cut his upper lip.

She returned to the mirror and massaged the cream slowly into her skin. It was singularly ineffectual.

The under secretary must still be married of course. The weekly magazines hadn't given any indication to the contrary, anyway. However, she wouldn't leap to conclusions. Back in her seat she glanced again at the fax before she rang. It was signed by the minister himself, though she was requested to phone the under secretary.

His voice was deep and attractive. He was from Oslo, but had a very distinctive pronunciation of individual words, a feature that made him sound special and easily recognisable, almost musical.

He didn't suggest dinner. Not even a miserable lunch. He was curt and impersonal, and excused himself for having to trouble her. He was being nagged by the minister of justice. Would a briefing be possible? The media were starting to badger the minister. A meeting would be a useful idea. With the commissioner herself, or the appropriate departmental head. But no lunch.

Right. If the under secretary was going to be so offhand, she could be too.

"I'll send you a fax of the indictment." That was all.

"Fine," he replied, and to her disappointment didn't even exert himself to argue. "Personally I'm not bothered. But don't come to me for help when the minister himself weighs in on you. I wash my hands of it. Good-bye."

She sat in silence looking at the receiver, feeling utterly rejected. He'd get no information at all. Not one single bloody word.

WEDNESDAY 25 NOVEMBER

The sound of the bell was so unexpected that she almost fell out of bed in sheer confusion. She was still sitting up reading, even though it was getting on for two in the morning. Not because the book was so especially enthralling, but because she had slept heavily for three hours after dinner. On her bedside table, which she had made herself many years before, were a candle and a glass of red wine. The bottle next to it was almost empty. Karen Borg was half drunk.

She clambered out of bed, bumping her head on the sloping ceiling. It didn't hurt. Her mobile was recharging in the socket over by the door. She brought it back under the covers before pressing the talk button.

"Hello, Håkon," she said, even before she knew who it was. It was taking quite a risk, since it was more likely to be Nils. But her instinct hadn't failed her.

"Hello," said a meek voice at the other end. "How are you?"

"How are *you*?" she countered. "How's the appeal gone?"

So she knew about it.

"The result didn't come out today. Or rather, yesterday. There's still hope. Only a few hours to go to

308

the start of the working day, and then the decision will be announced pretty quickly. I just can't get to sleep."

It took half an hour to explain to her what had happened. He didn't spare himself with regard to his own woeful effort.

"It can't have been *that* bad," she said, not very convincingly. "After all, you won the Court over to your side in obtaining custody for the principal suspect."

"Well, for a limited period," he replied grumpily. "We'll lose tomorrow, almost certainly. What we'll do then, I haven't a clue. And I've managed to drag you into it for committing an indictable offence: breach of client confidentiality."

"Don't worry about that," she said, dismissing it lightly. "I did think about the problem in advance and aired it at some length with my wisest and most experienced colleague."

Håkon was tempted to remark that the magistrate in the case wasn't exactly inexperienced, nor was Christian Bloch-Hansen a novice in criminal law. He was much more doubtful about the competence of Greverud & Co. in this sphere, but he held his tongue. If she wasn't worried, it was better to leave it like that.

"Why didn't you get in touch before you left?" he asked suddenly and accusingly.

No reply was forthcoming. She didn't really know why — why she hadn't let him know, nor why she couldn't answer now. So she said nothing.

"What do you actually want of me?" he continued, annoyed by her silence. "I feel like a yo-yo. You make rules for what I should and shouldn't do, and I try to

309

stick by them to the best of my ability. But you don't even do so yourself! What am I to think?"

There was no simple answer. She stared at a little print above the bed, as if the solution to the conundrum might be concealed in the blue-grey landscape. But it wasn't. It was all suddenly too much. She couldn't talk to him. Instead of telling him that, she put one slender finger on the cut-off button. When she lifted it, all the accusations had gone. There was only a faint, soothing buzz from the receiver and little grunts from the dog curled up on the rug.

The telephone announced itself again in a melancholy tone. It rang more than ten times before she picked it up.

"Okay," the voice said, from far, far away, "we needn't talk about us anymore. Just let me know when you want to. Whenever you like."

His sarcasm didn't penetrate the thin protective layer of alcohol that enveloped her.

"The point is that we have to have another interview. Can you come back into town for a while?"

"No, I'd rather not. I can't. I mean . . . I just can't face it. I've got a fortnight's holiday now, and intended not to see anyone except the old man in the local shop. Please, get me out of it if you can."

The mournful sigh wasn't lost across the ether. Karen had no desire to react to that, either. She'd done more than they could expect for this dreadful case. She wanted to forget the whole thing now, forget the poor young Dutchman, forget the horribly disfigured corpse, forget drugs, murder, and all the ills of the world, and

310

just think about herself and her own life. That was more than enough. Much more than enough.

Having pondered for a moment, Håkon came up with an alternative.

"Then I'll send Hanne Wilhelmsen down to you. On Friday. Will that suit you?"

Friday wouldn't suit her at all. But neither would Thursday or Saturday. If the alternative was to go into Oslo, she'd have to accept it.

"Okay then," she agreed. "You know the way. Tell her I'll mark the turning with a Norwegian flag, so she doesn't miss it."

Indeed he did know the way. He'd been there four or five times, along with various boyfriends of Karen's. More than once he'd had to resort to earplugs at night to avoid the torture of the noises from her room, the gasps of passion and the creak of bedsprings. He'd curled himself up as patiently as a dog in the narrow bunk and rammed the wax plugs so far into his ears that he'd had trouble removing them the next morning. He'd never slept very well in Karen's parents' cottage. And he'd often breakfasted there alone.

"I'll tell her to get there about twelve, then. I hope you continue to have a good night."

It wasn't a good night, so it could hardly continue being one. But her closing words made it a little better for Håkon at least.

"Don't give up on me, Håkon," she said softly. "Good night."

FRIDAY 27 NOVEMBER

It was no use trying to get reimbursement for the trip. A hundred and forty miles in a wretched official car with no radio or heater was so unenticing that she had decided to take her own. A mileage claim would have to go through endless administrative channels and would probably end up with a negative result.

Tina Turner was singing, rather too loudly, "We don't need another hero." That was fine: she didn't feel particularly heroic. The case was at a standstill. The Court Appeals Committee had rubber-stamped the release of Roger, and reduced Lavik's time in custody to a single week. Their initial elation on hearing that the Appeals Committee were also of the opinion that there was reasonable cause to suspect Lavik of felony evaporated within a few hours. Pessimism had soon wiped the grins off their faces and dampened their spirits again. From that point of view it was wonderful to get away for a day. A hungry man is an angry man, and in the department they were all feeling starved of progress and taking it out on their colleagues. The Monday deadline loomed like a brick wall in front of them, and no one felt strong enough to surmount it. At the morning meeting, which Hanne had attended before setting off, it had only been Kaldbakken and

Håkon who had evinced any faith at all in their still having a chance. As far as Kaldbakken was concerned the feeling was probably genuine; he was not one to give up until the whistle had blown. Håkon's touch of bravado was more likely playing to the gallery, she thought. His face was lined and his eyes red from lack of sleep, and he might have lost some weight. That aspect at least was a distinct improvement.

In all there were fourteen investigators on the case now, five of them from the drugs squad. Even if they'd had a hundred, the clock would be ticking just as inexorably towards Monday, the cruelly short time the three old fogies on the Appeals Committee had foisted on them. The decision had been a harsh one. If the police couldn't come up with more than they'd mustered so far, Lavik would be a free man again. Lab reports, postmortem reports, lists of foreign trips, an old boot, unintelligible codes, analyses of Frøstrup's drugs — everything lay piled up in the incident room like scraps of a reality with a pattern they recognised but couldn't assemble in a way that would convince anyone else. A graphological analysis of Van der Kerch's fateful death threat hadn't elicited any clear answers either. They had a few notes from Lavik's office as a basis for comparison, and a piece of paper on which they had made him write the same message. He had provided the sample without protest, pale but apparently uncomprehending. The graphologist had been noncommittal. He thought there might be a few similarities here and there, but had ultimately concluded that no definite resemblance could be

313

established. At the same time he stressed that it didn't *preclude* the possibility that it was Lavik who had penned the ominous note. He might have been playing safe by disguising his handwriting. A hook at the top of the *T* and a quaint curl on the *U* could be an indication of that. But as evidence, it was of no value at all.

She left the main trunk road at Sandefjord. The little holiday town looked less than appealing in the November mist. It was so quiet it seemed to be hibernating, with only a few hardy souls in winter clothes bracing themselves against the wind and rain gusting in almost horizontally from the sea. The gale was so strong that she had to grip the steering wheel extra tight several times as the squalls buffeted the car and threatened to blow it into the ditch.

A quarter of an hour later, on a winding, vertiginous country road, she saw the little flag. It was flapping ardently in red, white, and blue as if in stubborn homage to its native land, against a tree trunk apparently impervious to its agitation. That was no doubt one way to mark a forest track, but somehow she felt it was almost a desecration of the national flag to expose it like that to the forces of nature, so she stopped off to take it with her into the warm.

She had no difficulty finding her way. There was an inviting glow from the windows, in welcoming contrast to the desolate shuttered cottages nearby.

She hardly recognised her. Karen Borg was dressed in a shabby old tracksuit which made Hanne smile when she saw it. It was blue, with white shoulder inserts that met in a vee on the chest. She'd had one very similar herself as a child; it had served as playsuit, tracksuit, and even pyjamas before it finally wore out and proved impossible to replace.

On her feet Karen had a pair of threadbare woollen slippers with holes in both heels. Her hair was uncombed and she wore no makeup. The smart, well-dressed lawyer had gone to ground, and Hanne had to stop herself scanning the room in search of her.

"Sorry about my clothes," said Karen with a smile, "but part of the freedom of being here is looking like this."

Hanne was offered coffee, but declined. A glass of fruit juice would be nice, though. They sat for half an hour just chatting, then Hanne was shown round the cottage and duly expressed her admiration of it. She herself had never had any links with a place in the country; her parents had preferred to holiday abroad. The other children in the street had been envious, but she would much rather have had a couple of months in the country with a grandmother instead. She only had one grandmother, anyway, an alcoholic failed actress who lived in Copenhagen.

Finally they sat down at the kitchen table. Hanne took out the portable typewriter from its case and prepared to take the statement. They spent four hours on it. In the first three pages Karen described her client's mental state, his relationship to his lawyer, and her own interpretation of what he would really have wished. Then followed a five-page account which was in outline the same as her first one. The papers were neatly signed in the bottom corner of each page and at the foot of the last.

It was well into the afternoon, and Hanne glanced at her watch before hesitantly accepting the offer of a meal. She was ravenous, and calculated that she would have time to eat and be back in town before eight o'clock.

The food wasn't very sophisticated: canned reindeer-meatballs in gravy with potatoes and a cucumber salad. The cucumber didn't go with it, Hanne thought to herself, but it filled her up.

Karen put on an enormous yellow raincoat and high green rubber boots to accompany Hanne to the car. They talked about the surroundings for a moment before Karen impulsively gave Hanne a hug and wished her good luck. Hanne grinned and in return wished her an enjoyable holiday.

She started the car, put on the heater and Bruce Springsteen at full blast, and bumped off down the rough track. Karen stood and waved, and Hanne could see the yellow figure getting steadily smaller in the mirror, until it disappeared out of sight as she rounded a bend. That, she thought to herself with a broad smile, that is Håkon's great love. She felt certain of it.

SATURDAY 28 NOVEMBER

"Have you heard the one about the bloke who went to the brothel without any money?"

"Yeah, yeah," the others groaned, and the joker subsided mutely into his chair and sulkily finished off his red wine. It was the fourth dirty joke he'd tried, with minimal response. His silence didn't last long. He poured himself another drink, puffed out his chest, and tried again.

"Do you know what girls say when they have a really great . . ."

"Yes, we do," the other five cried in chorus, and again the comedian was forced to shut up.

Hanne leant across the table and kissed him on the cheek.

"Can't you give these jokes a rest, Gunnar? They're really not that funny when you've heard them before."

She smiled and ruffled his hair. They'd known each other for thirteen years. He was as mild as milk, thicker than a hunk of bread, and the most considerate guy she knew. In the company of Hanne and Cecilie's other friends he could never hold his own, but he seemed to belong, his hostesses loved him, and he almost counted as part of the furniture. He was the nearest thing they had to a good, old-fashioned friend of the family. He had the apartment next to theirs, and it always looked a tip. He had no taste, didn't bother much about cleaning, and found it a lot more agreeable to luxuriate in one of his neighbours' soft armchairs than to spend an evening in his own scruffy pad. He called in at least twice a week, and was literally a self-invited guest at all their dinner parties.

Despite the tiresome Gunnar and his jokes, it had turned into a splendid evening. For the first time since the discovery of the mutilated faceless corpse by the River Aker that wet September evening, Hanne felt relaxed. It was half past eleven now, and the case had been a pale forgotten spectre for the last two hours. It might have been the alcohol that had such a benevolent effect. After nearly two months of total abstinence five glasses of red wine was enough to make her pleasantly light-headed and seductively charming. Cecilie's persistent leg contact under the table had tempted her to try to break up the party, but she hadn't succeeded. Anyway, she was enjoying herself. Then the telephone rang.

"It's for you, Hanne," Cecilie called from the corridor.

Hanne tripped over her own feet as she got up from the table, giggled, and went to see who was daring to call at nearly midnight on a Saturday night. She closed the living-room door behind her and was sober enough to recognise the dejected expression on her partner's face. Cecilie put her left hand over the mouthpiece.

"It's work. I'll be bloody mad if you go out now."

With a look of anticipatory reproach she passed Hanne the phone.

"Would you believe we've caught the bugger, Hanne?!"

It was Billy T. She rubbed the bridge of her nose in an attempt to clear her head, but without discernible effect.

"What bugger? Who've you caught?"

"The boot man, of course! Bull's-eye! Shit scared, plain as a pikestaff. That's how it looks to us."

It couldn't be true. It was difficult to believe. The case hadn't just gone down the pan, it was flushed away and into the sewers. And now this. The breakthrough perhaps. A living person, actually involved, and under arrest. Someone who could give them some real information. Someone they could grab by the balls. Someone who could bring Lavik down into the same sludge the police had been wallowing in. An informant. Exactly what they needed.

She shook her head and asked if he could come and fetch her. Driving herself was out of the question.

"I'll be there in five minutes."

"Make it a quarter of an hour. I'll have to have a quick shower first."

Fourteen minutes later she kissed her friends good-bye and asked them to keep the party going until she got back. Cecilie went with her to the door, and was offered a parting hug, but drew back.

"I sometimes hate this job of yours," she said in a serious voice. "Not often, but sometimes."

"Who was it who sat all alone night after night in that godforsaken place in Nordfjord when you were on duty? Who had limitless patience for four years with your evening and night duties at Ullevål Hospital?"

"You," said Cecilie reluctantly, but with a conciliatory smile. And she let herself be hugged after all.

"He's as unblemished as a newborn babe. Not even a bloody traffic offence."

He was drumming his grubby fingers on the sheet of paper, which could have been the criminal record of the prime minister. Absolutely blank.

"And now," said Billy T., a grin spreading over his face, "with this clean sheet, let's see how convincing a story he can damn well come up with to explain why he brandishes a gun at the police on the street and why he's sitting there quivering like a piece of wet cod."

Good point. A lot could be gleaned from reactions on arrest. The innocent were frightened of course, but it was always a controllable fear, an emotion that could be held in check by reminding themselves that since it was all a misunderstanding it would soon be cleared up. It never took more than a quarter of an hour to calm the innocent. According to Billy T. this miscreant was still scared to death even after two hours.

There was no sense in starting an interrogation that night. She herself wasn't sober, and the wait would do the suspect no harm. He'd been charged with threatening the police, which was quite enough to hold him till Monday.

"How did you find him?"

"It wasn't me, it was Leif and Ole. Talk about luck. You wouldn't believe it."

"Try me!"

"There's this bloke we've had under surveillance for some time. Never got anything on him. He's a medical student, very well behaved. Lives a nice and respectable life in Røa, in nice respectable low-rise housing. Drives a car that's a bit too nice and respectable, and surrounds himself with anything but respectable ladies. But nice. The surveillance team were pretty sure he had an interesting little consignment in his apartment, so our boys decided to take a look. Jackpot. They found four grams, plus a decent bit of hash. Ole realised he'd be home later than he'd told his wife, because a full search of the apartment would take men and time. The guy had no phone, amazingly enough, so Ole went to the next-door neighbour, a chap of about thirty. Born 1961, to be precise."

His fingers were drumming again on the printout from the police database.

"Well, it may be disconcerting to have the police ringing your doorbell at half past nine on a Saturday evening, but not so devastating that you're paralysed with terror and slam the door in the officer's face."

Hanne thought privately it wasn't in the least surprising that someone should slam the door in Ole Andresen's face. He had hair down to his waist, which he boasted he washed once a fortnight, "even if it wasn't dirty." It was parted in the middle, like an ageing hippie, and between the curtains of hair projected an unbelievably large and pimply nose above a beard which would have been the envy of Karl Marx. Not unreasonable to be afraid, she thought, but maintained a diplomatic silence.

"It was the stupidest thing he could have done. Ole rang the bell a second time, and the poor bloke had to open up. It was a pity he gained a few minutes to himself in the flat, but the amazing thing was that when he eventually opened the door . . ."

Billy T. was roaring with laughter, becoming increasingly hysterical, until Hanne began to chuckle herself, even without yet being able to share the joke. Billy T. pulled himself together.

"When he eventually opened up, he had his hands in the air!"

He collapsed with laughter again. This time Hanne joined in.

"He had his hands in the air, like in a film, and before Ole could say anything at all — he'd only held up his police ID — the guy was standing with his feet apart and his hands against the wall. Ole had no idea what was going on, but has been in the business long enough to realise it was something suspicious. And there in the shoe rack was the missing boot. Ole pulled out my stencil and compared it. It was a direct hit. The guy just stood against the wall with his palms glued to the wallpaper."

They both choked with mirth till the tears ran.

"And Ole simply wanted to use the telephone!"

Perhaps it wasn't as funny as all that, but it was the middle of the night, and they were relieved. Bloody relieved.

322

"Here's what they found in his flat," said Billy, bending his ungainly body to pick up a bag at his feet.

A small-calibre pistol fell onto the table, followed by a well-worn boot, size ten.

"Well, it's not really enough to reduce him to such a complete state of the jitters," said Hanne with satisfaction. "He must have something else for us."

"Give him a Hanne Wilhelmsen special. In the morning. Let's get you back home now so you can carry on enjoying yourself."

Which was exactly what she did.

SUNDAY 29 NOVEMBER

"You're shaking like a piece of wet cod — a jelly, a leaf, whatever — you're shaking so damned much that unless you can cough up a doctor's certificate to say you've got an advanced stage of Parkinson's, I'll have to assume you're pissing yourself in fear."

She shouldn't have said that. A pool had appeared soundlessly beneath his chair, slowly increasing in size till it reached all four legs. She sighed aloud, opened the window, and decided to let him sit in wet trousers for a while. He was crying now too. A pitiful wretched weeping that didn't elicit any kind of sympathy, but actually irritated her enormously.

"Cut out the snivelling. I'm not going to kill you."

The assurance didn't help; he went on whimpering, tearlessly and infuriatingly, like a fretful, defiant toddler.

"I've got extensive powers," she lied, "very extensive powers. You're in deep trouble. Things will be a lot easier for you if we get some cooperation. A bit of give and take. Some information. Just tell me what your connection is with Jørgen Lavik, the lawyer."

It was the twelfth time she'd asked. She got no response this time either. Beginning to feel a sense of defeat, she handed over to Kaldbakken, who up till then had been sitting silently in a corner. Perhaps he'd get something out of the guy. Though she didn't really think so.

Håkon was depressed when she reported to him, as might be expected. It seemed as if the man from Røa would prefer the tortures of hell to reprisals from Lavik and his organisation. If so, the police hadn't made the breakthrough that Hanne and Billy T. had so exultantly assumed the previous night. But the battle wasn't yet lost.

Five hours later it was. Kaldbakken put his foot down. He left the whining suspect to his own devices and took Hanne out into the corridor.

"We can't go on with this any longer," he said in a whisper, one hand on the doorknob as if to make sure no one would steal it. "He's dog-tired. We ought to let him rest. And we ought to get a doctor to take a look at him: that trembling can't be normal. We'll try again in the morning."

"Tomorrow may be too late!"

Hanne was getting absolutely desperate. But it was no good: Kaldbakken had made up his mind and was not to be persuaded otherwise.

It was Hanne who had to convey the bad news to Håkon. He received it without a word. Hanne sat there momentarily undecided, but then thought it best to leave him alone.

"By the way, I've put Karen Borg's statement in your case file," she said before she went. "I didn't have time to make copies Friday evening. Can you do it before you go? I'm off. It's Advent Sunday."

This last was meant as an excuse, rather unnecessarily. He waved her out of the room. When the door closed behind her, he laid his head in his arms on the desk.

He was worn out. He was ready to go home.

The annoying thing was that he forgot to take a copy of the statement. He thought of it when he was halfway home in the car. Ah well, it could wait till the morning.

Although he was nearing pension age, he moved with the litheness of an athlete. It was four o'clock in the early hours of Monday morning, the time when ninety-five percent of the population are asleep. A huge, newly lit Christmas tree was blinking its illuminations to keep itself awake down in the entrance hall. There was also a pale blue light shining through the glass walls of the night duty room. Otherwise everywhere was in darkness. His rubber soles made no sound as he moved swiftly along the corridor. He clutched his impressive bunch of keys very tightly to prevent them jingling. When he reached the office with Håkon Sand's nameplate on, he found the correct key almost immediately. Closing the door behind him, he drew out a heavy rubber torch. It had an extremely powerful beam, which momentarily dazzled him.

It was almost too easy. The file was right in front of him on the desk, and the statement he was seeking was on the very top. He hastily flicked through the rest of the file, but there appeared to be no further copies of it.

Not in this file, at least. He ran the beam of the torch up and down the sheet. This was the original! He folded it hurriedly and stuffed it into the deep inner pocket of his capacious tweed jacket. He glanced round to make sure that everything looked as it had when he'd come in, went to the door, switched off his torch, and slipped out into the corridor, locking up behind him. Further along the corridor he opened another door, again with a key. On this desk too the case file was out, open in two untidy piles, as if it had outgrown its strength and fallen into an exhausted slumber. It took longer to check through this one. The statement wasn't where it should have been according to the arrangement of the file. He carried on searching, but when he couldn't find the eight-page document anywhere, he began a systematic inspection of the rest of the room.

He gave up after a quarter of an hour. There wasn't a copy. This was a cheering assumption, and not without logic. According to reports, Hanne Wilhelmsen hadn't got back to the office until about half past seven on Friday. She might not have felt much like waiting the twenty minutes or so it took for a copier to warm up.

His theory was reinforced when he'd searched the third and final office, Kaldbakken's little den. If neither Wilhelmsen nor the chief inspector had copies, there was every likelihood that the document only existed in the original. Which was now in his possession.

A few minutes later it existed no more. First it had passed through a shredder until it resembled a desiccated and malformed tangle of spaghetti, and then it lay in a dish for just as long as was needed for the flames to destroy it completely. Finally the remains were collected up in a sheet of toilet paper and flushed down the lavatory, which was at the far end of the corridor on the most invisible floor of the police headquarters building. Using an old lavatory brush, the man from the Special Branch removed the final particles of ash from the WC, and with that Hanne Wilhelmsen's rainy trip to the county of Vestfold was totally wasted.

Back in his office the man picked up a mobile phone and rang the number of one of the men he'd met in Platou Gata a few days previously.

"I've done as much as I'm prepared to do," he said in a low voice, as if out of respect for the somnolent building. "Karen Borg's statement has been removed from the file. It's bloody awful doing things like this to colleagues. You'll have to look after yourselves from now on."

He terminated the call without waiting for a reply. Instead he went to the window and stood staring out over Oslo. The city lay heavy and tired beneath him, like a drowsy whale glistening with the phosphorescence of the sea. He felt old and tired himself. Older than for many years. After a while his eyes began to feel gritty, and he had to screw them up to steady the dancing specks of light far, far below. He sighed and lay down on a small and very uncomfortable sofa to await the start of the working day. Before he fell asleep the full import struck him again of what he had done to his colleagues.

MONDAY 30 NOVEMBER

"It's not surprising this gang has managed to keep it all going so long. They have a hold over their people that I've never seen the like of. Not in the drugs world. Very strange. Is he still not coming clean?"

Kaldbakken was genuinely amazed. He'd done six years in the drugs squad and knew what he was talking about.

"Well, we can't exactly throw the book at him," said Hanne Wilhelmsen miserably. "Threats against public servants, even the police, don't qualify for more than a brief vacation in a pleasant little cell. From that point of view he has a lot to gain by keeping his mouth shut. He may appear to be scared out of his wits, but he's still got enough left to keep a cool head. He's even clever enough to admit he was the one who aimed a gun at Billy T. We'll have to let him go today; we've got no reason to detain him. No risk of losing evidence if he's admitted it."

Of course they could keep him under observation for a few days. But for how long? Twenty-four-hour surveillance of Roger from Sagene was already taking up a large part of their capacity. If Lavik were released today, they'd really have a problem with resources. It could be solved in the short term, but these guys were hardly going to do anything stupid in the next few days or weeks. It would probably be months before they resumed any interesting activities. The police would miss it, not willingly, but because budgets wouldn't allow such extravagance. Not even for a case with these ramifications. It was a raw deal. As usual.

Håkon hadn't said anything. Apathy had set in. He was anxious, fed up, and deeply disappointed. His grey temples had gone greyer, his acid stomach more acidic, his clammy hands clammier. Now all he had was Karen's statement. It was doubtful whether it would be enough. He got up dispiritedly and left the meeting without a word. An oppressive silence followed his departure.

The statement wasn't where he'd put it. He tried a couple of drawers absentmindedly. Could he have tucked it away somewhere? No, all he found were a few insignificant items he'd hidden out of sight of his guilty conscience. Now was not the time to confront previous procrastination.

The statement wasn't in his office at all. Odd — he was convinced he'd placed it right there, on top of the big pile. With a deeply furrowed brow he cast his mind back to the previous day. He'd been going to make copies; then he'd forgotten to. Or had he gone to the copying room? He went to check now.

The machine was running at full tilt, and a stocky woman in her sixties confirmed that there'd been nothing there when she arrived. To make absolutely certain they looked behind the machine and underneath it, but there was no sign of the statement anywhere.

Hanne hadn't taken it. Kaldbakken had already asked for a copy, and shrugged his shoulders dolefully, swearing he'd never seen it.

Håkon was getting seriously worried now. The document was the only hope they had of obtaining an extension of custody. Before going home the night before he'd scanned it as well as his red-rimmed eyes would allow. It was exactly what he'd wanted. Thorough and incisive. Convincing and well expressed. But what the hell had happened to it?

The time had come to raise the alarm. It was half past nine, and the application for an extension had to be ready to take to the Court by noon. The hearing should actually have been held at half past eight in the morning, but on Friday Christian Bloch-Hansen had asked for a few hours' postponement, which had suited the police admirably. He had a trial to attend in the morning, and would if necessary send an assistant to the important custody hearing. There were two and a half hours to go, which actually gave Håkon just about long enough to get the custody application dictated and typed, with no time to embark on a general search. But no statement, no custody order.

They abandoned the effort at about half past ten. The statement had totally disappeared. Hanne was upset, and took all the blame on herself; she should have done the copies straightaway. Her unreserved declaration of responsibility didn't really help Håkon at all. Everyone knew that he was the last to have had the papers.

Karen could come and repeat the statement. He could get a postponement of an hour, which would just about enable her to make it back from the cottage. She would *have* to make it.

But she didn't answer the phone. Håkon rang five times. In vain. Hell. Panic was setting in, clawing its way up his spine. It was an extremely unpleasant sensation. He shook his head violently as if that would somehow help.

"Ring Sandefjord or Larvik. Get them to fetch her. Immediately."

The commanding tone couldn't conceal his anxiety, though it hardly mattered — Hanne was equally fearful. Having spoken to the police at Larvik, under the mistaken impression that they were the nearest, she hurried back to Håkon's office. He was morose and unapproachable, and busy trying to construct something which might give an appearance of solidity. It wasn't easy with the third-rate and imperfect material they had.

That bloody boot man. Håkon was tempted to run down to the cells and offer him a hundred thousand to blab. If that didn't work, he could beat him up. Or maybe kill him. In pure and simple rage. On the other hand, both Frøstrup and Van der Kerch had bought their own tickets to the other side, so who knew, perhaps the police would soon have another suicide on their hands. God forbid. Anyway, they'd have to let him go in the course of the day. They'd wait as long as they could.

An hour later there was nothing more to be done. The secretary took twelve minutes to type what he'd dictated. He read it through with a despondency that increased with every line. She gave him a sympathetic look, but said nothing. Which was probably best.

"Karen isn't in the cottage."

Hanne stood at the door.

"Her car is there, and there's a light in the kitchen, but no sign of the dog, nor anybody. She must be out for a walk."

Out for a walk. His beloved Karen, the only straw he had left to clutch at. The woman who could rescue him from total humiliation, save the police from scandalous headlines, save the country from a drugs baron and murderer. She was out for a walk. Right now she was probably strolling along the shore at Ula, throwing sticks for the dog and breathing in the fresh sea air many miles and a hundred light-years away from a stuffy claustrophobic office at police headquarters with walls that had started to sway, constricting themselves and threatening to suffocate him. He could see her in his mind's eye, in her old yellow raincoat, with wet hair and no makeup, the way she always looked on rainy days at the cottage. Out walking. Out for a bloody walk in the pissing rain.

"They can take a walk too, the local police! The bloody area isn't that big!"

It was unfair to take it out on Hanne, and he regretted it instantly. He tried to moderate his outburst with a weak smile and a helpless movement of his head.

Hanne replied soothingly that she'd already asked them to do that. There was still time, and thus still hope. A swift glance at the clock prompted her to ask whether he'd given notice of the delay.

"I asked for a postponement till three o'clock; I got till two. There's an hour to go. I'll get longer if I can promise that she's coming. If not, the hearing will start at two."

Far, far away a yellow figure was walking along by the ravenously snatching winter sea and feeding it with stones. The boxer flung itself again and again into the rough waves, quivering with cold as only dogs do and yet not giving up, impelled by its canine instincts to pursue every object that was thrown. It had never had a chill, but it was shivering violently now. Karen Borg stopped and took an old jumper out of her rucksack and put it on the dog to keep it warm. It looked ridiculous with pink mohair wrapped round its front legs and flopping under its thin belly, but at least it ceased its trembling.

She had come to the end of the headland, and was hunting about for the nice sheltered spot where she so often sought refuge on days like this but always had difficulty locating again. There it was. She sat down on an insulated groundsheet she'd brought with her and took out a thermos flask. The hot chocolate had a distinct flavour of many years of ingrained coffee, but it didn't matter. She sat there for a long time, deep in thought, her ears filled with the noise of the sea and the wind whistling round the big rock. The dog lay at her

334

feet looking like a pink poodle. For some reason she felt troubled. She was desperate to find peace out here, but it remained unattainable. That was unusual; it had always come willingly to meet her here before. Perhaps it had found someone else and deserted her.

The police didn't find her. She didn't get to Oslo that day. She didn't even know she was wanted there.

It was doomed to fail. Without the slightest shred of new evidence, there was nothing more to put forward. This time Christian Bloch-Hansen took twenty minutes to persuade the Court that continued custody was a clearly unjustifiable and disproportionate measure. Mr. Lavik's legal practice was obviously suffering significantly from his detention. He was losing thirty thousand kroner a week. Nor was it just himself who was adversely affected: he had two employees whose very jobs were threatened by his absence. His professional and social standing made the present circumstances even more stressful, and the overwhelming media attention had not exactly improved the situation. In the unlikely event of the Court's continuing to believe there were reasonable grounds for suspicion of criminal behaviour, it should take into consideration the extreme burden posed in this instance by remand in custody. The police ought to have been able to produce more substantial evidence in a week, but they hadn't. Lavik must be released before irrevocable damage was done to his reputation. His health was also at risk: the Court could see for itself the condition he was in.

The Court could indeed. He'd looked a sorry sight last time, and there was no sign of any recovery yet. You didn't need to be a doctor to see that he was in a bad way. His clothes had drooped in unison with their owner, and the previously elegant young lawyer now looked like a tramp dragged in off the street after a grim Christmas lunch at a soup kitchen.

The Court was unanimous. The decision was dictated then and there. Håkon's profound depression was lifted somewhat when the judge reiterated that there was still reasonable cause for suspicion. But his heart sank again when he heard him express his condemnation of the police in fairly unequivocal terms for their failure to follow matters up, referring in particular to the lamentable lack of clarification of Karen Borg's statement.

The danger of destruction of evidence was also obvious, but unfortunately it was equally apparent to the magistrate that custody would indeed be a disproportionate measure given all the circumstances. The defendant was to be released, but would have to report to the police every Friday.

Report to the police! A lot of help that would be. Håkon appealed against the decision on the spot and asked for a stay of execution. That would at least give them one more day. A day was a day. Even if Rome wasn't built in such a short period, there were many other things that had come to fruition on the basis of a few extra stolen hours.

Håkon could hardly believe his ears when the judge stated that he could not grant that request either. He tried to protest, but met with a sharp rebuttal. The police had had their opportunity, which they had singularly failed to take advantage of. Now they would have to manage without the Court's help. Håkon responded aggressively that there was no point in appealing at all, and tore up the application in anger. The judge pretended not to notice, and brought the hearing to a close with a sardonic observation:

"With luck you might escape a claim for damages. If so, you can count yourselves extremely fortunate."

Jørgen Ulf Lavik was released that same evening. He immediately seemed to straighten up and fill his suit, growing several centimetres and putting on some of his lost kilos. As he left police headquarters he laughed — for the first time in ten days.

Which is more than Hanne Wilhelmsen or Håkon Sand did. Or anyone else in the great curved building on Grønlandsleiret, for that matter.

It had gone well. It really had gone well. The nightmare was over. They hadn't found anything. If they had, he'd still have been inside. But what was there to find? As fate would have it, only two days before his arrest he'd removed the key from beneath the filing cabinet and found a safer place for it. Perhaps the old man was right and the angels were on their side. Only the gods themselves could know why.

But there was one thing he didn't entirely understand. When he'd selected Christian Bloch-Hansen as his lawyer, it was because he was the best.

The guilty need the best; the innocent can get by with anybody. Bloch-Hansen had come up to expectations, and that was fine. He himself would hardly have thought of the breach of confidentiality angle in respect of Karen Borg. He'd done a splendid job as defence counsel, and had been perfectly correct and polite to him. But with no warmth or empathy or kindness. He had seemed indifferent, doing his job, doing it efficiently, but there had been something in his penetrating eyes that looked like a glint of animosity, even contempt. Did he believe him to be guilty? Was he refusing to believe in his convincing story, so convincing that he'd almost begun to believe it himself?

Lavik dismissed the thought. It wasn't important anymore. He was a free man, and had no doubt now that the case against him would soon be dropped. He would ask Bloch-Hansen to make sure it was. A real blunder, that thousand-kroner note, but as far as he knew it was the only mistake he'd ever made. Never, never would he put himself in that position again. There was just one task left, but he'd had plenty of time to plan it. Several days. But it still needed some fine-tuning, and it had come as a real gift when Håkon Sand had attributed the lack of further elucidation of Karen Borg's witness statement to her absence on holiday. The magistrate had been exasperated by the fact that the police had had problems contacting somebody in the next county, as if it were the other side of the world. Of course it wasn't. He knew exactly where it was. Nine years ago they'd organised a trip for the student representatives on the faculty committee, of

338

all political persuasions. He'd had a feeling at the time that the woman might have been a little in love with him, though the political gulf between them would have made any greater familiarity impossible. But there was talk of restrictions on student numbers, and they'd all set aside their political differences to make common cause against the planned admission reductions. Karen had offered to host the historic meeting. It had been more wine than politics, but as far as he remembered it had been an enjoyable weekend.

He would have to act fast, and it would be problematical getting rid of the troublesome mosquitoes he knew would be buzzing around him for a long time to come. But he'd manage it. He had to. If he could dispose of Karen Borg, they'd never get him. She was the last hurdle between himself and ultimate freedom.

The dark-blue Volvo came to a halt in front of the garage, skidding slightly on the slippery drive but finding its way home like an old horse returning to its stable after a hard day's work. Lavik bent over his pale wife behind the steering wheel, kissed her tenderly, and thanked her for her support.

"Everything will be fine now, darling," he said.

It didn't entirely seem as if she believed it.

Should he phone, or not? Should he go down there, or should he leave her alone? He wandered restlessly round his small apartment, which had the air of having for some time been a place he just passed through to get clean clothes and some sleep. Now there weren't any clean clothes, and he couldn't find sleep anywhere either.

Giddiness overcame him and he had to clutch at the bookcase to keep his balance. Luckily there was a dusty bottle of red wine at the back of the kitchen cupboard. Half an hour later it was empty.

The case was lost. Karen too, probably. There was no point in getting in touch with her. It was all over.

He felt dreadful, and broached a half-bottle of aquavit that had been in the fridge since the previous Christmas. The alcohol finally had the desired effect: he fell asleep. An evil and malicious sleep, with nightmares of being pursued by devilish gigantic lawyers, and a tiny little yellow figure calling to him from a cloud on the horizon. He tried to run towards her, but his legs were like lead and he got no closer. In the end she disappeared altogether: the yellow figure flew off, leaving him lying on the ground, a tiny little police attorney surrounded by cloaked vultures pecking out his eyes.

TUESDAY 1 DECEMBER

At last there was some kind of sense to all the fuss and glitter and gaudy plastic lights that were intended to transform the streets for Christmas — they were into December. The snow had returned, and the business community had eagerly taken note of the fact that the personal consumption of the people of Norway had increased a few percent during the course of the year. It raised expectations and inspired resplendent shop-window decorations. The lime trees on Karl Johans Gata, naked and self-conscious in their Christmas lights, stood in for their coniferous cousins. The solemn illumination ceremony for the massive spruce outside the university had taken place the day before yesterday. Today there was only a shabby Salvation Army officer enjoying the sight as he stood stamping his feet and smiling hopefully at the morning commuters hurrying past his collecting box without even a few seconds to spare for the tree in all its glory.

Jørgen Lavik knew he was being shadowed. Several times he stopped abruptly and looked back. It was impossible to work out who was following him. Everybody had the same blank gaze; only one or two gave him an extra inquisitive glance, as if they half recognised him and wondered where they'd seen him before. It was fortunate that the photographs in the press had been so out-of-date and of such poor quality that hardly anyone would have recognised him.

But he knew they were after him, which made things difficult, though at the same time it gave him a permanent alibi. He could turn the situation to his own advantage. He took several deep breaths and felt his mind clearing.

His visit to the office was brief. The receptionist nearly dislodged her dentures in her rapture at seeing him, and gave him a hug that smelt of lavender and old age. It was almost touching. After a couple of hours on the more urgent matters, he told her he was going to spend the remainder of the week at his cottage. He would be available by telephone, and took a number of case files, his computer, and a portable fax machine with him. He might drop in on Friday, since he had to report to the police then.

"So you can hold the fort, Caroline, as you have so ably over the last few days," he said in a complimentary tone.

Her mouth formed itself into a pallid smile again and her delight at the praise brought roses to her cheeks. She bobbed at the knees flirtatiously, but refrained from turning it into a curtsy. Of course she would hold the fort, and he should have a good holiday. He deserved it!

He thought so too. But before he left he went into the toilet to use the mobile phone he'd grabbed from his colleague's pigeonhole. He knew the number by heart.

"I'm out. You can relax."

His whisper was scarcely audible against the embarrassing gurgle from the defective cistern.

"Don't ring me, and especially not now," the other man hissed, but without hanging up.

"It's perfectly safe. You can relax," he repeated, to no avail.

"It's easy to say that!"

"Karen Borg is in her cottage at Ula. She won't be there long. You'll be quite safe. Only she can bring me down, and only I can bring you down. If I'm all right, you're all right."

He didn't hear the older man's protests; he had already hung up. Jørgen Ulf Lavik had a pee, washed his hands, and went back to his invisible stalkers.

He would soon have to have something done about his heart. The medication he'd been taking didn't work anymore. Not very effectively, anyway. He'd twice felt the hand of death, like the frightening and near-fatal blow that had prostrated him less than three years ago. Systematic exercise and a fat-free diet had certainly helped up to now, but his condition over the last few weeks couldn't be remedied by jogging or carrots.

They were onto him. In a way he'd been expecting it, ever since the snowball began to roll. It could only be a question of time. Even though the description in the *Dagbladet* of the presumed ringleader had been rather general, and could have fitted several hundred people, it was a bit too exact for the guys in Platou Gata. He'd been walking home from work one afternoon and suddenly they were standing there, as anonymous as the job they were doing, two identical men, the same height, the same clothes. They'd forced him into the car in a friendly, but very firm, manner. The drive lasted half an hour, and ended in front of his own house. He had denied everything. They hadn't believed him. But they knew that he knew that it was in the interests of all of them that he should be in the clear. Which put his mind at rest to some extent. If it came out how the money was actually spent, they'd all be finished. Admittedly he was the only one who knew where it came from, but the others had accepted it — and used it. Without ever asking, without ever checking, without ever investigating anything. Which made their position extremely delicate.

The real headache was Lavik. Had he gone out of his mind? It was pretty obvious he intended to kill Karen Borg. As if that would solve anything! He would be the prime suspect. Immediately. Besides, who knew whether she'd told others, or written something down that hadn't yet found its way into the hands of the police? Killing Karen Borg would solve nothing.

Killing Jørgen Lavik, on the other hand, would solve most things. The moment the thought was formed, it seemed his only recourse. The successful murder of Hans Olsen had effectively halted all problems in that branch of the syndicate. Lavik had just made matters worse and worse for both of them. He had to be stopped.

The idea didn't frighten him. On the contrary, it had a calming effect. His pulse was beating steadily and evenly again, for the first time in days. His brain felt alert and he could feel his concentration improving.

The best thing would be to eliminate him before he had time to send Karen Borg to whatever heaven was reserved for lawyers. The murder of a young and beautiful, and in this respect innocent, female lawyer would have far too many repercussions. A desperate male lawyer on drugs charges wouldn't die without causing a few ripples either, but still . . . One murder was better than two. But how to go about it?

Jørgen Lavik had talked about Ula. A cottage. That must mean he was thinking of going there. How he would evade the plainclothesmen who doubtless had him under constant observation, he had no idea. But that was Lavik's problem. His own was to find Lavik, find him without being seen by those same officers, and preferably before he got to Karen Borg. He didn't need an alibi: he wasn't in the police spotlight, nor would he be. If all went well.

It would take him less than an hour to find the precise address of Karen Borg's cottage. He could ring her office, or perhaps the local council; they could check in the land register. But that was too risky. A few minutes later he'd made up his mind. As far as he could recall, there was only one way down to Ula, a little track off the coast road between Sandefjord and Larvik. He would simply lie in wait there.

Relieved at having come to a decision, he immersed himself in the day's most pressing tasks. His hands were steady and his heart was beating regularly again. Perhaps he didn't need any new medication after all.

It was a bit more than a summer cottage — a substantial red-painted old wooden house from the thirties, completely renovated, and even in the gloom of December you could appreciate the idyllic character of the location. It was quite well protected against the elements, and though there was some snow on the approach to it, the rocky ground behind was scoured clean by the incessant wind off the sea. A fir tree swayed obstinately just a few metres from the west wall. The wind had managed to bend the trunk but not to kill the tree. It stood leaning away from the shore, as if it were longing to join its family further inland but couldn't tear itself loose. You could make out the contours of summer flowerbeds between the humps of snow on the lee side of the house. It was all neatly tended. It didn't belong to Lavik, but to his senile and childless uncle. Jørgen had been his favourite nephew when last his uncle had been able to feel anything of that nature. He had turned up faithfully every summer when he was a boy, and they had gone fishing together, caulked boats, and eaten fried bacon and beans. Jørgen was the son he'd never had, and he would inherit the beautiful summer cottage when Alzheimer's eventually, and probably in the not-so-distant future, met its only match — death.

Jørgen Lavik had spent quite a lot of money on the place. His uncle wasn't a poor man, and had paid for the essential maintenance himself. But it was Jørgen who'd installed a bathroom with a Jacuzzi, and a mini-sauna and a telephone. He'd also given his uncle a nippy little boat as a seventieth birthday present, in the certain knowledge that it would effectively remain his own.

On the journey down to the far end of the Hurum peninsula, he'd not once caught sight of his pursuers. There had been cars behind him all the way, but none of them had tailed him long enough to be likely candidates. Nevertheless, he knew they must be there, and was pleased about it. He didn't hurry himself parking the car, and demonstrated his intention of staying for a significant period by carrying in his luggage in several instalments. He wandered from room to room gradually switching on all the lights, and lit the paraffin stove in the living room to supplement the electric heater.

In the afternoon he went for a short walk. He strolled over the familiar terrain, but even now couldn't see or hear anything suspicious. He felt uneasy. Weren't they here? Had they abandoned him? They couldn't do that! His heart was thumping fast and nervously. No, they must be somewhere nearby. They had to be. He forced himself to be calm. Perhaps they were just very skilful. That was probably it.

There were a few things to fix. He must start without delay. He took his time on the doorstep, stretching himself and knocking the snow off his trousers at unnecessary length. Then he went in to make his preparations.

The worst of it was that everyone was so cheering. He was slapped on the back with a cry of "Nothing ventured, nothing gained," and given congratulatory smiles and other friendly expressions of support. Even the commissioner had taken the trouble to phone down to him to convey her satisfaction with what he'd achieved, despite the unfortunate outcome. Håkon mentioned the possibility of a claim for damages to her, but she just snorted. She didn't believe for a moment that Lavik would dare; after all, he was guilty. He was probably just happy to be free again and anxious to put the whole affair as far behind him as he could. Håkon could rest assured about that; in fact the officers tailing Lavik had reported that he was now out at a cottage on the Hurum peninsula.

The support didn't do much to boost his morale. He felt as if he'd been put into an automatic washing machine, subjected to the centrifugal force of a complete washing cycle, and shrunk. There were other cases lying on his desk with imminent deadlines, but he was totally incapable of action and decided to let everything wait till the next morning.

Only Hanne recognised how he actually felt. She came by in the afternoon with two cups of hot tea. He coughed and spluttered when he tasted the contents, having assumed it was coffee.

"What shall we do now, Mr. Prosecutor?" she asked, putting her feet up on the desk. Nice legs, he thought, not for the first time.

"Don't ask me."

He sipped the tea again, a little more cautiously this time. Actually it wasn't bad.

"We won't give up, anyway. We'll nail him. He hasn't won the battle yet, just a little skirmish."

348

It was incomprehensible that she could be so positive. It almost sounded as if she meant what she said. Of course, it might just be the difference between an active police officer and an official of the Prosecution Service. There were many avenues of retreat for him; he could find another job at any time. Assistant secretary in the Department of Fisheries, for instance, he thought glumly. Hanne, on the other hand, was trained as a police officer. There was only one possible employer for her: the police force. So she could never give up.

"Now you listen to me," she said, putting her feet back down on the floor. "We've got a lot more to go on! You can't lose your fighting spirit now! It's in adversity we have the chance to show what we're made of."

Banal. But probably true. In that case he was a wimp. He definitely couldn't tackle it. He was going home. Perhaps he might be man enough to cope with a few household chores . . .

"Phone me at home if there are any developments," he said, leaving his stoical colleague and most of his cup of tea.

"You win some, you lose some," he heard her call out after him as he trudged off down the corridor.

The plainclothesmen following him, six in total, had realised that it would be a long evening and a cold night. One of them, a narrow-shouldered clever chap with sharp eyes, had checked round the back of the house. About three metres from the wall facing the sea the ground sloped down abruptly to a small cove with a

349

sandy beach. It was only fifteen to twenty metres across, and bordered at each end by a barbed-wire fence with supports fixed into the bare rock. Private ownership of land was never so jealously guarded as at the seashore, the policeman thought, grinning to himself. On both sides of the wire there was a steep rock face five or six metres high. It would be possible to climb it, but only with difficulty. In any case Lavik would still have to come round onto the road by the house. The point was completely cut off by the road, which therefore had to be crossed in order to leave the area.

One man was stationed at either end of this stretch of road and one in the middle, and since it was only about a couple hundred metres, they had visual coverage of the entire length. Lavik couldn't get past without being seen. The other three took up positions around the cottage.

Lavik was sitting inside amused at the thought that the men outside, however many there were, must be freezing their arses off. He was warm and comfortable and hyped up with excitement as he embarked on his plan. He had an old-fashioned alarm clock in front of him, with no glass over the hands. With a bit of fiddling he managed to attach a wooden peg to the small hand. He plugged in the fax machine, put a sheet of paper in the feed, and tried it out. He set the hand just before three, placed the extended hand over the start button of the machine, keyed in his own office number, and sat watching it. A quarter of an hour passed, and nothing happened. He waited a few more minutes and began to worry that the whole scheme would have to be aborted. But then, just as the little hand made its tiny movement to the three, everything functioned perfectly. The peg on the end of the hand just brushed the electronic start button, but it was sufficient. The fax machine obeyed, sucked in the sheet of paper, and transmitted the message.

Encouraged by this success, he went quickly through the house plugging in the time switches he'd brought from home. He used them to economise on electricity, turning the electric radiators off at midnight and on again at six, so that the house was warm when they got up. It was soon done — he was accustomed to setting them. But the difficult part was still to come. He had to create movement while he was away: lights going on and off wouldn't be enough. He'd thought it all out beforehand, but hadn't put the idea to the test. It was hard to tell how it would go in practice. Hidden from view by the drawn curtains, he arranged three thin cords across the living room, tying one end of each to the kitchen door handle, and the other ends to different points on the opposite side of the room. Then he attached a kitchen towel to the first, an old pair of swimming trunks to the second, and a napkin to the third. It took a while to set up the candles in the right place: each one had to be up against its string, close enough for the string to catch alight when the flame burnt down to the same level. He broke off the candles to unequal lengths and fixed them in a base of molten wax, standing them on saucers. The candle by the string with the napkin on was the shortest, only a fraction of an inch above the taut thread. He stood and watched in eager anticipation.

Success! In just a few minutes the flame had come low enough to lick at the string, which smoked and then burnt through, and the napkin descended to the floor, casting a moving shadow on the curtains in the window that faced the road. Perfect.

He put up a new string to replace the burnt one, and got out a longer candle. Then he set the clock with the little hand just past one. In slightly less than two hours' time Jørgen Lavik would apparently send a fax to a lawyer in Tønsberg about an urgent matter which had been delayed by circumstances beyond his control; he apologised and hoped the delay had not caused any problems.

Then he changed into camouflage clothes, meant for hunting but ideal for his purpose. He lit the candles carefully and ensured once again that they were firmly in position. Then he went down to the cellar and slipped out through the door at the rear of the house.

Down on the beach he paused and waited for a moment. Hugging the wall of rock, he felt reasonably certain that he blended fully with the background. When he'd got his breath back he crept along to the spot where many summers ago he'd cut an opening in the wire to gain easier access to his neighbour's property, in order to play with a boy of his own age.

He crawled towards the road. They probably had it under observation along its whole length. Near the edge of the wood he lay and listened. Nothing. But they must be there. He continued parallel with the road, five metres in and hidden by the trees. There it was. The big concrete pipe that carried a small stream to the other side of the road, creating a bridge instead of a ford. He'd slithered through the pipe on countless occasions in his youth, but he'd put on several kilos and twenty centimetres since then. But he'd calculated correctly that it would still be big enough to take him. He got a bit wet of course, but the stream was only a thin winter trickle; the little pond in the forest above was probably frozen. The pipe continued for three metres beyond the road, because they'd allowed for a long-promised widening which had never materialised. With his head protruding from the other end, he lay quiet again for a few minutes to listen. Still nothing. He was breathing heavily, and could feel how debilitated he'd become from his days in prison. Though much of his loss of strength was compensated for by a potent rush of adrenaline as he darted swiftly and soundlessly into the undergrowth on the opposite side of the roadway.

It wasn't very far to run, and he was there in just over five minutes. He glanced at his watch. Half past seven. Perfect. The wood creaked a bit when he opened the door of the shack, but the police were at too great a distance to have any chance of hearing it. He slipped inside just as a car went past on the main road twenty metres away. Another one followed close behind, but by then he was already sitting in the dark green Lada and had found that even after being laid up for several months, the battery still had enough power in it to start the engine with a cough and a splutter. Although his uncle's mind was gone and he barely recognised him on his visits to the hospital, it was obvious that he got some enjoyment from the occasional drives in the Lada that Jørgen treated him to. So as a gesture to his uncle, Jørgen had kept the car in good condition. Now it was he who was reaping the benefit. He revved the engine a couple of times, drove out of the garage, and headed off in the direction of Vestfold.

It was bitterly cold. The police officer had to flap his arms and stamp his feet while remaining silent and invisible. It wasn't easy. He needed to remove his gloves to use his binoculars, which meant he wasn't using them very often. He cursed and envied this bloody lawyer for being able to sit and enjoy the warmth in a place that necessitated outdoor surveillance. A moment ago a light had been switched off in one of the upstairs rooms: surely he wasn't intending to go to bed so early. It was only eight o'clock. Hell, another four hours to the end of the shift. There was an icy blast on his wrist as he uncovered his watch, so he hurriedly pulled his sleeve down.

He could try the binoculars with his gloves on. There wasn't much to see. Lavik had obviously drawn all the curtains, which was understandable, since he wouldn't be so stupid as not to realise he was under observation. From that point of view it seemed rather foolish that they were making such efforts to remain invisible. He sighed. What a tedious job. Lavik was certain to hole up for several days, bearing in mind that he'd lugged in bag after bag of food, plus a laptop computer and a fax.

354

Suddenly he straightened up. He blinked rapidly to disperse the tears caused by the freezing wind. Then he tore off his gloves, flung them to the ground, and focused the binoculars more accurately.

What the devil was it casting those dancing shadows? Had he lit a fire? He lowered the binoculars for a moment and stared up at the chimney outlined in silhouette against the dark night sky. No, there was no smoke. What could it be, then? He put the binoculars to his eyes again, and now he could see it clearly. Something was burning. And burning fiercely. All at once the curtains were aflame.

He threw down the binoculars and raced towards the house.

"The house is on fire!" he roared into his radio. "The bloody house is on fire!"

The radio was superfluous: they could all hear him without it, and two of them came running over. The first one there smashed open the door, saw in an instant where the regulation fire extinguisher was, and hurtled into the living room. The smoke and heat stung his eyes, but he located the source of the fire immediately and fought his way across the room wielding the jet of powder like a frenzied sword before him. The blazing curtains scattered glowing fragments into the air and one landed on his shoulder, setting his jacket alight. He beat out the flame with his hand, scorching his palm, and went on undeterred. His colleagues had arrived, and one seized a woollen blanket from the sofa, the other unceremoniously ripped down a splendid Sami woven wall hanging. In a couple of minutes they had smothered the flames. Most of the room was saved. Even the electricity hadn't gone off. Lavik, however, had.

The three detectives stood surveying the scene as they recovered from their exertions. They saw the two remaining cords and discovered the little mechanism that had not yet sent off the fax.

"Bloody hell," the first swore quietly, shaking his painful hand, "the fucking lawyer's tricked us. He's conned us good and proper."

"He can't have gone before seven. The surveillance team swear they saw him look out of the window at five to seven. In other words he can't have more than an hour's start, hopefully less. For all we know, he might have scarpered only minutes before it was discovered."

Hanne Wilhelmsen was trying to calm Håkon's agitation, but without much success.

"Warn the other stations in the area. They've got to stop him at all costs."

He sounded breathless and kept gulping noisily.

"Håkon, just listen. We've no idea where he is. He may have gone home to Grefsen and be watching some comedian on TV and having a drink with his wife. Or driving round the city. But the crucial point is that we've got nothing on him that would justify another arrest. The fact that our surveillance team let themselves be duped is clearly a problem, but it's our problem, not his. We may well be tailing him, but he's not doing anything illegal by giving us the slip."

Even though Håkon was beside himself with anxiety, he had to admit that Hanne was right.

"Okay, okay," Håkon interrupted as she was about to continue. "Okay. I know we can't move heaven and earth. I understand what you're saying. But you *must* believe me: he's out to get her. It all fits in: the note about Karen that was taken when you were beaten up, her statement that vanished. He must be behind it all."

Hanne sighed. This was a new tack.

"You can't seriously think it was Jørgen Lavik who knocked me out? And that he was the one who sneaked up from a custody cell to your office and stole the statement and then got back down again closing all the doors behind him? You must be joking!"

"He needn't have done it himself. He might have accomplices. Hanne, listen to me! I know he's after her!"

Håkon was really frantic now.

"Will it set your mind at rest if we take the car and go over there?"

"I thought you'd never suggest it . . . Pick me up by the riding school in Skøyen in a quarter of an hour."

Perhaps the whole thing was just an excuse to see Karen. He couldn't swear that it wasn't. On the other hand, his dread lay like a physical knot of pain beneath his ribs, and was definitely not just a figment of his imagination.

"Call it male intuition," he said ironically, and sensed rather than saw her smile.

"Intuition's neither here nor there," she scoffed. "I'm doing this for your sake, not because I agree with you."

That wasn't entirely true. Since speaking to him twenty minutes ago on the phone she'd been getting an increasing feeling that his agitation might well be justified. It was difficult to put a finger on what had made her change her mind. His certainty, perhaps: she'd lived long enough not to ignore other people's instincts and presentiments. Besides, Lavik had seemed so demoralised and desperate when she'd last seen him that he might be capable of anything. Nor did she like the fact that Karen Borg hadn't answered the phone all evening — it might mean nothing, of course, but she didn't like it.

"Keep trying her number," she said, inserting a new cassette into the player.

Karen was still not responding. Hanne glanced across at Håkon, put her hand on his thigh, and patted him gently.

"Relax, it's good if she's not there. Anyway . . ."

She looked at the clock on the dashboard.

"Anyway, he couldn't possibly have reached there yet, not even by the most pessimistic reckoning. He'd have to find himself a car first, and in the unlikely event of his having one ready to hand near the cottage, he still couldn't have got away until after seven. Probably later. It's twenty past eight now. Stop worrying."

That was easier said than done. Håkon released the little lever on the right of his seat and let it recline as far as it would go.

"I'll try," he muttered disconsolately.

Twenty past eight. He was hungry. In fact he hadn't eaten all day. His elaborate preparations had taken the edge off his appetite, and his stomach had become unaccustomed to food after ten days of semi-fasting. But now it was rumbling insistently. He indicated and pulled off into a lit-up parking area. There was plenty of time for something to eat. He had about a three-quarter-hour drive left. Plus another quarter of an hour to find his way to the right cottage. Maybe even half an hour, since the students' meeting there had been so long ago.

He parked the Lada between two Mercedes, but it didn't appear intimidated by such exalted company. Lavik smiled, gave it a friendly pat on the boot lid, and went into the café. It was an unusual building, rather like a UFO that had taken root in the ground. He ordered a large bowl of pea soup, and took a newspaper to the table with him. He was in no great hurry now.

They had already passed Holmestrand and the tape had played both sides. Håkon was bored with country music, and hunted in the tidy console for something else. They didn't say much on the journey; it wasn't necessary. Håkon had volunteered to drive, but Hanne had declined. He was content not to, but less happy about the fact that she'd been chain-smoking ever since they passed through Drammen. It was much too cold to open the window, and he was beginning to feel sick. His own chewing tobacco didn't help. He used a tissue to get rid of it, but couldn't avoid swallowing the last few bits.

"Would you mind leaving the smoking till later?"

She was embarrassed and very apologetic, and stubbed out the cigarette she'd just started.

"Why didn't you say something before?" she asked in gentle reproof, throwing the packet onto the backseat.

"It's your car," he murmured, looking out of the window.

There was a fine layer of snow all over the fields, and here and there long rows of straw bales wrapped in white plastic.

"They look like gigantic fish balls," he remarked, feeling even sicker.

"What do?"

"Those plastic rolls. Hay, or whatever it is."

"Straw, I think."

He caught sight of at least twenty huge bales a hundred metres from the road on the left; this time in black plastic.

"Liquorice fish balls," he said, his nausea increasing. "Can we stop soon? I'm getting carsick."

"There's only fifteen minutes to go. Can't you hold on?"

She didn't sound annoyed, just anxious to get there.

"No I can't, to be honest," he said, putting his hand up to his mouth to emphasise the precariousness of the situation.

She found a suitable place to leave the road a few minutes further on, a bus stop by a turn-off to a little white house, which was all in darkness. It was as desolate a place as could be, on a trunk road through

Vestfold. There were cars rushing by at regular intervals, but no other life to be seen anywhere.

The fresh, cool air did him good. Hanne stayed in the car while he took a walk along the short track. He stood for a few minutes with his face into the wind; then, feeling better, made his way back to the car.

"Danger over," he said, fastening his seat belt.

The car coughed irascibly into life when she turned the ignition key, but faded immediately. She made repeated attempts, but there was no reaction to the starter motor at all: the engine had gone completely dead. It was such a surprise that neither of them said a word. She tried once more. Not a murmur.

"Water in the distributor," she said through clenched teeth. "Or it could be something else. Maybe the whole bloody car has packed up."

Håkon continued to say nothing, quite deliberately. Hanne got out of the car abruptly, and grimly opened the bonnet. A moment later she was back beside him, holding what he assumed to be the distributor cap; at least, it looked like a lid of some sort. She took several paper tissues from the glove box and rubbed the inside of the cap dry. She gave it a final critical inspection and went out to replace it. It was soon done.

But it didn't make any difference. The car was just as uncooperative. After two more attempts on the starter, she struck the steering wheel in anger.

"Typical. It has to be now. This car has run like clockwork ever since I bought it three years ago. Couldn't have been more obliging. And now it has to let me down at a time like this. Do you know anything about car engines?"

She gave him a rather reproachful look, and he guessed she knew the answer. He shook his head slowly.

"Not much," he said, with some understatement. The truth was that he knew nothing at all about cars, except that they required petrol.

Nevertheless he went out with her to take a look. It would be moral support: the car might be persuaded if there were two of them.

To judge from all the cursing, her search for the fault was not going well. He made a discreet withdrawal and felt queasiness rising in him again. It was cold, and he hopped from one foot to the other as he watched the cars zoom past. Not one of them even slowed down. They were probably on their way home and had no leanings towards human compassion on such a dreary and unpleasant December evening. They were easily visible, since there was a lone street lamp beside the timetable board at the bus stop. Then there was a gap in the regular, if not particularly heavy, flow of traffic. In the far distance he could see the lights of an approaching car. It actually appeared to be adhering to the seventy-kilometres-an-hour speed limit, unlike most of the others, and it had collected four cars impatiently tailing it close behind.

Then came the real shock. The street lamp briefly illuminated the driver as the car went by. Håkon was paying special attention because he'd made a small bet with himself that it must be a woman driving so slowly. It wasn't a woman at all. It was Peter Strup.

The import of this took a second to penetrate to the relevant part of his brain. But only a second. Recovering from his astonishment, he ran over to the car, which was standing with its bonnet agape like a pike in the reeds.

"Peter Strup!" he yelled. "Peter Strup has just driven by!"

Hanne jumped up, hitting her head on the bonnet.

"What did you say?" she exclaimed, even though she'd heard him perfectly.

"Peter Strup! He just drove past! Right now!"

So the pieces fell into place, everything fitted with a sudden click, difficult to take in, even though the picture was now as clear as day. She was livid with herself. After all, the man had been under suspicion the whole time. He was the most obvious candidate. The only one, in effect. Why hadn't she wanted to see that? Was it Strup's spotless reputation, his very correct manner, his photograph in weekly magazines, his successful marriage, his splendid children? Was it these elements that had made her resist the logical conclusion? Her brain had told her it was him, but her police intuition, her bloody overestimated intuition, had protested.

"Shit," she muttered, slamming down the bonnet lid. "So much for my damned instincts."

She hadn't even brought the guy in for questioning. How bloody stupid.

"Stop a car!" she shouted to Håkon, who obeyed her command immediately, taking up position at the side of the road and waving both arms in the air. Hanne got back into her own useless vehicle, gathered up her coat, cigarettes, and wallet, and locked it. Then she joined her overwrought and panicking colleague.

Not a single car showed any inclination to help. Either they drove by without appearing to notice the two people leaping and gesticulating at the roadside, clearing them by centimetres, or they hooted angrily and reprovingly at them as a traffic hazard and swerved round them as they tore past.

After nearly thirty cars, Håkon was on the point of despair, and Hanne realised that something had to be done. It would be far too dangerous to stand in the middle of the road, no question of that. If they phoned for assistance, it would probably be too late. She looked over at the unlit house, standing hunched and unassuming and closed up, as if trying to excuse its unenviable position only twenty metres from the main E-18. There was no parked car to be seen.

She ran up to the house. The little hut on the other side, barely visible from the road, might be a garage. Håkon wasn't sure whether she expected him to continue the attempt to stop a vehicle, but he took a chance and followed her, which met with no protest.

"Ring the bell and see if there's anyone at home, just in case," she called, and tugged at the shed door.

It wasn't locked.

No car. But a motorcycle. A Yamaha FJ, 1200cc. Latest model. With ABS brakes.

Hanne despised rice burners. Only Harleys were motorbikes. The others were simply two-wheeled conveyances for getting from A to B. Apart perhaps from Motoguzzi, even if that was European. Deep inside, however, she'd always had a sneaking affection for the more sporty type of Japanese machines, especially the FJ.

It looked as if it was in a roadworthy condition, except for the fact that the battery had been removed. It was December; the bike had probably been standing idle for at least three months. The battery was lying on a folded newspaper, neatly stored for the winter just as it should be. She snatched up a screwdriver and connected it across the terminals. Sparks flew, and after a few seconds the thinnest part of the metal began to glow faintly. Enough power in it, evidently.

"No one in," said Håkon breathlessly from the doorway.

There were plenty of tools on a shelf, more or less the same as the ones at home in her cellar. She quickly found what she wanted, and the battery was back in place in record time. She hesitated only for an instant.

"Strictly speaking this is theft."

"No, it's *jus necessitatis*."

"What?"

She hadn't quite caught it and thought he was talking nonsense in his excitement.

"Nothing. Legal Latin. I'll explain later."

If I ever get the opportunity, he thought.

Though it broke her heart to damage a new bike, it took only thirty seconds to fix the ignition. She snapped the steering lock with a rapid and hefty jerk. The engine burst into a promising growl. She looked round for a helmet, but couldn't see one. Naturally enough: there were probably a couple of expensive BMW or Shoei helmets inside the locked house in the warm. Should they force an entry? Did they have time?

Hardly. They would have to ride without them. There was a pair of slalom goggles on a wall-hook next to four pairs of alpine skis. They would have to do. She sat astride the bike and manoeuvred it out into the open.

"Have you ever been on a motorbike?" Håkon didn't speak, just shook his head vigorously.

"Well, listen: Put your arms round my waist, and do exactly as I do. Whatever it feels like, don't lean in the opposite direction. Do you understand?"

This time he nodded, and as she was putting the goggles on he mounted the bike and gripped her as firmly as he could. He was clutching her so tight that she had to loosen his hold before she let the bike roar off onto the main road.

Håkon was totally petrified. But he did as he'd promised. To allay his terror he closed his eyes and tried to think of something else. It wasn't easy. The noise was overwhelming, and he was as frozen as a wet kitten.

So was Hanne. Her gloves, her own everyday gloves, were already soaked through and icy cold. But it was best to have them on; they provided at least some protection. The goggles were also a help, though not much: she had to keep wiping them with her left hand. She cast a quick glance at the illuminated digital clock in front of her. They hadn't had a chance to put it right before they set off, but it told her that it was a quarter of an hour since they'd sped out of the side track. It had been 9:35 then.

There was no doubt that time was not on their side.

The silver-haired man was pleased to note that his memory had been correct: there was only one road to Ula. Although surfaced, it was very narrow and scarcely conducive to fast driving. At a sudden bend he saw a small lane bordered by thick bushes. He jolted another few metres down the road and found room to turn round where it levelled out. The frost had made the ground hard and easy to drive on, and he was soon strategically positioned with the front of the car facing the road but well hidden from it, and with a little gap through which he would be able to see any vehicles that came by. He put the radio on low and felt, for the circumstances, reasonably comfortable. He would recognise Lavik's Volvo. It was just a matter of waiting.

Karen Borg was also listening to the radio. It was a programme for long-distance lorry drivers, but the music was okay. She was starting the book on her lap for the sixth time, James Joyce's *Ulysses*. So far she'd never got beyond page fifty, but now she'd have a real opportunity to get into it.

It was warm in the spacious living room, almost too warm in fact. The dog was whining. She opened the verandah door to let it out. It didn't want to go, and just carried on with its restless wandering. She gave up and told it to sit, and in the end it lay down reluctantly in a corner, but with its head raised and ears pricked. It had probably caught the scent of some small animal. Or maybe an elk.

But it was neither a hare nor an elk in the bushes below the cottage. It was a man, and he'd been lying there for quite a while. Nevertheless he felt hot; he was wearing thick clothes and his adrenaline was running high. Finding the cottage had been easy. He had taken the wrong turning once, but he'd soon realised. Karen Borg's cottage was the only one that was occupied, and it blazed out its presence like a lighthouse. He'd found a good hiding place for the car only five minutes' walk away.

His head and arms were resting on a ten-litre can of petrol. Even though he'd been careful not to slop any over when filling it up, the fumes were burning his nostrils. He rose rather stiffly, picked up the can, and moved towards the house, half crouching. It wasn't really necessary, since the living room was on the other side facing the sea. At the rear there were only the windows of two bedrooms, both in darkness, and a toilet in the cellar. He tapped his chest to make sure that the monkey wrench was still there, even though he knew it was: he could feel it jolting against his ribs as he walked.

The door was actually unlocked. One hindrance less than he'd reckoned on. He smiled and turned the handle, infinitely slowly. The door was well oiled and made no sound as he opened it and went in.

The silver-haired man glanced at his watch. He'd been sitting there a long time now. No Volvos had come past, only a Peugeot, two Opels, and an old, dark-coloured Lada. There was virtually no traffic. He tried to flex his muscles, but it was difficult in a car seat. He didn't dare risk getting out to stretch his legs.

Madness! A motorcyclist with a pillion passenger came roaring by at a speed that was much too fast for the bad road. They had no helmets on either and weren't wearing leathers. At this time of year! It made him shiver to imagine it. The bike went into a great skid at the bend, and for a moment he was afraid it would slide right into his car. But the rider managed to straighten it up at the last minute and accelerated away. Crazy. He yawned and peered again at his watch.

Karen Borg had got to page five. She sighed. It was a good book. She knew that, because she'd read that it was. She found it insufferably tedious herself. However, she was determined to persist. But she kept finding little things to distract her. Now she was going to have another coffee.

The dog continued to be restive. It was best not to let it out at all: twice before it had stayed away a whole night and day in its hunt for hares. Strange, since it wasn't a hunting dog; it must be an instinct that all dogs shared.

Suddenly she thought she heard a faint noise. She turned to the dog. It was lying absolutely motionless, its whimpering had abruptly ceased, and its head was tilted to one side, ears pricked. Its whole body was quivering, and she knew that it had heard something too. The sound had come from below.

She went over to the stairs.

"Hello?"

Ludicrous. Of course there was no one there. She stood as quiet as a mouse for a few seconds before shrugging her shoulders and turning away.

"Stay," she said to the dog in a strict tone, seeing that it was about to get up.

Then she heard steps behind her and wheeled round. In an instant of disbelief she saw a figure bounding up the fifteen stairs towards her. Even though he had a cap right down over his ears she recognised who it was.

"Jørgen La . . ."

That was all she got out. The monkey wrench struck her above the eye, and she fell straight to the floor. Not that she would have noticed if she'd hit anything on her way down — she had already lost consciousness.

The dog went berserk. It hurled itself on the intruder snarling and barking with rage, jumping up to the height of his chest, where it fastened its teeth in his bulky jacket, but lost its hold when Lavik jerked his upper body sharply. It didn't give up. It clamped its powerful jaws on his lower arm, and this time he couldn't shake himself free. It hurt like hell. The pain gave him a surge of strength and he lifted the dog right off the ground, but to no avail. He'd dropped the monkey wrench, and in an attempt to retrieve it took the risk of allowing the animal to make contact with the ground again. That was a mistake. It let go of his arm for a split second and got a better hold higher up. That hurt even more. The pain started to make him feel bemused, and he knew he didn't have very long. At last he managed to grab the monkey wrench and with a murderous blow crushed the skull of the demented dog, which even so didn't release its jaws. It hung dead and limp in its death grip, and it took him nearly a minute to loosen its teeth from his arm. He was bleeding like a stuck pig. With tears in his eyes he scanned the room and caught sight of some green towels on a hook in the kitchen doorway. He quickly made a temporary tourniquet, and the pain actually receded. It would come back even more unbearably, he knew. Bugger it.

He ran down to the lower floor and opened the can of petrol. He poured its contents systematically all over the cottage. It amazed him how far ten litres went. It soon began to smell like an old petrol station, and the can was empty.

Steal something! He must make it look like a burglary. Why hadn't that occurred to him before? He hadn't brought a bag or case to carry things in, but there must be a rucksack somewhere. Downstairs. There was sure to be one there; he'd seen some sports equipment. He raced back down.

She couldn't make out what it was that tasted so peculiar. She moved her lips feebly. It must be blood. Probably her own. She wanted to go back to sleep. No, she had to open her eyes. Why? Her head was so damned painful. Better to go on sleeping. It smelt awful. Did blood smell like that? No, it's petrol, she thought, with a half-smile at her own cleverness. Petrol. She made another attempt to open her eyes. She couldn't. Perhaps she should try one more time. It

371

might be easier if she rolled over. The effort was agonising, but she slewed herself round almost onto her stomach. There was something preventing her from turning fully. Something warm and soft. Cento. Her hand slowly stroked the dog's body. She could feel it immediately: Cento was dead. She opened her eyes abruptly — the dog's head was right up against her own. It was battered in. She tried desperately to rise. Through her bloodied eyelids she saw the figure of a man outside the window, with his face up close to the glass, cupping his hands round his eyes to be able to see more clearly.

What's Peter Strup doing here? she managed to think, before falling back and crumpling over the corpse of the dog.

There wasn't much of value in the cottage. A few ornaments and three silver candlesticks would have to do. The cutlery in the kitchen drawers was all steel. It was by no means certain that any loss would be discovered anyway; with luck, the whole house would burn to the ground. He laced up the grey rucksack he'd found, drew out a box of matches from his inside pocket, and went towards the verandah door.

That was when he saw Peter Strup.

The motorbike wasn't very well suited to cross-country riding. She was also frozen solid, and realised that her coordination and strength were failing her. She stopped just a few metres along the forest track and dismounted, numb and aching. Håkon said not a word. It would be a waste of time even attempting to use the stand on the uneven ground, so she tried instead to lay the heavy machine carefully on its side. She had to drop it the last bit. The owner would be furious. She would have killed anybody herself in similar circumstances. They ran as best they could along the track — not exactly fast. Rounding a bend they came to an abrupt halt. They could see a frightening orange glow through the trees two hundred metres ahead, and above the bare trees yellow flames leaping into the sky.

In seconds they were running again — much faster now.

Jørgen Lavik hadn't quite known what to do. But his uncertainty was short-lived. He'd thrown three matches, and all of them hit the mark. Flames leapt up instantaneously. He could see Peter Strup tugging at the verandah door, which fortunately was locked. He was unlikely to go away, and must have spotted Karen Borg where she lay, perfectly visible from outside. Had she moved? He was sure she'd been lying on her back before.

It wasn't so certain that Peter Strup had recognised him. His cap was still pulled down low over his face, and his jacket had a high collar. But he couldn't take the risk. The question was which would Strup regard as the more important, catching him, or saving Karen Borg? Probably the latter.

He made up his mind fast, picked up the monkey wrench, and ran across to the verandah door. Peter Strup was so surprised that he let go of the handle and lurched back a few paces. He must have caught his foot on a rock or a stump, since he swayed momentarily and then fell backwards. It was the chance Lavik needed. He opened the door, and the flames, which by now had taken hold of the walls and some of the furniture, blazed up fiercely.

He jumped on the man as he lay there, and raised the wrench to strike. But a split second before the blow would have smashed into his mouth, Strup twisted his head out of danger. The wrench hit the ground harmlessly and dropped from Lavik's grasp.

Intent only on recovering his weapon, Lavik relaxed his guard. Strup wriggled over to one side of him and drove his knee into Lavik's groin. Not hard, but enough to make him double up and forget the wrench. In a fury, he seized Strup's legs just as he struggled to his feet. Down went Strup again, but with his arms free, and as he tried to work his legs loose by kicking out at his opponent, he got his hand inside his jacket. The kicking had an effect, and he felt his foot make contact with Lavik's face. Suddenly his legs were released and he was able to stand up. As he staggered towards the edge of the wood twenty metres away he heard a yell and turned to look behind him in trepidation.

Police officers Sand and Wilhelmsen had reached the blazing house in time to see a figure in hunting gear wielding a massive wrench charging after a man in a suit. They came to a standstill, too winded to intervene.

"Stop!" shrieked Hanne in a futile attempt to prevent the catastrophe, but the huntsman ignored her.

He had only three metres to go when there was a bang. Not very loud, but short and sibilant and very,

very distinct. The huntsman's face assumed a weird expression, clearly defined in the strong light from the flames, as if he were amused by a game he didn't really understand. His mouth, wide open as he ran, closed in a cautious smile, and he dropped the tool he'd been carrying, let his arms fall, looked down with interest at his own chest, and collapsed in a heap on the ground.

Peter Strup turned to the two police officers and threw down the gun, as an overt demonstration of his good faith.

"She's still inside," he shouted, pointing at the burning cottage.

Håkon didn't pause to think. He tore across to the open verandah door, not even hearing the warning cries of the others as he plunged into the inferno. He ran so fast that he couldn't stop until he reached the centre of the room, where the only thing as yet in flames was one end of a rag rug. But the heat was so intense that he could feel the skin on his face beginning to tighten.

She was as light as a feather; or perhaps he had suddenly acquired superhuman strength. It took no more than seconds to heave her up onto his shoulder, in a proper fireman's lift. As he swung round to get back out the way he'd come in, there was an almighty crash. The noise was deafening, like a gigantic explosion. The picture windows had done their best to withstand the heat, but had eventually succumbed. The powerful draught from outside made the roaring flames almost unbearable, and his exit was cut off. At least in that direction. He turned round slowly, like a helicopter with Karen as a broken, lifeless rotor blade. The smoke and heat made it difficult to see anything. The stairs were ablaze.

But perhaps not as engulfed as they seemed? He didn't have any choice. He drew a deep breath, which made him cough violently. The flames had caught his trousers now. With a howl of agony he leapt down the stairs, and could hear Karen's head bumping against the wall with every stride.

The fire had been considerate enough to blow out the cellar door. With one final effort he was outside, and the fresh air gave him the extra strength to run another ten metres away from the building. Karen toppled to the ground, and all he had time to notice before he himself lost consciousness was that his trousers were still on fire.

This had all been something of a failure. For one thing, Lavik could have got there before him. Not very likely, though, because murder is easier at night; and it would have been simpler for him to throw off the men tailing him after dark.

But it was boring just sitting there. He finally took the risk of a little walk outside the car — nothing had come past since the crazy motorcyclists. It was bitterly cold, but fine and dry. The frost crunched beneath his feet, and he stretched his arms above his head.

There was a faint pink glow reflected on the low cloud-cover where he imagined Sandefjord must be. He turned towards Larvik and saw the same there. Above Ula, on the other hand, the glow was more of an orange colour, and much more conspicuous — and he thought he could see smoke. He stared towards the light. It was a fire!

Damn and blast! Lavik must have beaten him to it. Or maybe he hadn't been driving the Volvo? Perhaps he'd changed cars to fool the police. He tried to remember what makes had gone past: two Opels and a Renault — or was it a Peugeot? No matter. The fire couldn't be coincidence. Arson was one way of taking someone's life. The man must be completely insane.

He was probably too late. It would be difficult to get Lavik now. The flames were so high that someone would be bound to notice them and call the fire brigade. In a few minutes the placc would be full of fire engines and firemen.

But he couldn't resist stealing a glimpse. Back in the driver's seat, he put the car in gear and drove slowly towards the conflagration.

"The ambulance is the urgent thing. Very urgent."

She gave the mobile phone back to Peter Strup, who stood up and put it in his pocket.

"Karen Borg is the worse of the two," he said. "But the burns on your colleague don't look good, either. And inhaling all that smoke can't have helped."

Between them they had managed to drag the two unconscious bodies down to the parking space where Karen's car was standing. Hanne hadn't hesitated to smash the window of the driver's door with a big stone. There was a woollen blanket in the car, and two small cushions. It was also draped in a tarpaulin that they'd removed and laid beneath the injured pair. They'd torn off a large piece first and filled it with ice-cold water from a little stream just below. Even though the water quickly ran out again, they both thought it had some cooling effect on Håkon's burnt leg. The heat of the fire could be felt right down by the car, and Hanne was no longer freezing. She hoped Karen and her rescuer were reasonably comfortable as well. The wound above Karen's eye didn't appear to be any more severe than the one she'd suffered herself a few long weeks ago; hopefully that might be some indication of the force of the blow. Her pulse was even, if somewhat rapid. Hanne had found some ointment for burns in the first-aid box in the car, and smoothed it on the worst areas before covering them with wet tarpaulin. It was rather like using cough linctus for tuberculosis, she thought wryly, but did it anyway. They were both still unconscious, which was all to the good.

Peter Strup and Hanne Wilhelmsen stood and watched the flames, now apparently nearly sated. It was a riveting sight. The whole of the upper storey was gone, but the lower floor was harder to consume, consisting in the main of bricks and mortar. But there must be some wood there too; even though the flames were no longer soaring high in the sky, they were finding plenty to occupy them. In the distance at last they could hear the sirens, almost mockingly, as if the fire engines were taunting the stricken cottage with their imminent arrival, knowing it to be too late.

378

"You would have to go and kill him," she said, without looking at the man by her side.

He gave a deep sigh and kicked at the frosty grass.

"You could see the situation for yourself: it was him or me. I'm lucky I had witnesses."

He was right. A classic example of self-defence. Lavik was dead before Hanne reached him. The shot had hit him in the middle of the chest and must have penetrated his heart. Strangely enough it hadn't bled much. She'd hauled him a bit further away from the burning building, since his immediate cremation would be of little advantage.

"Why are you here?"

"At this very moment I'm here because you've arrested me. It would be impolite to run off."

Too much had happened that day for her to be able to raise a smile. She tried, but the result was just a weary and unattractive contortion of the lips. Instead of asking him further questions she just raised her eyebrows.

"I don't need to say anything about why I came here," he went on calmly. "It's okay for you to arrest me. I've killed a man, and I'll have to make a statement. I'll talk about everything I saw here this evening. But nothing else. I can't, and I won't. You've probably been thinking I had something to do with the notorious drugs syndicate. Maybe you still do."

He glanced at her for confirmation or negation. Hanne's expression was totally impassive.

"All I can say is that you're completely wrong. But I've had my suspicions about what's been going on. As

Jørgen Lavik's former employer, and as someone who feels a sense of responsibility for the legal profession, and for . . ."

He broke off, as if he suddenly realised he'd said too much. A little moan from one of the patients behind them made them turn round. It was Håkon who was showing signs of regaining consciousness. Hanne crouched down by his head.

"Does it hurt badly?"

A weak nod and a wince were answer enough. She gently stroked his hair, which was singed and smelt burnt. The ambulance siren was getting louder, and subsided in an anguished wail as the white and red vehicle drove up to them. Following it came two fire engines, prevented by their size from coming all the way.

"Everything's going to be fine," she promised him as two strong men lifted him carefully onto a stretcher and carried him into the ambulance. "Everything's going to be fine now."

The silver-haired man had seen enough. Lavik was obviously dead, otherwise he wouldn't have been lying alone and unattended on the grass. He wasn't so sure about the two prostrate bodies in the parking area. But it didn't matter. His problem was solved. He retreated into the trees and paused to light a cigarette when he was far enough away. The smoke tore at his lungs, since he'd actually given up some years ago. But this was a special occasion.

"It ought to have been a cigar," he thought to himself as he returned to his car and trod out the stub in the brown leaves. "A fat Havana!"

A broad grin spread over his face as he set off back to Oslo.

TUESDAY 8 DECEMBER

They both made a good recovery. Karen Borg had
suffered from smoke inhalation, a minor fracture of the
skull, and severe concussion. She was still in hospital,
but was expected to be discharged towards the end of
the week. Håkon Sand was already on his feet again,
metaphorically if not yet quite literally. The burns were
not as bad as had been feared, but he would have to
resign himself to using crutches for a while. He'd been
granted four weeks' sick leave. His leg was excruciatingly painful, and after a week of sleepless nights and
large doses of analgesics, he couldn't stop yawning.
He'd also coughed up little black particles of soot for
several days after the fire. And he jumped every time
anybody lit a match.

He was relatively satisfied, however. Almost pleased.
They might not have solved the case, but they'd
brought it to some sort of conclusion. Jørgen Lavik was
dead, Hans Olsen was dead, Han van der Kerch was
dead, and Jacob Frøstrup was dead. Not to mention
poor old unremarkable Ludvig Sandersen, who'd had
the dubious privilege of opening the ball. The killers of
Sandersen and Lavik were known to the police; Van der
Kerch and Frøstrup had chosen their own way out.
Only Olsen's unfortunate encounter with a bullet

remained something of a mystery. The official opinion now was that Lavik was the perpetrator. Kaldbakken, the commissioner, and the public prosecutor had all insisted on that. It was better to have a dead, identified murderer than an unidentified one still at large. Håkon had to admit that the basis for the theory of a third man had gone — it had been Peter Strup's weird behaviour that had given rise to the idea, and now the top lawyer was out of the picture. He had conducted himself in an exemplary fashion. He accepted two days' custody without protest until the prosecution service dismissed the killing of Jørgen Lavik as having been without criminal intent. Self-defence pure and simple. Even the chief public prosecutor, who as a matter of principle believed that all murder cases should be brought to trial, had soon agreed to no charges being preferred. Strup's weapon was legally owned, since he was a member of a gun club.

The view of the majority, with some relief, was that there was no third man. Håkon himself didn't know what to think. He was tempted to go along with the logical conclusions of his superiors. But Hanne Wilhelmsen demurred. She insisted there had to be a third man who had attacked her that fatal Sunday. It could not have been Lavik. Their superiors, however, disagreed: it was either Lavik, or perhaps an accomplice lower down the hierarchy. Anyway, they must not allow such an insignificant factor to disturb the neat solution they had found to the whole affair. They bought it, all of them. Except Hanne Wilhelmsen.

✱ ✱ ✱

A strike. The third in a row. Unfortunately it was so early in the day that only one of the other lanes was in use. Four noisy young teenage boys were playing there, and they hadn't so much as glanced over at the two older men since their initial critical and sneering appraisal. So there were no spectators to see this piece of bowling skill other than his opponent — and he pretended not to be impressed.

The screen suspended from the ceiling above their heads indicated that they'd both had a successful series. Anything over 150 points was quite good. Considering their age.

"Another game?"

Peter Strup was asking. Christian Bloch-Hansen hesitated for a moment. Then he shrugged his shoulders and grinned. Just one more.

"But let's get some mineral water first."

They sat there, each with a heavy ball in his hand, sharing a bottle. Peter Strup was running his hand over the smooth surface. He looked older and thinner than the last time they'd met. His fingers were dried up and emaciated, and the skin was cracked over his knuckles.

"Were you right, Peter?"

"Yes. Unfortunately."

He stopped stroking the ball, put it down, and rested his elbows on his knees.

"I had such hopes for that young man," he said, with a sad smile reminiscent of an ageing clown who'd carried on too long.

384

Christian Bloch-Hansen thought he could detect tears in his friend's eyes. He patted him awkwardly on the back, and turned his gaze in embarrassment to the ten skittles standing rigidly to attention awaiting their fate. He could think of nothing to say.

"He wasn't exactly like a son to me, but at one period we were very close. When he left my firm to set up on his own, I was disappointed — maybe hurt, too. But we kept in touch. If we could, we had lunch together every Thursday. It was pleasant, and rewarding. For both of us, I think. Over the last six months, though, the lunches became rather sporadic. He was abroad a lot. And didn't give me such a high priority anyway, I suspect."

Peter Strup straightened himself up in the uncomfortable little plastic chair, took a deep breath, and continued:

"I was stupid. I thought it was a woman. When he got divorced the first time, I probably came over like a strict father. Lately when he started to withdraw, I assumed that his marriage was failing again and that he wanted to avoid my reproaches."

"When did you start to realise that something was wrong? Really wrong, I mean."

"I'm not quite sure. But towards the end of September I began to suspect that a member of the profession was up to something on the side. It all began when one of my clients broke down. A miserable wretch I've had for years. He burst into tears with a long tale of woe. It transpired that what he was most concerned about was to get me to take up the case of a friend of his, a young Dutchman, Han van der Kerch."

"Was he the chap who committed suicide in prison? The one there was so much fuss about?"

"That's right. You know yourself how some clients are always dragging their friends along to try to get help for them, too. Nothing unusual in that. But after whingeing on for ages he told me he knew there was at least one lawyer behind a drugs ring, virtually a gang. Or a mafia. I was thoroughly sceptical, but thought there was enough in it to warrant further investigation. So I tried initially to make contact with the Dutchman. Offered my services, but Karen Borg wouldn't budge."

He gave a short, dry laugh without a trace of amusement.

"That refusal almost cost her her life. Well, with no access to the main source, I had to approach it in a roundabout way. I felt like some tenth-rate American private eye at times. I've talked to people in the strangest places and at the oddest hours. Though, in a way, it's also been quite stimulating."

"But, Peter," the other man said in a low voice, "why didn't you go to the police?"

"The police?"

He looked at his companion as if he'd suggested a pre-prandial massacre.

"What on earth would I have gone to them with? I didn't have anything tangible. In fact, I think the police and I have had that problem in common: we've had hunches and beliefs and assumptions, but we haven't been able to prove a damn thing. Do you know when I

386

first got any positive evidence of my growing suspicions about Jørgen?"

Bloch-Hansen gave a slight shake of his head.

"I put one of my sources physically in a corner, that is on a chair without a table in front of him. Then I stood right in front of him and stared him straight in the eyes. He was frightened. Not of me, but of a feeling of disquiet in the market that seemed to be affecting everyone. Then I went steadily through the names of a number of Oslo lawyers. When I got to Jørgen Ulf Lavik he was noticeably uneasy, averted his gaze, and asked for something to drink."

The boisterous youths were going out. Three of them were laughing and grinning and tossing a jacket from one to another, while the fourth, the smallest, was cursing and groaning and trying to intercept it. The two lawyers remained silent until the glass doors closed behind the lads.

"What did that give me? I could have gone to the police and told them that by using what was perhaps a somewhat amateurish lie detector I'd got a nineteen-year-old drug addict to reveal that Jørgen Lavik was a crook. Please go and arrest him for me. No, I had nothing to inform them of. Anyway, I'd begun to see fragments of the real truth even then. And it wasn't something I could refer to a young attorney on the second floor of police headquarters. I paid a call instead on my old friends in the Intelligence Services. The picture we managed to piece together by our joint efforts wasn't a pretty one. To be more precise, it was ugly. Bloody ugly."

"How did they take it?"

"Naturally enough it stirred things up. I don't think it's settled down yet. The worst of it is that they can't touch Harry Lime."

"Harry Lime?"

"*The Third Man*. You must remember the film. They've got enough on the old man to make things hot for him, but they don't dare. It would get a bit too warm for them, too."

"But are they letting him continue in post?"

"They've tried to persuade him to retire. They'll keep on trying. He's had heart problems, fairly severe ones. There wouldn't be anything surprising about his retirement on health grounds. But you know our former colleague — he won't give up until he drops dead. He sees no reason to."

"Has his boss been told?"

"What do you think?"

"No, probably not."

"Even the prime minister has been left in ignorance. It's too horrific. And the police will never succeed in apprehending him; they don't even have the remotest suspicion."

The last frame went badly. To his annoyance Peter Strup saw his friend beat him by almost forty points. He must really be getting past it.

"Answer me one thing, Håkon."

"Wait a minute."

It was difficult getting his stiff leg into the car. He gave up after three attempts, and asked Hanne to slide

388

the seat back to its full extent. That made it easier. He wedged the crutches in between the seat and the door. The heavy gate of the yard at the rear of police headquarters opened slowly and reluctantly, as if it wasn't entirely sure whether it was advisable to let them out. At last it made up its mind: they could pass.

"What do you want an answer to?"

"Was it really so important for Jørgen Lavik to kill Karen Borg? I mean, did his case depend so very much just on her?"

"No."

"No? Just no?"

"Yes."

It pained him to discuss her. He'd limped over twice to the hospital ward where she was lying bruised and helpless. Her husband had been there both times. With a hostile look and demonstratively holding her pale hands as they lay on the bedcover, Nils had by his very presence thwarted any attempt at saying what Håkon actually wanted to say. She had been distant and discouraging, and though he hadn't expected any thanks for his lifesaving intervention, it hurt him deeply that she didn't even mention it. Nor did Nils for that matter. All Håkon did was exchange a few meaningless words for five minutes and then leave again. After the second visit he couldn't face another; since then not a moment had passed without his thinking of her. Nevertheless he was able to take some comfort from the fact that the case was more or less solved. He just couldn't bear talking about her. But he made a supreme effort.

"We wouldn't have got a conviction even with Karen's statement and testimony. It could only have helped us procure an extension of the custody order. When he was first released, Karen's role was irrelevant, unless we'd found additional evidence. But Lavik was probably not fully responsible for his actions."

"Do you mean he wasn't of sound mind?"

"No, not that. But you have to remember that the higher you are, the further you have to fall. He must have been rather desperate. In one way or another he'd convinced himself that Karen was dangerous. From that point of view it makes sense when our superiors maintain that he was the one who knocked you out. That memo may have caused his obsession."

"So now it's my fault that Karen was nearly murdered," said Hanne peevishly, though she knew he hadn't meant it like that.

She wound down the window, pressed a red button, and announced her business to a voice of indeterminate sex that crackled out at them from a perforated metal plate. The barrier was raised by unseen hands and she was directed to an empty space in the garage underneath the parliament building.

"Kaldbakken is seeing us straightaway," she said, assisting her colleague out of the car.

It was hard to imagine how a minister of justice could tolerate such wretched conditions. Despite the fact that the room was being redecorated, it was obvious that the youthful minister was still in residence. He stepped over rolls of wallpaper, squeezed past a stepladder on the top of which a can of paint was ominously teetering, gave them a beaming smile, and proffered his hand in greeting.

He was strikingly handsome as well as surprisingly young. He'd only been thirty-two when he took office. He had golden blond hair, even in midwinter, and his eyes could have been a woman's: large, blue, and with very long, beautifully curling lashes. His darker eyebrows, meeting above the bridge of his nose, formed a stark masculine contrast to all this lightness.

"Wonderful that you could come," he said enthusiastically. "After everything there's been in the papers over the past week it's difficult to know what to believe. I'd be grateful for a briefing. Now that it's all over, I mean. Quite an incredible affair, and very uncomfortable for us upholders of the law! I'm the one who's supposed to be responsible for these lawyers, and it's a nasty business when they hop over the fence."

His grimace was presumably meant as a fraternal gesture of acknowledgement of the state of the legal profession. The minister had been in the police force himself for three years before his appointment as a public prosecutor in record time at the age of only twenty-eight. He helped Håkon solicitously with one of his crutches that had dropped to the floor as they shook hands.

"Quite a spectacular rescue, I understand," he said as a friendly overture, pointing at Håkon's leg. "How are you getting on?"

Håkon assured him that he was fine. Just a little pain still, but otherwise all right.

"Let's go in here," the minister said, leading them into the adjacent room. Unlike his own it looked out not over the gigantic building site — where they were at long last trying to make something of what had for so long been a hole in the ground — but onto the helicopter landing pad on the roof of the Department of Trade and Industry.

This room was no bigger, only tidier. There were two magnificent Oriental rugs on the floor, and one of them must have been more than four square metres. They couldn't possibly be public property. Nor did the paintings on the wall look as if they belonged to the State; if so, they should have been in the National Gallery.

The parliamentary under secretary came in immediately behind them. Since it was his office, he drew up chairs and offered them mineral water. He was twice the age of his boss, but just as jovial. His suit was tailor-made, emphasising the fact that he hadn't given up the expensive habits acquired during thirty years as a successful barrister. His official salary was probably only pocket money for him, since he was still senior partner in a moderate-sized but much more than moderately prosperous law firm.

The account of events took a good half hour, and it was mainly Kaldbakken who did the talking. Håkon was dozing off by the end. Embarrassing. He shook his head and took a swig of mineral water to keep himself awake.

The reddish, richly patterned rugs were beautiful. From this side they appeared a different shade than from the door: warmer and deeper. The wall shelving seemed more in keeping with the office, a dark brown plain veneer, full of legal books. Håkon had to smile when he saw that the under secretary also had a penchant for old children's books. There was someone else who had, he remembered, though the powerful medication he was taking was affecting his ability to concentrate. Who was it?

"Sand?"

He gave a start, and made the excuse of his leg. "Sorry. What was the question?"

"Do you agree that the case is solved now? Was it Lavik who killed Hans Olsen?"

Hanne was gazing into the distance with an inscrutable countenance. Kaldbakken nodded decisively and looked him straight in the eyes.

"Well, maybe. Presumably. Kaldbakken thinks so. He's probably right."

Correct answer. The others began to gather up their things; they'd been there longer than planned. Håkon heaved himself up and limped over to the bookshelves. Then he remembered.

He felt quite dizzy for a moment and put too much weight on one crutch, which skidded away from him on the shiny floor: he went down with a crash. The under secretary, who was standing nearest, rushed across.

"Steady on, old chap," he said, offering his hand.

Håkon ignored it, staring at him in consternation for so long that Hanne had time to come over and get her arms round him. He struggled to his feet.

"I'm okay," he muttered, hoping they would ascribe his confusion to the heavy fall.

After a few more expressions of gratitude they were free to go. Kaldbakken had his own car. When Hanne and Håkon were out of earshot, he tugged at her jacket.

"Fetch those three sheets of code. Meet me at the Central Library as soon as you possibly can."

With that he hobbled off across the asphalt on his crutches at impressive speed.

"I can drive you," she shouted after him, but he seemed not to catch it. He was already halfway there.

It was very worn, but the picture on the cover was still clear. A handsome young European pilot lay helpless on the ground in his blue flying suit and old-fashioned leather helmet, being attacked by a savage horde of hostile black Africans. The book was entitled *Biggles Flies South*. He passed it to Hanne, who was still out of breath. She realised at once.

"South," she said, dropping her voice, "the code heading on the piece of paper we found in Hansy Olsen's flat. Oh, my God!"

She leant over his shoulder. In front of him was the complete set of the adventures of the British flying ace. She picked up *Biggles in Africa* and *Biggles in Borneo*.

"Africa and Borneo. Jacob Frøstrup's insurance documents. How did you suddenly come upon it?"

"We can be grateful for all the laborious routine work that's been done. In the long list of the contents of Lavik's office, I happened to notice that the Biggles series was among his books. It amused me, because I used to devour them myself as a boy. If the individual titles had been listed, I would have probably seen it then. But it just said 'Biggles books.'"

He ran his hand over the frayed, light-blue spine. His leg wasn't hurting anymore. Karen Borg was only a faint and distant image in the back of his mind. He was the one who had discovered the key to the code. For ten weeks he'd been jogging along behind Hanne Wilhelmsen. Now it was his turn.

"The under secretary had the same books. The whole set complete."

It was like a bombshell. There it was in front of them, in the form of three well-thumbed books for boys. Books that for some reason were on the shelves of an under secretary and in the office of a corrupt, deceased lawyer. It couldn't be coincidence.

In forty minutes they had broken the code. Three incomprehensible pages of rows of numbers were transformed into three seven-line messages. They were quite informative — confirming some of their suspicions. The amounts involved were huge. Three deliveries of a hundred grams each. Heroin. As expected. The letters, written in a hasty backhand — both of them were left-handed — gradually revealed all the collection points and delivery instructions. Price, quantity, and quality were stated, each message ending with a note of the courier's payoff.

But not a single damned name. Nor address. The places mentioned were obviously specific, but they were in code. The three collection points were given as B-c, A-r, and S-x. The destinations were FM, LS, and FT.

Meaningless. For the police. But obviously not for the people for whom the instructions were intended.

They were alone in the big room. Books towered above them in impersonal silence on all four sides, damping the acoustics and muffling the transmission of sound in the venerable building. Not even a class of schoolchildren in the next room could disturb the scholarly peace that resided within those walls.

Hanne struck her fist on her forehead in exaggerated recognition of her own stupidity, and then banged her head on the table for emphasis.

"He was in police headquarters the day I was knocked out. Don't you remember? The minister was having a sightseeing tour of the custody suite and was going to discuss unprovoked violence! The under secretary was with him! I remember hearing them out at the back."

"But how could he have got away from the group? There were so many journalists in tow."

"Lavatory key. He could have borrowed a bunch of keys to go to the lavatory. Or got one for some other reason. I don't know. But he was there. It can't have been a coincidence, it just can't."

They folded up the deciphered codes, handed in the Biggles books to the woman at the issue desk, and went out onto the steps. Håkon was fumbling with his chewing tobacco and getting into the swing of it again after a couple of prods with his tongue.

"We can't arrest a guy because he's got books on his shelves."

They looked at one another and burst into gales of laughter. It sounded raucous and disrespectful between the tall pillars, which seemed to shrink back towards the wall in outrage. Their breath formed puffs of mist in the freezing air before evaporating.

"It's incredible. We know there's a third man. We know who he is. A scandal of significant proportions, and yet we can't do anything. Not a damned thing."

There was really nothing to be amused about. But they were grinning all the way to the car, which Hanne had rather cheekily left on the pavement outside. She'd put a police sign behind the windscreen to lend legality to her inconsiderate parking.

"Well, we were right, anyway, Håkon," she said. "Which is rather nice. There was a third man. Exactly as we said."

She laughed again. More despondently this time.

His flat was still there. It looked quite alien despite its familiarity. The change must be in himself. After three hours' cleaning, finishing off with a thorough round of the carpets with the vacuum cleaner, he felt more relaxed. The activity didn't do his leg any favours. But it was good for his soul.

Perhaps it was foolish not to say anything to the others. But Hanne had taken over again now. They were sitting on something that could bring down a government. Or fizzle out like a damp squib. In either case there would be one hell of a stink. No one could blame them for waiting a while, biding their time. The under secretary wasn't going to disappear.

He'd phoned Karen Borg's number on three occasions and had always got Nils. Quite idiotic, he knew she was still in hospital.

The doorbell rang. He looked at the clock. Who would come visiting at half past nine on a Tuesday evening? For a moment he considered not answering. It would probably be someone making him a fantastic offer of a cut-price subscription. Or wanting to save his immortal soul. On the other hand, it could be Karen. Of course it couldn't be, but it might perhaps, just perhaps be her. He closed his eyes tight, said a silent prayer, and went to the entry phone.

It was Fredrick Myhreng.

"I've brought some wine," his cheery voice announced, and although Håkon had no great desire to spend an evening with the irritating journalist, he pressed the button and admitted him. Moments later Myhreng was standing in the doorway with a lukewarm pizza in one hand and a bottle of sweet Italian white wine in the other.

"Pizza and white wine!"

Håkon made a face.

"I like pizza, and I like white wine. Why not both together?" said Fredrick, undeterred. "Damn good. Get a couple of glasses and a corkscrew. I've got some napkins."

A beer was more tempting, and there were two slim half-litre cans in the fridge. Fredrick declined, and began knocking back the sugary wine as if it were fruit juice.

It was quite some time before Håkon found out what he had come for — when he eventually moved on from his own self-aggrandisement.

"Look, Håkon," he said, wiping his mouth punctiliously with a red napkin, "if someone did something that wasn't entirely above-board, nothing serious, mind, just not quite acceptable, and then he discovered something that was a lot worse, something that someone else had done, or for instance he found something that, for instance, the police might be able to use ... For instance. In a case that was much worse than what this bloke had done. What would you do? Would you turn a blind eye to something that wasn't really kosher, but not as wrong as what others had done, which he might be able to help clear up?"

It went so quiet that Håkon could hear the faint hiss of the candles in the room. He leant over the table, pushing away the cardboard box in which now only a few scraps of mushroom remained.

"What exactly have you done, Fredrick? And what the hell have you discovered?"

The journalist lowered his eyes guiltily. Håkon banged his fist down on the table.

"Fredrick! What is it you've been withholding?"

The national newspaper journalist had vanished, to be replaced by a puny little boy who was about to confess his misdemeanours to an enraged adult. Shamefaced, he put his hand into his trouser pocket and produced a small shiny key.

"This belonged to Jørgen Lavik," he said meekly. "It was taped to the underside of his safe. Or filing cabinet, I can't really remember which."

"You can't really remember."

Håkon's nostrils were white with fury.

"You can't really remember. You've removed important evidence from the premises of a suspect in a criminal case, and you can't really remember whereabouts it was. Well, well."

The whiteness had now spread into a circle round his whole nose, giving his face the appearance of a Japanese flag in reverse.

"Dare I ask when you 'found' this key?"

"Quite recently," he replied evasively. "And it's not the original, by the way. It's a copy. I took an impression of it and then replaced it."

Håkon Sand was breathing in and out through his nose very rapidly, like a rutting stag.

"You haven't heard the last of this, Fredrick. Believe me. Right now you can take your bottle of dishwater and go."

He shoved the cork violently back into the half-empty bottle, and the *Dagbladet*'s emissary was ejected into the unpleasant frosty air of the December night. Outside the door he stopped and placed his foot on the threshold to prevent their conversation being so abruptly terminated.

"But Håkon," he ventured, "I hope I'll get something in return for this? Can I have an exclusive?"

All he got for an answer was a very sore toe.

400

THURSDAY 10 DECEMBER

Having worked on it for less than a couple of days, they had reduced the possible locations to a very encompassable number: two. One was a respectable and serious gym in the centre of town, the other a less respectable, more expensive, and more multifarious health club in St. Hanshaugen. Both venues were devoted to physical pursuits, but while the former was legitimate, the latter's activities functioned with specially imported ladies from Thailand. It had taken a while to discover the manufacturers of the key, but once they found them, they succeeded in narrowing it down in just a few hours to the cupboard it might fit. In view of Lavik's shattered reputation they were all convinced that the specific one would be found in the brothel. But they were wrong. Lavik had pumped iron twice a week, as on checking the file they realised they already knew.

The locker was so small that the attaché case had only been squeezed in with difficulty. It now lay unopened, its combination lock still unassailed, on Kaldbakken's desk on the second floor, blue zone. Håkon Sand and Hanne Wilhelmsen were anticipating an early Christmas present and could hardly bear to wait for the leather-covered metal case to be broached.

The combination was no match for Kaldbakken's screwdriver. They'd fiddled about with the six numbered wheels just to satisfy themselves, but had soon given up. After all, the owner had no use for it anymore, even though it was still new.

None of them could understand why he'd done it. It was incomprehensible for the man to have taken such a risk. The only logical explanation was that he'd hoped to drag others down with him if he fell. He would have been unlikely to need such a thick bundle of documentation while he was alive. It must have been a real security headache for him. In a fitness centre, where he could never be sure that the owner wouldn't make an inquisitive round of his affluent members' lockers after closing time, he had stashed away a complete and detailed account of a syndicate none of the three readers had ever imagined they would come across, except perhaps in a crime novel.

"He doesn't mention the attack on me," said Hanne, "which must mean that I was right. It must have been the under secretary."

Kaldbakken and Sand were totally uninterested. If it had turned out to be the Pope himself who'd travelled north to commit violence on a defenceless woman, they wouldn't have batted an eyelid.

They spent a couple of hours going right through it. Some of the papers they pored over together, some they took turns to read. Occasional exclamations prompted them to lean over one another's shoulders. After a while they were no longer surprised at anything.

"This will have to go straight to the top," said Hanne when they'd finished reading and had put it all back into the damaged leather case.

She pointed her finger at the ceiling. And she didn't mean God.

The minister of justice insisted on a press conference that very evening. The Special Branch and the Intelligence Service had protested vociferously, but in vain. The scandal would be enormous if the media found out that they had kept the matter under wraps for more than a few hours. It was significant enough as it was.

The minister's striking appearance had taken a severe buffeting in the course of the day. His skin was more pallid and his hair less golden. He could hear the baying of the newshounds outside the door. For various reasons he had decided that the conference should be held in police headquarters.

"It's only you lot who'll come out of this affair with any glory," he'd declared sarcastically when the commissioner had expressed the opinion that they should receive the journalists in the government building. "We'll have the press conference under police auspices."

What he forbore to mention was that there was a virtual state of emergency in and around all the government buildings. The prime minister had ordered a tripling of security arrangements and had become increasingly paranoid about the media as the day wore on. Police headquarters would thus afford a welcome diversion.

Taking a few deep breaths he strode into the big lecture hall. It was fortunate that he had some reserves of oxygen, because the crush inside the double doors nearly suffocated him.

Håkon Sand and Hanne Wilhelmsen stood leaning against the wall at the back of the room. The affair was now totally out of their hands. It had progressed up the building at an unprecedented rate. All they'd heard was a brief message to say that the case could now be regarded as fully investigated and finally solved. Which was okay by them.

"It'll be interesting to see how they get themselves out of this one," said Hanne in an undertone.

"They can't get out of it," said Håkon, shaking his head. "This is something no one is going to emerge from unscathed. Except us two. The heroes. Us in our white Stetsons."

"The good guys!"

They were both wreathed in smiles. Håkon put an arm round his colleague, and she didn't push it away. A couple of uniformed constables gave them a furtive glance, but rumours had already been circulating for some time and were no longer so intriguing.

Where they stood they were practically invisible to the crowd up at the front of the room. Five powerful floodlights had hastily been rigged up by the technicians from the three TV channels, and that had left the back of the room in darkness compared with the fierce glare over the table where all the VIPs were sitting. Norwegian Radio and Television were broadcasting live. It was four minutes to seven. The press release, issued through the Press Agency three hours earlier, had said everything and nothing. No details, simply that the parliamentary under secretary had been arrested for a serious criminal offence, and that the government had convened a special session. In fact, everyone who could justify their presence, plus a few more, had got to the meeting in the chamber in double-quick time.

The commissioner opened the proceedings now. If it hadn't been for the whirr of the camera motorwinds, you'd have been able to hear the proverbial pin drop even from Hanne's and Håkon's position.

She seemed nervous, but brought herself under control. She had prepared some notes in advance, several A4 sheets that she kept shuffling backwards and forwards to no obvious purpose.

The police had reason to believe that the parliamentary under secretary in the Ministry of Justice was involved with, had quite possibly masterminded, a group whom they suspected of the illegal importation of narcotic substances.

"Another way of saying that the guy's a mafia boss," Håkon whispered in Hanne's ear. "Now we're getting the refined legal version!"

The shocked and excited buzz died down immediately when the commissioner resumed speaking.

"As we see it at the present time," she said, coughing discreetly behind her hand, "as we have reason to believe, the organisation consisted of two groups. The deceased lawyer Hans E. Olsen was responsible for one, the deceased lawyer Jørgen Ulf Lavik for the other. We

405

have reason to suspect that the under secretary directed both of them. He has been arrested and charged with the importation and distribution of unknown quantities of narcotic substances."

She cleared her throat again, as if reluctant to continue.

"How much?" one of the journalists ventured, without getting a reply.

"He has also been charged with the murder of Hans E. Olsen."

Now a ton of pins could have dropped unnoticed amidst the hail of questions.

"Has he confessed?"

"What grounds do you have for your suspicions?"

"What kind of money are we talking about?"

"Have you made any seizures?"

It took nearly ten minutes to bring the meeting to order. The head of the CID kept thumping the table, and the commissioner had sat back down in her chair, pursing her lips in mute refusal to answer anything until the room was quiet again. She looked older than ever.

"Don't see why she seems so tense," Hanne murmured to Håkon. "She ought to be damned pleased. It's a long time since anyone in our building has been able to claim such a triumph!"

The head of the CID finally succeeded in achieving silence.

"There'll be an opportunity for questions after reports from the various interested parties. But not before. We ask for your patience and cooperation."

Whether the general muttering from the journalists was an indication of assent was difficult to know. But at least the commissioner was able to continue.

"It seems that these activities have been in progress for some years. We think since 1986. It's too early to speculate on the possible total quantities." She coughed again.

"That cough comes on whenever she lies or feels threatened," said Håkon *sotto voce*. "From the information in the attache case, I made it fourteen kilos in all. And that was just Lavik's half of the business!"

"I made it fifteen," Hanne said with a grin.

The commissioner began speaking again.

"As for the particular circumstances surrounding the use of . . ." — her coughing now seemed almost a parody of itself — "the . . . use of . . . hmm . . . the profits from this illegal enterprise, I will hand over to the minister of justice himself."

She heaved a sigh of relief as all eyes turned to the young minister. He looked as if he'd received news of his father's collapse, his mother's death, and his own bankruptcy all on the same day.

"Provisionally, and I repeat *provisionally*, it seems that some of these . . . some of these . . . hmm . . . profits, let's call them, have been used for . . . irregular expenditure by our Military Intelligence Service."

Everyone realised immediately why the minister of defence was also there. His presence, seated beyond the end of the table at the far left of the row of VIPs, almost as if not really belonging, had raised some eyebrows.

But no one had had a chance to give the matter more thought.

It was hopeless now to try to stem the flood of questions. The head of the CID banged on the table again in an attempt to do so, but just looked increasingly impotent. The commissioner pulled herself together with a determined effort and, in a voice that was totally unexpected from so slight a figure, took command of the proceedings.

"One question at a time," she declared. "We're at your disposal for an hour. It's up to you to get the most out of it."

After a quarter of an hour most of them had a fairly good overview. The gang, or mafia, as everyone, including the VIPs on the panel, had now switched to calling it, had been organised on a strict "need to know" basis. The aim had evidently been that each one should know only his direct superior. The under secretary was thus safe from all of them except Olsen and Lavik. But this pair of subordinate officers had gradually felt over-confident, had gone too far, and adopted too active a role. There was reason to assume that they had taken considerable advantage of their unique opportunities to smuggle dope into prisons. The most effective payment method in the world. And enticement.

For a moment at least Fredrick Myhreng caused a hush to fall.

"Is it true there's been illegal political surveillance?" he shouted from the third row.

The speakers on the podium glanced across at one another, but none of them replied — in fact they scarcely had the opportunity before Myhreng persisted doggedly:

"My information is that there's rumoured to be near enough thirty kilos of hard drugs. That's an absolute fortune! Has it all been appropriated by the Intelligence Service?"

The fellow wasn't stupid. But nor was the commissioner. She stared at him for a moment.

"We have reason to believe that significant sums have been utilised by those in charge of certain surveillance operations, yes," she said slowly.

The more enterprising of the crime reporters immediately tucked their heads in their jackets to speak into the neat little mobile phones in their inside pockets, exhorting their editors to summon their political commentators. Everything so far would have been of considerable interest for them, too, though they wouldn't normally have expected to concern themselves with a press conference arranged by the police. But there could be widespread political repercussions when a politician of such eminence turned out to be a crook. Now that information about the use of the money had come out, it was only a matter of minutes before the first of the political commentators slipped in through the door and crept over to his colleague for a muffled briefing. He was gradually followed by another fourteen or fifteen of them. The hubbub from the crime reporters subsided, and some of them headed for the door after passing on the baton.

A flashy type from *Dagsrevyen* with the face of a forty-year-old but hair and clothes more befitting someone half his age held a giant microphone wrapped in winter fur towards the minister of defence.

"Who in the Intelligence Service was privy to this? How high up did the authorisation go?"

The minister wriggled in his chair and cast a pleading glance at his colleague from the Ministry of Justice. But no assistance was forthcoming.

"Well, it seems . . . As far as we can tell at present . . . Nobody knew where the money came from. Very few had any knowledge of the money at all. Further investigations are still in progress."

The reporter from *Dagsrevyen* wasn't going to be fobbed off so easily.

"Do you mean, Minister, that the Intelligence Service has spent many millions on one thing or another without anyone being aware of it?"

That was exactly what the minister did mean. He waved his arms and raised his voice.

"It is important to emphasise that this was not officially sanctioned. We have no evidence to suggest that many were involved, so it's incorrect to speak of the Intelligence Service *per se* in this respect. We're talking of a few guilty individuals, and it's those few individuals who will be called to account."

The reporter could scarcely suppress his incredulity.

"Do you mean there will be no consequences for the Service as a whole?"

When he didn't get a response straightaway he thrust the microphone right into the minister of justice's face

410

so that he had to jerk his head back to avoid getting a mouthful of nylon fur.

"In view of the fact that your closest colleague has been charged with such a serious crime, shouldn't you resign as minister of justice?"

The minister was now quite calm. He gently pushed the microphone further away, ran his fingers through his hair, and looked straight at the television camera.

"Yes, I think I should," he said coolly and deliberately.

The reaction was instantaneous. Even the cameras were stilled.

"I am stepping down with immediate effect," he declared, and evidently meant it literally. Without any indication that the press conference was being terminated, he picked up his papers, rose to his feet, and surveyed the assembly before squaring his shoulders and walking out.

The two police officers at the back of the hall felt sympathy for the young minister.

"He hasn't done anything wrong," Håkon murmured. "Only selected a bit of a rogue as a colleague."

"Good help is hard to get these days," said Hanne. "You're lucky from that point of view: you've got me."

She kissed him on the cheek and whispered good-bye. Hanne Wilhelmsen was off to do some late-night shopping. It was high time she bought her Christmas presents.

MONDAY 14 DECEMBER

There were only eleven days to Christmas. The weather gods were propitious, and were endeavouring for the sixth time in two months to decorate the city for the festival. Now it looked as though they might succeed. There were already twenty centimetres of snow lying on the broad expanse of grass in front of the curved grey building of police headquarters on Grønlandsleiret. The paving stones that led up to the entrance were as slippery as an ice rink, and only ten metres from the door Håkon Sand's painful leg slithered from under him. The taxi driver had refused to tackle an ungritted slope, and Håkon was perspiring from the effort of toiling up on foot. The hill must have been constructed with malice aforethought.

He struggled to his feet again and limped into the warmth. As usual the foyer was full, and as usual the darker-hued immigrants were sitting on the left, shabby and sweaty in their garish, old-fashioned winter coats. Håkon stopped for a moment and scanned the floors above. The building was still standing at any rate. Things were much worse for the Intelligence Service.

The furore was far from abating. The newspapers were bringing out several editions a day, and there had been additional television news bulletins three days running. The immediate resignation of the minister of justice had plainly been an attempt to save the government, but it was extremely doubtful whether it would succeed. The situation was still uncertain. The Intelligence Service now had a belligerent investigation committee on its back, and there was already open talk of radical restructuring. A book published only a few months previously, on the relationship between the Party and the Secret Services, was enjoying an alarming resurgence of topicality. A new edition with a huge print-run had gone to press. A conservative politician who had long maintained he had been under illegal surveillance without being able to get a response from any quarter was now being taken seriously.

Håkon didn't mind being removed from the case, nor was he particularly bothered by the total lack of any express recognition from his superiors. It was only colleagues at his own level who gave him due credit for what he'd achieved. The job was done, the case was closed. He'd been free at the weekend on both Saturday and Sunday. It had been ages since that last happened.

When he reached the door with the peeling Walt Disney characters on, he stopped and fumbled with his bunch of keys. Once inside, he was brought up sharply by the sight of the figurine on his desk.

It was Lady Justitia. For an instant he thought it was the commissioner's own, and was at a loss to understand. But then he realised that this one was bigger and shinier. It was presumably new. It was also more stylised; the female figure was more erect and the sculptor had taken liberties with the anatomy. The body was too long in relation to the head, and the sword was raised at an angle above the head, not resting down by the skirt. As if poised to strike.

He went over to the desk and lifted the statuette. It was heavy. The bronze was russet and gleaming and had not yet begun to oxidise. A card fell to the floor. He put the figure carefully back on the desk, and with his injured leg extended stiffly to one side he bent down and picked it up.

He tore it open.

It was from Karen.

Dearest Håkon, I thank you for everything with all my heart. You are my hero. I think I love you. Don't give up on me. Don't phone, I'll ring you soon. Yours (believe it or not as you will), Karen. PS: Congratulations!!! K.

He read it again and again. His hands were shaking as he caressed the radiant copper-bronze statuette in front of him. It was cool and smooth and pleasing to the touch. Then in utter amazement he had to close his eyes tight and refocus — he was sure he'd seen it move.

The Goddess of Justice had peeped out from behind her thick blindfold. She had gazed straight at him with one eye, and he could swear that for a split second she had winked. And smiled. A wry, enigmatic smile.

Also available in ISIS Large Print:

Headhunters

Jo Nesbø

Roger Brown has it all. He's the country's most successful headhunter. He has a beautiful wife and a magnificent house. And to maintain this lifestyle, he's also a highly accomplished art thief.

At a gallery opening, his wife introduces him to Clas Greve. Not only is Greve the perfect candidate for a position with one of Roger's high-profile clients, he is also in possession of "The Calydonian Boar Hunt" by Rubens, one of the most sought-after paintings in the world.

Roger sees his chance to be rich beyond his wildest dreams and starts planning his boldest heist yet. But soon, he runs into trouble — and this time money is the least of his worries . . .

ISBN 978-0-7531-9054-8 (hb)
ISBN 978-0-7531-9055-5 (pb)

Fear Not

Anne Holt

The snow-covered streets of Oslo are the very picture of Christmas tranquility. But over the tolling bells for Christmas day, a black note sounds. As first light breaks, Bishop Eva Karin Lysgaard is found stabbed to death in the quiet city centre. DI Adam Stubo heads up the police investigation, but it is Johanne Vik, criminal profiler, who infers an unlikely pattern from this shocking murder, and who suspects that a bitter and untempered hatred has been unleashed upon the city of Oslo. A hatred that is not yet satisfied . . .

ISBN 978-0-7531-8938-2 (hb)
ISBN 978-0-7531-8939-9 (pb)

Frozen Moment

Camilla Ceder

One cold morning, in the wind-lashed Swedish countryside, a man's body is found in an isolated garage. The victim has been shot in the head, and run over repeatedly by a car. Inspector Christian Tell, a world-weary detective with a chequered past, is called to the scene. But there are few clues to go by, and no one seems to be telling the truth.

Then, a second brutal murder. The methods are the same, but this victim has no apparent connection with the first. Tell's team is baffled. Seja, a reporter and witness, thinks a long-unsolved mystery may hold the key to the killings. Tell is drawn to Seja, but her presence at the crime scene doesn't add up, and a relationship could jeopardise everything. For the inquiry to succeed, the community must yield the dark secrets of its past . . .

ISBN 978-0-7531-8924-5 (hb)
ISBN 978-0-7531-8925-2 (pb)

Evil in Return

Elena Forbes

Bestselling novelist Joe Logan walks out into a hot summer's evening in central London. The next day his body is found dumped in a disused Victorian crypt at the Brompton Cemetery. It was no ordinary murder — he'd been tied up, shot and castrated.

Detective Inspector Mark Tartaglia is convinced that Logan's personal life holds the key to his violent death, but unravelling his past proves difficult. Following the overnight success of his debut novel, Logan had become a recluse. Was Logan just publicity shy or did he have something to hide? Then the body of a second man is found in an old boathouse on the Thames — killed in an identical fashion. Can Tartaglia find the link between the two dead men before the killer strikes again? As he soon discovers, nothing in life or death is straightforward.

ISBN 978-0-7531-8872-9 (hb)
ISBN 978-0-7531-8873-6 (pb)

1222

Anne Holt

1222 metres above sea level, train 601 from Oslo to Bergen careens off iced rails. Marooned in the mountains with night falling and the temperature plummeting, 269 passengers are forced to decamp to a centuries-old mountain hotel. But when dawn breaks one of them is found murdered.

Retired police inspector Hanne Wilhelmsen is asked to investigate. But Hanne has no wish to get involved. Her pursuit of truth and justice has cost her the love of her life, her career and her mobility: paralysed from the waist down by a bullet lodged in her spine.

Trapped in a wheelchair, trapped with a killer and by the deadly storm outside. And there are rumours about a secret cargo carried by train 601. For Hanne there are too many unanswered questions; do they wait for help? And what if the killer strikes again?

ISBN 978-0-7531-8806-4 (hb)
ISBN 978-0-7531-8807-1 (pb)

ISIS publish a wide range of books in large print, from fiction to biography. Any suggestions for books you would like to see in large print or audio are always welcome. Please send to the Editorial Department at:

ISIS Publishing Limited
7 Centremead
Osney Mead
Oxford OX2 0ES

A full list of titles is available free of charge from:

Ulverscroft Large Print Books Limited

(UK)
The Green
Bradgate Road, Anstey
Leicester LE7 7FU
Tel: (0116) 236 4325

(Australia)
P.O. Box 314
St Leonards
NSW 1590
Tel: (02) 9436 2622

(USA)
P.O. Box 1230
West Seneca
N.Y. 14224-1230
Tel: (716) 674 4270

(Canada)
P.O. Box 80038
Burlington
Ontario L7L 6B1
Tel: (905) 637 8734

(New Zealand)
P.O. Box 456
Feilding
Tel: (06) 323 6828

Details of ISIS complete and unabridged audio books are also available from these offices. Alternatively, contact your local library for details of their collection of ISIS large print and unabridged audio books.